Karina Natalia Vasquez is a fantasy romance author based in England. She is of Peruvian and Spanish descent and adores anything that has dulce de leche in it. When she isn't writing, she is reading fantasy, romance and fangirling over Star Wars. You can usually find her holed up in her room, cuddling her two dogs, collecting crystals for her superstitious mind or daydreaming in the hopes that she will magically end up in a Fae kingdom one day.

By Rina Vasquez in Solaris and Crello *trilogy*

A CITY OF FLAMES
A KINGDOM OF SHADOWS
A WORLD OF RUINS

A WORLD OF RUINS

RINA VASQUEZ

WILDFIRE

First published in paperback in 2024 by
WILDFIRE
an imprint of HEADLINE PUBLISHING GROUP

1

Cataloguing in Publication Data is available from the British Library

ISBN 978 1 0354 1441 3

Typeset in 10.18/14.8pt Adobe Caslon Pro by Jouve (UK), Milton Keynes

Printed and bound in Great Britain by Clays Ltd, Elcograf S.p.A.

Headline's policy is to use papers that are natural, renewable and recyclable
products and made from wood grown in well-managed forests and other
controlled sources. The logging and manufacturing processes are expected
to conform to the environmental regulations of the country of origin.

HEADLINE PUBLISHING GROUP
an Hachette UK Company
Carmelite House
50 Victoria Embankment
London
EC4Y 0DZ

www.headline.co.uk
www.hachette.co.uk

For my yaya . . . we did it

ZERATHION

EMBERWE

AURUM CASTLE

CITY OF FLAMES

AERIS

ISLE OF ELE

UNDARION

SEA OF SERENITY

OCEAN OF STORMS

NARALIA'S VILLAGE

SCREAMING FORESTS

ÍENTS

OLCAR

TERRANOS

THALORE

MELWRAITH

PART ONE
THE RESCUE MISSION

Darius

Noctura Night

I find myself gazing at an obsidian ring I fashioned from one of my scales many years ago. The den is crowded tonight, with many shifters celebrating Noctura. One child bumps her hip into my table, and I glance at her. She shoots me an apologetic smile, and the warmth from it fills my core.

Deftly taking out a small pouch from my pocket, I pass it over to her.

She opens it up and gasps. 'Is this the magic dust from the Isle of Elements?'

I nod, chuckling when I feel her excitement. 'Make sure your mother doesn't see it, or I won't hear the end of it.'

Margie might love me, but she often told me off – sometimes for as little as swearing in front of her.

'Oh, thank you, thank you, thank you! You are the best, Darius!' As she runs off, I smile and return to looking at the ring while nursing a mug of ale in my other hand.

'Are we ever going to see Miss Misty again, Darry?' Tibith's enthusiastic question pairs with the fluttering of his ears as he climbs onto the table.

Hearing that nickname brings another smile to my lips, one that appears too quickly whenever I even think about her.

'Naralía,' I say. 'Her real name is Naralía.' I bring the mug up to my lips and scoff. 'Or *Nara*, as she says, and no, I don't think we will.'

From the side, I can see Tibith blink in confusion. When I told him to stay behind while I went to the ball, he worried I would be caught. He isn't used to me being this bold, inserting myself into situations amongst Venators. So, seeing how affected I am around *Goldie*, all he can do is wonder. I'll tell him more about who she is to me eventually, but after tonight, I doubt I will see her again despite me still having her scent of jasmine on my clothes.

A sensual thought crosses my mind, about our dance and how close she was to me. I shift on my chair, grumbling as I take another swig from my mug, hoping to drown her out of my head with alcohol.

An hour later, it still doesn't work. I've only achieved a new-found hatred for Cutler, who seems to think he can beat me at Liars' Dice.

Tibith then talks my ear off, explaining how he wants all the bread in the world, but although I usually always listen to him, this time, I cannot focus. Otis comes by and whispers something into my ear. On any other occasion, I would have happily agreed with him.

By the time male shifters are slurring their words and women have taken their children up to bed, I stand and flick a few coins onto the table. I tip my head at a couple of people I know more than others and whistle over at Tibith to come follow. He lifts his head and smiles as he trots behind me and into the warm night air.

I pause by the doorway, staring up at the crisp moon, marvelling at how large it looks tonight. An attractive beacon of light.

'Come on, that's it—'

I frown, dropping my head to look to my right. It appears to be Gus, with an Ardenti dragon named Fernah, aiding one of her hatching eggs.

Tibith and I look at each other before waltzing across the grass field. Likely hearing us, Gus glances behind his shoulder and chuckles as he spots me.

'Darius,' he says, holding up a hatchling that can barely open its eyes. 'Leaving already?'

'Cutler was getting on my nerves.'

This time, Gus lets out a howl of laughter. He often finds the simplest things I say hilarious. 'You should cut him some slack. He looks up to you; everyone does.'

I shift uncomfortably on the spot, and I am relieved Gus doesn't notice. I may take pleasure in being the centre of attention, but having people look up to me leaves me with too much space to mess things up.

Clearing my throat, I decide to involve myself before Gus can say something I am not in the mood for. I roll my shirtsleeves up and crouch beside him, with Tibith staring curiously from the side.

Gus turns his head as I grab one of the colossal eggs with the dragon hatchling still inside. 'Looks like that one is having too much fun inside; it doesn't want to leave.'

Fernah rumbles in response, lowering her head to the ground. I chuckle as I move my hand over the scaly exterior of the shell, helping the creature to emerge from its home. 'It likely is better in there than out here.'

'But it looks so small, Darry! How can a whole dragon fit inside an egg?' Tibith asks inquisitively.

I slant an amused glance his way. 'How do you think you came into this world, hm? You once hatched from an egg, too, Tib.'

Tibith gasps, pawing at his plump figure as if wondering how he himself could fit somewhere so small. I think he forgets he was once the size of a thumb. 'Did you hatch from an egg too, Darry?'

Before I can answer, Gus huffs out a laugh. 'Have you taught him nothing about our species?'

I shrug. 'He knows the important stuff.'

Gus's brows shoot up. 'Rolling around in gold isn't what one might consider *important*.' He slides his gaze towards Tibith. 'Shifters don't hatch from eggs, boy. We're a much more evolved species of dragon. Thank Solaris and Crello for that.'

Fernah doesn't like that answer, as she stirs and growls at Gus, baring her sharp teeth at him.

I straight-out laugh as I slap Gus on the shoulder with my free hand. 'Now I'm starting to see why you are single.'

For a moment, something odd passes across Gus's features, but not long enough for me to question it as he clears his throat and looks down at the nest.

'There we go,' he says, directing my attention back to the few hatchlings already by their mother. Some have a red shine to them: Ardenti. Others pure obsidian: Umbrati.

The one in my hands, though, is still shy to emerge. 'Come on, little guy,' I encourage. 'I promise it is not so bad out here.'

Gus snorts, and I give him a quick smirk.

'Of course, the food could be better, but what can we do? Gus seems to be fine with serving everyone meat that is slightly off.'

'Watch it.'

I grin, knowing there's a scowl on Gus's face. 'Maybe gold will tempt you.' I reach into my pocket and take out my gold coin and flick it in the air. Leaning in, I hold the coin in front of the egg. 'Between you and me, this is my most prized possession. It belonged to someone . . . exceptional.' *Still does.*

Slowly, the cracks in the eggshell widen, and a soft glow spills forth from the emerging fissures. The dragon within is determined to break free now, and I marvel at its resilience as a sleek black snout pushes against the confines of its shell.

Soon, the hatchling's wings burst free from the crack, and I have to wipe away the excess gunk coating its leathery skin. I bring the hatchling towards my chest and look over at Gus, laughing as the dragon squirms in my hands. My heart swells with a profound sense of connection with the hatchling's accomplishment.

As I look over at Gus, he smiles at me proudly. 'It seems to like you, Darius.'

I click my tongue. 'What can I say?'

'Maybe it can smell Miss Nara, Darry!'

I stiffen at her name, and the hatchling almost slips from my grip. *What is it about you, Goldie, that has every living thing so enamoured?*

My mood shifts, and I clear my throat as I gently place the dragon next to his mother and rise to my feet, gesturing for Tibith to come along.

I'm walking away when Gus says, 'You're still heading off early?'

I throw him a thumbs-up without looking back.

'Not even going to celebrate your birthday?'

I pause before slowly turning to look at him. A slow blink follows before I narrow my eyes. 'How did you know that?'

He sighs, taking his time to get up from the ground. As he straightens, he smiles down at me. 'Tibith.'

My eyebrows almost hit my hairline as I drop my gaze to the orange furball beside me. He looks up at me sheepishly, an apology already circling his eyes.

'Were you ever planning on telling anyone what today was?'

A huff pushes through my nose, and I shake my head at Gus. 'I don't need to when Tibith can do that for me.'

'You're twenty-six, Darius.'

No kidding.

'Sooner or later, you'll be of age to become a full-fledged shifter. Maybe you should think about settling down and . . . finding someone to spend your life with.'

'Is this another way of saying I need to stop stealing people's clothes after I bed them?'

He glowers. 'I'm serious.'

I grin. 'And when am I not?'

Gus is clearly annoyed, meaning I have done my job here and can leave. I turn to walk away and smile as I quickly assess what I can steal away from him.

'You do realise that relying on thievery has its limits,' he remarks, stating the obvious. 'But if you joined . . .'

The implication has me shaking my head. Fists clenching at my side, I twist around to confront him.

'Darius, I—'

'I accepted your friendship because I thought you understood me,' I assert, my tone cutting through the warm air like a warning. 'You didn't ask questions, and I didn't care whether you attacked Sarilyn's castle or her people. I may have helped you and the rest of your group on a few occasions, but that's it.'

He tries to talk, but I don't give him that chance.

'So, if you want to see me around here again, stop asking me to join you. You stay on your path, and I'll stay on mine.' I back away, watching as his expression sours. My hand slips into my pocket, fingers wrapping around the ring. I pull it out, casting it a lingering look before my gaze rises once more.

Solaris, I despise you.

I know. But do you despise me that much to take me down with you . . .
Naralia?

My mind replays that memory as I flip the ring between my
thumb and forefinger. A smile lifts the corner of my lips, envisioning
Goldie's face, the anger reddening her cheeks, and the way she was
still beautiful, even while hating me.

Without another thought, I hand the piece of jewellery over to
Gus. 'Here, before I go, I need you to take this,' I say.

Gus takes a long look at it, his eyes widening when he realises
what the ring means. 'A scale ring?'

I nod, taking a deep breath. 'I want you to throw it away.'

He starts to shake his head, but I firmly plant the ring in his
hands. 'Darius—'

'I'll be seeing you, Gus,' I dismiss him, not even sparing the ring
a final glance as I turn my back on him and stride off.

Tibith follows beside me, leaping to catch up. 'Why do you want
to throw that ring away, Darius? You said it was special!'

'I've said a lot of things, Tibith,' I respond, my eyes fixed on the
pathway leading into the woods. 'I guess I was wrong this time.'

CHAPTER ONE

NARA

'You need to concentrate, Nara. You're overthinking it.'

I squeeze my eyes shut, then open them and turn to face Gus, who is standing a few metres away from me in the Aerian training fields. He has his arms crossed over his chest as he analyses my stance, sensing how discouraged I am that I don't seem to possess any source of power, despite what I thought after we found out three months ago that I was the reincarnation of Solaris.

'I'm starting to believe I am no Solaris,' I huff, flexing my gloved hands in front of me as if that will conjure up my power, or at least summon an animal like I have done in the past.

Gus cocks his head to the side and smiles through his thick beard. 'And yet only yesterday you were grinning at the fact you beat a shifter – one who has never trained in combat before – in a sword fight.' My silence makes him breathe out a sigh. 'Have you considered that perhaps you do not want to accept this change?'

I shrug, even though I know he is not entirely wrong. Changing means that I am no longer who I once was. It's too much pressure, too much of a burden, to see others place their hopes in me.

Flames charge through the winter air as a few phoenixes fly towards us, stopping me from entering another self-doubting conversation with Gus. As they land, I realise my brothers and Link are atop them. Having the Aerian headquarters be airborne on floating landmarks meant you had to travel within Aeris by riding with phoenixes or dragons, many of which Gus had managed to save.

Illias is the first to jump off a phoenix's back as its gold- and scarlet-feathered tail thrashes against the grass. Illias then jogs over to me, his arms out, and squeezes me into an embrace, and I chuckle, rocking us back and forth on our toes. 'How is training coming along?' he asks.

I open my mouth, but Gus answers before I do. 'She is getting there. She has the fighting down thanks to her time as a Trapper and Venator trainee, but in terms of power, she just needs to stop doubting herself.'

Offence takes refuge in my chest. 'That is not—'

'Give her time, Gus,' Idris cuts in, his hands in his trouser pockets. 'It was only a year ago she was still trapping pixies and carving flowers out of wood for a living.'

'Not to mention falling for a shifter.' Illias chuckles and shakes his head as he steps away from me. It seems I have no say in this matter. Everyone is speaking for me.

'Are we forgetting she is a reincarnation of Solaris?' Iker adds, still in disbelief since he first heard about it months ago. 'Our sister is a deity – who would have thought!' He frowns. 'I wonder what that makes me? Semi-powerful?'

'Nothing,' Idris deadpans. 'It makes you nothing.'

'If it helps, Nara,' Link says, a small smile colouring his lips as he comes up beside Illias, 'I always felt there was something special about you. It was just a matter of time before we figured out *what* exactly.'

I smile, having missed Link's soft reassurances. That is until I hear the landing of a creature behind me and Rydan's voice as he dismounts a sleek black Umbrati dragon with shadows curling around its talons.

'And alas, my heart breaks, for I was not chosen to be your other half, Ambrose. But I suppose sometimes even the deities can make mistakes.'

I turn to him and cock a brow, only for him to wink back at me. 'Maybe you should try explaining how you would woo me in the bedroom again?'

Idris starts coughing uncomfortably, and I bite my lip so that I don't burst out laughing.

Rydan shakes his head, pulling off the tips of his gloves. 'Unfortunately, not today, Ambrose.' His expression turns sour. 'Hira would like to see you; they are all holding a meeting right now in the common area.'

Any tinge of laughter or humour drains from my body. I look over my shoulder at my brothers, acknowledging the worried glances they share with Gus. I turn and give Rydan a nod as I head towards Gus and ask him to take me to the meeting.

He accepts and shifts before I mount him and slide my hands over his leather skin. No matter how much time passes, I can never get used to not seeing Darius's unique silver scales. Letting out a sigh, I pat the side of Gus's neck, and he takes off into the sky towards the Aerian headquarters. Fog ahead shields the grand open spaces of the palace, where Aerians flash into flames and become phoenixes. Despite the chaos spreading across Zerathion with Aurum's return, I'm still able to take a moment to admire the Aerian architecture. Roofs made of red stone and marble curve around the entrance to the balcony, while gossamer leaves that shimmer in emerald hues hang from the surrounding trees.

As Gus lands, I hop off and rush inside before he can return to his human form. I half jog and half walk past spacious rooms glowing in the winter light. When I reach a set of golden doors with a phoenix engraved on them, I push through and into the great hall where Freya, Leira, her wife Aelle, and a few Phoenix warriors are waiting. Gus catches up to me, shaking his head, though he is now used to me escaping him.

My mood further deflates when my eyes snag on russet hair as Lorcan looks up at me from across the round glass table.

I ignored him for three months, making sure he couldn't come anywhere near me, but lately, it's harder to avoid him when we all live in the same place, especially now that I know . . . he isn't a Rümen any more.

Recalling the moment I found out Lorcan was alive, my vision fogs up, and I'm suddenly back in that hallway where I bumped into him.

'—I cried for you . . . I mourned you.' My voice cracks uncontrollably as I stare at Lorcan after having pushed myself off him. 'Darius mourned you.' Agony ruptures through my heart as I think of Darius and how he is not here to soothe away all the rage I feel, and for one blinking moment, I let myself picture him. I let myself believe he is beside me, his eyes burning into mine with that golden fire.

I run my hands through my hair, frustrated, as I bite down on my tongue to make the image fade.

Lorcan looks at the ground solemnly when he says, 'I know.'

You do not know. You do not know the half of it. 'How . . . how is it—'

'I did die that day.'

Intense silence cuts through the frostiness of the hallway.

'And I accepted it.' Shame takes over his expression as he looks up. 'But the leader of the Aerian warriors . . . she took my body back here, Nara. She felt something in me – something alive and worthy.'

Staring at him, I'm not sure where he is going with this.

'See, they have this belief.' The apple of his throat moves visibly as he swallows. 'A belief that life can be reborn.'

A rebirth from the ashes . . .

Recognition of what he now means tightens a coil around my chest. 'You're a phoenix.' I don't pose it as a question; it is more of a statement that I need to hear myself say.

He nods slowly as if conscious of admitting it. 'Aerians believe my ancestry dates back to them, that perhaps my mother was never exactly mortal, and that is why I became Erion's first successful Rümen.'

'Nara,' Hira speaks, pulling me out of my memories with a welcoming smile. She moves her long raven hair to the side, showing off the typical Aerian armour she wears – a burgundy chestplate over leather attire, to match the banners inside the hall. If I have learned anything from the past few months staying here, it is that the three Aerian leaders take great pride in being warriors. Since I first met Hira that night at the Noctura ball, she made sure to impress that onto me, despite now knowing who I was.

'Thank you for joining us,' she says. 'We appreciate, with all the training you are undertaking, that you have enough time to spare and give us a chance to speak with—'

'Any news?' I interrupt her, anxiety dripping from my words.

Her lips thin into a closed smile as she gestures for me to take a seat. I remain upright, causing her to awkwardly clear her throat as she walks around the table and plants her hands against it. 'We have received word from the princesses of Terranos that Aurum is no longer there.'

My hands begin to clam up. 'Where is he?'

'Princess Arlayna believes he has returned to Emberwell to finish what Sarilyn started.'

Hope blooms inside my chest, and my breath comes out in short bursts. Excitement is taking over at the prospect of good news for once. 'Then if he is there, we can find a way into the castle and free Darius.' I glance at Freya and Leira. 'How is the preparation for the unbinding spell coming along? I assume that is why I was brought here to this meeting, right?'

Freya grimaces, biting her lip as she looks at her aunt and Aelle for guidance. Leira seems at a loss, and I do not like it one bit.

'Even if Aurum is there with Darius,' Hira's voice ripples across the room, 'Freya and her aunt are beginning to believe the spell wouldn't work. Aurum used his blood in the Isle of Elements to bind their souls together. Our research tells us that simple witchcraft cannot sever that tie.'

My eyes slide to where Lorcan shifts from his statuesque pose. He stares at the floor with enough focus to burn a hole through it. 'So, what then?' I say to Hira and begin to tap my fingers against my thigh.

'Aelle has been able to locate where Aurum is hiding the Elemental Stones inside the castle through her scrying. In the meantime, I'll have Leira and Freya keep searching for a way to free—'

'But that's not good enough!' I lose all patience, raising my voice. I have kept myself busy and let everyone else take the reins so I could focus on building up my strength, but I can no longer hold in my frustration.

'Nara—' Gus touches my shoulder, but I shrug him off, taking a step forward.

'I have waited three months,' I say. '*Three* months where I have had to suck it up and listen to everyone tell me that it won't be long until he is back here with all of us. How much longer must I wait while he is stuck with his deranged uncle, who is likely torturing him right as we speak?' Guilt wraps around my heart, imagining the terrible things he must be going through. I don't want to believe the worst has happened, and I *don't* want to think we will never get him back. 'The longer we spend planning what to do next, the more Aurum gains control over everything else around him. He did it three hundred years ago; he did it in Terranos with me and Darius, and he will do it again.'

'We understand your frustrations—'

'No, you don't understand!' My lips wobble, and I bite down hard. 'Darius probably doesn't even know I am alive,' I whisper, and everyone inside the room takes turns looking at each other and then at me pitifully. I do not want pity; I want everything to go back to normal. 'If it were him in my position, he would have done everything to get me back by now.'

I just know that he would have torn the whole world apart and wouldn't have waited just because others told him to. I feel like I am failing him right now.

'We are trying everything, Nara,' Freya says quietly, and I don't even realise she is now at my side. My gaze locks with her hazel eyes, and for a second, I feel as if I am drowning in something I can't control.

I need to get out of here.

Backing away, I mouth my apologies to her before I cast everyone else one final stare and storm out of the room.

CHAPTER TWO

'Why do you look so sad, Miss Nara?' Tibith sits upon my knee, his paws patting the tears that are running down my cheeks. I'm leaning against the window ledge, my legs raised to my chest, a melancholy smile creeping across my lips. I've worked hard to maintain a cheerful attitude for Tibith all these months. I guess today is just one of those days where even carving into the wooden window frame does nothing to calm me.

'Would you believe me if I said these were happy tears?' I cough out a laugh, wishing it were true, as I fiddle with the coin necklace Darius gave me.

Tibith shakes his head, and his fur tickles my fingers when I run them through the sides of his face. 'Y-you don't need to lie to me, Miss Nara. Those are tears for Darry, aren't they?'

I stroke his stomach to get a giggle out of him. 'Have you always been this smart?'

He grins. 'Darry has told many that I am a genius!'

A fist clenches around my heart, and I almost let out a whimper before I tamp it down.

Tibith notices the anguish in my expression and pouts. 'He will come back, right, Miss Nara?'

That has been my only hope since I woke up here in Aeris.

'When has he not?' I whisper, smiling, before the door to my room opens, and I wipe my eyes with the sleeves of my tunic. My smile disappears, and I look over my shoulder at Freya. She walks up to the ledge, bunching her violet dress in her hands, and sits down. Tibith glances at her with a thrilled squeak and slides off my knee. We watch as he clambers onto the single bed and positions himself against the pillow, falling asleep within seconds.

'I apologise for what happened during the meeting with Hira,' Freya says. 'We really have tried everything, Nara.'

I slowly turn my head to look at her, and though the corners of my lips lift, the smile feels broken. 'I know that.'

Freya tilts her head, curls dangling from her updo as she stares at me like she understands that *nothing* is fine with me. We have spoken less since I arrived here. She busied herself with finding a way to help Darius while I occupied myself training with Gus. I have rarely seen Freya except when she showed me her new-found powers as a witch. Telekinesis comes naturally to her, like many of her kind. I suppose it goes hand in hand with other mind magic for witches and how in tune she is with my emotions.

I confess with a shaky breath, 'I am just frustrated with it all. I mean, here I am, supposed to be this deity reincarnation who will bring life back to Zerathion, yet I am limited in what powers I have. The man who I am annoyingly in love with is locked away and . . . and I am letting him down each day I spend here without figuring out a way to get him out.'

'Maybe this is how it had to be.'

Her response makes my lips fall and I frown.

'They always say Solaris and Crello shared the skies,' she explains. 'But they were also separated until they were finally able to reunite. It sounds like you are living through that right now with Darius.'

'But I didn't ask for this.'

'Then what did you ask for?' The intensity of her gaze burrows deep into my soul. 'The Nara I met would have told me that she is confident she is far better than Solaris.'

I stare back in silence and almost chuckle.

'Let's not forget you've broken hands, killed, talked back to my father when he was the General, and helped a dragon thief steal a pendant from the palace.'

My eyes suddenly sting with her words.

'What happened, Nara? Because I *know* you and I know that all you have done these months is either act all tough just to torture yourself or busy yourself with writing who will be the first to die on your kill list.' She raises her brows. 'Aurum being number one.' With a sigh, she says softly, 'What would Darius say if he were here?'

I blink, looking at her like a child missing their mother. Images float inside my head. Darius's golden eyes, his mischievous smile, and that stare he would hold me with that spoke a thousand love letters.

I am here.

I have a purpose.

I cannot and never will be daunted.

I press three fingers against my heart and whisper, 'That it is okay to be vulnerable.'

Freya nods with vehemence and smiles. I shake my head and slide my legs off the ledge as I wrap my arms around Freya. 'Solaris, how I have missed your encouraging words.' I close my eyes as she rubs my back. 'Every moment I was in Terranos, all I could think of was how wonderful you would find it. You don't understand how much I needed you there with me.'

She separates from our embrace, clutching my face in her hands. 'And I needed you at the den with me.' She sighs, letting go and looking away briefly. 'So much happened while you were gone. I—'

'I know,' I say to reassure her. 'You don't need to tell me—'

'I kissed your brother,' she blurts out, snapping her head back at me. 'Idris.'

My eyes widen and, almost comically, all I can say is, 'Oh.'

'It's been killing me not to be able to tell you all this time. I am so sorry, Nara. I mean, it didn't mean anything. He can hardly look at me now and—'

I grab her hand before she can spiral into one of her panicked monologues. She looks at me grimly as if I am irritated with what she has done. She could not be more wrong. 'Idris . . . is the hardest person someone can get through to. Trust me, I have had to live with it for twenty-two years of my life. But I have seen how he looks at you now for a long while, and if he is avoiding you right now, then he clearly does not realise how lucky he would be to have you, so don't apologise. There is no need.'

A reflection of the moon shines in her hazel eyes as she takes in my words. A smile almost touches her lips, but it falters, and I wonder if there is more to it. Lately, I feel that something is on her mind, and she doesn't want to let me know what it is, or maybe she can't.

'Nara, I—' she starts, but the door to my room creaks open and Iker's head pops through.

'Oh, uh, I didn't realise Freya was here. I'll just leave—'

'No, stay.' Freya stands up, darting her gaze from Iker to me. 'I need to go find Leira. She and Aelle wanted to teach me the differences between certain herbs. Apparently, star anise *doesn't* help our psychic visions, although I have yet to have one.' She laughs, and I want to tell her not to go, but she doesn't give me a chance as she hurries past Iker and leaves the room.

Iker keeps glancing back at the door as if hoping Freya will reappear.

My brows draw into a frown, seeing how restless he is as he paces around and runs a hand through his short curls. 'You never come into my room unless you want something, so what is it?'

He halts, turning to me with a bemused look. He lets out an incredulous laugh. 'What if I wished to spend quality time with my little sister? We were apart for months—' One raised-eyebrow look from me, and he sighs, dropping onto the edge of my bed. 'Fine, you got me.' A pause. 'I need your help in ridding someone.'

Well, that is not what I expected, and by my reaction, Iker can also see the sudden worry.

'Not in that sense,' he amends quickly, and the rise in his voice has me shush him before he can wake Tibith up. 'It is more of a *forgetting your feelings* situation.'

That does not make it any better.

Puffing my cheeks, I blow out a breath and lean forward. 'Iker, I can't even command any creatures as of lately. Solaris, it feels like I've lost everything! What makes you think I have the power to do something like that? And besides, making you forget someone isn't exactly part of Solaris's magic. You would likely have more luck with a witch or shifter than me.'

Iker inhales. Something is clearly bothering him.

'Why do you want to forget your feelings towards someone?' I wonder as to why, of all things, he desires this. For the entirety of my life, I have seen Iker only care for three things: writing, his siblings and using his trickster mind to outsmart villagers. This . . . This is different.

He looks at the palms of his hands and frowns like he wishes to devise a solution to the state he has found himself in lately. 'It . . .' He expels a restless breath, and his eyes snap to mine. 'It would be easier that way.'

I have no response except to feel the same ache he must feel. Knowing I cannot help him the way he wants to be helped unravels a cord of devastation inside me. Iker may not have the same pride as Idris or the kindness Illias emits, but he does care. More often than not.

'Look, forget I asked. It was stupid of me,' he mutters as he gets up to leave, but I can't help thinking I might know who this someone he wants to forget is.

'Iker,' I say before he can leave my chamber. Almost like he does not want to look my way, he hangs his head and takes a deep breath. 'Does this person happen to be one of my friends?'

He hesitates for a moment. 'Yes,' he whispers before shutting the door behind him.

I sit back with the heaviness of that answer. I do not know every detail of what happened while I was away from my brothers, but if I am sure of one thing, it is that something must have occurred for Iker to desperately want to erase *Freya* from his mind.

CHAPTER THREE

E arlier this morning, Gus agreed with Rydan that he should stand by, with Iker and Illias, watching me train in case any 'reincarnation' power of mine surfaced. Nothing in the books had prepared us for this possibility. No myth, legend or history book I have read before had even hinted at such a thing. There was that book back in Olcar's library . . . But I doubt even that would have been useful to me now.

'That's it, Nara,' Gus says in encouragement from behind. 'Focus on what lies within you . . . Feel the air around you, the ground at your feet—'

I squeeze my hands into fists at my sides. The wind pummels into my lungs and whips my hair in every direction as I stand at the edge of a grassy cliff. I do what Gus says – as I have been doing for months, even when nothing happens.

'I will bet you ten gold coins that she manages to move the ground or something.'

My lips bunch to the side when I hear Rydan bidding, but I keep my eyes closed and my back facing his.

Iker claps his hands. 'I like the sound of that. How about we throw some drinks into the mix? Spice it up a little bit.'

'I'm not vouching for you if you get your drunken self in trouble again for breaking shit . . . and *you*, I doubt you have that much money, Rydan,' Illias scoffs.

'On the contrary, Ambrose number two, I have that and more.'

'I believe him,' Iker says.

'Can Miss Nara have Darry's magic?'

'Boys—' Gus tries to intervene, but it doesn't do much. I'm no longer concentrating.

'Tibby, of course she could have the Golden Thief's magic. They likely share that and—'

I groan, twisting on my heel, as I plant my hands on my hips and stare at Rydan.

He points his index finger at me, clicking his tongue as he blows me a kiss. He knows how much of a nuisance he can be, yet he has never cared. It's a quality I admire and also want to strangle him for.

'Must you always chat nonsense?' I huff, and Illias looks at me with an apologetic grimace on Rydan's behalf.

'Well, I suppose that's all the training for today.' Gus walks over, his attention on me. 'I don't want you to overwork yourself.'

'Overwork myself? Nonsense. Why don't Rydan and I spar for a bit?'

Rydan gasps dramatically. He almost sounds as if he is choking. 'Ambrose, why would you risk losing against me?'

I roll my eyes, unbuckling my belt. As if on cue to the noise, the two dragon whelps playing around on the fields come over and nudge their snouts against my calves. I stumble forward and glance over my shoulder at them.

Mischievous little creatures.

Zuru and Naryx are their names. Zuru is a female Merati with an onyx coating and horns that are beginning to grow, while Naryx is a male who embodies all the colours of an Ardenti dragon. Red, orange, and even hints of blue flicker in the sunlight. They are siblings, though still too young to do much, but the way their slit eyes gaze at me and always want to be nearby has my heart spilling out to them.

There is something about the idea that these little creatures were once inside a shell. Gus loved informing me of how he assisted in so many dragon births. Shifters, dragons . . . the whole lot.

I turn, smiling down at them both, and they purr before Tibith steps between us, fluttering his leaf-like hairs at them.

'I hope you are not taking Miss Nara away from me!' he yells, and immediately jumps back when Naryx hisses at him and spits out a small fireball onto the ground.

Amusement makes my brows rise as I look at Tibith. He has his arms wrapped around my calf. 'What did I say about being nice to them?'

He whimpers up at me. 'But they ate the bread Miss Freya gave me yesterday, Miss Nara!'

I click my tongue, shaking my head with mirth, when Gus says from my side, 'And they will eat you next if you try and rile them up.'

I fire him a look of stern disapproval as Tibith buries his face into my leg, and a rumble of laughter leaves Gus's throat. For a weakening moment, it reminds me of Darius – his playful side. Throughout this time, I have considered Gus a guardian, and I understand why Darius thought so highly of him. Still, there were times I would picture Darius whenever Gus spoke to me, and it never made it easier.

'We'll talk later, Nara.' As the wind weaves through Gus's shoulder-length hair, he pats my shoulder. 'Hira wanted me to enforce some barriers between shifters and the off-bound areas,' he says with a gentle smile, reminding me of the ongoing feud between the Rocs and Phoenixes. Only recently have I found out that a Roc is what a phoenix once used to be before turning against the sun, thus becoming dark and horrific in its phoenix form. Their history was never in any book I've read, but after spending time here, I'm fortunate to know that Phoenix warriors are always loyal to their kingdom, protecting their civilians from the manipulations of a Roc.

'You should come by and visit the rest of us,' Gus says. 'They've been asking for you.'

I nod, not giving him a definite answer. I know he means visiting the shifters down at their quarters. Hira made sure to provide them with a homely place near the Aerian palace, but I'm unsure if I can handle questions about how the rescue mission is coming along.

Gus flashes into his dragon form, taking off as I clock Link running towards Illias. Illias picks him up, spinning him around before they share an intimate kiss. They are in their personal love bubble as I smile at them. On the other hand, I see Iker rolling his eyes at the scene before my gaze travels over to Rydan, whose eyes aren't on us. They're on Lorcan as he talks to a few other training Aerians far out in the fields. My eyes narrow, suspicion twisting my insides, urging me to approach Rydan. I glance at Tibith's tight grip on me and tell him to wait here. He doesn't look convinced, but after I reassure him that Zuru and Naryx won't eat him, he lets go, and I head towards Rydan.

'All right, spill,' I say, and he jerks around, blinking in surprise.

'Spill what? My undying love for you? Because I already did that, Ambrose, and I have to say I'm a little offended—'

'Why have you been avoiding Lorcan?'

He balks, shock almost making him stutter. 'I haven't.'

I wish I could hear his heartbeat like shifters can, but luckily, I don't need to when his lying skills are worse than most. 'I understand I was preoccupied with . . . well, what I am now, but it doesn't mean I haven't noticed, Rydan. For one, all you've done is spend your time near me, and while I have somewhat come to appreciate your blabbering, I know there's something on your mind.'

Haven't we all got something on our mind these days? Nothing is as it was a year ago.

Rydan rips his focus away from me, and dark clouds herd over us as if ready for a storm. He is thinking, trying to grasp my words, and losing. His chest deflates with a heavy sigh when those deep brown eyes bounce back to me. 'I took it hard when I heard he had died at the Venator trials, and then when I found out he was still alive, it was worse. Everyone else quickly adjusted to it, but I didn't know what to say. I still don't. Link is the only person who has been beside me for it all.'

Empathy punctures my heart. The first few days after the Venator trials, Rydan was different. I noticed. In fact, I was one of the few that did, and yet I did nothing. I let the selfishness of my own grief triumph over others'.

'Do you like him?' I say, breaking the sudden silence.

His scoff is full of disagreement. 'I like many people, Nara—' He stops, seeing the intensity of my stare, and cracks. 'All right, fine! Solaris, it's not as if this is the first time you have suggested such a thing,' he mutters, and while I *have* teased him about it in the past, I never realised how strong his feelings really were. 'It's nothing, though. He prefers women with anger issues and thinks I am a pest, so I should probably keep my distance.'

I scowl at him before lowering my head as disbelief reigns over me. 'Solaris, it's odd how similar we are about certain things.'

He laughs. 'I don't believe I am an angry little woman.'

'Little?' I frown at him, and outrageous offence takes over my tone. 'I'm above average height, you toad!'

'Mmm, I love it when you speak dirty things to me, Ambrose.' With a grin, he winks.

He truly knows how to ruin sentimental moments.

I glare, clearly in no mood for his antics. 'Just talk to him. You never know what could happen.'

'Are you saying that because you never thought you would fall in love with the Golden Thief?'

My heart begins to rattle. I lick my lips, feeling them freeze over with the cold weather. 'No,' I breathe. 'I have always been in love with him.' My view of Rydan's puzzled features blurs as I focus on my brother and Link talking to one another. 'I just needed to remember.'

You're all I've ever wished for, Goldie.

'Nara?' The clearing of someone's throat awakens me back to reality, and Rydan's eyes widen.

He whispers as he looks down at his hands. 'Did I just summon him?'

The fact he believes he can do that makes me almost laugh before I peek over Rydan's shoulder and see Lorcan standing there. He looks nervous, his lips twitching as if unsure whether to smile or keep a straight face.

'I uh—' he starts, but I know what he wants.

He wants to talk.

CHAPTER FOUR

I t seems somewhat nostalgic.

The reality of having Lorcan here by my side as we walk past the training grounds.

Male and female warriors in burgundy armour blast each other with fire onto the sandy terrain, and I simply watch them. Study them even, as if that will miraculously aid me in becoming Solaris. But I know that thought is too illogical under these circumstances. I am not a phoenix, not like Lorcan.

My gaze slips from the phoenixes to the side profile of his face. I look at how his jaw is coated in auburn stubble, and his hair is slightly overgrown. It might seem so silly to others that something minuscule, such as not shaving or growing their hair out a bit too long, is noticeable to me. But when Lorcan was a Venator, I never saw him be this carefree with his looks. He needed to present himself with this image of power. A second-in-command. Now here he is, a phoenix. What he was meant to be.

He casts me a sideways glance, thinking I am already looking away, but I am not, and it is obvious I have made him uncomfortable by outright staring at him. He clears his throat and points to the palace in the skies before us. 'I see you are close to the shifters residing here.'

'Solaris,' I mutter under my breath.

'Is something the matter?'

I shake my head as frustration slices across my chest, deep and agonising. 'Don't do that.'

'Do what—'

'The small talk, the idea that everything is perfect right now,' I sigh before stopping our walk and facing him. 'This is not the same as before, Lorcan.'

He looks away, ashamed. 'I am just not sure how to speak to you any more. You ignore me and act as if I am still dead and not here to help. It's been three months, Nara.'

I close my eyes and exhale a breath. I do not want a reminder. 'Did you think three months is all it would take for us to go back to normal?'

He bites the inside of his cheek, his face still turned away from me, as if he is intent on not answering that.

'I spent longer than that, thinking you had *died* the day of the trials.'

Lorcan's gaze falls to the grass below, a distressed sigh escaping his nose.

'I don't hate you for what you did to my father. It wasn't you.' I confess what I have been unable to face for so long. He finally looks at me – looks at me like there is hope for us again. I can see it; I notice it because it is the same look he gave me when he visited me in the dungeons the day before the trial. 'But,' I whisper, and my throat suddenly burns, 'you were still one of the first to break my trust.'

A heartbreaking shock pierces his eyes. It's almost tangible between us, with his guilt for me. And yes, I might have once thought it was the queen that broke me, but she was only part of what came after.

Having nothing else left to say, I start walking away. I've only gone a few steps before he says, 'He spoke of you, you know.'

I pause.

'A lot.' Lorcan chuckles. 'Actually, it became the only thing he would talk about.'

I slowly turn on my feet as Lorcan's eyes stare at the clouds. He smiles, and it looks almost boyish. 'The girl with golden hair and fierce eyes. Of course, I didn't make anything of it until I met you for the first time in your village.' He lowers his gaze, that smile fading into something sadder, and as the Phoenix warriors fly above us, keeping a watchful eye on trainees within their domain, Lorcan remains still. 'Deep down, I knew it was you, and the more you two met in secret, the more I knew I was losing you to him.'

Losing me to *him* . . .

'Lorcan,' I sigh, sinking my teeth into my lower lip. 'You didn't lose me because of him, because you never had me.' I should feel wrong for saying this to him, for letting my admission ruin whatever chances he might have imagined for us, but I don't. He deserves the truth. No matter how harsh it may be. 'And the truth is, I do not think you ever loved me. Not properly.'

He looks like he is about to interrupt me, but I raise my hand.

'I think you were infatuated,' I admit. 'And I believe the side of me connected to animals and creatures played a part in that, too.'

There is a stagnant pause, and I step towards him. He stiffens, unsure of my next move, as I hesitantly place a hand on his chest. Though I can't see the scar he once had through his clothing, I imagine it is gone, like the rest of the scars on his hands are.

'You were given a second chance to live,' I whisper, my eyes looking up at his. 'And you deserve to be loved, but that person is not me.'

He's shaking his head. 'No one will dare to after everything I have done in the past.'

I allow a slight titter to escape me as I drop my hand and take a step back. 'You would be surprised how forgiving the people of this world can be.'

His brows slant downwards, wondering what I mean by that, but I don't intend to spill anything. It is not my place.

'Goodbye, Lorcan.' I smile as if this is our truce for now.

He nods sagely. 'Goodbye . . .' an amused smile dots along his lips – '*Miss Ambrose.*'

I nod in gratitude as an Aerian warrior opens the large double doors of the base where the surviving shifters are staying. The building used to be a garrison for retired Aerian warriors; I have learned that Aerians treat one another like family and aren't accustomed to any rules such as the royals from other kingdoms have. I was always told they were the more rebellious of our four peoples, but really, they just accepted everyone as equals.

The Aerian woman smiles, her pale skin a jewel under the sunset. I then notice a few other Aerians walking towards the palace. They are wearing the usual Aerian armour, with the difference being the letter T carved in obsidian against their chestplate.

Trackers.

They are different from warriors. They are knowledgeable geniuses who investigate potential threats across Aeris. With the concern

I see across their leonine features, I can guess they are on their way to inform Hira about more Rocs.

As they disappear behind hedges, I enter the garrison and am hit with a powerful memory of my time visiting the shifter's den in Emberwell. But here is a hall full of them. Men, women, children, creatures Darius has saved, and dragons rest on long tables. A few are standing on the second floor, looking down at the others over the banister.

Despite what our world is facing, they are still enjoying themselves and acting like one giant family. This is why I don't like coming here often. Other than their endless questions, they remind me too much of Darius.

A child in plaits runs across to me with a whelp on their tail, while a goblin and what must be a pixie by the size of his enormous ears smile at me in recognition.

None of the shifters know who Darius and I truly are to the world. Gus had decided to keep that bit a secret. Having certain people know is already too much pressure, and I don't want more of them to rely on me.

'There is the Goldie!'

An agonising ache immediately has my breath drop to my stomach as I hear that nickname. I look to the right of me as the blond locks of Cutler come into my line of view. He's smiling from ear to ear with a tankard in his hand, not realising the significance of that one word.

My fingers twitch at my sides. 'Do not call me that.' It's a soft-spoken order, but I am so close to sending a punch his way.

He frowns, pressing his drink against his chest. 'It is what Darius called you, is it not?'

I know he does not mean it as a discourtesy, but I still take an infuriating footstep towards him and part my lips to go off on him, but a voice from behind stops me.

'Leave her alone, Cutler.'

I turn as Aelle strides over to us. Her brows slant as she looks at Cutler like a mother would at a misbehaving child.

'You and I both know you would not be acting this confident around her if Darius were here,' she says, side-glancing at me with a smirk, and I cannot thank her more for it. Ever since she and Leira stayed with the shifters back in Emberwell, Aelle has become like a mother to them all.

Cutler sighs, dropping his head in resignation. 'Yes, you are right.' He pouts before his eyes flit up at me with sheer embarrassment and waves his drink. 'I guess I will see you around, Nara.' He joins a group of other shifters by the table, and I blow out a huff as Aelle chuckles.

'Thank you,' I say as she wraps her arm around me and squeezes me into a quick hug. 'I was so close to punching him in the balls.'

'What balls? He has none!' She throws her head back, roaring with laughter as her copper hair shakes with the trembling of her body. Soon, I begin chuckling too. 'No, but on a serious note . . .' She wipes her eyes, clearing her throat. 'How are you?'

And here come the questions . . .

'Starving.' I smile.

Her brow jumps. 'That is always your answer. Do you think I don't know when you are lying by now? I could tell even if I weren't tuned in to your emotions.'

Despite how right she is, it's not hard to decipher my true feelings. Sighing down at her, I link arms with her and walk down the middle of the hall. 'I guess, if you must know, each day I am hoping I will wake up from this nightmare.'

She stops, turning me with her. 'Dearest.' She fixes the collar of my maroon shirt which is tucked into my dark leather trousers. 'Who says this has to be a nightmare?'

'Well, it is not exactly a joyous time.'

'It neither has to be joyous.'

I can only stare at her, wondering what form of consolation she is trying to give me this time. I have had enough from everyone else but all it has left me with is a hollowed chest.

'You love that man, do you not?'

Her question fills my heart with something so overwhelming that I can only nod before my voice breaks on the word 'Deeply.'

Aelle's eyes crinkle as she smiles before noticing the golden coin around my neck. She presses her palm against it and looks up at me almost maternally, much like Leira does. 'Then *that* should be enough to keep you from thinking this is all a nightmare.'

The soothing note of her voice has me drawing backwards, my gaze watery as I clutch on to my necklace. 'Have you seen Gus?' I clear my throat and avoid looking at her.

She sighs, and a beat of a second passes by before she acquiesces to my need to change subjects. 'He was in here not long ago, playing some music on the piano at the far end of the hall.'

I frown. 'Piano? Since when does Gus play?'

'Since he was a child, apparently. You should have seen him back at the den; he kept us entertained most nights. According to others, it was the first time he had played in a while.'

I lose focus for a moment, and my mind seems to spin as I think of something that *has* to be just a coincidence.

'Margie, have you seen Gus?' Aelle asks a passerby.

Margie purses her lips. 'Last I saw of him, he went into the kitchen with your wife and that bubbly niece of hers.'

My gaze snaps back to her, brows furrowed. 'Freya?' She had told me this morning she would be visiting the Aerian children at the campsites in the nearby villages until nightfall.

Aelle hums a 'yes', though she focuses more on what is behind Margie. 'Ayru!' she shouts, startling me. 'You better not be eating that tapestry!'

I glance towards an Ardenti dragon who looks up with bewildered eyes and a piece of hand-sewn phoenix tapestry still inside his mouth.

'Apologies, Nara.' Aelle touches my arm as she starts walking. 'I need to ensure Ayru doesn't destroy what the Aerians humbly gave us.'

I nod, bidding her goodbye as I dart through the shifters and head towards the end of an empty hallway where the kitchen door is ajar. I press my hand against it, hearing voices as I peek through and spot Leira and Gus standing behind oak countertops. Freya is on the opposite side, sitting on a wooden stool with her face buried in her hands.

'How long do you plan on hiding this from her?' Leira hisses, her head shaking as she stares at Gus.

'She is going through enough, Leira. She does not need another thing to bring her down.'

'And do you expect to keep it from her like you did with *him* all these years?'

'You know it was not easy.'

'It *was*, Augustus!' Leira smacks her hands down against the counter, making Freya flinch. 'It has *always* been easy, but you kept choosing the hard way, and now you have dragged me and my niece down with it.'

I glance between them as heaviness takes over my chest, leaving me breathless.

Gus lowers his gaze, the tendrils of his dark hair covering his face and making it hard to see his expression. 'She will hate me for it.' He sighs with desperation. 'And *he* will hate me for it—'

'He is your son!'

The air inside my lungs stills.

No.

I didn't know you could play.

I can't. That was all I knew.

Whose music, was it?

My father's.

'And right now,' Leira's voice quivers with an exhale, 'he is being held against his will by Aurum. *Fix it* before Zerathion ceases to exist.'

Disbelief wracks my entire body. I have no control over myself as I barge into the kitchen, watching all three heads turn in my direction.

My eyes lock on Gus's wide gaze as my lips twitch angrily. 'It was you. All this time, you were Darius's father.'

CHAPTER FIVE

'Nara.' My name, coming out of Freya's mouth, fades into a whisper as she rises from the stool. Sorrow tears her expression apart, but I shake my head, focusing all my might on Gus.

'We didn't—' Gus's voice is low and firm, but I cut him off by slamming the door shut behind me, creating an echo to fill the panic inside everyone standing here.

'Didn't what?' I speak. 'Think I would show up here today?'

They all share guilt-ridden looks.

'Didn't think I could handle something so—' My hand flickers around the place. 'Secretive? Something that, *apparently*, I am not ready to find out about?'

Gus starts towards me like he is trying to keep me from lashing out or, worse, trying to kill him. 'It is not your burden—'

'It does not matter whether it is my burden or not!' My shouting is so raw it grips my throat and scratches the surface as I swallow. 'You are his *father*.'

He closes his eyes, running a hand over his mouth and beard. I shake my head, annoyed that I never saw the signs. The mannerisms, how he sought out Darius back in Emberwell to join him, and the paternal instincts.

'All this time that he has confided in you.' I quell the temper in my voice. 'That *I* have too, and you've just kept it one big secret.' My eyes are like daggers, aiming them straight at Gus. 'You should be ashamed of yourself.'

Gus doesn't respond. He knows better.

I glance over at Leira's fallen stare, then at Freya. 'How long have you known?' I ask her, my voice cold with betrayal.

She fidgets, playing with her fingernails. 'Leira and I only found out during the time you were away in Terranos, but Nara, I swear I wanted to tell you—'

'But you didn't,' I cut her off, and she winces at my tone. Of all the people, she is the last person I would expect to keep this from me. 'None of you did.' I look at the other two. 'Because all I am to everyone here is this girl who can barely control what she is supposed to be.'

Leira shakes her head, concern suddenly contorting her delicate features. 'That's not true. We do not think that at all.'

Lies, lies, and more lies. 'Then what do you think? Hm? Because everyone around me is acting like I am slowly losing my mind.'

She sighs, cupping her mouth with one hand as she turns away from me.

'And maybe I am!' I raise my hands before smacking them down on my thighs. 'Maybe this is the price I pay for still being alive!'

'Nara.' Leira looks at me again. She sounds like she is begging me to stop.

I relent because I know I cannot do much else. Heaving a breath to control myself, I straighten my back as I say, 'Aurum must have gotten rid of all the steel within the castle walls by now.'

Gus's gaze darts up at me. A worrying frown takes over him, much like Leira's.

'We will depart for Emberwell tonight,' I tell them, and immediately they all give each other panicked looks as if I am proving my insanity. 'And *you* –' my gaze cuts to Gus – 'will tell Darius yourself who you are to him.'

'We can't—' Gus's words are immediately interrupted as I storm up to him, raising a pointed finger.

'You once ordered an attack in the city because the Queen despised you all,' I snap. 'I have even killed some of your people because of it. And yet you stand here, ready to tell me we cannot go rescue Darius, who happens to be your son and the man who spent his whole life believing you abandoned him?'

He flinches at the word, shaking his head at me. 'Nara, this is different. You know ordering an attack when his life is tied to Aurum's is risky—'

'Then we will find a way to untie it!' My voice cracks. I'm desperate, and they know it. 'He is Crello's reincarnation. You cannot tell me there is no way to free him.'

'No,' Leira says quietly, her stare focused on the counter instead of me. 'There isn't any way we can find as of right now.'

Heavy breaths stab my chest as I look between the three of them. I'm begging them to change their minds and pleading for them to listen to me, but they do nothing.

'There will be no departure tonight, Nara.' Gus's voice is authoritative. 'That's an order.' He passes by me to open the door. When I turn to him, my blood sizzles and spits as I try to hold back my urges to react physically.

'You know what? I changed my mind. I am so glad Darius doesn't know who you really are.' Pure venom seethes through my lips as he freezes and looks back at me. 'You would only have disappointed the image he already had of a father even more.'

I do not wait for whatever reaction my words cause him as I shoulder past him and march out of the kitchen, feeling my soul shredding to pieces.

Aerian guards are preparing to open the palace doors when Freya catches up to me along the cobblestoned bridge and tells me to stop. My fingers flex at my sides, and begrudgingly I turn around. She is a few feet away from me as the curls of her hair flap around her face uncontrollably in the wind.

'We have nothing to discuss, Freya. Just go back to the garrison,' I say, about to turn my back on her.

'You always do that.' She sounds frustrated – looks it too as she shakes her head. 'Shut everyone out when all we want is to help.'

My brows rise comically at that word. 'Help?' I repeat in bewilderment. 'You think keeping *that* from me helps?'

'You were so focused on your training, I . . . Gus did not want to make you any worse. But if you let me explain . . .'

All that I can answer back with is a sardonic laugh as I mutter, 'Pathetic.'

Freya looks at me, regretting having said all that. Her hazel eyes are dark and sombre against the grey skies.

'I am not a child,' I say. 'I can deal with it all just fine.'

'Can you?' She finds strength in her voice, which I have not often witnessed with her, but when I have, it is enough to frighten me. She is just as angry and frustrated, and perhaps it is because she knows me. She knows I haven't dealt well with anything so far, and she knows I am spiralling.

Still, I do not have it in me to answer the question as my gaze tears through her, and I turn to leave.

'Just like that, you walk away,' she shouts after me. My feet come to a stop as I glance at the ground beneath me. I hear her scoff, 'Solaris, you do not change.'

Suddenly, all I see is white.

I whirl, marching my way up to her. 'I have changed!' I yell. 'That is the problem. I have changed so much that I do not even recognise myself!' My legs are shaking, and my lips are quivering with anger at her and who I am right now. Freya stays still, her chest heaving as I step closer. 'And do you know what I get from it all? *Pity.*' I spit the word out as if it didn't belong in my mouth. 'Pity from you, from my brothers, from Hira – *I am so sorry about what happened to you. I know how hard it must be to take on the role of a deity when you are just a mortal.*' Exhaustion takes over me, but I can't help everything I say to her. 'You all act as though one of these days I will break. And you know what? I am so sick of it, and most of all, I am sick of *you!*'

Regret is imminent. I stumble back as if I have hurt myself, but no, it is Freya who I have hit with the damaging words, and I can see it. Her face falls, the spark I always seem to see in her fades, and as I'm about to reach my hand out to her, a wave of air lifts me from the ground, and I'm knocked back against a pillar. A groan splits from my lips as I land palms first on the ground. My head spins as debris crumbles at my sides, and the echoes of more than one person shouting my name surround me. I lift my head, seeing the violet glow in Freya's eyes. She gasps as they return to her normal colour, and tears slide down her cheeks. Rydan runs to her as Idris and Illias hoist me up by my arms, and Iker's gaze darts back and forth, torn at the event that has just happened.

'Frey—' My throat hurts as I try to speak. I wish I could take back what I said, but Freya wipes the teardrops from her face, turning to Rydan as he leads her away.

CHAPTER SIX

'I said I was fine, Illias.' I swat his hand away as he keeps grabbing my face to check for bruises.

He scowls down at me, using his Aerian maroon tunic sleeve to wipe dirt off my brow. 'Just because you hated whenever I would try and clean your cuts up after a fight at the village doesn't mean you can still push me away and act like it is nothing.'

I stir on the edge of my bed. Iker is staring at me from the doorway while Idris leans against the window of my room, looking out as day slowly turns into evening.

'What happened between you and Freya for her to react this way?' Illias asks as I take hold of his two fingers and sigh.

I shake my head to the ground, unable to erase the wounded look on Freya's face. 'Like I said, it was a silly argument,' I whisper. 'I shouldn't have said the things I said to her.'

'What *did* you say?' The question comes from Iker.

My eyes fly in his direction, and I open my mouth, keen on saying whatever comes to mind, but I am stumped. Telling my brothers that

Gus is Darius's father will cause more chaos than there already is. They trust Gus too much.

Idris must notice the turmoil going off inside my head as he says to the boys, 'Leave us for a moment.'

My shoulders stiffen, and I shift on the edge of the bed. Talking with Idris alone means he's going to lecture me; and that is the last thing I need. The last time he wanted to speak to me was to chastise me for falling in love with a criminal who is also a dragon shifter.

A grimace sneaks up on my lips as I imagine how this conversation will go, but Iker scoffs, shaking his head at Idris, which startles Illias and me. And before he turns to face him, I catch a small glimpse of contempt in his eyes. A look I have rarely ever seen on Iker.

'What is it that you have to say that you can't say in front of us?'

Illias looks over at me, his eyes wide and knowing as if he has dealt with this too many times now. Idris doesn't even utter a word at Iker, his stoic gaze unbreakable.

'Come on—' Illias tries to yank Iker away, but he is unable to move him from the spot.

Iker shoves Illias off, and I stand up with blunt force, not liking this sudden hostile situation between my brothers. 'No, I want to know,' he says, jerking his chin at Idris. 'What is it, brother? The role of a father figure in our family gone to your head?'

'Iker. *Stop*,' I warn.

'Why is it always us two having to leave? Do you not tire of being so demanding?' He steps into Idris's space, squaring off as he pushes him. 'So controlling—'

'Enough.' I jump between them, pressing my hands against their chests before they can enter a brawl that Illias and I will have to break up. 'Don't you see what is happening?'

The harsh look in both their eyes settles to something gentle as they land on me, and whatever possessed them to act this aggressively towards each other stops.

I lower my hands. 'Nothing is right any more.'

'Nothing has been right since you left home, Nara,' Illias whispers, and I bob my head knowingly.

'Yet do you believe any of this is helping us right now?' I gesture to the whole room, metaphorical meanings and all. 'I just got thrown through the air by my best friend. Iker and Idris clearly have something to resolve, while the previous king of Emberwell is alive and a danger to our world. I don't know about all of you, but I am tired of this, so can we just *please* focus.'

The whole room lapses into silence. I know they agree with me. Too much is at stake. We are no longer in our village dealing with dragons or goblins stealing from our cottage. This is mightier than all of that.

'Illias,' I say, looking over as Iker's head hangs low, his curls dangling over his forehead. 'Take Iker somewhere else to calm down.'

As Illias nods, heading out of the room with Iker, I take a long-deserved breath before returning to reality.

'And you!' I spin around to look at Idris with an accusatory finger pointing in his direction. 'What is the matter with you?'

He raises a bushy brow. 'Shouldn't I be asking you that, considering the incident outside?'

My head tilts, and I throw him a look as if to say that it's a stupid question. Before Iker tried to confront him for his own reasons, I knew Idris would have asked me this either way.

'Why do you ignore Freya?' I say, making his eyes jump until he reverts to his stone-like expression.

'What does that have to do—'

'Why do you *ignore* her? Or better yet, what is happening between you and Iker? I have never seen him like this, so what have you done?'

As he shakes his head, he makes a noise at the back of his throat, almost like he wants to laugh. 'You sound just like Father once used to.'

'Why? Because I am calling you out on what I've witnessed lately?'

'Because you're quick to blame me.'

My brows pull together, and I wonder why he believes that. I might have been too young to remember specific moments between my father and Idris, but I never once felt he blamed him for anything. 'I—' My tone is lighter. 'I am not blaming you, Idris. I am simply—'

'Worried?' he cuts in, giving me a pointed stare. 'As am I, Nara.'

I look away, knowing he definitely thinks of me first. I cannot fault it when I have an urge to look after him too.

'I kissed her.'

My head swings in his direction at an abnormal speed. His gaze is elsewhere, not wanting to look at me after confessing to kissing my best friend. Though I already know about it, it doesn't mean I would have mentioned it. 'And do you . . . regret it?'

It takes him five seconds to answer. 'Yes.'

I scoff. 'Liar.'

The silence between us melts into me. It is the kind where I do not know if he will answer or if he will walk out of that door like he used to do whenever I confronted him about anything. I steel myself for the second option and stare at my brother as he turns his back to me. He runs both hands through his chestnut locks, and I wait. I wait for it—

'I do not want to commit to someone.'

My eyes struggle not to widen.

He turns to me, despair and exhaustion consuming his expression. 'Freya is young and too full of life to have to deal with me.'

Hating how he thinks so low of himself, I shake my head frantically. 'You are not some broken man, Idris.'

'But I am also not ready.' He shoots me one of those severe looks before sighing as he walks up to the window. 'I don't know if I ever will be, and I don't want to keep her waiting in hope that we *will* be someday.'

'And Iker?'

'He started spending quite some time with Freya while you were away. I suppose somewhere along the way, he developed feelings.'

I suppose it would have been hard not to under the circumstances they were all in.

'Does Freya know this?'

He shakes his head. 'I thought Iker was being childish at first, liking her to annoy me, but something snapped in him when he saw Freya upset because of me.' He looks over his shoulder at me. 'We've argued so much ever since.'

A heavy sigh pulls out from my chest. I can see how much this hurts him. Yes, we might have all argued as a family back in the village about the most nonsensical things, but never about love. Idris knows heartbreak; he has loved and lost, and I think, in many ways, he understands me more than Illias and Iker do when it comes to Darius.

'Miss Nara!' Tibith's little footsteps tap across the floor as he runs inside the room. He jumps onto my calf, hugging it tightly as he says, 'I have missed you tre-tremendously, Miss Nara!'

I chuckle as he releases my leg, and I kneel to bop his nose. 'As I have you!'

He giggles, rubbing his belly. He has no idea what happened with Gus or Freya, and I would like to keep it that way.

As I look up, my smile falls when I see Idris start to walk away.

'Idris,' I call, and stand as he turns to me. 'Father wouldn't blame you for any of this.'

He tries not to show any emotion, but fails as his forehead scrunches and he looks at me like he could just cry.

'He would be proud of how great a big brother you have been to us all.' My heart cracks open as I smile at him. 'And even if you don't believe it, you will be ready one day. Whoever that may be with.'

A strangled sigh comes out of him as he looks off to the side. He nods in thought before darting his gaze back to me. He doesn't mention anything about what I have just said to him, but I understand this is his way of accepting it. 'I forgot to tell you. When you have time, I have a gift waiting for you inside that chest box.'

I look behind me at where he points and I narrow my eyes suspiciously, heading towards it. 'A gift? Another one?'

'Consider it your late birthday gift.'

A gasp lodges in my throat as I pry the chest open to reveal a leather saddle. Tibith climbs up onto my shoulder as I lift the harness out of the box and run my hands over my name embossed on the side.

'I know you are . . .' He trails off as if he can't quite grasp what I am. 'But I thought you might need one, considering you have a close bond with almost every dragon here, especially Fernah.'

My eyes shoot up at Idris. I can't stop myself from grinning. 'You made this yourself, didn't you?'

'With the help of Illias and Iker.' A note of soft laughter makes his chest shake. 'It is the only time we did not butt heads.'

My voice cracks as I laugh too and take another look at the saddle.

When I lost the dagger Idris gave me, because of Aurum, I thought he would never craft me anything else, but I should know better by now.

Too emotional to speak, I mouth 'thank you' to him.

'Don't thank me.' He gives me a stern look. 'Just go find Freya. I've already disappointed her once; don't let another one of us Ambroses do the same.'

I don't get another word in as he walks out the door.

CHAPTER SEVEN

I knock on Freya's door a second time, only to be met with absolute silence. My gaze darts to Tibith standing beside me, wearing a curious expression as to why we are here. I purse my lips to the side and knock a third time.

'Freya, are you in there?' My voice sounds unusually fragile. When I don't hear anything, I go to turn the doorknob, but I'm stopped before I can do so by Hira's voice floating through the hallway. I mutter a curse word and step away from Freya's door as Hira approaches me with the widest of smiles.

'Hira.' I bow my head and force a smile of my own towards her.

Her expression softens into something a lot like sympathy. 'I heard what happened today.'

I would have imagined so.

Feeling uncomfortable, I clear my throat and apologise, but she shakes her head as if I shouldn't have to.

Her long raven hair is tied back into plaits as she holds a wooden staff in her left hand. 'Is there a reason you two fought?'

Tibith tugs on my leg, shying away from Hira as I look down at him. I exhale a tense breath, still not wishing to discuss what happened in front of him, but I know he partly understands something is not right.

'Things are . . . rough around here,' I tell her, making a poor attempt at a conversation with a phoenix leader, no less. 'As you can imagine.'

Hira narrows her fire-stricken eyes as she hums in agreement. I almost open my mouth to speak again of something else but shut it when she says, 'I have been meaning to show you something.'

Great.

I press my lips together in a tight line to hide my grimace. The timing cannot be more wrong and despite the fact I have not answered, Hira turns away from me and starts marching down the hallway.

'Come along,' she says. 'We won't be long.'

Tibith and I look at one another. He does one slow blink while I glance back at Freya's door and sigh.

Who am I to turn Hira down?

When Hira said she had something to show me, I thought that meant within the Aerian palace walls. Not the campsites just north of Aeris. As Tibith and I jump off Hira's phoenix form, I squint past the rosy glow of clouds settling above mountains. There's a pull at my heart, knowing that over that horizon, across the sea, lies Emberwell.

Hira walks up ahead through stiff mountainous pathways. The higher we go, the colder I become. Wrapping my arms around myself, I let Tibith nestle his shivering body into my chest.

'What is this place?' I ask as the biting cold fills my lungs, and I breathe out puffs of mist.

Hira uses her staff to guide her as we reach a point where, surprisingly, the cold subsides, and there are mismatched summits made of granite. 'Pintock Mountain,' she says.

My foot scrapes across the ground, and I frown as dust flies into the air. I kneel, rubbing two fingertips through the dirt.

'What is it, Miss Nara?' Tibith whispers.

'Ash.'

'Here is where the ceremony of a phoenix's rebirth occurs.'

I look up to find Hira's sharp gaze staring at me. The fire blazing in them reflects how meaningful this place is for Aerians.

'When a warrior goes through training and proves their loyalty to the Aerian leaders, we take them here to celebrate.'

I stand, thinking of all I have heard from Aerians over the past three months. How their allegiance is also to Solaris and Crello.

Glancing at my surroundings, I try to imagine what it must feel like to be *reborn*. 'I suppose this is where you also took Lorcan.'

Hira nods and leads me towards a cave crafted within the walls of the mountain. I keep Tibith by my side, trying to figure out why Hira brought me here. If it is to remind me of who Lorcan now is, I do not need it. I have only known Hira briefly, and most of our interactions have resulted in tense silences or my impatience to save Darius.

'Pretty!' Tibith says hypnotically at the glimmering red gems encrusting both sides of the granite walls. I pull his paw back before he can touch anything that might break.

'Ruby,' Hira comments, almost amused as the reflections of the crystals bounce off her armour. 'They are the gems of our ancestors' beaks; they shed the jewel once they decide it is time to pass on.'

I look back at them, each one beautiful and shaped differently from the rest. Like Tibith, I am enthralled and barely hear Hira call out my name as she heads deeper into the cave. I follow, stopping behind her as we hit a dead end.

My eyes narrow. I don't want to offend her by asking if this is all she wants to show me, but before I can say the wrong thing, she lifts a palm, pressing it against the wall. An orange glow ignites from underneath, illuminating the wall with flames as it slides open.

I blink as I walk inside with her and Tibith. My gaze roves around the enclosure. Phoenix wings are carved on the walls where weapons such as spears and swords are hanging. I glance at the crystallised ceiling, smiling as Tibith squeals with delight at every piece of treasure this place holds.

A tapestry hangs to the side of me, a piece of artwork depicting all three revered leaders of Aeris – Hira and her two sisters. I study the piece, noticing how Hira is at the centre, adorned in robes of ethereal flame – the embodiment of dawn. Beside her, Ara stands regal and enigmatic, draped in twilight hues that mirror the fading sun above them. Finally, the third sister, Col, is cloaked in the star-studded darkness of a cosmic sky. Her dark gaze holds something so mysterious, much like the constellations around her.

I tip my head to the side, the tapestry stirring a memory of what I once saw in Emberwell – a wall painting of Solaris and Crello as their hands joined to let the power of our world flow from them.

'Nara?' Hira calls to me, and as I turn, an instant wave of shock forces itself through my lungs when I see the two crowns resting atop plinths at the far end. One is of gold and resembles a halo as the solar flares soar outwards; the other is a wreath of starlight and crescent moons. 'Forged from the power of a phoenix's fire itself.' Hira admires them as she waltzes up to the plinths. 'They are beautiful, are they not?'

Extremely. 'When were they made?'

'Long before you existed.'

I stare at them as if I will fall prey to a trance sooner or later.

'Though it is rarely spoken or written about, there were always tales that someday a deity representing Solaris and Crello would be born.' Hira goes to touch the sun crown, but her hand stops in midair, and she retracts it. 'To this day, I remember my mother speaking of it with others. Whether it was to be a vessel or resurrection, they never gave up on the hope that this possibility of reincarnation would eventually help rebuild what our world has become.'

And she believes that it can be me and Darius.

My sigh brings her gaze towards me as I shake my head. 'I am not so sure I can help when I am so powerless.' I stare at my palms, my lips twisting as I try to conjure some form of magic from my fingertips.

Nothing comes.

I sigh.

'Perhaps the power of Solaris isn't necessarily how you imagine it to be.'

I frown at her as she walks towards me, pressing her hand against my back and guiding Tibith and me out of the cave. Over my shoulder, I glance at the crowns before they disappear as the wall slides closed.

'What do you mean by that?' I go on to ask.

'A dragon's power involves one of three,' she says. 'Shadow, mind or fire – save for your love. A phoenix can incinerate anything in its wake yet create everlasting youth with the touch of its feather upon someone's skin. Then, of course, there are the merfolk who admire Crello for the tides, and their magical power to manipulate water.' As she comes to a stop, she turns to me. 'And finally, Elves. Nature . . . darkness – much like Solaris and Crello, wouldn't you think?'

'I'm not sure I am following.'

She chuckles as if she thought that would be the case and resumes walking us out of the cave. 'Every species has a role in this world, and they accept what it is, even humans, but the point I want to make is that you seem not to want to accept your purpose. Or to believe that you do not deserve to be Solaris.'

I slow down my steps, looking downcast. I don't wait for her to stop as I say almost timidly for once, 'Solaris created life alongside Crello, but what they gave, they could also destroy.' My head tilts up, and I find Hira's powerful gaze on me. 'What if I end up destroying what I wish to salvage?' Am I afraid? Yes, now more than ever, even if I *still* struggle to admit it at times.

Hira blows out a breath of understanding. 'What is life without a little destruction?'

When I don't answer, she raises her brows and turns her back to me.

'You are wrong, you know,' I say out loud. Her head twists to the side, and I'm staring at her sharp profile as I add, 'Everyone might have a role in this world, but not all accept it. Why else do you think there are Dark Elves, Venators . . . Aurum? Sometimes, I believe not all of us are destined to be part of a world like this.'

She hums, mulling it over. 'Which is why we intend to defeat Aurum.'

Even then, there will always be something.

And as much as I want to voice that, I decide otherwise.

'So, how do you propose we do that?' I ask. 'We do not have the Northern Blade, and while Darius is bound to him, we are nothing but entertainment for Aurum.'

She spins around and gives me a forlorn smile. 'From what I know of Aurum, he has only ever craved power. Being a Rivernorth was never enough for him, but you and Darius share something he does not have.'

I frown, failing to see her point.

'You were both placed here to serve a purpose.' She gestures her hand out. 'So, perhaps it was an act from Solaris herself for you to survive the injuries Aurum inflicted on you back in Olcar, and it also may be that the reason our world is slowly dying is because we need you and Darius to protect it.'

Hira's words plant themselves inside my mind. A seed, feeding me information until it grows. She believes everything has a plan that will work itself out, and *maybe* she knows that if I went to Emberwell now, if I tried to save Darius, I would be altering her perfect destiny.

A destiny in which I don't get to make my own choices.

'I know . . .' She sighs. 'I know that you wish to rescue Darius right now. But if there is any chance we can find a way to get him back without harming him, then shouldn't we at least try and wait it out?'

I stare at her impassively. She is telling me to stand down when that is all I have done so far. How much longer must I wait? How much longer must I stay here?

Hira's serene smile does little to change what I feel and want right now as she touches my shoulder. 'I am sure that Darius, a royal Rivernorth descendant, would agree if he was in your position.'

That is where she is wrong.

I shift away from her touch because no matter what everyone might think Darius would do, *I* know that he would have gone to me the minute something felt wrong. Darius isn't just a Rivernorth. He is also a Halen and the most wanted thief in Emberwell. He would stop at nothing to get what he wanted.

The shifting wind suddenly picks up, dragging what looks like a flower through the air. I let it get closer before capturing it in my hands. As I open them, I see the five white petals. Delicate, beautiful, and not a plant that should be found on these mountains. Bringing the flower to my nose to smell the fresh fragrance of jasmine, I close my eyes and inhale, letting my mind wander into memory.

'*Here,*' Darius once said in Emberwell, as he plucked a jasmine flower from a woman's basket.

'*What's this for?*'

'*You always smell of jasmine.*'

I picture his smile and the careless shrug he gave me, and it suddenly feels like someone is ripping my chest apart. I clutch the flower tightly to me, thinking it can spur something magical to fix this loss, but I know it cannot. Not from where I am standing.

My gaze, fierce and in control, flies wide open onto Hira, staring at me with a curious frown. 'You're right,' I say, not planning to let go of the flower. 'I shouldn't risk myself against Aurum.' I smile at her, but even then, it is tense. 'Like you have said before, he might want me to fall into whatever sadistic plan he has in mind.'

'It is for the best, Nara.' Hira gives me a gentle squeeze on the arm. 'I am glad you understand now.'

I nod and watch her walk past me. Turning to Tibith, I see him tilt his head up at me, his usual big eyes narrowing with acute suspicion. I squat and hand him the jasmine flower. My smile is no longer strained as I look at his ears, flapping excitedly.

If Aurum wants me to walk into one of his traps, then let it be decreed that I will do everything in my power to escape it.

CHAPTER EIGHT

I close my bedroom door and turn just in time to see Freya rise from my bed. I pause beside the entrance, staring at her as if the apology I intended to say earlier will once again manifest in me.

Freya picks at her lower lips, making them bleed, and an uneasy gust of air appears to encircle us as her gaze is drawn to the ground. 'Where is Tibith?'

'With Link,' I say curtly. As soon as my outing with Hira ended, I searched for Link, knowing he wouldn't ask questions about where I was headed in such a rush.

'Right, I—' She rubs the back of her neck, and I hate this. I hate how awkward we are.

I walk towards her, but she backs away as if she is afraid. Shock guts me like a twisted blade as I jerk to a stop. 'Freya, you know I wouldn't hurt you, right? With everything that happened—'

'I am not scared that you will hurt me; I am scared I will hurt *you* again.'

The chamber fills with silence.

She blames herself when it is not her fault.

I shake my head as a sigh escapes her lips in an almost sob, and she runs her hands through her tight curls. She stops me before I can speak.

'I should have told you about Gus. Or at least forced him to say something.' She paces the room. 'I wanted to do the right thing, but the more I kept it from you, the more everything became worse.'

My eyes track her nervous movements. The jittering of her fingers as she plays with them and the constant lip-picking. I had been the one to snap at her, to argue, and to egg her on until she used her magic on me. It shouldn't be her apologising, and it shouldn't be her carrying the weight of it all.

'You didn't do anything wrong, Freya,' I whisper. 'I am the one who keeps dragging you all down with me.'

She shakes her head. 'That is not true, Nara—'

'When I was five,' I cut her off, and a chuckle escapes my lips as I recall the faintest of memories, 'my only friends were my brothers. Then, when I turned six, I met someone who I never thought would be the man I am in love with today.' I let out a deep breath. 'But when I was twenty-one, I met the greatest person that I could finally call my best friend. Someone who, despite my lack of social skills, still cared for me and fought by my side even when she wasn't sure of the outcome.'

Freya gives me a look on the verge of tearing up.

'You couldn't hurt me,' I say, 'even if you tried. I only hope that you can forgive me for how I have acted all these months.' And if she didn't want to, I would not blame her; I have been too hard to bear sometimes. Not even I can stand myself at times.

'Solaris.' She sniffles, wiping her nose before she rushes towards me and wraps me in her arms. 'Why must you always make me cry?'

Her words have me chuckling. 'I am hoping it is for the right reasons, not the wrong ones.'

She grabs me by the elbows and looks into my eyes as we part. Her cheeks are tear-stained. 'You do know you aren't dragging any of us down, though, right?' I opt to stay quiet, and she lets go of me. 'Nara, you quite literally have the world's weight on your shoulders. You're Solaris, for—'

'What if I don't want to be Solaris?' I murmur a little too fast. Freya frowns, and I sigh, lifting my gaze to the ceiling as I laugh and shake my head. 'I should have never been chosen.' I look back down. 'I am not *you*, Freya. I am someone who used to trap animals for a living. How can it be that I am the world's . . .' I struggle to find the word before I spit out in shock, 'saviour?'

She stares at me. Usually, I can guess what she is feeling or thinking, but right now, she is giving me nothing to help me figure her out.

Her gaze drops to the floor as she whispers, 'Used to.'

'What?'

'You said you *used to* trap animals.' Hazel eyes flash up. 'That is the past. It is no longer who you are.' She pauses for a few seconds, her lips pursed in thought. 'But I also think you are too scared to let go of that.'

The space between my brows grows smaller as they furrow, and the back of my eyes sting. Despite it likely being the witch side of her, it is also the first time in a while that someone has read between the lines of the chaotic thoughts running through my mind and questioned them further.

And yes, I might be scared to let go of my past.

It was easier then.

'Before . . . the only people I used to care for were my brothers,' I say, a knot forming inside my throat. 'Now there is so much at stake, I fear I won't be able to protect everyone.'

Freya takes my hand. 'And that is okay.' Her smile is so kind and forgiving of the world. 'You have to remember, Nara, we can protect ourselves. Your brothers? They've handled everything on their own while you were gone. Idris spent so much of his time teaching self-defence to younglings; Illias trained himself with no help; Link is no longer afraid of anything; Rydan matured – to an extent; and Iker? He took on the task of teaching children how to read and write. He even taught them to build traps for any intruders.' She nudges my arm playfully. 'Like his sister used to.'

I make a tragic little noise at the back of my throat as I hold back a cry and smile. Seldom have I ever felt such pride, and knowing that while I have been away, they have all adapted to their new lifestyle without me makes my chest tighten.

Freya touches my cheek. 'Solaris or not, you are still the bravest soul I have ever met, and I am with you even if you wish to venture off into the wild again or face Aurum head-on.'

It's hard to stop myself from pulling her into an embrace again.

'Do you truly mean all that?' I ask, and the echo of her vibrating laugh makes me smile.

'Of course I do.'

I rear back, a plan already forming in the depths of my mind. 'Then would you be willing to help me tonight?'

Freya's mouth is half open as she frowns. She stutters, 'Well, I didn't think you would ask for my help this soon, but I suppose I should have seen it coming.' She sighs. 'What is it you need help with?'

'Going back to Emberwell.'

She blinks, her face the perfect statue of a shocked person. 'I am assuming this will involve getting Darius back.'

I nod and lick my lips. 'I know that everyone says we should wait, that if we can figure out a spell to undo Darius's bond with Aurum, then maybe it will be safer. But I can't do this any longer, Freya. The more time he spends there, the more I feel that I am risking losing him altogether.'

She takes my words into consideration. Freya is used to this side of me. She is no stranger, after all, to what occurred back in Ember-well. 'I—' She takes another moment to think. 'Of course—'

The second she is about to finish her sentence, the door to my chamber opens wide with a stumbling Link as he holds Tibith in his arms and Rydan grinning from ear to ear.

'You can count us in, Ambrose.' Rydan puffs out his chest, looking overly excited for a mission I have yet to describe.

My eyes narrow at the three of them. 'Were you eavesdropping behind the door?'

Tibith nods as Link shakes his head, and Rydan purses his lips.

'Define eavesdropping?' Rydan drawls.

'Listening in on one's conversation when you shouldn't,' Freya deadpans, causing Link to try to object by raising a finger.

'I would just like to state I was not part of this—'

'Then why did you hush me when they were speaking?' Rydan hisses at him.

'Because otherwise, they would have heard us.'

'What does Illias see in you—'

Link immediately takes a defensive stance towards Rydan, and my eyes roll to the back of my head.

'Must you both argue right now?' I cut them off mid-argument and set my shoulders back as I exhale. 'You know I did not want Tibith to be involved in any of this.'

Link bows his head at that reprimand, and Tibith jumps out of his arms. He trots towards me on all fours before standing on two legs.

'Oh, please let me come, Miss Nara! P-please, please, please!'

I sigh, disappointed at how difficult it is to deny him anything.

'I can help get Darry back!' He rolls around the room faster than the human eye can detect. 'And I am g-good at missions, Miss Nara; remember when I helped Darry trick you!'

My smile softens at his enthusiasm. It wasn't so long ago that he did, in fact, aid Darius in one-upping me at the jeweller's shop. 'I do.'

His feather-like hair flutters as he squeaks in delight, and I turn to Freya. She looks at me cautiously. Is she wondering when she will catch a break from my schemes?

The answer is likely *never*.

'There is something I need you to do.' My stare tells her everything.

I have a plan.

One that might not work, but one that I do hope does.

'Hira mentioned you, Leira and Aelle have managed to locate the Elemental Stones.'

Freya nods fervently.

Good. 'I will need you to scry for them one more time. This time deeper.'

Another nod comes from Freya as she mentions she will need to borrow the scrying mirror from her aunt and a dark room so that she can concentrate on using her magic.

Everyone else then joins in to listen as I draw out the details and see Link nod confidently as I mention his and Rydan's involvement. I almost burst with pride at how much Link has changed since his first days as a Venator trainee.

'You know, Ambrose,' Rydan says after I finish and everyone starts to leave except for him and I. He leans against the doorway and tucks his hands into his pockets. 'If we make it out of this alive, I think I deserve a kiss at least.'

His grin does not crack.

I eye him up and down, knowing this is just a farce because he still won't speak to Lorcan. 'You have a stain on your shirt.'

His brows crease together as he glances at his clothes and I smile, feeling like myself again as I waltz out the door.

CHAPTER NINE

A few hours later, I'm rushing Freya to the garrison where the shifters reside. The night is brisk, chilly and wet, but it makes no difference to the dragons, who are rolling in mud and grass outside the doors. Freya quickly grabs on to my arm as we stand before Fernah, an Ardenti dragon and mother to both Zuru and Naryx. She is the smallest of the adults we have here in hiding but large enough to ride.

As she lifts her head, a rumbling purr vibrates from her fire-red chest, and the most beautiful golden eyes meet mine.

'It's as if she knows you plan to ride her,' Freya whispers, and I chuckle while hitching the saddle Idris made for me up against my chest.

'She knows I have a soft spot for her.' I walk to Fernah's side and she lets me strap on the leather harness without so much as a protest. As I step back, I let her rise and my head falls in line with her chest.

'You have a soft spot for every dragon,' Freya says, and we both laugh, knowing that she is absolutely right. However, our high spirits soon plummet as someone calls out to me.

Freya's eyes widen as I mutter under my breath and turn to where Gus stands. His eyes shift from Fernah to Freya, then lastly to me.

'Gus!' Freya squeaks. 'We—we were just seeing if Idris's gift to Nara fits Fernah.' An awkward silence falls as Gus stares at us, causing Freya to fidget with her fingers. I put my hand over hers and stop her.

'Is there something you need?' I keep my tone cold and distant. His gaze darts to mine, and the mood around us shifts to something worse than when I found out who he was to Darius.

Guilt.

It is not enough, though. Not enough for me to forgive him for keeping this secret for so long.

'We need to talk, Nara.'

'No, we don't.'

He doesn't look like he will leave without being allowed to explain.

'Nara.' Freya tugs my arm, and I drag my stare from Gus to meet hers. 'It is all right. You need this.'

My lips twist and I frown before I open my mouth to tell her how I do not, but she raises her brows at me as if I have no choice.

'I will wait by the stables in case the boys come through there,' she whispers and walks past Gus, offering him a not-so-nonchalant smile that I hope he does not catch on to.

Luckily, it seems he doesn't as he rests his hands inside his trouser pockets and strolls slowly towards Fernah and me. He turns to face her, a wistful smile pulling at his lips as Fernah drops her head and purrs in obedience.

When Gus starts to speak, I don't know what to make of it. 'Darius was there when Fernah's whelps first hatched.'

The statement doesn't surprise me. In fact, it warms me to know Darius witnessed something so miraculous.

I move closer to Fernah and place my hand over her leathery skin as she breathes in and out. 'What was it like?' Even though I did not want to speak with Gus, he has quickly reeled me in by telling me this.

He chuckles, looking over at where I am standing. 'As if I was with his mother again.'

My gaze steadies on Fernah. Her head swiftly lowers so her eye connects with mine. The vertical slit of her pupil looks as if it expands, hiding most of the gold colour. To think I once believed in ending these beautiful creatures. I still hate myself for the past me that sought out revenge on them.

'When I first met Aurelia,' Gus says, 'I didn't know she was a Rivernorth.'

I can't help but let my eyes stray from Fernah to Gus. He is shaking his head, looking far off into the distance.

'I used to stay away from anything royal back then,' he continues. 'So, when I heard that Sarilyn had ended the Rivernorth reign, it didn't matter to me. What mattered was that the dragons were now in danger under her rule. I formed alliances with other shifters, saved as many of our kind as I could, and when the den was built, Aurelia stumbled into my path.' As he tips his head back and smiles, all I see is Darius. 'She was ethereal and passionate about all the dragons. Although she had quite a temper, too. She detested me bossing her around because, according to her, she could take me on quite easily and win.'

'And did she?' I'm overcome by my curiosity. Gus's amused gaze drops to look at me.

His smile widens. 'A few times, yes.'

Humour swirls in my chest, and I blow out a rushed breath through my nose, wishing I could have had the chance to meet Aurelia.

'Why did you leave Darius?' I ask the question that truly matters.

The smile on Gus's face vanishes. He looks at the ground and rubs a thumb across his bearded chin. 'I didn't. When I found out Aurelia was who she was, all I could focus on was protecting her from Sarilyn. It became my sole purpose to the point she felt suffocated. She thought by being with me, she would eventually drag me down with her problems, and when she became pregnant with Darius, I was ecstatic. But I knew this meant a long life of sheltering him, too. And a month after Darius was born, I found she had left the den with the plan of handing Darius to a few witches she knew, but . . . I guess she never followed up with that idea.'

Witches . . . Could they be the same witches who removed Darius's Rivernorth symbol on his hands?

I look at the ground and swipe my foot across the cut grass. I wonder what would have happened if Darius had stayed with the witches instead of his mother. Perhaps he would not have witnessed her death, and perhaps he would not have suffered so much at such a young age.

'I looked for her for so long, wishing she would just come back to me, but . . .' Gus never finishes that sentence, so I glance up at him.

'And then you found Darius years later,' I say, remembering when I first learned that Gus wanted Darius to join him.

A chuckle forms at the base of Gus's throat as he smiles fondly. 'I knew he was my son with just one look.'

'Then why didn't you tell him?' *Why didn't you try?*

He shakes his head, a sombre expression taking hold of his features. 'Because he already hated his father by then. He thought I abandoned him, and I guess it was easier to lie than tell the truth.'

'So you asked him to join you instead.' My voice sounds more accusatory than I intended it to be. I watch as he visibly swallows the guilt down his throat and nods.

'I did, and even when he rejected my proposition each time, I didn't care. I was just glad to have found him.'

'But Gus, you can't keep this from him for ever. There will come a day when he finds out, and it will only worsen things.'

He sighs understandably, but I can only say so much. *He* must be the one to break the news, not me, not Freya, not Leira, only him.

I look over at Fernah, marking her territory against other larger dragons wanting to invade her space. Sighing, I say to Gus after a minute or so, 'Apparently, you can play the piano.'

There is a note of silence. 'Since I was a child, I have played. Stopped when Aurelia left.'

'I heard Darius play once.' I glance at him. 'He told me it was all he knew and that it belonged to his father.'

Something glimmers in his eyes, carrying a mixture of humour and melancholy. 'That was the only piece I ever taught Aurelia. It was my love letter to her before Darius was born.'

And now Darius knows it, thanks to his mother.

I realise I'm smiling, and it is not much, but for the slightest moment, I let that anger I felt over not knowing who Gus was to Darius dissipate. We turn towards the dragons, focusing on them as I cross my arms over my chest to keep the cold from snapping at my fingers.

'Nara?' Gus says. 'On the night of Noctura . . . Darius gave me this.'

I snap my head to the side and watch him dig through his pocket, retrieving an obsidian ring. My eyes narrow as he draws closer and stares at the ring in his palm.

'When a dragon shifter marries, it is customary that the male makes his bride's ring using one of his scales.'

My confusion only escalates as he looks up and sticks his hand out for me to take the ring.

'I don't know when he made the ring, but that night, he told me to get rid of it,' he says, and I forget how to do a simple task such as blink. 'I assume whatever might have happened was enough for him to no longer want it.'

I look at the ring again, then at Gus, as he patiently waits for me to grab it.

Darius had this ring on the night of his birthday, the same day I helped him steal the Rivernorth pendant, and the same day he realised my feelings for Lorcan.

'Yet you never did throw it away,' I rasp, trying to soothe my throat as I palm my neck and end up finding the coin necklace Darius fashioned for me to wear in its place.

Gus looks at the coin and watches as I twist and turn it between my fingers. 'You know,' he chuckles, 'he took that coin with him everywhere he went. And whenever I asked him why it was so important to him, he would say it was the only piece of gold worth obsessing over. Then, when he brought you to the den, I figured out what he might have meant by that.'

I tighten my grip on the coin until my hand aches, but I don't care. I don't care at all.

'That is why I kept the ring, Nara,' Gus says. 'Because I knew he would regret it otherwise. And I am certain by now all he wishes to do is ask for you to marry him.'

My lips carve into a smile because he had, in fact, asked me to marry him, and if he had asked me a third time, I would have finally said yes. It was our game. A silly one that only ever mattered to us.

'Thank you,' I whisper, unconsciously reaching for the ring. Once it is in my grasp, warmth swirls all around me as if Darius were here with me. As my eyes well up with tears, my smile widens and I have trouble focusing on the ring.

'I should also tell you that I know you plan on heading to Ember-well tonight.'

The grin on my face disappears all too fast as my head snaps up, and panic drowns my features. 'Wh—'

'Hira told me about your outing earlier today,' he cuts me off with a level of calmness as though his reason will make this any better. 'As soon as she told me you agreed to back down from rushing to get Darius, I knew it was a lie. You never agree to anything lightly.'

I place the ring inside the pocket of my trousers as I shake my head and prepare myself for an excuse. 'Gus—' My mouth is like a gaping fish, opening and closing as I try to think of what to say, until someone else's voice I recognise interrupts us from behind, and Gus's eyes flicker over my shoulder with a knowing smile.

'Which is why we also figured you would try to do something like this sooner or later.'

I whirl to find Idris, Illias and Iker standing with their hands in their pockets and sheaths tied to their waists.

Shock doesn't begin to cover what I feel right now. 'How did you . . .'

'I might have told Illias.'

Link.

I look to my right as Link comes to a running stop with Rydan, Tibith and Freya, trying to catch up to them.

'I'm sorry.' Link sighs. 'I just couldn't keep something like this from him.'

Right, I should have known. Those two are inseparable, and Illias is also known to not keep secrets for long.

'Well, well, well.' Rydan claps his hands once as he catches his breath. 'Would you look at that, I am the only one who kept my word and—'

'So did I.' Freya's eyes roll as Tibith ignores everyone by tipping his head to each side while staring at Fernah.

As Rydan points an accusatory finger at Freya, firing himself up for an argument, I look back at my brothers. I take two steps at a time, swinging my arms back and forth like I used to do whenever I was in trouble with Idris.

'I'm guessing you're here to stop me from going through with it,' I say, and what would usually follow was him doing exactly that and then me disobeying him.

Yet he surprises me when he chuckles softly and says, 'Not at all.' My brows knit together. 'I always give you a hard time when it comes to letting you do what you want, and I know that I struggle to accept the concept of you—' He pauses with a grimace, twisting his lips as he looks off to the side.

'Loving,' Illias aids him, earning himself a glare from Idris and a snort from Iker.

'*Involving* yourself with a shifter,' Idris corrects him. 'But if you believe you can get him back from the clutches of Aurum, then I will follow you. We all will.'

I am so used to the assertive look in Idris's eyes that whenever he accepts me in spite of my antics, I can't help it; all my emotions tumble into me, knocking me off balance. When I was a child, I used to hate it. I thought he was only trying to teach me a valuable lesson by conceding to my wishes. Now, I savour every moment and every second he does it.

As I embrace my brother, I spot Lorcan standing idly by one of the pillars near the garrison. My shoulders hitch from the tension, and I step away from Idris as Lorcan walks across the grass.

'Oh, Solaris,' Rydan mutters. 'Don't tell me you are also coming, Lorcy?'

'He's not,' I snap. Truce or not, I still don't trust Lorcan enough to come with me, let alone to a place where everything went wrong to begin with.

'Nara.' Gus's voice sounds like he is trying to reason with me. It's as if *he* is on board with this.

I shake my head up at the sky. This is insane. All of it.

'You were going to go at this alone, to begin with—'

My eyes narrow as I force my gaze back down to Lorcan and stop him before he can carry on. 'I *had* Freya.'

Rydan's overdramatic gasp doesn't go unheard as he mutters to Freya how offended he is that I didn't mention him.

Lorcan sighs, his steps slow and careful not to spook me as he comes forward. 'I know that city like the back of my hand, Nara. I can help you.' He looks me straight in the eyes. 'But I need you to work with me. Just this once.'

He is asking me to do the exact thing I can't seem to do just yet. To trust him.

I glance at everyone who is here. They all surround me, waiting to hear what my final decision is. Only Freya has that look in her eye where she knows I'm secretly asking for some guidance. She smiles and tilts her head to reassure me that everything will be fine.

'What about Hira?' I peer up at Lorcan. It's been a matter of hours since I last saw her, but I can already imagine how disappointed she will be with me.

Lorcan rubs the back of his neck, pulling at the lengths of his outgrown hair. 'She will . . . *understand* once Darius is safe and with us.'

He doesn't sound convinced, even to himself, but this is a risk I am going to take regardless of anyone standing in my way.

'Then . . .' My attention sweeps to everyone else just as the wind picks up, dragging my hair across my face. 'If we are to do this, we will need a new plan.' One that might or might not end in chaos.

Gus steps forward. 'Where do we start?'

CHAPTER TEN

The streets of Emberwell are silent. Void of any civilians save for Lorcan and me. Grime coats the roads, even those of the once-prestigious Chrysos Street. I'm careful not to step on broken debris as nausea stings the back of my throat at the ruins of my once-home.

This is all my fault. I waited too long.

A rat skitters across my boots, and Lorcan is about to unsheathe his sword as if to attack it. I grip his arm and send him a warning look.

'Are you really going to try to kill a rat when we have other pressing matters at hand?'

He blinks, still holding on to the hilt of his sword. I roll my eyes, wishing I had chosen someone else to accompany me through this part of the plan. Letting go of him, I continue on our pathway as thick heat blows with the wind, contrasting with Aeris's winter weather at night. However, this feels different. Emberwell might always be warm, but it was never this blistering, even in the supposed hotter months. Can it be that it's worsened after Aurum used the Isle of Elements?

The thought hurts my head, and I try to shake it away when another gust of wind picks up. A torn flyer lands by the edge of my boot. When I pick it up and turn it over, my chest caves in at the sight of Darius's sketched face.

His *Wanted Thief* poster.

'I always hated seeing those all around the city.' Lorcan chuckles.

I stare at the sketch for a few more seconds before pocketing it away and turning. 'Because you despised him?'

Lorcan's smile fades over my cutting gaze. 'It wasn't because of that.' He sighs. 'It's just . . . It's just hard to believe that the last time I was here, all I was was a monster that should have never been created.'

My expression falls with regret. 'You weren't a monster, Lorcan,' I say. 'Rümens are intelligent, frightening, yes, but all they ever seek is to protect their herds. Isn't that what you tried to do?'

One of his eyebrows pops up, and a twitch of his lips tells me he's amused. 'And you know this first hand?'

'I *experienced* it first hand.' As soon as those words fall from my lips, Lorcan goes silent. I turn again, walking towards the end of Chrysos Street before I stop, curse under my breath and whirl to find Lorcan following closely behind, staring down at the ground like a lost animal. 'All right, look,' I say. 'I know that since we arrived here, all you've tried to do is make this less awkward between us, and I get it. These past few months haven't been *easy*.' My lips twist into a grimace as I think back to how many times I avoided him and still do even after our earlier conversation. I huff, shake my head and wipe the sweat from my forehead. 'I know that I forgave you for what you did in the past, but this still doesn't mean I can trust you easily.'

I hope he understands that, and I *hope* that the peaceful truce we have doesn't dissolve into what it once was.

Betrayal.

'I know,' he whispers, but he doesn't meet my eyes.

A familiar silence hangs between us, one that cuts through the smell of fear in the streets. After a minute of it, I say, 'I'm not sure how Darius will react to seeing you alive, and I'm not sure how he will feel about finding out you are a phoenix. But I know that he has never stopped thinking of you as a brother, and I can only hope you will accept him as the same.' I pronounce those last words so forcefully that he finally looks at me.

The colour of his green eyes flashes with something I recognise often in them these days – remorse. 'He told you about my father, didn't he?'

The muscles on my back go taut. 'I can't say I am your father's biggest fan.' I turn my back on him, my legs heavy from walking for too long. 'If he were still alive, I don't think I could contain myself very well around him.' I'm near the jewellery shop where I met Darius, and I find myself slowing down as I glance around at the silent streets, the worn-down town houses that were once so lively.

'I think he would be afraid of you.'

My brow shoots up at the sound of Lorcan's soft voice behind me and I snap my head over my shoulder.

He runs a hand over his chin, smoothing the scruff of his stubble. 'He was always quite the coward.' He shakes his head. 'I suppose that is where I got it from.'

The cumulative effect of all the times I have referred to him as a coward causes my eyes to shut momentarily. When I think about apologising, I open my mouth only to immediately close it. What good would it do to apologise and tell him I no longer believe that? He hasn't proved anything to me yet, just given me spoken promises with no action to back them up with.

'I loved him,' he says, standing beside me, and I just . . . stare at him. 'I loved him because he was my father. But how he treated Darius . . . ' His nostrils flare and he puffs out a long breath through his nose. 'I never once tried to stop it.'

What is it with the Halens that all they do is blame themselves?

I walk up to him and place my hand on his arm. He turns, looking at how I've touched him, at how I don't even wear a glove over my scar any more. 'But you still made sure to look after him.' He isn't looking at me, even as I try to meet his gaze. 'Despite your differences, despite the times you were pitted against each other as children, you still treated him like family, and that is all Darius has ever wanted.'

A family.

Both he and Tibith wanted that, and we almost had it. The three of us together, my brothers, my friends.

We can still have it. A whisper of a promise echoes inside of me, but it is the sudden frown on Lorcan's face that has me snapping out of it all.

'Nara,' he says, not looking at me but instead out ahead. I turn to where his attention is focused and find smoke pouring through the streets. I run without waiting for Lorcan into the city's centre and stop as soon as I see what has become of the Neoma Tree.

It is now nothing but charred wood and broken branches. Ashes scatter the ground, the few marigold leaves of which barely are left, are no longer vibrant like they once were.

I jerk forward with the urge to run towards it, but Lorcan pulls me back by my elbow.

'Nara, wait.' He bites down on the word *wait*, and I frantically shake my head.

It's burnt. It's all burnt. Aurum— '*He* did this, he—'

'Stay where you are!'

My eyes widen as Lorcan mutters '*Shit*' under his breath. Two Elves wearing the armour from Terranos come out of one of the hidden roads. Their arrows are nocked as they aim them at us, and then more and more guards come forth from every direction.

CHAPTER ELEVEN

Lorcan and I are shoved and dragged around as the Elven guards take us past the castle bridge. My eyes scan to whatever else might be different in Emberwell. No Venators are around; only Elves who once served Dusan and are now in the hands of Aurum and Thallan.

I watch as the dark sky has a faint blue light igniting the horizon.

It will soon be sunrise . . .

'Keep walking.' An Elf nudges his shoulder into me, and it takes all my powers of restraint not to react.

I clench my fists and begrudgingly allow them to manhandle us.

Just be patient, Nara.

As the doors to the castle open and we step inside, the only thing that can calm me down is repeating the mantra. But to my surprise, nothing has changed. The same gold walls shine beneath sconces, and crystallised windows adorn the hallways.

Lorcan and I exchange glances as we both notice a putrid odour in the air, similar to the smell of leather burning. And then I see it.

Passing the threshold into the throne room, there are charred bodies piled on top of one another lying at the far end, near the dais. I can't put a number on it; maybe a dozen of those could have been Venators. It's difficult to tell from how unrecognisable they look, but the dragon's crest still prominently shows.

My stomach twists and physical pain has me almost bending over, but the tug from an Elf forbids me from doing so.

'Nara,' someone says, and hearing that voice again sends a pang of nausea my way. 'What a pleasant surprise.'

The Elves in front of me step off to the sides, giving me a clear view of Aurum sitting on the throne. His dark hair is shorter than when I last saw him, his clothing different, now matching Emberwell's bright style. His legs dangle off the arm of the chair as he toys with a flame within his palm. He's not looking directly at me, but just the sight of him brings back unwanted memories of that night.

'I was beginning to think you wouldn't ever come.' He turns his head, revealing a golden eyepatch covering his left eye and a ghastly scar slipping diagonally beneath it all the way to his cheek.

My lips almost twitch into a smile, remembering that *I* did that – that *I* caused that, and it never fully healed.

Regardless, I try to lunge forward only to be held back. 'What have you done to the tree?' I demand.

He smacks his lips together, raising a finger as he drops his legs from the throne. 'Ah, yes, *that*.' He leans forward, steepling his hands. 'I always hated that tree from a young age. I must say it felt great burning it down along with mortals. I mean, who knew that a bleeding tree could make you feel so . . . *defenceless*?' He rises from the throne and strides down the dais with slow steps. 'Of course, it doesn't do much to me. I am a true-blooded Rivernorth, but Darius? Well, half Rivernorth or not, he was easier to manage with some of it in his system.'

'You—' My rage erupts within me enough to damn him and everyone in here as I lurch forward, only to be yanked back by the shoulders this time. I struggle against the Elf's grip, wishing to wipe Aurum's vile smile away.

That repugnant—

'Now, Nara, what did I tell you about siding with a thief?'

My blood stops pumping through my veins and every ounce of colour in my face drains away at the familiarity of that graceful voice. A voice that hides the most sinister history.

Sarilyn surfaces from behind the throne in a flowing red gown with a plunging neck, still so beautiful and dangerous. She isn't wearing her crown, but even without it, she doesn't stop being *Queen Sarilyn*, the one who tried to rip me apart.

She narrows her stare down at me as she slides up beside Aurum and drapes her jewel-covered hand over his shoulder.

What is happening?

'Then again,' she says, 'I can't say anything, can I?' Her gaze flickers towards Lorcan beside me, and her lips lift into a smirk. 'Nice to see you are alive and well, Deputy.'

Lorcan glares up at her, and I shake my head, dazed, as I lock eyes with Sarilyn.

'You're working with him?' *This can't be real.*

She lifts her shoulder. 'He came at me with an interesting proposition.'

Aurum chuckles. 'She couldn't stay mad at me for long. Sure, she tried to kill me and ruled over *my* kingdom for centuries. But it was either side with me, or— Well, you can use your imagination.' He wraps an arm around her waist and squeezes. It makes it almost impossible to keep myself from being sick all over this floor. 'She made the wisest decision.'

It doesn't make sense. It's ludicrous that the Queen – someone who despised Aurum and ended most of his bloodline – would now be with him despite the consequences if she disagreed.

My shoulders turn rigid, disappointment oddly coursing through my veins. 'I don't know what I expected,' I say. 'I suppose you both truly do deserve each other.'

Sarilyn's smile is forced. A look I have often received from her in the past. 'And how is the Golden Thief?' She offers me a concerned look. 'Oh, silly me.' She laughs. 'He is not even with you.'

Aurum joins in with a snicker, and I have never heard such a hateful sound in my life. A sound I wish to burn to the soils of the earth.

I cast a glance over to the windows, praying for the sun to rise soon before setting my scornful gaze on Aurum.

'Don't give me that look, Nara.' He pouts mockingly as he gestures to the throne hall. 'After all, this is all on you.'

His remark increases my temper to a burning point. I won't let myself give in to the blame. This is what he wants – to see me destroyed. 'Where. Is. He?' I demand.

Aurum roughly lets go of Sarilyn and she almost stumbles before recovering. 'What makes you think he wants to see you?' The disgust in his voice overpowers the expanse of the room.

Simultaneously, a slash of violet and blue warms the sky from outside. Lorcan and I share a knowing glance with each other as my lips twitch. I raise my chin just as I see Aurum tilt his head, arrogance rippling across his face. 'I guess I will have to see for myself, won't I?'

The look Aurum gives me would frighten the world. His lips

pinch in fury, and as I smile up at him, the sunrise comes, illuminating the perfect flame over the horizon.

Warning bells begin to chime, confusing the Elven guards. The one holding me lets go of my arm just enough for me to jerk it free and spin to grab his blade before pushing him. Then, as dragons and shifters storm through the castle doors, the ground trembles, dust billows and flames erupt from Fernah flying above me with Tibith on her back.

We strike the first attack on the Elves. Mayhem breaks out, and I grin as Tibith waves at me with a small dagger in his grip.

I take that as my cue to run towards the fight.

Chapter Twelve

I swing my blade around, driving it into one of the Elf's necks as I search for any sign of my brothers or Freya. It has been minutes since the first warning bells rang, and I knew it was no Elf. It was my brothers, following the orders I gave each of them after they joined alongside me.

Rydan and Gus have teamed up at the far end of the castle, fighting against a formidable Elf. Shadows swirl in Gus's hands as he uses them on his attackers, and I spin, feeling a flicker of memory spark at the edge of my vision – a memory from mere hours ago, me telling Gus I needed to speak with the shifters, that my plan required their help.

'You will wait in a different location near the forests,' I tell all the shifters beside their dragons and creatures as I stand upon an oak table.

The transition of the past to now flashes before me as two other guards rush through the crowd, wielding Elvarune magic that Arlayna once spoke of to launch fragments of broken glass towards me. I yank the dagger out from my victim, dodging left and right as I narrowly escape the shards of glass.

'But how are we supposed to know when to attack?' one of the shifters asks from within the crowd.

Before the guards can reach me, a sword slices across both their necks, decapitating them in one fleeting movement as the final chimes of the bell sound in the distance.

I turn to my brothers and face them, my friends and all. 'When the bells start to ring at sunrise.'

Two heads, followed by their bodies, roll onto the ground, exposing a breathless Link. His golden-brown hair is mussed to his forehead, blue eyes wide and full of adrenaline.

Partially in shock, I manage to nod a thank you to him, and he flashes me a bright smile before he turns to fend off another guard. Lorcan flies up ahead in his bright red phoenix form, spitting out balls of fire as Elves launch their arrows, narrowly missing him by an inch. I try to get a look towards the dais, but a raging Elf blocks my view, snapping his blade at me. I parry the attack and shuffle backwards, catching sight of Fernah from the corner of my eye as she roars and breathes out a stream of fire down onto some of Aurum and Thallan's lackeys.

My lips curve into a smile, but my pride is short-lived when the Elf strikes again and my dagger is knocked out of my hand.

As I dive to the floor, I see Aurum across the hall with Sarilyn at his side, and I grab the leather hilt with my hands. He's a silhouette against the destruction surrounding us all as some shifters I know try to ambush him, but when they get too close, he shoots them out of the way with shadows and fire like they're nothing more than an inconvenience.

My chest heaves with every breath, a mixture of anger and determination, knowing half of those powers were stolen. Invincible or not, most of that magic belongs to Darius.

The thought fuels my rage tenfold, and I roll onto my back as a sword meets the side of my head, snipping the ends of my hair off. A female Elf, snarling at me, stands over my figure, and I swipe my leg across hers, causing her to fall. It gives me enough time to rise as another comes at me from the side.

As he closes the distance, I thrust my blade through his throat. Blood spurts out, covering my face as I grit my teeth and dig deeper, hearing how his chokes intensify. When I yank the dagger free and the Elf drops, I freeze as I see Ruvyn – the young Elf I remember who was recently sworn in and had protected Arlayna when we went horse-riding.

He stares across at me. His sword is down at his side, and his innocent brown eyes are wide as he struggles with whether to fight me or not. When a few seconds pass, he drops his head and backs away, disappearing into the masses of his comrades fighting against our dragons.

My hand tightens around the hilt of my blade, and I shake off the bitter taste in my mouth at the cruel fate that some of these Elves are just doing what they are told.

I watch as swords clash in a symphony of metallic sounds and flames salt the air. I inhale it all at this moment, remembering I am here to get to Darius. I cannot let anything else affect me.

With a deft flick of my wrist, I flip the blade in my hand, a surge of energy coursing through me as I weave through the Elven adversaries, effortlessly slicing and dodging their strikes.

'Rydan,' I call out, my voice cutting through the chaos as someone deflects my attack by spinning and severing the tip of my blade. Rydan turns to me through the clash of his weapons against his assailant. 'Sword!'

He nods in understanding, executing a quick kick to the Elf's stomach, and tosses the steel sword towards me. The blade catches a glint of sunlight as it charges through the air, and I grab it with my right hand in time to gain the lead as I thrust it through the male Elf's abdomen. Victory washes over me and I whirl, aiming the sword at the next person. However, before the impact can land, my wrist is seized in a powerful grip.

With the blade in midair and my ragged breathing feral, my heart and soul react first, sparking emotions I've been craving for too long.

My surrounding noises are a mash of swords clanging, screams echoing and mayhem, but even through all that, I watch as my forearm is carefully lowered and I am faced with familiar golden eyes.

A half-smile adorns his lips, and something immediately pulls at my stomach. He looks like the same handsome shifter I fell in love with, dressed in a black jacket threaded with gold decorations and a shirt underneath it, yet strangely nothing, no scratch or sign of injury, is visible on him.

'Now, who might you be?' Darius murmurs and my heart cleaves in two.

Time seems to stutter, and the world around me blurs. His gaze, once filled with love and recognition, is now devoid of the familiarity we once shared.

I try to speak; I try to move, but he acts fast as his expression turns cold and his smile fades into something cruel. His hand clutches my throat and I yelp, dropping the sword as I reach for his hold on me.

'Darius,' I gasp, my fingers clawing at his hand to free myself. 'It's me!'

He doesn't loosen his grip, no matter the struggle, no matter the fear I have on my face as I plead with my eyes for him to let me go. He sees me as a threat and stares at me relentlessly, his eyes burning with a look of rage that I only ever witnessed when someone did him wrong . . . when someone would hurt *me* like he is doing right now.

'Darius!' I cry again, this time tearfully. My eyes blur in a tumult of confusion and heartache as I desperately hold on to him.

The air seems to thin, draining me of all strength just as I feel his grip on my neck finally loosen and he collapses onto the floor, unconscious.

Gasping for air, I press my hands to my throat as the precious taste of oxygen fills my lungs back up, and I face Freya. She is panting and staring down at Darius with her mouth agape as purple flames of magic dance around her outstretched palm. The violet gleam in her eyes soon fades as she looks up at me and asks, 'Are you okay?' while holding on to a small wooden chest with her other arm.

It is the stones I asked her to go in search of while we distracted Aurum.

From behind Freya, the swift footfalls of my brothers echo as they race towards us, their momentum halting abruptly as they take in the gravity of the situation. My gaze then drops to where Darius lies, and a collision of emotions barrels into me, disorienting my reality.

I don't nod; I don't say if I am okay. I simply lift my eyes and steady myself because I need to – because I can't afford to waste time.

'Let's get him out of here.' I cannot tell if I am even speaking. I'm still too dazed, but without hesitation, my brothers spring into action.

Idris and Iker seize Darius's arms and begin dragging him away from the castle's onslaught. I bring my thumb and forefinger to my mouth, a sharp whistle piercing the air as I aim it at Gus. He swivels his head, acknowledging me before his gaze slips to Darius, and he freezes.

The familiar ache I sensed mirrors across his countenance. His brows draw together in pained unity, and hesitation lingers on the corners of his lips before he averts his gaze, instructing the shifters to withdraw.

Surveying the crumbling surroundings, I search for Link and Rydan amidst the falling pillars and collapsing roof. Suddenly, a hand clamps on to my arm, instinctively prompting me to twist away, ready to deliver a defensive strike. It's only when I recognise it is Rydan with Link behind him that relief washes over me. Grabbing the collar of his shirt, I follow his lead as he guides me towards the exit doors.

I cast a final glance over my shoulder just in time to witness Aurum by the throne chair, extending his index finger towards me. A sinister grin spreads across his face, making it a promise and a threat that this is far from over. And as the doors to Aurum's castle seal shut behind us, I accept it, knowing that, at least right now, the stones are in my possession.

CHAPTER THIRTEEN

'Now, who might you be?'

I zone in and out of focus as Hira speaks from her throne. I watch as her lips move, as her fire eyes flame from anger and I do nothing to fix it.

'Now, who might you be?'

My head slants to the side as another phoenix named Col, seated beside Hira on a winged throne, shakes her head in disapproval.

'Now, who might you be?'

The third phoenix, Ara, can't even look at me.

'You disobeyed a direct order!' Hira slams her staff against the marbled flooring, and I think she expects me to flinch, to react, to at least show how worried I should be. 'Do you realise the dangers that *my* people face now that you have the stones?'

Col scoffs. 'Aurum won't show mercy; he will come here, swords at the ready, to take back those stones and his nephew, and when he does, you know we cannot take any more responsibility. We've already risked too much by letting Hira take so many of you into our land.'

I bite the inside of my cheek. The thought has already crossed my mind one too many times. 'The treaty no longer exists. If you choose not to fight, then you are no better than Aurum,' I say, and I notice Hira shake her head at me.

'You should never sacrifice yourself for love, Nara. It does not end well.'

What she says sparks something rageful inside of me, and I cannot tamp it down in time. 'I didn't just do it for love,' I snap. 'I did it for everyone.'

Hira's steely gaze does not falter as I march towards the three Aerians seated in place.

'Our world is slowly dying, Hira,' I say. 'Soon, the real threat won't be Aurum; it will be that our crops are dying, the animals struggling, and we are fending for what is left of it all. So, yes, maybe it was selfish of me to go after Darius when he doesn't even remember who I am, but I do not regret it. Sometimes, a sacrifice must be made, and I chose what I felt was right. We were only delaying what would come sooner or later.'

The following silence feels heavy against my chest as the three leaders ponder my words. I'm unsure what to do with my hands or legs as I stand there waiting for them to berate me for talking this way to such Aerian warriors. Warriors who can tear me apart in their Phoenix form just as quickly.

'You should never have brought them here, Hira.' Col is the first to speak as she chews on her tongue with a furious gleam in her eyes. 'You and your soft spot for humankind—'

'Enough.' Hira snaps her head towards Col and effectively shuts her up with just one glance. 'Remember your place.' As Hira looks at me, a gentle smile peels her lips back, though it is barely noticed by her sisters. 'She is Solaris's reincarnation, after all.'

A few quiet beats pass as relief sweeps over me. Hira has a softer soul than her siblings. I have noticed it ever since I first met her on Noctura night.

'Well, if—' Ara starts to say, when the double doors are pushed open and Link and Rydan burst through with Tibith.

From their dishevelled appearances and wide eyes, I instantly know what this is about.

Darius.

I'm charging down the brick stairs to where the dungeons are situated within the palace. Link, Rydan and Tibith are hot on my trail, telling me to calm down, but it's futile to even suggest that.

'Now, who might you be?'

I shake my head and the bright light from the sconces stings my eyes. After our attack on Aurum, my brothers took an unconscious Darius to the infirmary to rest. According to Link and Rydan, when he awoke, he began to attack Aerians despite his inability to use his powers. It took over five warriors to subdue him and throw him in a cell for their own safety.

'Now, who might you be?'

I grab hold of the coin around my neck and clutch it tight as I stop beneath an archway where Gus stands with a torn expression on his face. Water drips from the brick ceiling, and flashbacks to the time Darius was inside Emberwell's dungeons make my throat thicken.

'Miss Nara, why am I not allowed to see him?'

Glancing down at my feet, I see Tibith's big round eyes looking up at me, and my heart might as well just shatter to pieces. 'It is safer if you stay up there with the rest,' I say quietly, knowing that Tibith won't understand why. He thinks Darius remembers him; he *thinks* it is all just a matter of Darius needing rest, and he will be better again.

I so wish it could be.

'Ambrose,' Rydan says. 'Do you really think—'

'Take him to your room and do not let him out until I am back,' I order, and I can see it in his eyes that he wants to reason otherwise. I pin him with a stare that says I am not up to negotiating. He and Link start to turn away from me, but their gazes remain on me as they look over their shoulders. Tibith soon follows them, his head hung low and ears flopping downwards with disappointment.

I heave back a breath, squaring my shoulders before I whirl around to face Gus. 'Please?' My voice cracks with desperation. 'Let me speak to him.'

'Nara, he doesn't—' He's lost for words, anger swirling in his eyes like the ones Darius beheld me with back at Aurum's palace. 'Whatever Aurum has done, Darius only seems to believe in another reality. One where *you* do not exist.'

His answer feels like I've been struck with a whip one too many times.

'Now, who might you be?'

'His life revolves around the idea that he grew up with Lorcan and Rayth, that Aurum never died, and that Tibith, you, Terranos, none of it crossed his path.'

I feel Gus's hand touch my arm in a comforting way, and looking up at him, I make the conscious decision that whether or not he knows me, it will not stay this way for long. I promise that. 'Then I will make him remember,' I say and barge past Gus as I hear him sigh before calling out my name. But it is too late to start listening because, as I round the hallways of the dungeon, I pause by one of the cells where Darius sits against the wall with one knee raised to his chest and the other straight out in front of him as his head lolls back.

The small, barred window above him doesn't let in much light, but I can still make out his face in the dimness as the flames from the sconces behind me flicker. A few skeletal bones scatter the ground, and I shake my head, despising the thought that he was brought here because he wanted to defend himself.

His eyes are closed, but he smiles as if he knows I am here. 'I'm receiving so many visitors today,' he drawls, deep and teasingly. He tips his head forward and gestures to the tiny space around him. 'Welcome to my humble abode; please, come sit.'

My lungs feel as if something is compressing them, two walls closing in on me and crushing my organs. I can't find the words I want to say, so I stare silently.

'No?' he says. I don't answer. 'Fine. Suit yourself.' He drops his head back against the wall, quickly dismissing me.

Devastation slams across my face like a crushing blow. 'Do you truly not know who I am?'

He pops one eye open to look at me. 'Should I?'

I shake my head, wishing I could reach inside his mind and thrust it back to reality. A reality where he remembers me. 'Yes, very much so.'

He stares at me. He is no longer wearing the jacket I first saw him in. It is just his shirt, unbuttoned and ripped.

'All right.' He suddenly rises to his feet and makes his way towards the bars. I don't make any movement to step back, even as he closes in on me and leans against the cell wall. 'Then what are you to me? Because I highly doubt I would be close with a mortal.' He cocks his head to the side, a cunning smile twisting his lips as he studies me. 'My uncle says humans are only useful for one thing: following orders. *You* don't strike me as someone who follows orders.'

'Not when they are set by your uncle.'

He chuckles. 'You hate him.'

'As do you.' My heart crashes against my ribcage as I watch him tilt his head and smile at me like I am something of an oddity to him. An anomaly in this world.

'What is your name?'

I want to scream.

Just hearing him ask me that feels like a punch to the gut. 'You already know what my name is.'

'I don't think I do.'

'Darius, I . . . We were—' The unfinished words bottle up inside my throat before I sigh out of frustration. I turn my back to him and run a hand through my hair as I try to get a grip on myself. 'Do you remember the first time we met?' I slowly twist around upon his silence. It's difficult enough having to look at him, but it's worse knowing that when *he* looks at me, all he sees is a stranger. 'We were children,' I whisper, letting a tearful laugh escape me. 'We played for hours, and then I gave you this coin.' Gently, I reach for the coin necklace. His stare burns through it, yet there is no hint of reminders in his eyes. 'It is also the first time you made me forget who you were in order to protect me.'

As I step forward, there is a severity in his eyes, and he pushes himself off the cell bars.

'The second time we met,' I say, 'you were running away. We bumped into each other and dropped our carvings. The sun and the moon. Yours belonged to your mother, which she gave to you, and mine was one I'd made myself, because of how much I love to carve. Then, the third time we met was at a jewellery shop. You were stealing, and all I wanted to do was capture you. Do you remember *that*?'

He eyes me with a brutal look, one that digs into the pit of my chest. I let a second go by, wondering if it is my imagination, but I know better now that what I see is finally a faint recognition as his features soften, and he turns his head to the side, finding solace in staring at the brick walls instead.

Desperation clings to me like an unwelcome guest, and from my pocket I pull out the ring Gus gave to me. 'This ring.' I raise it to the side of my head. 'This ring *belongs* to you.'

His eyes dart to the obsidian-cut jewellery.

'You handed it to Gus the night of your birthday. Noctura. The same night I helped you retrieve your mother's pendant. It is made from *your* scales. A ring for a wedding. *Our* wedding.'

I wait, holding my breath before his smile turns lethal.

'Do you want to know what I remember?' His grip tightens around the cell bars as he tilts his head to the side and scoffs in my direction. 'You raiding the palace and then kidnapping me. So, to answer your question, no, I don't remember you. You mean *nothing* to me . . . You never will.'

The words sting to hear, and he knows it.

Embarrassment pricks the back of my eyes over how much of myself I have just laid out for him. Every moment we've shared is gone, *vaporised* from his mind. The first moment we met, the dance we shared at the Noctura ball, the den, the Screaming Forests, Terranos . . .

To keep the tears from falling, I clench my teeth and raise my chin, holding Darius's gaze for five more seconds until I finally turn and walk away.

Gus is still there where I left him, waiting with his hands tensely plucking at his ebony hair in anticipation of my return. When he sees me again, he sighs with relief. His mouth moves as though to speak, but I pay him little attention. I know he's telling me we'll figure it out, but my gaze drifts to the keys at his waist that I presume unlock

Darius's cell. I think back to another time when he told me I was all but an asset to him, that I meant nothing, and it had turned out to be a lie.

'He's lying,' I whisper, and Gus snaps his mouth shut as I slowly drag my eyes up to him. *'He's lying.'*

It all happens within a matter of seconds.

Me snatching the keys from Gus, and him yelling my name as I storm off in the direction of Darius's cell.

'Nara, don't—'

I whirl and press my forearm against Gus's chest. 'Stay here,' I order, and he looks as displeased as ever. 'If I need your help, I will call for it.'

He gives me a look as though he thinks I am mad. I suppose I am. 'He almost killed you once,' he says, 'Do you think he won't try it again?'

It is a risk that I do not care about. I will happily tempt fate with Darius if it brings us a step closer to recovering his memories. 'Two minutes,' I say. 'Just give me two more minutes.'

A steady beat of silence cuts between us.

He sighs. 'Two minutes, Nara, and then I'm coming to get you.'

CHAPTER FOURTEEN

Darius turns around as the keys unlock the door to his cell and I enter. I slam the door closed behind me and charge up to him, raising an accusatory finger. 'You're lying.'

He raises an eyebrow in bemused curiosity like he had not expected me to come back, let alone be in the same cell as him. 'Beg your pardon?'

'You tell me that you don't remember me, and fine, I suppose you do not. Whatever Aurum did to you, he succeeded in removing me from your mind completely, but you lie when you say I am nothing to you.' I dare to take another step; my eyes alight with confidence. 'Deep down, you know there is something that you can't seem to understand when it comes to us. You feel it, but you can't put your finger on it, and do you want to know why I believe that is the case?'

His eyes narrow, begging me to enlighten him.

'Because I know you,' I whisper almost tauntingly, but he doesn't react – doesn't even move away from me. 'You used to tell me I kept myself guarded from everything. That I did not want to show people another side of me because, secretly, I was afraid of the consequences. Yet you are doing that right now. You're refusing to let yourself remember because you know that if you do, all the bad and all the worst moments in your life will come back.' I have hardly done anything, but somehow I am breathless as I stare him down.

Now is when I imagine it can go either way. He attacks me again, or he lets me be.

Instead, a slow smile spreads across his face. A smile that can melt away ice and damn anyone who witnesses how beautiful it is. 'Has anyone ever told you that you have wonderful golden hair?'

I take a step back, feeling like I am now suffocating. 'Yes.' I frown, much to his amusement. My throat burns with all sorts of sensations, not expecting him to say that of all things. '*You* have. Many times.'

He purses his lips and hums. 'Have I now?' His smile grows deeper and flirtier. His old self. 'What else have I supposedly said or done?'

'That you love the night.'

He nods. 'I do.'

Suddenly, it feels like before – like the games we always played. 'You also learned how to bake.' I don't realise I am taking a few steps closer to him until my chest brushes against his shirt. 'Pies mostly, since they are my favourite.'

I feel his murmur against the top of my head.

'Interesting,' he says.

I glance up at him. 'You have also always struggled to sleep on beds, due to the childhood you had with your stepfather. In fact, the first time you laid on one was while I was with you. You treated it like a delicate animal, unsure of how to position yourself.' I forgot how much I craved being with him, being so close to him now that the scent of rosewood fills up my lungs. My hands ache to touch him as they flex at my sides. 'You're annoyingly playful and far too vain, but you are also thoughtful . . . compassionate. You care for everyone but yourself, and when I wanted to hate you, I couldn't.'

The tiniest bit of recognition rips through the gold threads of his eyes and hope kindles like a fire inside my chest, only for it to die out as he looks over my shoulder at someone else.

'Lorcan,' he says, surprised. 'Now, I don't recall you being alive.'

I glance back as Lorcan and Gus stand outside the cell, waiting for me.

'In fact,' Darius tilts his head, 'I thought I killed you?'

What?

My head spins as I look at Darius. His eyes are on Lorcan, narrowed and full of wicked amusement.

'That night at the cottage, you died along with your father,' he says. 'I left you to burn in that fire.'

Whatever Aurum has said to Darius, he now believes in another story.

The idea that Aurum might have utilised Merati powers to make Darius forget how much the night Rayth died affected him makes me sick to my stomach.

And when Gus says, 'Nara, come on, let's go,' I hesitate to follow him.

Darius's fingers wrap around my arm, and I instinctively turn to him. 'Nara,' he says thoughtfully. 'Your name is Nara?'

I struggle to get my words out as I nod, but all I want to say is *Yes, remember me, please, please, please remember me.*

The sound of an unsheathed sword makes Darius's gaze break away from me, and I beg for it to return.

'No need to draw any weapons, Lorcan.' Darius cocks an eyebrow; his hand is still holding my arm too tightly, as if he does not want to let go just yet. 'I'm not going to kill her.'

Something finally snaps inside of me, and I yank my arm free from his touch as I glower. 'You already tried once.' To prove it, I tilt my chin slightly to show him my neck. There are no bruises, thanks to Gus giving me his blood, but the memory is still there. The hatred and unfamiliarity in his eyes as he strangled me.

'Yes, well.' Darius's eyes land on my neck, sweeping over the length of it. 'Apologies for that. Although you did try to harm the king of Emberwell.' His tone is clipped, and I stare at him, so shocked to hear him say something like that. *The king of Emberwell.* Aurum is no king.

You are supposed to be, Darius.

'You're not yourself,' Lorcan says behind me.

Darius's eyes flicker his way. 'Neither are you.' He seems to be watching Lorcan closer this time. 'What are you?'

'Your brother,' I snap. 'He is *your* brother, and you never killed him. You could never, even when *he* might have wanted to kill *you*.'

Darius's eyes slowly make their way back to me, but by then, I've already turned around to leave. And as soon as Gus lets me out of the cell, I look towards Darius again. My breath halts and my eyes become heavy with hurt as he doesn't once turn away from my gaze.

I barely notice Lorcan grabbing the keys from my hand until he slams the cell door shut and twists the key to lock it.

'What are you doing?' I hiss out a whisper and catch his wrist.

'He tried to attack the Aerians, Nara,' Gus answers instead. 'Do you really think we can let him roam freely?'

I begin to protest. 'But keeping him locked away—'

'Don't worry about me, Goldie.' The name has my head turning at an alarming rate.

Goldie.

Darius doesn't realise the effect the nickname has on me. It's as if it came naturally to him. He scans the cell with a shrug before fixing his gaze on me. 'Like you said, not the first time I've been locked up.' His grin tells me he's teasing and messing around, but I hate knowing the truth to it all.

I struggle to leave him here. Gus is touching my shoulder, trying to get me to leave, and at last I shrug him away as I storm off, hearing the dragging of Lorcan and Gus's boots behind me.

'Tell everyone to gather in the common room tomorrow mid-morning.' I say the order without looking back. 'We have much to discuss.'

CHAPTER FIFTEEN

I tap my fingers absentmindedly against the arm of my chair as I watch my brothers and friends shout at each other across a sizeable oval glass table in a furious debate on what our next approach should be.

Aelle and Leira are on each side of me and are the only ones who are quiet compared to the rest. After I mentioned that Darius remembers a different reality from what is true, they both gently touched my arms with a comforting smile. On the other hand, Gus and Lorcan could not attend the meeting. With the after-effects of attacking Aurum's castle, the dragons and shifters require the most assistance.

'We have the stones to open the portal, right? So why don't we go in and recreate the Northern Blade?'

My fingers still at the sound of a frustrated voice, and I look over at Iker as he rubs his temples.

I think of answering, but Freya's one step ahead. 'It is too much of a risk,' she says. 'The Isle of Elements is already on the verge of destruction; bringing back Aurum took too much of a toll on it.'

Everyone glances at one another in silence before looking towards me for a further explanation.

I sigh, straightening up from my slouched position. My mind is still spinning from my conversation with Darius down in the cells.

'Using the Isle of Elements can also be more harmful than good,' I tell them. 'Before Darius and I entered, the previous ruler of Terranos told us how there is always a consequence to whatever we ask the Isle for.'

'What was the consequence for Sarilyn?' Illias asks, his brows knitted into a frown.

My eyes slide to him, and I wonder about Sarilyn. I hate that it bothers me knowing she is working with Aurum, even after everything that happened.

With a clear of my throat, I say, 'She lost her powers.'

'A sorceress without power . . .' Link voices pensively before those blue eyes brighten with an idea. 'Maybe we don't need to use the Isle of Elements.'

I sit up even straighter, focusing on Link only.

'Nara is a vessel for Solaris, as Darius is for Crello, right? So, they both must have some kind of power that acts like the Isle of Elements.'

Right . . . Solaris.

I try to hide the sudden depletion in my mood again, but from the corner of my eye, I see Idris staring at me, noticing as always. He has to. Looking out for anything that happens to me is second nature to him.

'All I can do is sometimes connect with animals,' I mumble, glancing at my reflection on the table instead. 'I believe I can do no more.'

'Then how do you propose we do this?' Leira asks me, her curls tied back in an updo just like Freya's, jostling from the whirl of her head towards everyone. 'Even with Darius's life tied to Aurum's, nothing would affect him unless it is the Northern Blade.'

'We could use gold to trap Aurum, then cut him up into pieces, send each body part to different kingdoms, and lock it deep, deep, deep down in an impenetrable chest.'

I blink, and then *all* of us look over at Rydan, who is sitting at the far end of the table, staring down at his nails as if he hasn't explained the most twisted plan to ever come from his lips.

Our silence has him lifting his head. 'What? I'm merely voicing what Nara would likely do.'

I screw up my face. 'I wouldn't do that!' It isn't torturous enough for a man like Aurum.

Rydan arches an eyebrow with a level of skepticism that has me shaking my head.

'Look,' I sigh. 'Sooner or later, Aurum will come searching for the Elemental Stones. Aelle has managed to keep them safe—'

'I do not have them,' Aelle interrupts. I frown at her. 'Freya has them.'

Snapping my head at Freya, she fires me a sheepish smile.

'I figured out a way to protect them,' she says. 'Well, actually, I spent the entirety of the night altering the stones.' Her gaze flits to Leira. 'We thought that perhaps there was a way to keep them more hidden from Aurum.' From beneath the layers of her bodice she reveals an oval locket with a phoenix engraved on it. She unclasps it and tries to pass it over to me, but I shake my head, trusting what she has done with it will be in safer hands with her. 'You mentioned the stones work when they are brought together, so I figured that perhaps drawing the essence of their power into one solid place could help.'

And that would be the locket . . .

I give Freya the first smile of the day, proud of how far she has come as a witch. She did not have to go to such lengths, and I feel horrible that I was away tossing and turning in bed while she fought to find a way to keep the Elemental Stones hidden together.

'How does it work?' Link asks as Freya fastens the locket around her neck once more.

'It is simple.' She grins at him and for a split second I notice Iker's dreamlike smile, while Idris looks away from her. 'You simply open the locket, and the portal should open too.'

'Seems like if that falls into the wrong hands – cough, cough, Aurum – we are all doomed. You should give it to me, Frey Frey. I'm good at looking after things.'

Leira scoffs. 'Oh please, Rydan – Nara left you in charge of Tibith this morning, and I haven't heard from him since you went to talk to the phoenix Trackers outside.'

My neck almost breaks as I snap my head to face Rydan, my eyes wide and blazing with anger.

Rydan's face pales. 'I can see you are mad at me, Ambrose, but he is safe.' He slowly raises his palms out in front of him, as if that will save him from what I might do. 'In fact, I left him in your room. He said your cot was cosy—'

'I'm going to count to three—' Luckily, I don't even get to start as Rydan shoots up from his chair and stumbles into a run out of the room.

I hear a few chuckles around the table, then Aelle asks me, 'Is there anything else you would like to say, Nara?'

I wrack my brain to come up with something but fall short. 'No,' I say and shake my head. 'No. I think we have exhausted all our thoughts on this matter. I think we just need to continue looking for a way to remove Darius's link to Aurum. I wrote to the princesses of

Terranos, hoping they might be able to help.' Although I'm not holding on to too much hope when they are trying to repair the damages after Dusan's death. But if . . . if we could get hold of a Galgr, then maybe we can salvage *something*.

Leira and Aelle nod, looking at Freya expectantly before I dismiss everyone. I'm the last to rise from my chair as I gaze towards the narrow windows. I waltz over, feeling the heat from the winter sun warm my face. I see a few dragons with black scales and fiery red wings flying among the phoenixes. Amidst them is Fernah, with her whelps on her back.

I smile.

At least here, they are content as long as they get to fly in the skies.

'Here.'

My head rears at the sight of a shiny red apple shoved before me. I turn my head to where Illias stands beside me, then to the closed doors through which everyone else has left.

I frown, and my lips form a pout. 'I'm not hungry—'

'When was the last time you ate a proper meal?'

I make a noise at the back of my throat, annoyed. 'You are almost starting to sound like Idris.'

'Please,' Illias scoffs. 'Idris would have force-fed this to you by now.'

I fix him with a smug smile. 'And he would have failed.'

He chuckles. 'Oh yes. Just like that time you didn't want to eat the broth he prepared.'

I hum in agreement and drop my head on his shoulder, staring at the dragons flying around. 'I believe that was the first time he realised how much trouble I would be.'

'You *and* Iker,' Illias remembers with a sigh. 'He is the one who copied you by throwing the broth all over Idris.'

Recalling that night with a chuckle, I hook my arm through Illias's. It had been a few days after the death of our mother. With what little food we still had, Idris cooked us dinner. It was the first time we sat down as a family without our parents there.

'It wasn't the worst meal in the world,' I say, wistfulness resonating deep in my chest. 'I thought it was the most incredible thing he had made for us since our mother's death.'

He tilts, making me shift to look up at him. 'But you weren't ready for something like that.'

I wasn't. But what I would give to have a moment like that again at our old cottage, knowing that our only problem back then was the possibility of goblins invading our home in search of food and treasures.

Illias takes both of my arms and spins me around to face him. When the light hits his brown curls, it makes them appear almost golden.

'Make sure you eat.' He kisses the top of my head and places the apple on the table before walking out.

Later on, that same evening, once the sun sets, I spend hours with the dragons outside the garrison, eating the apple my brother gave me while I make a promise to myself that I will get Darius's self back.

He is still there; I know it.

CHAPTER SIXTEEN

're you going to stand there and watch me all day, Goldie?' Darius sits opposite me inside the cell, munching down on a piece of bread and mutton I fetched earlier today from the kitchen. I don't like the idea he is in here; everyone knows that. The least I can do is feed him properly, something the phoenixes didn't want after Darius tried attacking them

'*Goldie*,' I repeat, and Darius stops chewing. 'That is what you always used to call me from the moment we first met.'

He stares at me, and I don't think he realises how his gaze drops to my lips. When he finally notices, he clears his throat and resumes eating away. I watch as he carefully swallows, his throat bobbing. 'I take it that it means something to you.'

'To the both of us,' I say.

He doesn't like that response. His jawline tenses and he drops his food onto the plate, rubbing his hands together to brush the crumbs away. Pressing his palms against the ground, he leans back. 'Why are you here, Nara?' He releases a stiff laugh when I don't answer and motions his head towards the plate. 'Other than to bring me food and attempt to get me to remember you.'

I want to look away from his scrutinising stare, but it is impossible to do so. His eyes are honey, and all I want is to drink them in. 'A few months ago,' I start, 'I found out that you had erased my memory of when we were children. I spent over half my life not knowing who you were, yet you remembered *everything*. And the other times we saw each other as adults, you did not tell me because you thought you were not worthy of me.' The tragic beat of my heart pounds with the memory of that day. 'But you *are*. That is why I will do anything I can to make you remember.'

I can feel him pulling away from me again, and he looks at me like he is so conflicted.

'We need you to come back to us, Darius,' I whisper. '*I* need you to; Tibith needs you—'

'Tibith?'

I nod. 'A Tibithian. You befriended him and taught him how to speak years ago.' His head slants and I grow desperate once again. 'He is your best friend.' *And he misses you.*

Darius mulls over my words and, almost as if he is curious, he goes to speak, but the words never fall from his lips as he looks over my shoulder.

'Nara?' The small female voice has me standing up and turning to see Freya there with an apologetic grimace on her face. 'The Elven princesses are here to see you.'

My lips part in shock. I didn't think they would appear here this soon. 'What? How—'

'Do you really want to question why they are here after the whole world is in a mess because of Aurum?' The sassy response elicits a chuckle from Darius, and I glance behind me, noting how he is watching us both.

Sighing, I tell Freya, 'You make a good point.' As I offer her the keys to the cells, she touches my shoulder, and suddenly I find it difficult to move.

'*Go*,' she says. 'I will keep an eye on him; don't worry.' She shoots me a look when I seem reluctant to leave her here. 'I'm a witch connected to his dragon side, Nara. Maybe I can help in some way.'

She's right, but with Darius's state of mind, I can't stop being concerned for everyone.

Dusting the dirt off my tunic, I nod to Freya and leave the cells, but not without hearing Darius say to her, 'Hello, witchy.'

'Arlayna,' I breathe in relief as I spot her in the foyer beside Faye and Aeron. Both princesses are dressed in casual Elven travel attire, with their dark hair in carefully crown-braided updos. They look no different from when I last saw them, except now their expressions seem more worn down, and the glow in Faye's usually mischievous face looks dull compared to how I had seen it months ago.

'It is so good to see you, Nara.' Arlayna wraps an arm around me, squeezing me gently as she takes in the different colours of the Aerian Palace. 'After you wrote to us, we didn't know whether it was a good time to visit you now or—'

'Never,' Faye cuts in, earning herself a quick scolding from Arlayna.

Aeron acknowledges me with a nod before walking towards the large panel windows and staring outside at the approaching sunset. I notice his armour is still the same as before: emerald armour plates and a carved crown made of branches and stars. The only noticeable change is that his once cheekbone-length blond hair is now well past his chin.

I wait until he is at a safe distance from hearing us. 'How come he is not with Aurum?'

Arlayna's gaze keeps flitting back and forth between me and Aeron. 'When Thallan took over, half the Elven army stayed with him while the others went with Aurum. Luckily, Faye convinced Thallan that Aeron should stay with us as he is her personal guard.'

'I'm quite good with my words.' Faye grins.

A soft chuckle leaves me, but Arlayna doesn't seem to be in the right mood to joke with her sister as she clears her throat and says, 'We read in your letter that you managed to get Darius back.'

My smile falls from my lips. I try to get it back, but it just does not feel sincere any more. 'Yes,' I say. 'I imagined the news would have travelled fast regardless of whether or not you had read my letter, although I'm surprised Thallan hasn't tried to attack us, considering he and Aurum are allies now.' I lead the three into one of the palace's spare chambers.

'That is what we wanted to talk to you about,' Arlayna says behind me as I close the doors and urge the princesses to sit on a sofa by the open windows. 'Thallan is too busy making *personal* changes to Terranos to fight side by side with Aurum—'

'Which includes trying to infiltrate Thalore, where the Dark Elves are,' Faye adds as I sit opposite them.

'Kirian,' I find myself voicing aloud.

Faye nods. 'Last we heard was that Thallan is trying to strike deals with him.'

I shake my head, thinking how unlikely that is. I have met Kirian, and despite it not being for long, his actions gave me the impression he would never listen to someone from Olcar, let alone the new ruler of Terranos. 'I doubt Kirian is stupid enough to trust in Thallan.'

'No, but he is a nightmare to deal with,' Arlayna grumbles and my eyes widen with intrigue as I look towards Faye for an answer.

Faye leans forward, giving me a secretive wink. 'They write each other strongly worded letters.'

That annoys Arlayna as stormy grey eyes fire daggers in her sister's direction. 'The point is, he seems to trust only two people.' She turns to me. 'You and Darius.'

The thought baffles me. 'Us? The same people who snuck into his place to retrieve one of the stones?'

Arlayna chuckles softly. 'It looks as if he admired you both for going to the extreme of gathering the stones.'

'And now that the treaty is broken, everyone and everything is in a mess,' Faye agrees with a nod. 'The merfolk of Undarion are not delighted to hear about any of this and have even taken to blaming you for what has occurred.'

The heaviness of the situation pushes against my chest. Of course, the last thing I need is for the people of Undarion to despise me for what happened.

'We know this is all a lot, Nara,' Arlayna tries to sympathise, 'given what has gone on in the past few months, and believe me, we want to help you, but—'

'It is not your fight,' I tell them, my eyes darting back and forth. 'You are both already dealing with the aftermath of your uncle's death, and Thallan, I—' I glance at my hands which are joined together in front of my lap. 'I wouldn't want to drag you into this.' Into any of it.

Arlayna nods solemnly, her gaze drifting to the floor. 'We have brought over what you asked for.'

I perk up despite the atmosphere of the room. 'A Galgr?'

'Yes. She was hard to capture, but—' She clears her throat. 'We kept her hidden from the sun.'

'Thank you—'

'We should warn you, though,' she cuts me off. 'Despite a Galgr's ability to restore memories, we don't know to what extent Aurum has messed with Darius's mind. This isn't just about remembering, Nara. You mentioned he believes he has lived a different life. This could make things worse.'

'And you should also know that Aurum's intentions are not to just take over kingdoms.'

The male voice startles me into snapping my head up at Aeron, now standing at the edge of my settee. He was so stealthy in coming over that I had not even heard him.

'During his visit to Olcar a few weeks ago, he spoke to Thallan about why he needed to return to the Isle of Elements.' He looks at Arlayna and lingering passion ripples from their pores and I wonder if anyone else has discovered their connection. 'He is slowly decaying.'

My brows scrunch into a frown as Aeron's hazel eyes meet mine.

'I believe the consequence of what the Isle gave him were that his youth would be taken away,' he says. 'It won't kill him, but one day, sooner or later, he will look like death itself.'

My vision goes in and out of focus, and I glance down at my hands like that will help me regain control. If Aurum returns to the Isle of Elements, I am certain the world will suffer gravely, more so than it is right now.

'Why did you not inform me of this?' Arlayna sounds betrayed.

Aeron whispers, 'I did not wish to worry you, princess.'

It goes quiet until I manage to push out a breath from my lungs and drag my gaze back up to Aeron. 'Then why didn't he go back?'

'I'm not sure.' His nostrils flare as he thinks about it. 'I believe he is waiting for something – something that doesn't just involve reversing his decaying looks.'

That puts a bitter taste in my mouth, but at least now I know. It means I am prepared to face Aurum again. 'Thank you, Aeron.' A tight-lipped smile. 'For telling me this.'

With his hands clasped behind his back, he bows his head at me, but the doors suddenly burst open and I jump from my seat, already sensing something is wrong.

Freya has her arms out wide as she holds on to the wooden double doors. All she manages to say is 'Nara,' before I sprint out of the chamber without saying a word to Arlayna, Faye or Aeron.

I rush down to the prison cells, my heart beating louder than the stomps of my feet against the ground.

I skid to a halt outside Darius's cell and go completely still.

He's curled up on the floor, sweat glistening on his brow as he clenches the sides of his head. And through chafing gasps, he mutters, 'Thirty-one, thirty-two, thirty-three—'

Freya finally reaches the cells, her ringlets tousled from running.

She throws me the keys and I yell, 'What happened?' as I burst through the cell door and throw myself on the floor in front of Darius.

'He—' Freya stumbles on her words, panicked. 'He was fine, but then—I—I felt this pain come from him and—'

'. . . forty-four, forty-five, forty-six—' Darius continues counting, and dread stabs at my stomach, seeing him in this state.

'Go get Gus.' I look over my shoulder, and when Freya doesn't budge, I shout, 'Now!'

CHAPTER SEVENTEEN

D arius never stops counting.

Forty-seven, forty-eight, forty-nine . . . It goes on as if it is all his mind will allow.

When part of his shirt rides up, I notice a mark on the left side of his abdomen that I haven't seen before. A symbol darker than the tone of his flesh, of two straight lines and an arrowhead going across as if pointing to . . . north?

I reach out to it and mutter his name helplessly, but at the slightest touch, his eyes roar to life and the world starts spinning. As solid hands squeeze my shoulders, my back slams against the wall and I see stars swimming in my field of vision. A gasp shakes my chest, and I react, drawing my blade from its sheath and pressing it to his neck with equal rapidity.

I'm stuck in between his legs and can't move. Both of us are choking on our own air and staring at each other with wide eyes as he holds me captive and my heart pounds in my chest fiercely. Darius's hands loosen somewhat around my shoulders, but not enough for me to try to break away, and I swear to Solaris and Crello that he feels the need to brush the few strands of hair off my face.

'Go on, try to kill me again,' I whisper, and his jaw locks dangerously. 'If that is what you want, then I will drop this dagger and let you do it.'

His grip on me tightens again, but he is struggling. Internal rage slices across the irises of his eyes, and it is like I can see the wounds he is so desperately trying to heal on his own.

'You can't, can you?'

'I want to.' He breathes harshly through his nose, his eyes slipping as I catch them drifting towards my mouth.

My lips part, missing the way his once felt on mine. He looks so wild and so untamed right now that it threatens me wholeheartedly. 'Then,' I breathe, 'what is stopping you from doing so?'

Silence dominates the cell, and then Darius's gaze flashes to mine. '*You*,' he says hoarsely. 'And I don't know why.'

'Because part of you still remembers me.'

He shakes his head. 'No.'

I nod. 'Yes, you do.' To prove him wrong, I slowly lower the dagger and let it clatter against the floor beside me. My eyes flutter closed, and I put my faith in him, where others wouldn't.

He once asked me if I trusted him, and I did – I do. Whether it is stupid of me to or not, I can't help but do so. Everyone else I have put my trust in has failed me, but Darius never did, so let me be right just this once.

'If you truly wish to harm someone, then it should be me, not her.'

My eyes pop wide open as the voice comes from the other side, thinking Freya and Gus will be there, but they are not. Lorcan is.

Darius finally lets go of me and we both rise from the floor, turning to Lorcan as he stalks through the open cell door.

I jump in front of him, seeing the harshness in his expression as he clutches the hilt of his sword. It reminds me too much of the past and what he used to be like. 'Lorcan, wait—'

He doesn't stop, not until Darius huffs out a laugh.

'So, I should start listening to you now?' A slow smirk. 'Brother?'

Lorcan's shoulders are tense at the mention, but he tries so hard to hide that it has affected him. 'If you wish to be helped, then yes.'

'Helped?' Darius seems to be acting aloof, like nothing has happened, as he crosses his arms over his chest. 'Helped with what exactly?'

Lorcan remains quiet for a few steady beats, his jaw moving back and forth before his gaze slides over to me. 'Let's go.'

I shake my head because that is the last thing I want to do. I don't want to leave; call it a death wish, but there was a moment where Darius himself knew he wouldn't and will never kill me, even if Aurum demands it, even if he tries with all his might.

My back connects with the hard front of Darius's chest, not realising he has stepped closer to me.

He chuckles bitterly. 'Always the ignorer,' he says to Lorcan. 'Maybe if you didn't walk away from things, Rayth would still be alive.'

My heartbeat quickens.

'Too bad I killed him, right, Lorcan?'

Behind me, I can feel how calm Darius is, but Lorcan . . . his green gaze turns turbulent, feral almost, as his fists clench and the atmosphere crackles with thunderous rage.

Panic flickers in my chest but before I can diffuse the situation, Darius is pushing me aside as Lorcan lunges forward and his fist connects with Darius's jaw. Shock has my limbs lock up, and seconds later, Lorcan is on the ground, Darius is on top of him, and punches are flying around.

I'm yelling at them to stop, but they're too deep into their rage, and Darius, despite his lack of power and strength, keeps overpowering Lorcan. If I don't stop it, he will bash Lorcan's head to the ground.

Blood then spurts from Lorcan's mouth and as Darius raises his fist in the air, I quickly pick up the knife I have used before. But as I turn around, I see the phoenix flames emanating from the base of Lorcan's hand. Before Darius can pummel him again, Lorcan uses his palm to blast him across the cell.

The brick wall cracks and smoke burns a hole through Darius's shirt, but it doesn't seem to affect him. His dark brows are slanted and his eyes flare as he stands up and stalks towards Lorcan with a dominating type of darkness.

When Lorcan tries to do the same, I leap in between them, pointing my dagger at Lorcan first.

Deep green eyes, darkened by the dull lights, look at me. 'Nara, get out of the way.'

I bark out a humourless laugh. 'So that you can end up killing each other?' Heavy footsteps sound behind me, gaining closer, and I spin with the tip of the blade just about scratching the surface of Darius's chest.

He stills and lifts his palms into the air, surrendering as he eyes the dagger then me.

'Don't,' I warn, glancing back at Lorcan. 'You told me you had changed?'

Regret swallows him and he backs away, shaking his head at the ground. 'Nara, I'm—'

'I don't want an apology.' I shake my head. 'Not again.'

The more I hear an apology, the less it means something to me.

My voice quivers with anger. 'I am *tired* of it.'

Understanding graces his features though he is despondent at my words.

I whirl back to Darius, my dagger still grazing his chest. 'And you,' I pant. 'This is not *you*, and I will prove it to you.'

His golden gaze takes on a look that shows me he accepts my challenge.

Dropping the blade to my side, I turn to see Freya and Gus speed to a stop outside the cell. Confusion wracks them both as I pass them.

'Freya,' I say, motioning her to follow me, before leaving the dungeons and my thoughts behind me.

CHAPTER EIGHTEEN

I had called all my brothers and friends to the foyer where Arlayna and Faye were still standing as soon as I left the dungeons. Freya bombarded me with question after question and once I told her what happened, she was on board straight away with helping me get answers.

Soon after, some Aerian guards brought over the cage where the Galgr was being kept and we all stood in a circle around it.

'Is it frightening? Pretty? Creepy?' Rydan is the first to ask as we all stare down at the burlap covering the cage.

Dark skies have settled over the clouds, marking night-time, and I roll my eyes at Rydan before swiping the burlap off. Grey scaly arms slam against the cage, causing Rydan and Iker to jerk back. No one else reacts, and if they did, then they did an excellent job at hiding it as the Galgr's face slowly appears behind the shadows of her small prison.

Hollow eyes snap at me instantly and sharp teeth shine through her sinister smile. 'Solaris,' she hisses, and I glance opposite me where Freya is, then past her towards the princesses, both with straightened spines and cautious glances between one another.

Arlayna has never liked this part of interacting with the Galgr.

The Galgr sniffs the air, tilting her head towards my brothers. 'The Ambrose siblings. All together again.' She snickers. 'Though a bond that ties a family together can also loosen with each passing day.'

With one step, Idris erases the gap between him and the Galgr's cage. 'What did you say?'

'The writer and the crafter.' The Galgr grins, her dull-coloured lips stretching wide and horrifyingly.

I approach Idris, lightly touching his arm as I look over at Iker. His solemn eyes jump from a confused Freya to Idris. 'Don't listen to her,' I say, adjusting my tone to sound soothing and calm. 'Galgrs can also manipulate.'

'Wise observation, Solaris.' The Galgr taps her sharp fingernails against the metal bar. 'I also see that you wish to help your other half – the dragon with three powers, the reincarnation of Crello.'

'Your kind are known to resurface memories, old and new,' I say. 'I need you to do that for him too.'

A few seconds of silence tick by before her hand slumps onto the floor and she turns her head. 'I cannot.'

I am starting to despise that word.

Anger bubbles up my throat and everyone can see it; they can feel me losing it. I march two steps forward, almost slamming my hand down on the Galgr's cage. 'You managed to restore a forgotten memory of mine once. Why can't you do it again with him?'

She cocks her head in an unnatural way that makes a cracking sound. Another slant of her head to the left, and she eventually answers. 'Because his soul is slowly breaking.'

'Then how do we fix it?' Freya demands.

'You do not.' The Galgr's black tongue darts out, long and oozing a strange substance I never saw the last time. 'If he is breaking, then he must do so alone.'

That is just absurd. She is lying. She has to be.

I shake my head. 'No,' I say. 'No. There is always a way, and you know there is.'

She moves closer to the edge of her cage. 'What do I get in return if I am to help you?'

'Your life,' I answer. 'I think getting to live seems fair under these circumstances.'

'Nara, think about—' Idris is saying, but Iker presses his hand to Idris's abdomen and stops him.

The Galgr grins. What I have said must have enticed her. 'No wonder you were chosen,' she drawls. 'All those years of waiting for the fierce trapper to be born, and the result did not disappoint.'

'Tell. Me.' I am done with her teasing remarks.

Somehow, her hollowed eyes darken as her expression falls serious and her sigh sounds like the hiss of many snakes at once. 'A source,' she says. 'In order to restore his memories, you must reach the source of what memory is important to him.'

I ponder over her words, not knowing what to make of them. I had tried to get him to remember so many things at once that the idea of trying again seems futile.

'That's great!' Rydan clasps his hands together, grinning at me as I look over my shoulder. 'We already know it will likely have Nara in it.'

The Galgr hums, amusement seeping through her terrifying tone. 'But which?'

Rydan's grin drops almost comically. 'Well, I was hoping you would tell us that part.'

'I have said enough,' she says, angling her head as if to look at me. 'It is up to her now.'

I slowly shake my head, wanting a better answer, *needing* a better answer.

But begging is not enough. Dropping to my knees wouldn't even be enough. The Galgr told me the things she wanted to tell me, and I was too daft to think the outcome would be positive.

Drained and frustrated, I go to turn away when her hand darts out, seizing my wrist tightly. Fingernails dig into my flesh as I gasp out in pain and my head snaps towards the ceiling.

The world around me fades into darkness as an unseen force envelops my senses and images begin to materialise across my vision, emerging from the shadows like apparitions. Faces and fragments play out before me – a blur of colours, each with a detail etched with a haunting clarity as Darius appears. I don't know where we are, yet there we stand in front of each other. An overwhelming tide of emotions sweeps through me, and it is as if I can feel everything, every painful thought, every bit of sorrow and uncertainty as he pleads with me over and over to kill him with a blade pressed to his heart and my hands wrapped around the hilt.

I can taste the saltiness of my tears, I can hear the crack of my heart, and then, as abruptly as it began, the vision recedes. I desperately try to reach out for Darius, but he becomes a speck in the distance, and soon I'm falling, falling, falling until everything stops.

A dull throbbing ache resonates in the back of my head as I come to, and a blurry vision of Tibith's bright face appears above me.

'Miss Freya, she is awake!'

I can barely make out the scuffle of voices as Freya's curls tickle my cheek, and I scrunch up my face, shielding my eyes.

'Oh, thank Solaris—' Freya is saying when the image of the Galgr materialises and I jerk up into a seated position, almost knocking heads with Freya.

'The Galgr,' I gasp, my hands violently grabbing at my clothes and legs.

Freya takes hold of my shoulders, leaning over the bed I am on, her wide eyes written with concern. 'Nara, stop. It's okay—'

It's not. It's not, it's not.

'The Galgr – she showed me something.'

'And she also made you black out completely.' The soft linen mattress beneath me rocks as Freya sits by my side.

Another person speaks, and I look up to see that it's Idris by the doorway of . . . the infirmary?

'She's gone, Nara,' he says, and it only takes a split second for me to register the meaning of his words.

'I was never going to kill—'

'I know,' he says softly, and feeling dazed, I sink into the cushion of my bed and glance at the environment I find myself in.

A female with long blonde hair is at the edge of a cot opposite me, her bent phoenix wing being attended to as she remains in half-human form. I look to my right, and a few more warriors rest upon beds before my gaze settles on Iker, almost nodding off to sleep in one of the chairs, and Idris and Link by my side.

'Miss Nara, you should lie down, Miss Freya said you had a terrible fall!' As Tibith climbs onto my knee, my gaze rips away from my brothers, and the infirmary's sterile scent wafts past my nose.

My smile is so weak that I'm unsure if I should even call it a smile. 'I'm fine, Tibith. Especially now that you are here.'

His ears flutter.

'Nara,' Link says warily. 'What happened in there?'

I direct my attention to him.

Honestly? I am not sure where to begin.

I struggle to get the right words out but ultimately find my way. 'I don't think she was trying to harm me.' I look at everyone else. 'I think she was warning me of what could come.'

Illias exchanges glances with my two other brothers. A look that speaks of a million worries.

Freya, however, lifts her gaze to Idris and says, 'You should have let me speak with it. I could have helped.'

Idris's cold features seem to soften at the same time as Iker rises from his chair and walks up to the cot.

'The Galgr hurt our sister,' Iker states, the weight of his words carrying that fierce protectiveness the three of my brothers share. 'We weren't going to take any more risks.'

Idris agrees with Iker for once, nodding at him. 'The creature likely put thoughts into Nara's head. Why should we trust it when it hurt her?'

I shut my eyes as Freya tries to reason and I exhale a tense breath. There is no use explaining to my brothers why the Galgr did what she did. Yes, I have come to realise they are ruthless creatures, killers in fact. But what she showed me . . . what if it was a look into the future? What if . . . what if Darius asking me to kill him comes true?

I cannot, I cannot do—

'Nara?' Freya's voice cuts through my contemplative thoughts, pulling me back to the present.

'Sorry.' I shake my head, wincing once I remember the hit I must have received from the fall. 'I—'

Lorcan's appearance by the doorway prompts me to stop talking. His hair is tied back and his clothes aren't the usual burgundy armour. Instead, he looks . . . comfortable in his casual red shirt.

'Can we talk?' he says, and I huff. It is the only question he knows to ask around me.

I glance at everyone else and nod that it's fine for them to leave the infirmary. They all kiss the top of my head before walking out one by one, with Tibith toddling behind and squeezing past Lorcan.

An awkward sense of restlessness and quietness in the air doesn't seem to disappear, even with the whispers of Aerians talking to one another as Lorcan comes to the foot of my cot.

'I heard about that—' he starts to say.

'Galgr,' I clip, and shift my weight on the bed.

'You're still mad about what happened, aren't you?'

My eyes snap up at him.

The answer must be clearly written across my face because he quickly adds, 'Look, I think it's best if I stay away from him. At least for now.'

Guilt consumes him as he looks directly at the bed and not me.

I sigh a big breath, surrendering to the vexation I felt previously. 'He still loves you.' His jade eyes flicker up at me. 'Whatever Aurum taught him to believe doesn't mean he stopped being your brother.'

'Stepbrother,' he rectifies with a frown.

I give him a pointed stare. 'You're making this really difficult, you know that?'

The first form of a smile marks his lips, and though we are far from how we once used to be, I surprise him with a closed-mouth laugh.

'I know,' he says, a smile lingering through his words. 'Just . . . take it easy, Nara. We'll get there with him. I think he might even be as stubborn as you, if not more so.'

I roll my eyes. 'He wishes.'

Lorcan taps his hand against the wooden post of the bed twice and chuckles before walking backwards towards the door.

Tipping my head to the side, I watch him in curiosity and think back to what Leira once said.

'A beast no less, though a heart of gold.'

I'm starting to see that maybe that *beast* has always been Lorcan without us knowing.

'Ah, Lorcy!' Rydan stumbles through the doorway, almost face-planting into Lorcan. He rears back, grinning as he looks Lorcan up and down. 'You look . . . well?'

Lorcan's face is an unreadable mask as he tersely mutters, 'Get out of the way, Rydan,' and strides away.

My lips contort into a grimace as Rydan approaches. 'And I thought *my* flirting skills were bad.'

'Ambrose, there's a difference between your flirting and mine.' He drops onto the bed, nearly crushing me as he leans against my legs. He points. '*You* can't; *I* can, just not when I actually do like someone.'

Ouch.

'And yet it never worked with me.' I try to push him off me, but he remains firmly in place.

He just clicks his tongue and smirks instead. '*Yet*. I give it five years before you're obsessed with me. It's in my five-year *Get Ambrose to Love Me* plan.'

'There won't *be* any five years if you keep cutting off the circulation in my legs.'

He looks down just as I manage to wriggle my legs free and promptly raise them to my chest, using the motion to shove Rydan off the bed. He hits the floor with a thud, and before he can make a complaint, Arlayna's gentle knock on the side of the door cuts him off.

I invite her in with a smile while Rydan struggles to get up from the floor. He rubs his rear end with a pinched expression, and I ignore him, turning my attention to Arlayna. I try to get up, but she shakes her head, lightly touching me by the shoulders as she pushes me back down.

'Goodness, Nara,' she scolds with a *tsk*. 'You know how dangerous Galgrs are. We should never have come.'

'It was worth it,' I grumble as she holds on to my wrist and I stare up into the grey clouds of her eyes. 'How else would I know Aurum is slowly decaying?'

Her brows furrow, a hint of uncertainty crossing her features. 'Listen, Nara, it pains me to say this, but . . . ' She pauses, sighing. 'If you ever need an ally, Kirian would be your next hope, more than the people of Undarion.'

I stay quiet.

'Even with the possibility that Aurum may be suffering from the Isle's consequences, he has still taken most of our soldiers. So just . . .' She bites her lip. 'Think about it.'

I can see the weight of the stress bearing down on her, not just for me but for her family and her people back in Olcar.

Covering her hand with mine, I offer a soft, reassuring glance. 'I will,' I whisper. 'Thank you, truly. Not just for this but for everything you have done for us.'

She smiles, aiming her eyes at the floor, and begins to speak, but Aeron's voice interrupts, calling out to her.

He gives me a farewell nod as Faye comes up beside him, looking tiny next to his height. Arlayna then bids me goodbye before I watch the three of them depart from the infirmary.

Rydan's whistle catches the attention of Aerians trying to rest. He doesn't seem to notice their glares. 'That tension.' He shakes his head, eyes wide. 'Looks like the princess wants some of the guards—'

'Don't finish that sentence.' I glower. 'Besides, Arlayna knows she can't be with him.'

Rydan chuckles, his brows rising as if he knows a secret that I don't. 'Oh, I wasn't talking about her.'

I frown and he winks at me, his brown eyes sparkling with mirth.

'I'll see you tomorrow, Ambrose.' He walks up to the doorway and looks over his shoulder at me. 'Unless you feel like joining me in bed later, which I perfectly understand—'

I throw my pillow at him, though he perfectly manages to dodge it and leaves me here with the rest of the Aerians.

CHAPTER NINETEEN

I wake up the next day with a new positive outlook towards Darius and me. Most will think I am stupid to try to go back to the dungeons and visit him, but avoiding him won't help our situation any better.

After the princesses left with the Galgr, Freya, Link and Illias all tried to dissuade me from going through with it, not to mention Idris's reaction when he found out the actual truth of what happened between Lorcan and Darius. But instead of arguing with me, he left the room with a whispering grumble about how he was getting too old for this.

When I descend the steps into the dungeons and walk along the hallways, I see Darius lying on his back, knees up and his forearm draped over his eyes as I arrive outside his cell. I spot the mark on his abdomen again, and I remember how I told Freya about it after what happened yesterday. She said it was a linking rune and promised to investigate it with Leira and Aelle as a way to break his connection with Aurum. But time is moving fast, and I am wondering how long we have left until Aurum comes in search of the stones and Darius.

'Do you usually stare at people without saying a word, Goldie?'

I blink over at Darius, though he still doesn't seem to move his arm away from his eyes. 'And are you always this perceptive?'

His laugh wraps around my throat like a lover's grip, making it hard to swallow. 'Your scent is quite powerful.' He sits up and turns to look at me. The small window above him casts a shadow over his face. 'Reminds me of a jasmine flower.'

I roll my bottom lip between my teeth. 'Is that so?'

He slowly nods, narrowing his eyes as he rises to his feet. Striding towards me, it's as if he forgets there's a barrier between us. He inspects the metal bars with furrowed brows and shakes his head, turning away from me. 'So, what will we be doing today? A nice stroll around the palace? Perhaps a visit to the main towns? Or, my favourite, eating a fine meal with the Aerian warriors? I must say I do quite fancy some mutton with a nice tankard of ale to accompany it.'

His sarcasm is duly noted. I hate him being here as much as he does.

Sighing, I want to tell him how sorry I am, but I am no better than everyone else who keeps him locked up here.

'Hello, Darry!'

Oh, Solaris, no.

I glance to my right, where Tibith is now waving animatedly at Darius. Panic swirls in my chest, anticipating that Darius will react in a way that will upset Tibith.

Yet when he whirls around, his head slants to the side in curiosity, and he smiles. 'Hello, and you are?'

'Do you not r-remember me?' Tibith twirls around before puffing out his chest with confidence. 'I am Tibith, your greatest friend and thieving partner, as you like to say!'

My lips peel back into a grin, and when Darius laughs, all my worries seem to float away.

Darius kneels and leans forward as if about to let Tibith in on a secret. 'Tell me . . . Tibith, right?' A nod from Tibith has Darius continuing. 'If you are my *greatest* friend, what are some things I enjoy doing?'

Tibith beams. 'That is easy! You like to steal bread with me; you don't like sleeping on beds, so you give me all the cushions to sleep on; and you enjoy spending time with Miss Nara without wearing any clothes—'

'I think he gets it, Tibith.' My cheeks flush with mortification, but Darius looks at me and cocks an eyebrow.

A smirk forms in the corner of his mouth. 'Had you started with that, Goldie, I would have been much more willing to comply.'

My lips twist in disapproval, but that only makes Darius chuckle as I turn away from him and crouch down. 'Come on, Tibith.' I jerk my head in the direction of the stairs.

His ears droop and I know that means he is disappointed. 'But I want to stay with Darry.'

'We can visit him tomorrow.' Softness eases my tone, and I smile at him to seal the promise. It was selfish of me to keep him away in the first place, despite knowing Illias would argue that it was me protecting Tibith from uncertainty.

Tibith gives me that look again. The one it is hard to say no to. 'Really?'

I nod and stand up. When I look back at Darius, his attention is solely focused on me. Tibith and I turn around and head out of the cell. Tension trembles between us like an unbreakable rope as Tibith waves goodbye, and Darius shakes his hand once back at him.

As we leave the dungeons, I squint my eyes at the sun carving its pathway across the brick archways of the palace grounds. Tibith and I look at each other, and I keep that promise that he will see Darius again – the very next day, we bring him breakfast, and it starts to feel like before. When it was us three against the centipede, us three against poisonous vines, and us three against Renward.

When the second day came, Tibith left Darius and me to be by ourselves. He brought a loaf of bread he took from the palace kitchen and he wanted us to share it. 'Bread is the most romantic food of them all, Miss Nara,' he'd said, and I suppose I couldn't let him down by declining.

During the evenings, Gus would come by, though it never became easier watching him and Darius converse when I knew the truth, and he did not.

On the third day, Darius wanted to play a game. A game of guessing things about me. And when he showered me with teasing insults rather than compliments, I found myself smiling more than usual. Until, of course, he brought up Gus.

'Are you close with Gus?' he had asked out of curiosity.

Shame turned sour in my mouth as I looked down at my hands instead of at Darius. 'He has been as kind to me as he has been to you.'

He had mulled my words over, and there was a moment there where he saw right through me. He wasn't sure what exactly it was, but I hadn't done a perfect job at hiding my guilt, and despite his memory loss, he recognised my mannerisms of unease. Perhaps he could even feel the slight quickening of my heartbeat.

Thankfully, on the fourth day, it was all forgotten as he used a fork from his supper and bent it into the shape of a poorly made flower. He handed it to me with a smile that dented his cheeks, and I laughed before sniffing it and telling him it smelled nothing like a flower.

That was the first time in days that I had witnessed a genuine laugh from him that I hadn't seen in a while.

Then, once the fifth day came, I asked him to tell me a story. He didn't understand why and even insisted he was not a storyteller. My rebuttal was that it was one of the many things he enjoyed. He studied me thoughtfully, and it wasn't long until he began a tale about a thief and his search for the golden princess.

I do not think he ever realised it was *his* life that he was retelling, and as the sixth day dawned, I brought Freya along with me. Together, we thought she could try to use her magic to sever the link between Darius and Aurum.

In the dim light of the cell, Freya extended her palm towards Darius's rune; the only thing separating them was the cell doors. I waited and waited and waited as I fixated on Darius, our eyes locked. Then a vibrant purple glow emanated from Freya's hand until . . . she stopped and turned to me, disappointment etched across her face as she shook her head.

It hadn't worked.

On the seventh day, Darius's mood was no longer like the days before. He was . . . much more contemplative, let's say.

Tibith and I visited him as soon as we awoke, not even attempting to try to eat breakfast with everyone else. I took plates of fresh fruit and pastries and rushed down to the cell so that I could see him. Except, it has now been over an hour, and he hasn't touched his food. Not once, and neither has he spoken.

With Tibith playfully rolling around in the far-left corner of the dungeons, I inhale a deep breath as I go to speak, but he cuts me off before I can even begin.

'Do you know how the Rivernorths first came to be?'

The slow scanning of his eyes on me has my skin tingling.

I nod. 'I have heard things, yes.' Hira has even mentioned the tragedy of the Rivernorth line before, but I know . . . I *know* that bloodline can be salvaged with Darius.

'My uncle says they were the first of the dragon kind. Born out of the Northern Rivers, immune to steel, and hard to kill with just any weapon.' He cocks his head. 'Sounds ludicrous, doesn't it?'

I look towards Tibith, who is now watching us with glowing eyes. 'With a world like this, hardly.'

Darius's hum has a lilt to it. 'True.'

My chest is heaving with a sigh that I can't seem to evade as I face him again. 'What else has your uncle said?'

He smiles. 'Trying to get information out of me, Goldie?'

I shrug. 'Perhaps. Unless you wish for me to bribe you, I have a few gold antique pieces I could steal for you.'

He raises an eyebrow in interest at my offer. 'Where?'

I laugh and straighten up, brushing the dirt from the side of my leather trousers. 'Oh, I can't tell you that.' As Darius lifts himself off the floor, he grabs on to one of the bars while leaning his shoulder against it. 'It's too risky, especially for someone who recalls never being a thief himself.'

He knows I am goading him. My taunt practically makes his eyes brighten with pleasure as his head bobs while humming. He searches his trouser pockets for something before taking out a sharpened bone pick and waving it in front of us.

My eyes dart to the mound of bones by the side of his cage, and trepidation mixed with desire swims in my vision as I glance back at Darius. He's smirking at me as he picks at the lock with the skills of a professional.

The gate clangs open and I stumble back, watching Darius exit the cell.

'Darry, you are free!' Tibith squeaks, earning a soft chuckle from Darius.

I shake my head, my jaw almost hanging wide open. 'How did you—'

'I figured out a few days ago that I am rather good at lock-picking.' He eyes the bone pick before throwing it over his shoulder as he takes a step towards me, then another.

My feet shuffle backwards the closer he gets. 'And yet you haven't tried to escape.' When there is no room left behind me except for an empty cell, I grab on to the bars. Darius, however, cages me in with both hands on either side of my head.

'I've come to quite enjoy talking to you these days.'

'So, you have willingly spent time inside this cell when you could have been out there, free?' The thought is thrilling.

He grins. 'Sounds *ludicrous*, doesn't it?'

Repeating that phrase turns me red as I watch the words roll from his lips in pure seductive bliss and find myself breathlessly saying, 'Yes, truly inane. The Aerians would not be happy in the slightest.' I attempt to sneak a peek elsewhere, but his gaze pulls me in; I can't control it. I swallow. 'Neither will Gus or Lorcan—'

'Are *you* happy, though?' He's staring at my mouth, and I'm not sure how much longer I can restrain myself.

'Delighted.' The word comes out softer than I would have liked.

The answer excites him. He leans in and whispers against my ear, 'So, if I were to kiss you, would you try to lock me back inside?'

Solaris.

'I never wanted you to be locked in in the first place,' I say equally quietly. 'You just happened to infuriate almost everyone living inside the palace.'

He looks at me, and my legs almost buckle.

'Tibith?' He keeps his eyes fixed on me even as Tibith hums in response. 'Close your eyes.'

I don't look to see if Tibith has closed his eyes because the next thing I know is that my restraint is long gone, and I'm grabbing

Darius by the neck of his shirt as his lips smack against mine in desperate need.

Three months is too long to have gone without feeling the touch of his lips. *Three months* is a crime against us, knowing that I do not want this moment to ever end.

My legs are sore and sensitive from being wedged between his, and yet we're animals fighting to kiss each other harder. His hands are in my hair, rough and eager, making a groan sound low in his sternum.

He is kissing me as if he needs me in order to live. As if he thirsts for me.

His stubble scratches my face as our heads move to the motion of our lips. It doesn't feel like enough, and he knows it just as much as I do. I'm greedy for more of him, for the taste and scent of his skin upon mine.

Until he breaks off the kiss, jerking away from me as if I have stabbed him right in the heart.

I'm breathing wildly, my chest heaving as my lips tingle at the loss of him.

He runs a hand over his mouth and shakes his head. I can't tell what he is thinking; I can hardly think myself. All my mind keeps yelling is for him to tell me he remembers. To tell me our kiss *did* something.

'I shouldn't have done that.'

Five words – five words that ruin me.

He can't look at me. He doesn't want to.

I glance over at Tibith, his eyes wide and despondent as he stares at the both of us.

'Why?' I whisper, and anger surges me forward when Darius doesn't answer. 'Is it because you're afraid to remember who we once were?'

His jaw pops, yet he still does not reply.

Frustration swells inside my chest and I can't contain the burst of energy that leaves me. 'Say something, for Solaris's sake!'

'It's because he won't let me!' He turns to me, forcing the words out through clenched teeth. I balk, and his expression softens with remorse as he adds quietly this time, 'He won't let me remember.'

I hate what he means by that, and I hate it even more that I can't do anything to fix it myself.

I reach out and wrap my hands around his arm to bring us closer. His eyes widen in shock as his head whips around to look at me. 'He is not your family,' I say. 'He never was. He's hurting you, Darius, and I know that you are stronger than this.'

Our eyes lock, and a shadow of aching torment passes over his eyes. It is as if he is too exhausted to fight for himself. Whatever Aurum did in those three months makes my stomach turn at the thought.

'What did he do to make you like this?' I whisper with muffled rage.

He drags his gaze from mine to the empty and cold prison hallway. He has a vacant look to him suddenly as he says, 'Nothing. He did nothing.'

Tibith toddles over and grabs my calf. He looks up at me with a heartbreaking gaze, feeling for the one person who has stood by him for so many years.

I want to call Darius out on the lie but can't. Part of me knows that he doesn't believe it to be a lie. Inside his mind, he thinks he is telling the truth. That *everything* Aurum has told him is true.

I bite my lower lip; frustrated tears blur my eyesight, and then the worst thought comes to me – the very vision that the Galgr showed me, where Darius was in front of me, just how he is now, his expression pained as he begged me to kill him.

Stop, just stop, I beg my mind. My head turns to the side, my breathing becoming heavier the more I think about it.

I won't let it happen.

I can't.

I *won't*.

Squeezing my eyes tightly shut for a second, I take a deep breath before putting on a front as if the kiss had never happened, as if the vision of Darius asking me to kill him never existed, and I force myself to smile. Even though it feels as if I am dragging a knife across the sides of my lips. 'Can you still fly?'

He blinks from his stupor and swivels his focus back on me.

His brows push together into a pensive frown. He looks saddened. Disappointed even. 'Not on command.'

Suppressing the surge of anger that wells up my throat in response to the extent of Aurum's control over Darius, I opt for another feigned smile. 'Then we will search for a loophole.' I pivot away from him, whistling over at Tibith to follow before glancing briefly over my shoulder. 'I assume you'll know how to ride a dragon, considering you are one.'

A chuckle escapes his lips, lacking complete sincerity, but he nods and saunters over to me. 'Lead the way then, Goldie.'

CHAPTER TWENTY

The clouds part as Fernah's dragon wings lift me into the sky. With a grin stretching from ear to ear, I turn to check whether Darius is around.

His chuckle can be heard as he rides through the fog on top of an Ardenti that is breathing fire. My smile doubles, and I glance behind me, seeing Tibith strapped in his own leather saddle, excitedly warbling.

Fernah swerves left, right and centre in the wind before disappearing below the clouds. I tilt my head back and grin like we're in a race as Darius and his dragon trail behind. It's almost as if up here, we don't need to be scrupulous about the horrors we face on land. I can breathe and not feel as though I am suffocating.

It's freedom. *My* freedom.

'This is so much fun, Miss Nara!' Tibith yells, and I laugh.

In the distance, I can see the grassy cliff where Gus has previously taken me for training. Fernah swoops down towards it as a shadow falls over my head. The sight of Darius racing ahead motivates me to outrun him, and I call out Fernah's name. She speeds up, creating a rhythmic sound with her wings.

My sight homes in on the cliff, passing training grounds and forests.

We make it within a second of Darius almost beating us. Fernah's soft landing pushes some grass up off the ground as I unclip myself from the saddle and jump down, making sure to grab Tibith.

As I set him on the grass, he wobbles on his feet, looking unsteady after the ride, before he ends up falling flat on his bottom. I turn to look at Darius as his feet land on the ground. His hair is windswept, which makes me want to run my hands through it and mess it up even more.

Grinning, I say to him, 'I win.'

He chuckles, peeling the leather gloves I gave him off his fingers. 'So, how did you learn to ride a dragon?'

I rub Fernah below her snout and she purrs. 'I didn't until I came here. I had only ever ridden a dragon once before Fernah.' My gaze shifts over to Darius. 'And that dragon was you.'

He lifts a brow, giving me an expectant look as he smirks.

I roll my eyes. 'Glad to know that your shameless thoughts have never left.'

'Well, did you enjoy it?' he asks, and my cheeks flame bright red. His grin is the most mischievous I have ever seen come from him as he crosses his arms over his broad chest, the muscles practically ripping his shirt apart. My heart quickens. 'When I took you out flying, I mean.'

I cough, attempting to clear my throat. It hardly works. 'You dropped me,' I deadpan. 'On purpose.'

He finds the thought thoroughly amusing as he tips his head back and laughs. The vision soothes me, and I chuckle alongside him. It is like we are back to our old selves for just a short second. One in which Darius has his memories back, and I'm content with him.

I storm up to him and try to smack him across the chest, but he captures my hand and rests it against his heart. I swallow back my laugh, almost choking as I stare up at him.

Darius watches my reaction and gorges on it like it is a feast as I glance at the position of our hands and feel the soft beat of his heart beneath my palm.

Am I lying now, Goldie?

The night before his capture back in Emberwell slips into my mind, just as it has done so many times in the past. He would do this whenever he wanted to prove something. Now, I do not care what he has to prove because all that matters is that I can feel it, that I can touch him and know he is real; he is here with me, and he is trying.

He closes the gap between us with a single step. My hand stays on his chest, but my breathing stops as he hooks his finger around the coin necklace and stares at it.

It's your birthday gift.

I was irreversibly in love with you. I am irreversibly in love with you, Nara.

My body shivers at his attention and the crease along his forehead as he studies the coin. It is a similar look to the one he gave me the first day he was here. The look where he knew this meant something more than his mind was letting him remember.

'It's not just any coin,' I utter, my mouth parched as his gaze flicks up to meet mine. 'It's a gold coin.' I offer a smile, hoping he recalls the significance from all those years ago when I handed him this very coin.

The corner of his mouth starts to lift, and I can't help but mirror his expression.

'Shit.' My smile falls as soon as I spot Gus shifting into human form at the edge of the cliff and marching towards us, looking as if he is ready to kick up a storm with me. The added wind surrounds him as it blows his shawl and hair, reminding me of the times Idris would show up with the same furious expression.

Darius goes to take a step in front of me, but I stop him with a shake of my head.

'Do you have any idea how worried I was when I went to check the cells and found the door open and you and Darius both gone?' Gus is seething, completely, utterly mad.

'I know—'

'Idris is this close to forming a fleet to return to Emberwell, thinking you are there.' His thumb and forefinger, barely touching as he shows me, are enough to imagine.

'You needn't worry,' Darius says, a smirk moulding his lips. 'She is in safe hands.'

Gus's gaze shifts from me to Darius, his brows rising in disbelief. 'Safe hands?' he scoffs. 'Please, you are hardly to be trusted right now.'

Darius clicks his tongue, touching his heart as if to say Gus's comment wounded him. Yet it's clear that this is his way of playfully messing with him.

Gus looks sternly at him, and I tug at his arm, ushering us away from Darius as I guide him to the cliff's edge.

He is shaking his head by the time we stop walking and I face him. 'Whatever your reason may be—'

'He is making progress,' I tell him quietly, glancing back at Darius to check on him as he crouches down to talk to Tibith. Clearing my throat as I see him staring at us, I say to Gus, 'I think the reason why he might stop himself from wanting to remember is that Aurum's influence is too strong.'

Gus looks at me with a deep frown. 'Have you mentioned this to Leira?'

I nod. 'She thought that would be the case if Aurum had full control over Darius's powers.' I bite my lower lip in thought as Gus remains silent. 'What if the answer is you?'

His back goes rigid.

'You're his father, Gus. Maybe there is a way you can—'

'Nara.'

His warning tone irks me.

'Would you, for once, put aside your fears of how he would react around you, and help him?'

The sigh that escapes him resonates with a mix of aggravation and shame. He pinches the bridge of his nose, and as my eyes return to Darius, I watch as he throws his head back in laughter, engrossed in whatever Tibith is saying.

'If it meant saving your son,' I whisper, my focus still on Darius, 'would you not at least try, despite the consequences?'

No response comes, and even when I tear my gaze away from Darius to look at Gus, his eyes are elsewhere.

His chest rises with a deep breath. 'I should take you back to the garrison. Your brothers are waiting there.'

I make no effort to conceal my disappointment at the sudden shift in conversation. 'And Darius?'

Regret grips him by the throat as he lowers his voice and looks at me. 'You know it is not my choice, Nara.'

That means he is going to take him back to the dungeons.

Frustration slithers its way up my spine. 'He is not a threat any more.'

'I know,' he says, and that frustration turns into anger as my eyes well up with furious tears, and I turn the other way to face the view beyond the cliffs. The vast expanse below reveals valleys veiled in mist and rolling hills painted in hues of green and gold. For once, I hate how beautiful it looks, how even as Gus's footsteps fade behind me, I wish for nothing but to be up in the air again.

CHAPTER TWENTY-ONE

The garrison is a mess.

Shifters, goblins and any other creature who was fortunate enough to survive Emberwell are yelling out their protests and need for answers.

Answers to what will come next.

Gus is trying to calm most of them down, but it's not enough to keep them at bay. They are as infuriated as I would imagine them to be after we attacked Aurum's castle.

My brothers are at my side, as are my friends, watching it all unfold across the hall. On the other hand, Darius returned to his cell despite how opposed I was and still am to it. But with the Aerians already angry with me, this would have been the final straw.

I close my eyes as if to drown out the noises from everyone around me.

'How much longer must we remain here?'

There goes that.

I peel my eyes open and look at one of the shifters, who has spoken out for the rest of the people here. The others agree with him, murmuring and banging against the tables.

Gus waves his hands to quieten the crowd. 'We are doing our best—'

'That's what you said last time!' another chimes in, and the shifters clamour in another array of protests. 'Where is Darius?'

Gus glances back at me; tension carves lines across his forehead, and I shake my head at him. Most of the people here are as stubborn as I am. They won't listen, even if we are to gift them with a bigger place to stay in the meantime.

'You don't need to be here to witness all of this. Go get some rest, and we will meet later.' I lean in to my brothers, whispering, but all three turn to me and scrunch their faces together at the same time.

'That's insulting. Do you know how entertaining this is?' Iker says, and Illias slaps his abdomen, drawing out an oomph from him.

'We're staying,' Idris adds with finality, straightening his shoulders as he looks forward, ending our discussion.

I know he is still mad at me for vanishing off with Darius, but I am not about to apologise for what I did, and he already knew that from the moment I appeared inside the garrison. 'Idris—'

'What has the mortal to say in all of this?'

I freeze, looking out at the flock of shifters.

'She is the reason for Darius's capture in the first place!' the woman yells. She is the only one standing now, as she points accusingly at me. 'We listened to her when we invaded the castle, and now, after everything we have done, she decides to stay quiet?'

Anger hits my throat, and I spring forward to say my part, but Freya jumps to my aid.

'Nara has nothing to do with this,' she says, and it's a different side to Freya I now see. She's fierce and a leader, unlike most. 'She is the one who has ensured your safety – she stepped up when no one else would. Mortal or not, she is part of you, and you will respect her as much as you do Gus.'

Silence settles over the hall. Everyone's attention is on Freya and Freya alone. I sense Idris tense beside me, and before I can look up at him, my gaze snags on one of the tables as a cup tumbles onto the floor. Dice scatter out from it, landing in a perfect line.

Liars' Dice.

The very first game Darius and I played back at the den.

Every single muscle of mine seizes as I think of that moment. A moment that changed so much of what I knew back then. And even as the sudden rumblings of horse hooves from outside creep closer and the warning bells chime, I only focus on those dice. But as the doors are busted open, and I turn to see Lorcan and a dozen Aerians behind him, I realise what we are up against.

'Aurum!' he shouts, what I have dreaded for so long, and my stomach buckles as the shifters inside rise on alert. Chaos reigns in the Aeris lands as people push each other towards the front.

I whirl to my brothers as Link and Rydan draw out their weapons and Freya ignites her magic into the palm of her hands.

No, no – I need more time.

'Nara, go!' Idris is yelling, but it doesn't register until I glance back at the dice. Idris grabs my shoulders, shoving me so that I start moving, but I plant my feet down on the ground and hold on to him.

'Darius,' is all I say. As I turn to look, I see Gus guiding a few children to some hiding spots at the end of the hall. When he finds my gaze, he gives me a stern nod, and I immediately know what he is implying.

I twist my head back at Idris. He's looking at me with a strangled expression, stuck between being an older brother or an ally.

'Damn it, Nara.' He squeezes my arms, choosing the latter.

'Find a dragon and ride out of here, the three of you.' I don't care if they can fight better than a goblin; I do not want Aurum near them. 'Head to Terranos if you have to, but just, *please*, get to safety.'

Idris hesitates, his jaw ticking more by the second.

'We will, as long as you do too.' Illias touches Idris's shoulder, struggling to drag him away from me. 'Be safe, Nara. For us.'

I nod and my chest heaves in and out as I stare at the commotion unfolding before me. Lorcan is on the other side, lining people up as explosions of dragon fire fill the skies from outside the windows. As I make my way through the mayhem and snatch the cup and dice from the floor, my feet jump into motion and propel me forwards. Everyone who is left charges towards the doors, ready for a fight, but as I make it outside, I sprint in the other direction, where the palace lies and Darius is.

CHAPTER TWENTY-TWO

I'm running as fast as possible through the palace's hidden passageways. I focus only on the thought that Darius is still in the dungeons and that I have to get to him before anything can happen. My feet ache and my emotions tangle along with the pain.

I make it to the dungeons, my burgundy tunic catching the surfaces of the walls and ripping apart as I make it down the steps. It doesn't matter, though; what matters is that I reach Darius. I raise one of my hands up as I skid around the corner and slam against the wall.

Darius rises to his feet, worry so potent across his features that he stalks towards the bars of his gate in three swift strides. 'Goldie? What's wrong?'

I'm panting as I rush over to him. I lift the cups stacked with the dice inside and say between breaths, 'You said Aurum won't let you remember.'

He stares at me, his gaze sharpening with concern.

'Fine, then,' I say, 'we will do something different. Something that follows *my* rules.'

Darius takes in what I am saying with shrewd eyes. 'And that is?'

'We play a game of Liars' Dice.' I plop myself onto the ground, sitting cross-legged. Darius watches me as I unstack one cup from the other, managing to fit it through the bars of the cell. 'You know it, right? After all, you are a well-known champion within the shifters.'

Acknowledgement shines in his eyes. Even if he does not intend to play, I have him fascinated by this sudden arrangement. The sounds of what might be happening outside do not reach this far down the dungeons, but that doesn't make it any less daunting as I rush to set up the game.

My fingers tremble as I drop the dice into my cup, then pass the other five through the bars. Worry gnaws at the back of my mind, believing this is a pointless plan and that all I am doing is endangering everyone else due to the slightest hint of hope inside me from playing this game.

'We play one round.' I stare at the dice, concentrating on each black dot. 'If you win, I let you out of here, and you can go with Aurum.'

'And if *you* win?'

I pull back a breath, forcing myself to look up at Darius. When I do, he has already sat down opposite me with the cup in his hand and a gaze that watches me with every intention of devouring me. 'Then nothing happens.'

He clicks his tongue. 'Doesn't seem fair, Goldie.'

'Yes,' I answer, lifting my chin. 'I suppose it does not.'

His brows scrunch together, and I know he must wonder what the endgame is here. 'All right then, Goldie,' he says with a slow nod. 'I'll play your game.'

Perfect. 'There is one thing you must know before we start,' I say as we begin rolling the dice inside our cups. 'For every time we go to say our numbers, we must ask the other a question, and we must answer it truthfully.'

He keeps his gaze concentrated on me before forcing a slow nod. We both then slam our cups upside down on the ground. I inhale deeply, glancing at the dice hidden beneath.

Darius gestures his hand out towards me and smirks. 'Ladies first.'

'Why do you believe you killed Lorcan back at the cottage?' I jump straight into a heavy question.

Darius's immediate reaction is nothing, but it's hard to ignore how his hand tightens around the cup.

He looks at me with reflective gold eyes. 'It is not a belief when it is what happened.'

Now, my fingers grip the base of the cup with too much force. 'Three fours.' I don't acknowledge his answer. 'Your turn.'

'Who gave you that scar?' He nods at my arm, and I glance down at the injury I once despised wholeheartedly.

'Lorcan,' I whisper. *But you already knew that from before.* 'We were young. He didn't know right from wrong.'

Visible anger cuts across Darius's eyes. The veins along his neck strain from the effort to keep himself from asking more, but the old him, the one who lived a real life, understands why Lorcan did what he did.

'Four fours.'

He turns his head to the side, and it feels as if there is a knot in my throat, rendering me powerless to speak up. I know that my next question will dip into unknown territories, so all I can offer him is a relaxed breath. 'If you believe your uncle is a good man,' I start, 'then why do you not question as to why he took your powers and controls your very being?'

His gaze comes crashing down on me in a punishing way. 'He is doing it to protect me.'

Liar, I want to shout, but that is not part of the game. At least not yet, not until one of us believes the other has bid more than what we have.

Frustration curls the sides of my lips into a downward frown. 'Five fours,' I clip.

The air around the dungeons is taut, pulling its strings at us as we glance at our dice here and there.

Darius rolls his shoulders back and inhales deeply through his nose. His stare is relentless. 'Why is it that you want to play this game?'

I tuck my bottom lip between my teeth and think. I already know why I want to play this game, but the whole truth doesn't come out. Only part of it does. 'The first time we played this together . . . you took me to the shifter's den. It is also the first time I realised that hating you was just a façade.'

Darius never stops watching me. Watching me speak, watching how the words form and spill from my lips as if they are magic. His attention makes my heart bubble up with nerves, and then he says, low and raspy, 'Six fives.'

I tilt my cup just enough to see how many dice I have again. Two fours, three threes. I lift my gaze to Darius's and take a slow breath. I'm staring at him, mapping out his face so that I can remember it and never forget it, unlike how he forgot me. My lashes flutter against my cheeks as I glance at his hands, and suddenly, an echo of remembrance calls at the back of my mind – a memory of when Darius and I were travelling through the Screaming Forests.

'Have you ever fallen in love?' I'd asked Darius after he saved me from the Galgrs.

'Yes.'

'What's it like?'

'Frightening.'

'Is that all?'

'Love is different for everyone, Goldie. Sometimes, a simple glance is all it takes to fall in love with someone.'

'I've only ever heard that in stories my mother would tell me.'

'And how did your mother and father fall in love?'

'On Noctura night, when they were children. My father saw her dancing as the gold dust fell from the sky, and he's always said since that moment he loved her.'

Darius's smile from that night flashes across my mind.

'Well then,' I had said. 'How can you know when you're in love with someone?'

'When it hurts.'

As I return from the vivid words Darius once spoke to me, my heart stumbles over a beat.

I look up at him, my lips parted, as I try to catch a breath and ask the very question that stops time. 'When do you know you're in love?'

He is hit with a barrage of feelings all at once. His brows draw together, and his chest heaves as his attention suddenly shifts to the left. I can tell his head is swirling, trying to process the question I have laid on him.

I wait and wait and wait.

And when he finally looks me in the eye, it is pure agony. 'When it hurts.'

Hearing those words is both a relief and a blow to the heart. He never says that he remembers or that he recognises the words from that same night, too, and I know that what I am about to say will make me lose. 'Eight fives,' I whisper, his eyes closing as if he knew I would bid a higher number.

'Liar,' he rasps, disappointment dripping from his deep voice.

We both lift our cups to reveal the amount we have on our dice. He has four fives and two sixes.

I shut my eyes and bite my lower lip before exhaling. 'You win.'

He doesn't sound satisfied. 'I guess I did.'

I put on a brave face as I stand up and force myself to look at him. 'You're finally free to go.' I don't know where my voice went, but it is no longer here with us. Clearing my throat, I fetch the keys out of my pocket. 'No need to pick the locks any longer.'

He's against the cell door now, his jaw cemented tight as I unlock the gate and hold on to the bars, believing that will keep me from wanting to collapse. I keep my concentrated gaze on the key wedged in the lock, sensing as Darius walks out of his cell.

How can you know when you're in love with someone?

When it hurts.

Pain engulfs me as I clench my eyes, expecting him to have run off now to find Aurum.

But then he says, 'Nara.' And I turn.

I hardly have time to take in the look on his face before he's on me in two quick strides, cupping my face so that his lips are firmly planted on mine.

A strangled noise between a moan and a plea tears through his lips against mine, and I take it. I take everything he is giving me. The soft strokes of his tongue with my own, the gentle touches of his hands in my hair, my back and my heart.

'I'm sorry,' he murmurs, and I shake my head, kissing him harder. 'I do remember.' He nips my lower lip and I let loose a hungerful sigh. 'I remember everything.'

I do remember.

I remember everything.

His tears hit my face as he clutches my cheeks and kisses me over and over again, whispering in between. 'I tried,' he says. 'I tried so hard not to let you go.'

I don't know what he means by that, and I don't bother to ask because all I care about right now is this moment.

'Please don't forget me,' I breathe, my lips over his, as I touch his face, wondering if this is real. 'Never again.'

He shakes his head, his nose rubbing against mine. 'Never—'

A slow clap ricochets off the dungeon walls, and I jump back from Darius. Cold dread dampens my back as Darius and I glance to the right, where Aurum and Sarilyn stand side by side, looking at us with the smuggest of grins imaginable.

No, Solaris, please, not now.

CHAPTER TWENTY-THREE

'Nice to see that *true love* can indeed break even the most powerful mind magic.' Aurum's smile is viperous. 'Pathetic, truly, but what can I do when my only nephew becomes weak over a mortal?'

Darius quickly takes on a protective stance, pushing me behind him while he glares at Aurum and shields me with an outstretched hand across my midsection.

Aurum watches the action with cruelty alongside Sarilyn. I'm used to seeing her in a gown, but now she's wearing a suit of golden armour that fits her like a second skin and is just like Aurum's. Panic smashes across my chest like fragile glass as I think of my brothers, my friends . . .

'Oh, Darius, how you disappoint me. I thought we were family.' Aurum's grinning, arms opened wide as if to greet us.

Darius's hand hardens into a fist. His harsh gaze targets Aurum as he says, 'You're a sick bastard.' He charges at him, set on doing harm, but Aurum's grin widens as he raises his arm and shadowed hands form out of the ground, seizing Darius's ankles.

'Don't forget, I still own you,' Aurum says mockingly while toying with the shadow magic at his fingertips. 'As long as you have that mark on you, you can't do anything.'

Anger ebbs out of me as I unsheathe my dagger and run towards him. Predatory green eyes slide over to me as he creates a massive shadow that drives me back into the wall. Hot stings spread all over me as I scream and land on the ground with my palms flat on the rubble.

Pushing through the throbbing pain, I rise to my knees, but something heavy pushes me back down and I groan, unable to move. My gaze fixes on Aurum as he stretches his hand to me. He clenches his fist, and the weight on my back crushes me bit by bit.

As my mouth fills with a heavy metallic substance, I immediately spit blood out in front of me. Aurum's slow, lethal steps then stalk towards me, but Darius shouts for his attention, making him pause and turn. I look up to see Darius free from the shadows and now, behind Sarilyn, pressing one of her blades against her neck.

'Touch her again and I swear I will take pleasure in slicing this knife across your precious Sarilyn.' Darius is furious compared to Sarilyn's confident stance, as she holds her head high and doesn't show any sign of fear in her dark gaze.

Aurum's chuckle comes out as a scoff. He looks back and forth between Darius and me. 'Even without your powers, you're a brave little shit,' he says to his nephew, prompting Darius to draw blood from Sarilyn's neck. She stutters a gasp but does not try to fight out of it. 'Go on then, kill her. I can easily make you stop with a click of my fingers.'

'Darius,' I croak, seeing his gaze shift to where I am. Anguish clouds his eyes with a veil of hesitation. The blade in his hand trembles, and he struggles to keep his grip on it as Aurum manipulates his mind and the dagger clatters onto the ground. Darius stumbles away from Sarilyn, and at that exact moment, Aurum whistles, beckoning a few Elven soldiers.

They rush in, not giving me enough time to recover as two of them yank me up from the ground. A third, who I recognise from my time with Arlayna, stands before me, his green regretful gaze elsewhere as he places my hands in shackles. It is the same boy from the night we rescued Darius.

'Ruvyn,' I whisper. He doesn't look at me, his dark hair shielding most of his face. 'You don't have to do this. Arlayna would not want this.'

He yanks at the chain connecting to the shackles and shakes his head. 'I no longer answer to the princess.' He turns away from me before I can speak, and the two other Elvens holding me by the arms look towards Aurum as more Elves haul in someone else, beaten and bruised.

Terror slices across my heart when I realise it is Gus.

He is thrown to the ground, his eyes flickering up to meet mine with apologetic need.

'Ah, there you are, finally,' Aurum says gleefully as Sarilyn watches on from the shadows of the dungeons. 'I was beginning to wonder if they had left anything of you at all.'

A trail of blood follows beneath Gus as he holds his abdomen, but an Elf quickly presses the heel of his boot down on Gus's back. He cries out in pain, and I squirm to let myself free.

'What did you do to him?' I demand and glance over at Darius. His gaze is fixed on me, and as his eyes lower to the shackles on me – the same ones restraining him – he seethes with anger.

'Well, after I took hold of . . .' Aurum begins, his voice dripping with malicious amusement, '*most* of your little friends, and what is it again? Ah, yes, those interesting brothers of yours. Augustus here enlightened me to a terrific truth, in accordance with the fact that I freed your siblings and took him in their place.'

A wave of nausea burns my throat as I choke back the panicked fear that my brothers never made it to safety.

Furiously shaking my head, I attempt to lunge at him, but a sharp cry escapes my throat when the Elf beside me yanks at my hair, forcefully pulling my head back.

Darius yells, trying to draw the Elf's attention as he breaks free from Aurum's lackeys, but it is useless. Aurum's power takes hold of him, and he freezes on the spot as if trapped in an invisible cage with no way to escape.

Aurum's smile widens. 'Although now I've changed my mind.'

'You said you'd let them go!' Gus chokes from the ground.

'I'm funny like that.'

With his free hand, Gus raises it towards Aurum, shadows swirling around his palm as he conjures blades aimed at him.

Aurum dodges them, letting a few hit an Elf behind him. As the Elf crumples to the ground with blood spilling from his head, neck and chest, Aurum turns to Gus. 'Is that any way to treat your brother-in-law?'

The air stills.

Aurum chuckles. 'Oh, that is right; I forgot.' He glances back at Darius. 'He doesn't know, does he?'

Gus's eyes turn to slits. 'Don't—'

'This is why, Darius.' He shakes his head in faux shame, walking up to him. 'I told you that you were siding with the wrong people.'

No, no, no, no.

'Aurum!' I shout, but the grip on my hair has me barely able to move an inch of my neck.

He strolls behind Darius before leaning forward as if he is about to let him in on a secret. His gaze is directed at Gus as he says in a venomous whisper, 'Even your own father has been lying to you all these years. He is the one, after all, who left you and your mother to focus on becoming the leader of those delinquent shifters.'

I see the colour drain from Darius's face and jerk my arms, wanting to break free from the Elf.

'No,' I whisper as he looks down at Gus, and the betrayal sinks in. I can only feel a surge of helplessness as Gus pleads with him from the ground, and Aurum watches the exchange with a sadistic gleam in his eye.

'Darius.' Gus's voice cracks with vulnerability. 'I never left your mother. He's lying—' The pressure from the Elf's boot on Gus is enough for him to stop talking.

'Now that that's over, here is what will happen.' Aurum strides past a devasted Darius, his gaze so vacant it hurts. 'While my soldiers—'

'Dusan's soldiers,' I grit between my teeth. From the corner of my eye, I see the slightest hint of a smirk form on Sarilyn's lips before she looks away.

Aurum comes closer to me, his smile dripping with hate. 'While *they* slaughter those stupid Aerians. You, the shifters and everyone you love will come back to Emberwell with me.' He stares at how defenceless I am right now and chuckles. 'I am sure you are looking forward to your new home.'

'You're not going to touch her, I swear—' Darius, fuelled by mounting anger, seems to recover enough to turn towards us.

Aurum doesn't acknowledge him, keeping his filthy eye on me. 'Oh, don't worry, Darius, I'll be kind enough to let you share it with her.' With one click of his fingers, the Elves begin to drag Gus and

Darius away. 'But first, you and I are going to have a chat about the stones.'

'Nara,' Darius calls out as he's pushed and pulled. 'We'll get everyone out, I promise, okay? Don't let him break you. You're stronger than him. Nara!'

I lose sight of him, and my heart splinters into pieces. Tears sting my eyes, but I refuse to let them fall as I look at Aurum. 'You can wonder where the stones are all you want, torture me to get the answers, but I will never tell you.' My smile is malicious as I stare into the only eye visible and then look closer at a deteriorating slash of black and green across his jaw. 'I would rather see you completely *rot* before you can return to the Isle.'

Aurum's smirk falters at the realisation that I know what is happening to him. His confident veneer starts to crumble, and I revel in it.

His gaze narrows and the dungeon seems to darken along with his rage. 'I'm going to enjoy ruining every little bit of hope you have left.' His words are laced with venom. He takes a step back, tilting his chin upwards – a signal to the awaiting Elves.

Yanked forward, the sharp sting from the Elf's grip on my hair reverberates throughout my skull. I pass by Sarilyn, nailing her with a vicious glare before I am forcibly claimed as Aurum's captive.

PART TWO
RUINATION

DARIUS
THREE MONTHS AGO

Darkness engulfs the small, dank dungeon chamber. The air is heavy with the acrid scent of dampness and Venators captured under Aurum's command.

I get up from the ground and stretch my arms outward, only for steel chains to clink against each other as I find myself shackled to the cold, unforgiving wall.

'Great,' I mutter with a sigh, flexing my hands to ease the soreness.

'It is . . . far cosier here than Olcar's prison, wouldn't you say?' Aurum's voice echoes through the grim space as I look up at the flickering flame of a solitary torch casting an eerie shadow across his face.

I scoff, my roughened demeanour preventing a smile, yet I can't help but laugh at the scar across his eye, a reminder of Nara's defiance. Pride courses through me as I recall that moment.

'Ever thought of decorating in here?' I mock.

Aurum's smile is sickening, reminding me of the unfortunate reality that I am related to him. 'Say, Darius, how long has it been since we left Terranos?' He strides from one side of the dungeon to the other with his arms behind his back. 'Days, weeks, months?'

Seventeen days.

Seventeen days of hearing Aurum relentlessly telling me I will never see Nara again.

'I mean, by now, you would think the people you so terribly care for would come for you.' He stops and slowly spins on the heel of his boot to look at me. 'It makes one question whether they care about *you*.'

My resilience starts to crack as I grit my teeth. 'They'll come.'

He frowns. 'Are you sure?' Drawing himself forward, he whispers in sinister satisfaction, 'Because I would have thought if Nara was so in love with you, she would be here. Unless she's—'

I feel a surge of anger forging a storm within me as I lunge at him. The urge to break free only gets stronger when he rears back and merely chuckles at my struggle.

'Oh, Darius.' He shakes his head, watching me. 'The strength you hold is just as much a weakness. Your mind and your love for her will be your own demise.'

'Say what you want about me, but don't you *dare* speak of her again.' My tone carries a dangerous edge, but Aurum only revels in the rage he is causing.

'Ah, love,' his voice drips with malice. 'How easily it can shatter someone.'

I look elsewhere as my fists clench at the sides. 'You don't know what you're talking about.'

'On the contrary. I know *too* much, but unlike you, I was smart enough not to let my feelings cloud my judgment.' He steps into my sight and smirks. 'Pity, though. If Nara had not met you, perhaps she wouldn't be caught up in all this.'

The damp air in this cell seems to carry the weight of my

helplessness as his lips twist into a sneer. He wants me to feel guilty –
to blame myself for having brought Nara into my world.

I don't want to give him that satisfaction. But as night and day go
by, I slowly know that I'm losing it.

'Then again,' he continues, 'it was predestined after all, wasn't it?'

The corners of my mouth curl into a smirk as I tilt my head, wanting to prove him wrong. 'As will be your death.'

Aurum goes silent, the veins on his neck straining and bulging as
all the control he has over himself cracks. He raises a hand and my
body instantly responds to the unseen force of power.

Pain plunges into my chest, images of moments with Nara flash-
ing in my mind. When we first met, the ball, our intimate moments,
each one fading as Aurum digs through my head, tormenting me
both physically and mentally.

As he stops, I crumple onto my knees.

Breathless, I laugh. 'Is that all?' I say, lifting my head. 'Felt like a
tickle.'

He emits an irritated hum, his smile tinged with annoyance
before he goes again. This time, it feels as if my brain is on fire, burning at every memory. I grit my teeth, clutching the sides of my head
as I try to power through it. Sweat trickles down my face and the
chains rattle as I pull against them.

It feels like a lifetime of torture until he finally stops and I gasp
for air. Sickness churns inside my stomach, and if I had any food in
me, I would have for sure emptied it all out on this floor.

Aurum carefully kneels before me, a small silver blade now in his
grip. 'I want you to answer a question.'

The cell throbs with an agonising thrum of my aching body as I
lift my gaze, and each pulse of my heart echoes the seething rage I
feel towards him.

'If you get it wrong, you will use this knife to stab yourself five times in your leg.' The order grips me tight, forcing me to nod as he hands me the dagger. He stands before me, a taunting smile playing on his lips. 'Who is Naralía Ambrose to you?'

'The future queen of Emberwell.' My words come out strained, a rasp in the distance.

Aurum's jaw twitches and fighting the urge not to raise the blade to my thigh fails me as an invisible force compels me to drive it through skin and bone. I grunt at the impact, blood spilling from the top.

One.

I draw it out and go again.

Two.

And again.

Three.

And again.

Four.

And again.

Five.

'Let me ask again,' he says. '*Who* is Naralía Ambrose?'

My anger boils over. I know whatever I say will be wrong.

Blood stains the cold floor but I will myself to look Aurum in the eye. A feeble grin marks my lips as I whisper, 'The sun.'

Another wave of compulsion beckons me, and the blade sinks into my leg.

One.

I grit my teeth against the searing pain.

Two.

I dig the blade even deeper this time.

Three.

I grow weaker by the second.

Four.

Even against my will, I can't stop.

Five.

Aurum repeats the question again and again and I give him the same answer each time.

As I yank the dagger out of my leg, I'm visibly spent. My vision is blurry, and the pain no longer feels like it is real.

I wait for the question to come again, angling the blade at my thigh once more. Aurum then leans forward with sadistic satisfaction, narrowing his eye.

'This time,' he whispers, 'do both legs, and don't stop until I tell you to.' He stands back, watching and revelling as I lift the bloodied weapon.

'Ah.' He stops me, and there is a moment where I almost believe he might make me not do this, but it is just my mind playing tricks. 'Count out loud for me.'

My jaw tightens, and the air ripples with a promise that I will destroy him. Even if it takes my life along with it.

'One,' I say, thrusting the blade into my thigh. 'Two . . .' The numbers climb steadily, each pronounced with agony. The knife pierces my flesh, creating a sickening harmony with the growing pool of my own blood.

I reach seventy-two before the world dissolves and I fall unconscious to my suffering.

Chapter Twenty-Four

Nara

The study doors close with a thud, leaving me in the dimly lit room with Aurum at his desk and Ruvyn beside me. His grip tightens on my upper arm, a silent betrayal lingering since our return to Emberwell and my shackles were finally released. His gaze remains fixed straight ahead, determined to disregard my presence.

'Nara.' Aurum chuckles, raising his boots onto a desk piled with vellum sheets. 'How was the journey back here? I would have asked that we meet in the throne room, but –' He clicks his tongue – 'repairs are still being made since your last visit.'

'Where are you keeping my brothers?' I demand.

He sighs, dropping his chin against his chest, feigning boredom. 'They are unharmed, if that is what you wish to know. As are your friends, Darius and my courageous brother-in-law, if you were wondering.'

I huff, shaking my head. 'Why don't you just kill me already,' I say. I see no reason why I am here if it isn't to torture me with his plans. 'I am sure that is what you have been dying to do.'

His upper lip twitches. 'I like to hunt.' He takes a deep breath and

smiles as if my misery is feeding into his sick pleasure. 'Call it the predatory dragon in me.' The way he savours those words sends a twisted
shiver up my spine, and I notice my breathing quickening as he rises
from the gold-threaded chair to walk towards me. 'But . . .' He points. 'I
would much rather watch you struggle. See how those pretty blue eyes
slowly become haunted by seeing the people you love suffering.'

My shoulders tense as he draws his hand out and traces his fingers along my face. I turn my head, physically repulsed by his touch.

'It is only when you plead with me for death to come,' he whispers, 'that I might consider killing you.'

I whip my head back to him, and before I can retort an insult, I
notice something on the side of his neck. Black veins slither outwards
from every direction, much like the slow decay on his face.

He catches on to my gaze and responds with a restrained smile,
bringing a finger-lit flame to his neck. 'Nothing a bit of fire can't fix,'
he remarks, wincing as the red glow of flames licks away the decay.

I glare. 'Careful, too much fire and you might just burn.'

He laughs. 'Not for an Ardenti.'

'But you're not one, are you? Those abilities belong to Darius.'

He takes a step back, smoothing a hand over his tightened jaw.
'Not any more.'

I shake my head, disgusted by his words. 'What made you like
this? You had everything, a family, a kingdom—'

'And yet it was never enough!' He loses it then, his neck straining
with the force of his words. He narrows his eye at me, seeing how I
remain calm through his outburst and instantly corrects himself by
fixing the collar of his tunic and smoothing back his hair with a
chuckle. 'I wonder what Solaris would think of you being here.' He
turns to me. 'Knowing that the wondrous reincarnation – the vessel
of the sun! – is now at my mercy.'

I watch him in silence, my rage knowing no bounds as he walks towards me again.

'Would the deity of our world be proud?' he whispers. 'Or would it be disappointed, just as your old boss was when I told him you failed your mission back in Terranos?' His smile holds a touch of arrogance and excitement as he stares at my reaction slowly unfolding.

'Ivarron,' I whisper, horrified. I jerk from Ruvyn's grip, inching my face closer to Aurum. 'Where is he? What did you do to him?'

Aurum throws his head back, a sadistic laugh echoing through the room as he strides towards his desk and sits back down. 'Apparently, he was in love with your mother. Even tried to say he was protecting you all these years.' He shakes his head in complete mockery. 'And they say *I'm* terrible.' Sighing, he feigns regret and taps his fingers along the desk. 'Shame I had to kill him. He would have made a great ally if he hadn't been so . . . untrusting.'

Hearing his heartless remark, a storm of emotions stirs within me. My jaw clenches and anger burns in my eyes, yet beneath it all, I can't deny how the thought of Ivarron dying upsets me. We had such a complicated bond that I did not even know he loved my mother. Deep down, I should have known, with the way he despised my father and how he always said I reminded him of *her* . . .

I raise my eyes, keeping my chin hanging low. My voice quivers with a growing temper. 'Do you really think you can keep us here? That the people of Aeris won't come for us? That Lorcan, Hira—'

'Will save you?' He chuckles. 'Lorcan does not care for you any more. Not after I struck a deal with the Aerian leaders.'

My face must be priceless because it only makes Aurum's smile grow.

'Hira's land and people go unharmed as long as she lets me get what I want.'

Me and Darius . . .

'Hira would never do that,' I whisper, shaking my head at the thought that Hira could betray us this way.

'You are right,' he says. 'She wouldn't. Which is why she is no longer alive.'

Ice sweeps through my veins as every ounce of air vanishes from my lungs.

She is no longer alive.

'The other two warrior leaders, though, accepted the deal with no problem. Although did you know Hira was Lorcan's real mother?'

Aurum's filthy joy as he speaks numbs me. He won't stop smiling as he talks, tells me the truth, and lets me in on a secret that must have broken Lorcan just as much as it did when Darius found out about Gus.

'Shocking, isn't it?' His golden eyepatch snaps towards me, the other eye squinting with delight. 'Whatever plagued her to fall for a mortal is beyond me, but oh, you should have seen the look on Lorcan's face when he found out. I suppose he and Darius aren't so different after all.'

'What is wrong with you?' I spit, anger simmering beneath the surface of my words. 'You killed her, you—' My rage spikes; I can't do it any more. Strength takes hold of me as I push myself free from Ruvyn and launch myself across Aurum's desk.

Aurum jumps from his chair as I try to reach for him, but Ruvyn's hands wrap around my waist, turning me away before I can get him.

A mangled cry tears from my throat as I pull at Ruvyn's hands, but he keeps me within his grip.

Aurum walks around his desk, grinning while watching me thrash in Ruvyn's arms. He leans forward; our faces are so close that

I could bite off his nose. 'I would do it all over again just to relive how good it felt to see the life drain away from her useless body.'

Flames dance across his fingertips as he shows them off in front of me, and for a second, I stop fighting. I stop trying to free myself because I realise something that makes me laugh so much that I cannot breathe.

Aurum's confusion only fuses my laughter. 'What are you laughing about?' he grits.

I watch his flames die out, and my amusement fades into a disdainful smile. 'That even though you are a Rivernorth, you still feel *that* threatened by your nephew that you had to take his powers.'

He looks mad – so, so mad.

Good.

'You want to know what I was once told?' I chuckle, riling him up. 'That Darius is the rightful king to Emberwell. Not Sarilyn, not you, *him.*'

He snaps, gripping my jaw between his hands and squeezing until I feel the bones crack. 'Where are the Elemental Stones?'

I wince beneath his feral gaze, but I don't want to give in. I *won't* give in. 'Go on, do your worst.' Heat flares from my nostrils. 'I will *never* tell you where the stones are, and I will never bow down to you.'

We stare at each other, and his jaw clenches the more I choose not to back down – the more I show that I am not afraid of him.

Right up until the doors to the study open and an Elf interrupts us.

'Sorry—the-the Queen has asked for the prisoner's presence.'

'*Sarilyn,*' Aurum corrects him, seething between his teeth all the while maintaining his gaze on me. He releases his forceful grip on my jaw, and I draw a deep breath, my fingers instinctively massaging the soreness in my jawbone as Aurum swipes a hand over his face.

He doesn't say anything as the Elf and Ruvyn take me away, and I stare at him, knowing that I got inside his head.

CHAPTER TWENTY-FIVE

B eing bundled from one place to the next, bound again and helpless, isn't how I imagined I would spend my time in this place.

The cruel embrace of memories tightens around me as I find myself standing by the doorway of the same chamber where I once stole the Rivernorth pendant. The room is adorned with vibrant hues, just like before. The only change is the absence of the charm.

I think about how the last time I saw it Darius had passed it to Ivarron, and now . . .

A sigh escapes my lips as my gaze shifts towards Sarilyn.

She's sitting on a plush silk settee, with a glass of wine in her hand and her golden gown taking up most of the space as her eyes survey me. There is a long pause between the moment she sips from her wine glass and her finally rising and walking towards the decanter on the opposite side of the chamber.

As soon as I entered, she demanded I be unshackled again and dismissed the Elven guards. The amount of freedom she has entrusted me with is unsettling. It leaves me perplexed.

'You look like you're starving,' she says, her back to me, while I hear her glass being refilled. 'Would you like anything to eat? I can have one of . . . *Aurum's* lackeys bring us something.' She turns, her smile strained. 'If you'd like.'

My eyes narrow as I watch her move from one end to the next. Hunger is far from what I am feeling right now. 'I'd sooner starve to death than eat anything you have to offer me.'

Her laugh is one I do not miss. 'Oh, I forgot how much I loved that sharp tongue of yours.'

'Why am I here?'

She is still chuckling. 'I guessed you would want a breather from being with Aurum.'

I fist the side of my tunic. 'It's not like you to care about me.'

Her gaze burns into me with curiosity and amusement, finding anything I do or say entertaining.

'I mean, isn't this what you wanted?' I grit. 'Me and Darius imprisoned for what happened after the trials.'

'Darling, that was long ago now. So much has happened since then. You freed Aurum; parts of Emberwell were destroyed; humans and Venators began to rebel against Aurum's commands once he returned . . .' She waves a hand. 'You know the rest.'

'And yet here you are working for him. Funny how life can change in an instant.'

Any semblance of humour dissolves from her face. 'It's called survival. Do you really believe that I want Aurum back in my life?' She scoffs. '*I* was the queen here. I *saved* you humans from eternal slavery, and all I got back in return was your rebellion.' She turns to me, raising her glass to toast. 'So, if joining Aurum's side means living, then I will be the greatest ally he needs.'

I watch her tip her head back and down the contents of her glass in a way that would make you forget she is royalty . . . or *was*. I note how scared she must be if she is going to this extent.

Survival is only a means to a possible end.

'You being with him won't solve anything,' I say. 'It just proves you to be a coward and nothing more.'

She hums something sarcastic under her breath.

'You won't win.'

Her dark eyes watch me with piqued interest.

'Neither you nor Aurum will.' I take a step forward. 'And when you lose, I will make sure to put you through the same misery you put me through.'

She's silent as she stares at me with a cunning smile, and I turn away from her, not wanting to deal with Aurum or her any more.

'Eighty-three days,' she says, and I hate that I can't tune her out; I hate that I whirl around instead of walking out to where the guards are and leaving her. 'It took Darius eighty-three days to finally forget you.' A hole forms inside my chest, growing bigger the more she explains. 'He endured every torture method known to mankind, each one ending in Aurum asking him one simple question.' She walks towards me, each step slow and deliberate to hurt me. 'Who is Naralía Ambrose?'

Something is ripping away at my strength and clawing at my heart.

'His answer would always be a smile followed by the words that you were his queen . . . his sun.' She smirks before whispering, 'Do you want to know what finally broke him?'

'No,' I answer, but it is no use; she will continue regardless.

'It was when Aurum made him believe you had died.'

I shake my head, my whole being burning like wildfire, unable to be stopped.

'Darius was too weak by then, slowly falling apart. All it took was for Aurum to slip into his mind one more time and show him that *you . . .'* She taps my forehead with her finger once, twice, thrice. 'No. Longer. Existed.'

'Stop.' I clench my teeth and pain radiates from my jaw and temples.

'Aurum not only made him forget you, but he would force him to kill mortals from the streets, biting them—'

No, no – I cover my ears and clench my eyes shut. 'Please, stop—'

'Even if he finally remembers you, he will never be the same—'

'I said stop!'

Everything goes silent except for the sharp-pitched buzz in my ears.

The floor shudders beneath me with the force of my voice, and then I open my eyes as I stumble, the side of my body knocking against the door.

With my chest heaving, I notice the ground is splintered and cracked all the way to the settee, split in half. Sarilyn is on the floor, tendrils of black hair across her face as she tries to stand.

Frantic, I glance at my hands outstretched in front, and something so raw within me pulses to life. A golden light emanates from my palms before it fades again as the Elven guards enter with their weapons drawn.

Sarilyn wipes blood off the side of her lips with the back of her hand, her chuckle catching me off guard as she signals for the Elves not to do anything. 'I always knew there was something special about you,' she says. 'Even when the seers told me about a reincarnation, I never thought that to be true. I believed in possible wars, a future where the world could be destroyed, because that was at least plausible, but then you stumbled into the city, hoping to become a Venator, and I just had this *feeling*.'

Disbelief knocks me off my feet, and Ruvyn catches me by my arm, keeping me upright.

Sarilyn is grinning as she comes closer. 'But when the trial came, I finally knew you were the vessel when you managed to bring those Rümens to their knees.'

When I don't speak, the Elves start to pull me along. In a blind state of daze, I follow, dragging my feet along until Sarilyn calls out my name.

'Tell me,' she says with a tilt of her head. 'If it means saving Zerathion, is the Golden Thief worth dying for?'

I hold the moment between us with such stillness and my heart in my throat.

Slowly and knowingly, Sarilyn's lips curve into a smile. A smile where she can see the answer in my eyes, I do not have to even say it.

CHAPTER TWENTY-SIX

Darkness envelops the narrow passages of the dungeons as I am escorted by Ruvyn and a few other Elves further ahead. I flinch when I hear the distant echoes of prisoners begging to be let out and I see the faces of captured shifters I know and Venators I once trained with inside cells, beaten and half-conscious.

I swallow my regret, wishing I could break them out, but soon they disappear from my sight and my heart quickens with each step as I desperately scan the occupants of each cell, searching for my brothers and friends.

As we turn the corner, the flickering torchlight illuminates a corridor with rows and rows of prison cells. As we walk past, I soon catch my breath and I spot familiar faces.

'Freya!' The name escapes my lips in a breathless whisper as I pull my arm free from Ruvyn and run towards the cell bars. Link, Rydan and Freya all rise from the ground and rush to meet me from their side of the cell. I reach for them within the small space allowed, grabbing Link's arms and gripping him tightly. 'You're all okay . . . I—' I check their faces for any injuries as a few Elves yell from afar, wondering what is happening. 'Where's Tibith?' I ask when I don't see him.

'We managed to get him out before Aurum got to us,' Freya says, a mixture of relief and concern flickering across her eyes, much like mine. 'He should be safe with the Aerian survivors and hopefully Lorcan.'

I nod, trying to forget what Aurum told me as tears well in my eyes and I press my forehead against the bars. 'I will get you all out of here, I promise.'

'We know,' Rydan and Link whisper simultaneously, with Link tightening his hold on my arm. I look up to see the three of them smiling at me before Ruvyn grabs me and drags me away.

'Let her go!' I hear Freya shout while I stumble backwards and my panic surges as I lift my eyes to Ruvyn.

I blink away my tears. 'Ruvyn, you have to listen to me,' I say, but he seems to focus ahead, his dark brows screwing together as if he's struggling not to face me. 'Aurum is not someone you should trust.'

'I don't trust anyone, let alone a prisoner.'

I shake my head. 'I can help you, I can—'

'Be quiet,' he grits, trying to remain stoic as he slows down to a stop and glances at the other Elves. Their sharp-shaped ears are in sight as they turn their heads to the side. Time seems to hang in suspense as I look towards them and then back to Ruvyn, his fair skin now tinged red with fear.

My eyes narrow, a sense of disconcerting reality becomes apparent and the gravity of my realisation presses down on my chest. I whisper, 'He threatened you, didn't he? Aurum?'

He must have threatened so many lives because that is him. *That* is Aurum.

Ruvyn's head dips and at last he sighs. 'He saw I hesitated when you last came.' The quiet pain in his voice is a sharp sting to my heart. He snaps his gaze up at me. 'He will kill my mother if I defy him.'

The thought of Aurum ruining so many lives has my chest caving in. He is using so many people, so many innocent lives and turning them against everyone else.

'I can protect her,' I quickly say, but he looks like he is about to protest. 'Arlayna and Faye would—' A rough hand clamps on to my shoulder, jerking me away from Ruvyn.

'Move,' the Elf orders, and I glance at a conflicted Ruvyn. 'You're relieved of your post, Ferncrest. Report back to Aurum.' With a forceful shove, I'm pushed ahead as I look over my shoulder and Ruvyn hesitates to leave his position.

If I can just get him on my side—

My thoughts are pulverised into dust once we stop by a secluded area of the dungeons and I recognise the same set of iron gates where I killed that Ardenti . . . where Darius had been locked up after his capture.

The lever is pulled and I shake my head, watching the door lift before I'm shoved inside. I hear the heavy sound of the doors closing behind me with a clang, sealing me within the confines of my very nightmare.

As my eyes adjust to the large cell, I see him. Darius. He stands at the other end, his eyes meeting mine with concern.

'Darius.' I call out his name in a soft embrace as I take steps towards him. I'm ready to collapse in his arms and stay there for eternity, but all I can think as we walk towards each other is if he will forget me again. If this isn't real, and that none of it ever was . . .

He captures me in his embrace, the force of me rushing into him slamming against his chest. The side of my head lies against him, and I let out a relieved breath. 'Goldie,' he says into my hair and pulls back. His hands, which had held my waist, now trace a path across my shoulders before framing my face as his eyes sweep over me in an intense search. 'Did he hurt you?'

I shake my head.

'Nara,' he says my name with urgency like he doesn't believe me, but I cut him off with a cocked brow.

'*I* was the one who tried to hurt him.'

He stares at me then, unable to help the proud smile forming on his lips as he embraces me again. 'I just wanted to be sure,' he whispers, and I nod against him in reassurance. 'Is Tibith—'

'He is safe,' I say, not to worry him, though I still can't help doing so myself.

At that moment, the doors slide open. Darius and I turn in time to witness a stumbling figure being pushed onto the floor before the gate is closed back up again.

'Gus,' I whisper, rushing over to help him.

He grabs on to my hand and then gets up on his knees. 'I don't have long.' Blood coats the side of his face, some of it fresh and trickling down from his forehead. 'Aurum conceded to my wishes of speaking with you both—'

'If it's advice you're going to give us, you should have stayed in your cell.'

There it is. The cold tone – empty and dull at the same time – coming from Darius.

I cast a glance behind me. Darius is in the same spot as I was before, his golden eyes darkening with anger towards Gus.

'I . . . I understand how much you must hate me right now,' Gus says, no longer needing my aid to stand. He takes a deep breath. 'But if we are to survive—'

'I've survived a lot without you before. Why would I need your help now?'

'Darius,' I say softly, coaxing him to listen. 'We need him.'

When Darius looks at me, he seems to relax. The harshness in his expression fades into something tender.

'I never meant to hurt you.' Gus limps forward, his voice pleading. 'I loved you and your mother so much.'

The moment Gus utters those words, Darius reverts to his stoic demeanour before meeting Gus's eyes. His shoulders tense, the veins on his forearms pulsating as he clenches his fists. 'Hurt me?' His tone freezes the room, and then a biting laugh escapes his lips. 'No, hurting me would be if you had stayed with us and then left. But *you* . . . ' He points at Gus, shaking his finger up and down. 'You left us long before that, didn't you?'

'It wasn't like that.'

'No?' Darius cocks his head to the side. Crossing his arms over his chest, he starts to pace. 'All right then, where were you when I first shifted?'

I sigh. The wound is too fresh. Throughout most of his life, Darius has navigated it alone; his pride won't allow him to forgive Gus, at least not now, not *yet*.

'Where were you when I was on the streets having to fend for myself?' Darius pauses, his voice gradually rising. 'Where the fuck were you when my mother died?'

Gus drops his head, crestfallen.

'I don't care if you loved my mother or if half the things you want to say are true,' Darius confesses in such a calm tone despite his deep hatred for Gus. 'You are not my father.'

My heart shatters upon seeing the devastation colouring Gus's features. He stumbles backwards as if waves of sorrow are crashing into him, and he can't push through them.

We knew this would be the outcome of Darius finding out, and though I thought I was prepared for it, begging for Gus to tell him, I now understand why he hesitated for so many years.

As I watch him open his mouth to speak, there is no longer any time. The Elves pry the door open once more and barge in, capturing Gus by his arms.

I jerk forward, but Gus shakes his head for me not to.

'Remember everything I have taught you about harnessing your powers?' he says low enough for only me to hear as he darts his gaze to the cracked stones marring the entire cell. I frown and slowly nod despite it never having worked all the times we trained. 'You have it within you to use them . . . You just have to accept yourself for who you are.' Though he doesn't say the name, I know he means Solaris.

He is dragged out at that moment, with me trying to follow after him as the door closes, and I slam my hands against the iron gate.

A tight breath lingers within my chest, and I release it with a sigh as I lower my forehead against the gate. Gus doesn't know what happened with Sarilyn, and neither does Darius.

No *one* except Sarilyn and I know.

Turning around, Darius and I stare at each other from across the dungeon. For a heartbreaking second, that resilience he had against Gus cracks, and he looks just as vulnerable as any of us before he averts his gaze.

I silently walk up to him. He doesn't ask me what Gus said just then, and I don't ask him about Gus in return. Instead, I head to one of the four walls surrounding us.

Closing my eyes, I picture the glow in the palm of my hands, the hunger for power buzzing through my veins.

Even if he finally remembers you, he will never be the same.

I swallow the burn of those words down my throat as I look at my hands, but nothing manifests except for the unsettling tremors wracking my bones.

Darius appears beside me as I gaze up at him. There is a profound way in which he looks at me this time – a gaze infused with a power that fortifies my strength and deepens my understanding.

The shaking of my hands stops. And not having noticed before, I glance down to see that the chains he must have picked up from the ground are now in his hand. He moves closer towards the wall, and without looking back, he starts to swing the chains against it with unrestrained force.

CHAPTER TWENTY-SEVEN

It has been hours since they took Gus out of our cell. Darius and I have relentlessly tried to find a way out by breaking through the walls – to find a weakness that perhaps could help us. But the more we kept at it, the more Darius grew weak from his link to Aurum and would collapse onto the ground.

I urged him to take a break, and while my determination was undeterred, the increasing difficulty of getting us out was becoming more exasperating.

Now as I claw at the stones, I push and slam my palm against it.

The dungeons have become darker, and the slit in the ceiling tells me it is night. I take a step back, heaving a breath as I glance to my left, where more large, heavy chains lie. The same ones that once held the Ardenti dragon Sarilyn made me kill.

I find myself clenching my fists, frustration fuelling my inner rebellion to fight. Turning to the wall again, I start to think of my brothers and unleash cries that strain my throat as I strike with full force.

My bones tremble with vibrant pain pulsing through my knuckles

Hoping to have sourced some power into me again – like Gus believed I could – I withdraw my hand, but the wall remains steadfast and my frustration manifests into blinding anger as I raise my other first.

I miss the wall just as Darius wraps his arms around my waist, pulling me back in a protective embrace. I pant, my breaths ragged as he spins me around, redirecting my focus towards him. Concern darkens his golden eyes, and gently, he takes my still-clenched fist in his hand.

I wince and he steadies his touch, quickly looking me in the eye before focusing on the bloodied, macabre mess that is my broken knuckles.

'It was worth a shot,' I mumble, wanting to get my point out before being berated.

'It isn't if it results in you hurting yourself.' His voice sounds calm, but I know he is worrying.

I huff, snatching my hand away from him and sitting down instead.

He does the same, both of us now cross-legged.

'Sometimes I wonder if you like to injure yourself just so that I get to touch you,' he teases, the familiarity of his smirk comforting me as he grabs my hand again.

I give him a look that has that arrogant smile of his widen. 'Don't make me regret having ever fallen for you.'

He chuckles before swiftly ripping part of his shirt. 'We wouldn't want that now, would we?' He cocks an eyebrow and I narrow my eyes as the tear of clothing echoes through the air. I watch his teeth sink into his wrist, producing droplets of blood. He then uses that same piece of fabric and smears his blood on it.

His hands work deftly and his attention is solely focused on the stained shirt as he wraps it around my fist.

'Dragon blood?' I angle my head with a smile.

He finishes tying the knot. 'It's the only thing that luckily still works.'

A weight of shame settles on my shoulders and I look away, finding that exact spot where I once faced the Ardenti.

'It was here, wasn't it?' Darius's voice echoes, and I turn my head. He's staring at me now, fixating on how a sigh departs from my lips. 'Where Sarilyn ordered you to kill one of us.'

'Yes,' I whisper, not seeing the point in lying.

He gives me a subtle shake of his head and averts his gaze. 'I should never have let you help me.' His jaw tenses. 'You'd be safer—'

'I wouldn't,' I reply quickly, hoping he sees how wrong he is to blame himself. 'I was never going to be safe in this life, Darius. We both weren't.'

He's still looking off to the side, his brows furrowed like he believes otherwise. Under other circumstances, I know he would have teased me about anything, but all I can hear is Sarilyn's voice telling me how Darius would never be the same after he remembered.

'Do you . . .' It's as if someone was crushing my windpipe because my words come out choked. '. . . remember your time here with Aurum?'

Darius snaps his gaze back to me and it pierces through mine. The anticipating answer lingers between us as he focuses on me and finally says, 'No.'

I should feel relieved by that answer, but I don't. Part of me knows it is a lie because if he remembers everything he said in Aeris, that will include his time here.

My tongue darts out to wet my lips, and I say his name, only to be silenced by the sudden movement of him coming closer. He places his hands at the sides of my waist, gently running the pad of his thumb over my clothes.

I draw in a breath, having missed this, yet the lingering guilt persists. Just knowing how much he has endured gnaws at me, and the thought of him being tortured snakes through my mind, weaving into the crevices of regret and poisoning my chest and heart for not having rescued him sooner.

Dropping my head against his chest, I close my eyes, and all I can mumble right now is, 'I'm sorry about Gus.'

I can feel the rise and drop of his chest as he sighs. 'I should have known it was him.' He forces out a laugh. 'He always treated me differently. In ways, I thought that was only because he wanted me to join him.'

Pulling back, I search his eyes for something that will tell me that he has room to forgive Gus regardless of it all. 'His intention was never to leave you; he didn't—'

'Goldie—' he breathes, snapping his eyes shut, but I'm nowhere near finished.

'No, listen to me. Even before you were born, he wanted to protect you and your mother – and when I found out, I was mad at him myself, but if you think—' I stop when I see he is now smiling at me. Attractive lines carve indents into his cheeks and I frown. 'What is it?'

He shakes his head, his smile never faltering. It makes my heart ache. 'I do not care one bit if Gus *is* what he is to me. What matters is that I have *you. Alive.*'

My chest sinks and my head falls against his chest once again. His fingers run up and down my spine as I whisper, 'For now.'

He stops, touches the sides of my arms and pushes me back so that I look at him. It isn't anger in his eyes; it's fear, and I badly want to kick myself over it. 'Don't say that.'

I capture my bottom lip between my teeth, looking down at his lap and apologising. Despite the cold, damp air clinging to the stone walls of this dimly lit dungeon, this is the only place I feel safe with him right now.

But then my gaze fixates on the dark colour of his clothes, and images of Sarilyn in that room and the fractured floor beneath us ignite inside my mind.

'Something happened.' I sound distracted. 'Something with Sarilyn.'

He cocks his head.

'I knocked her to the ground,' I say. This time he shoots me one of those cocky smiles I now love more than anything, and the look he is giving me is as if he is proud.

'I never *touched* her,' I clarify, brows all the way up to my hairline.

The glow in his smirk fades upon realisation, only to swiftly return. It transforms into a radiant smile before he seizes the sides of my face and kisses me. First once, then repeatedly. He's grinning, solidifying my confusion.

'What—' I can barely get the word out as he plants another kiss on my lips, and I chuckle. 'Did I do something?'

He shakes his head slowly as he presses his forehead against mine. 'I just missed you.' He kisses me again, whispering, 'So, so much.'

My smile trembles against his lips as I touch his hand. 'I wanted to get you out sooner – I did, I really did—'

He shushes me, shaking his head. 'I hate it when you apologise.'

I laugh, closing my eyes. 'Why is that?'

'Because I prefer it when you're insulting me.'

I grin. 'If it's an insult you want, I have many. Ones that start off with how much of a punchable face you have.' *Kissable*. Kissable face, but he knows that anyway.

'Much better,' he breathes before capturing my lips fervently. A sharp gasp escapes me as he grips my waist, and I press a hand on his chest to steady myself. The kiss isn't slow; it never is between us. Darius feeds into my hunger for him, his tongue teasing my own as if he wants to savour me, every moment.

My head arches back as he angles his neck, deepening the kiss and consuming me with his all. And as he pulls me onto his lap, we draw back, looking at each other. His eyes reflect a determination that matches my own. Despite the circumstances, a glimmer of hope dances in his gaze as he strokes the side of my face, and I smile like I am in a dream.

Just then, for this moment, I remember what I want, which is to be forever with him.

'Darius—' I whisper, my heart unbridled with love. 'Marry me.'

CHAPTER TWENTY-EIGHT

Darius freezes beneath me, hearing the words we'd once promised each other. 'I thought we had decided I would be the one to ask you on the third try?'

I shrug, humour pulling the corners of my mouth into a gentle smile. 'I changed the rules.'

His smile lights me up aflame. Holding on tight, he flips me over so that I'm underneath him, and I squeal with laughter.

Through the darkness, I manage to see the glow in his eyes and rummage through my pocket, content when I pull out the ring he'd once made and show it to him. 'Is that a yes?'

He chuckles and nods without hesitation. 'When would I ever say no to such an offer from you?' Sliding his hand beneath me, he lifts me from the ground and keeps me tight against his chest. 'Although we have no one to wed us right now, Goldie.'

'Then we will do it,' I say. 'Just us.'

With a soft smile, he takes a small step back from me, and I already miss his touch.

I chuckle as he clears his throat, fixing the collar of his ripped and bloodied shirt before he whispers my name and looks me in the eye. 'In the presence of—' He glances around. 'No one.'

I laugh louder.

'I, Darius.' Leaning closer so that he grins against my lips, he continues, 'Take my beautiful, stubborn Goldie as my wife. To love and to annoy you all my life.'

I can't stop smiling as tears fill my eyes.

'I make a vow to be there for your friends and your family, even if that means sacrificing my own life with it.'

A chill runs over my body as he says 'sacrifice', but he doesn't notice the slip in my smile because I don't let myself think about it for long. I won't let this moment be ruined by the thought of never seeing him again.

Darius takes a deep breath that expands his chest as he looks at me like I am his source of determination and salvation. 'You deserve it all, Nara, and I will do everything to ensure you have it, because the day you don't smile, I will know I have not done my job right. I dream of your smile, of that laugh that comes out of you when you feel free. I don't ever want to stop hearing it, and if that day ever comes, I will rip worlds apart just to hear it again.'

Tears kiss my cheeks as they roll down, and the cool touch of the ring he crafted for me presses against my skin as he slides it onto my finger. Even in the grim darkness of the dungeons, it still shines with a silver sheen as I tilt my hand.

With a sniffle, I glance up at Darius. 'I don't have a ring,' I whisper comically.

His chuckle is soft and a whisper in itself. 'You're all I need.'

I rest my hand at my side. Excitement floods my system as I stare at him. My thief, my dragon, my king. 'I, Nara,' I say. 'Take you, Darius, as my husband.'

He smiles.

'To love and respect you and to fight you for eternity if you misbehave.'

We both laugh, and he nods, looking to accept that proposition with no trouble at all.

I wipe a stray tear from my cheek. 'I never thought—' My throat thickens with emotion. 'That I would marry someday, especially not someone who drives me insane half the time.'

He smirks.

'But I did think I would eventually find an adventure . . . and it just so happens that adventure was you all along.'

Darius can't take his eyes off me. His gaze lingers on every curve of my mouth as my vowing words settle between us, and it is the most enchanting feeling.

'I'm helplessly in love with you, Darius,' I tell him with a crack in my voice. 'I always will be.'

Everything comes to a standstill as he slowly exhales. He closes the gap between us, dropping his forehead against mine.

'That's it,' he whispers, and my heart leaps. 'We're husband and wife now, Goldie.'

I smile like a child, wrapping my arms around his neck and biting my lower lip as I stare up at his face.

His eyes are on my mouth. 'May I kiss the bride?' he murmurs against my lips, and my smile stretches even wider.

'I'll kick you if you don't.'

He palms my face in less than a second, pressing his mouth against my lips. His tongue instantly seeks permission, and I let him, opening up and kissing him back with hunger. The taste of desperation grows between us as our fingers clumsily reach for each other's clothes, ripping them apart.

He sinks to his knees, his unwavering gaze fixed on me as he hooks his thumbs inside my trousers. Their deliberate descent, gliding along my skin, stirs an ache in my core. I tip my head back and release a weighted sigh doused with arousal.

Grabbing my thighs from behind, he keeps a tight hold on me as he drags his bottom lip across my skin, sucking and kissing up my thigh. My legs start to tremble, and I know he can feel it because his grip burns into my flesh as he squeezes.

I gasp, my breaths coming out scattered as I look down at him kneeling before me. 'Don't stop,' I say to him when his head nears that mound where no one but him is allowed to go.

'I don't plan to.' His voice vibrates against my skin, sending a shiver of pleasure through me before he withdraws his hands from my thighs.

I feel him rise, and I frown, looking at him. 'You just did.'

A chuckle rolls out of him as he picks up his shirt and tears off another piece of his sleeve. 'Just trust me.'

Annoyingly, as always, I do trust him.

He holds up the dark piece of fabric between his hands and leans towards me.

'What are you—' I start to say when the cloth wraps around my eyes, and I'm plunged into darkness.

I breathe heavily, feeling every bit of my senses heighten. I want to yank the blindfold off, but something in me tells me not to move or even make a sound as I stay on the spot, waiting.

Anticipation builds inside my chest, knowing he is walking around me, teasing me with his steps. His featherlight touch slides across my bare shoulders and then traces along my back's contours as if memorising every curve.

I press my body against his chest and lean into him, rubbing my backside against his front. As if I am tormenting him, his forehead drops against the top of my head with a deep groan.

A sound I've come to adore the most.

I roll my hips into him to hear it again, and I feel him swallow. A slow, deliberate sigh escapes my lips, content with how I make him feel. Right then, his palm cups me between my legs and I draw in a sharp gasp, bordering on a yelp, as I lift myself onto my toes. His other hand comes over my abdomen, keeping hold of me as if he doesn't plan to let go.

'Darius,' I whimper his name, biting down on my lower lip as his fingers part my folds.

'I want you to open your senses,' he whispers against my neck. 'Every touch, every sound . . .'

A breathless nod is my only response.

Using his other hand around my midriff, he presses his thumb against the lower part of my abdomen. It seems to intensify the feeling of his fingers rubbing against my crotch as I writhe in his grip.

'What do you see?' he asks, the sensuality of his voice sending a thrill through me.

'No—' I gasp when he pinches at the right spot. 'Nothing. I'm blindfolded, remember?'

His chuckle is deep and rougher. 'Try again.' Two fingers slide into me and I jump, unable to escape his hold. Each stroke and crook of his finger swirling in the right direction sends me into a frenzy. I'm whimpering, moving against him as I try to focus on what he's asking of me.

What do you see?

'I see—' A vision of Darius appears. He's at the den, laughing by one of the tables. 'You.' Music thrums inside my head as I picture him now spinning us around while we dance. We're happy; we're *free*. 'I see us.'

With each thought I conjure, Darius's fingers work in tandem. My knees bend, allowing him to reach a deeper part of me that draws out a guttural moan.

All I see are moments where he and I are together, focusing on a future where we will thrive every day.

Our bodies are slick with sweat, the scent of our arousal pervading the air and overpowering the must from the dungeons.

'We're going to get out of this, Goldie,' he tells me, his fingers thrusting in and out of me at a fast pace. 'And when we do, I'm not letting you go.'

I shake my head. 'You better not.' Pressure builds at the base of my mound and I dig my fingernails into his arm.

'Do you want to know what I see?' His lips graze my neck and I nod, my moans vibrating against him. 'Me and you, every hour, every minute, every second.' My legs begin to shake, my body tensing. 'I'm yours, Goldie, forever yours.'

His whisper hurtles me over the edge. I cry out through the pleasure, spasming in Darius's arms. But it's not over, as he yanks the blindfold off my eyes and turns me around. I gasp as he lifts my legs around his waist and drops me to the ground with one deep thrust of his cock inside me.

I bite my lip, holding back a sob, having craved this for so many months, since we were last together in Terranos.

Our pace is fast, almost animalistic. We need each other, we *yearn* for each other.

I cup his face as he pounds in and out of me, my lips parting, letting him moan into my mouth.

'Harder,' I breathe.

Our foreheads meet, his rumbling groan buzzes up my spine, and I start to lose it all over again.

My lips skim his ear and I smile. '*Deeper.*'

'Goldie,' he whispers, releasing another moan when I tighten up around him. 'My Goldie.'

We look each other in the eye, each movement of our bodies intertwining, pushing us into oblivion. 'My thief.'

Within seconds, the orgasm hits us both at the same time. I shake with immense pleasure, panting and making sounds that I wouldn't be surprised if the guards can hear them.

Darius strokes my hair, moving strands away from my face as I smile in blissful exhaustion at him. He kisses my forehead, his eyes still burning with such exhilaration that I can imagine him wanting to do it all again and again.

Collapsing beside me, he grabs me by the waist as he effortlessly pulls me to his chest and nestles his head in the crook of my neck.

My heart grows with a mixture of love, defiance and a touch of fear. Fear of the consequences we might face tomorrow, the next day or the one after. But right now, what matters is that Darius and I are married and that despite where we might be, I'm his wife, and he is my husband.

As exhaustion takes over, I unwrap the makeshift bandage across my knuckles, smiling when I see it healing already.

For minutes, we find peace in each other's comfort, our breathing steady as he moves his fingers up and down the side of my body. As I stare at the walls around me, I sigh. 'What if we aren't able to get out of this one?'

He lets out a deep and hard breath as I twist around and peer up at him. He turns his head to the side, his gaze tracing my features. 'You'll think of something, Goldie.' He presses a soft lingering kiss against my lips and whispers, 'You always do.'

CHAPTER TWENTY-NINE

I wake up with a smile on my face and turn to face Darius.

Except he is not there.

And I'm not where we were last night.

I jerk upright with a gasp, rising to my feet and pivoting in a slow circle as I scan the cramped cell. Four stone walls envelop me, their surfaces shrouded in darkness and grime. Above, a rhythmic dripping sound echoes, and I lift my head to see where it is coming from, yet the absence of light makes it impossible.

My chest tightens, and each breath I take starts to feel like a struggle as I search aimlessly for a way out.

I shout Darius's name, but my voice cracks and I yell in frustration.

Until a mechanical creak reverberates through the cell, drawing my attention. I turn, witnessing a cascade of light seeping beneath the wall as it gradually rises.

Sand is the first thing I see, accompanied by the pungent odour of decay lingering in the air as the wall grinds to a halt.

Nails dig into my skin as I clench my fist, and I let out a shaky breath as I move towards the arena. I hiss as the sun burns through the sky and onto my skin. Raising my arm to my forehead, I can finally see how the arena surrounds us as the crowd's cheers and jeers blur in a less enthusiastic cacophony. When I look at some of them – children, families, men and women – I notice most are crying, as if they are here against their will.

I shake my head, and the nightmare of being here before crashes against my chest, chipping away at the last chance to breathe.

The same sound I heard when my cell opened comes from my right. Darius steps out, but this time, our eyes meet in a different way. He looks tormented – tormented by himself. My gaze slides to his hands, and I notice how he rubs his thumb against his ring finger before the flash of a chain around his ankle catches my attention.

Aurum must have done something last night – he must have come in and seen us together and—

'Nara!' His voice causes a spurt of nausea to rush up my throat.

The crowd settles and I glance up at where he and Sarilyn are seated – the same place Sarilyn once sat with the General, watching us and dragons fight each other, just for their sick pleasure.

'I'm sure you've missed this place as much as the rest,' he gloats, grinning as he leans back against his seat. 'Sarilyn tells me you never completed your Venator trials. A pity. I'm certain you would have made an *excellent* dragon hunter.'

I hate how he looks down at me as if he knows I can't do anything. It makes me wonder how a man so cruel as him can sleep so soundly at night.

'So,' he continues, 'being the generous man that I am, I am allowing you to fix that.'

Every muscle in my face tightens as I stare at him, dreading what he is implying.

'You and Darius,' he drawls. 'Will *fight* to the death.'

My lungs stop working.

I look over at Darius whose murderous gaze is set on Aurum.

'Oh, don't look at me like that.' Aurum grins. 'Today is a special day. I'm allowing you to use your powers. Isn't that exciting?'

'Darius and I would never fight each other if it meant death!'

Aurum's gaze is calculating as it meets mine. '*He* does not have a choice.' His one eye cuts to Darius before he flicks his fingers and Darius clenches his eyes shut, wincing.

I feel helpless as ever. 'Stop!' I say, but even my voice betrays me.

'Oh, come on, Nara.' Aurum chuckles. 'We will make things interesting. We will even give you a few knives to make it fair.'

An Elf on one of the stands tosses a few jagged-shaped daggers into the pit, not caring if they hit me or Darius. Luckily, they fall in front of us.

'I won't do it,' I say, baring my teeth at Aurum. 'Just kill me already!'

'Nara—' Darius's low warning voice captures my attention but only for a short second.

'I'm afraid you must,' Aurum says, and my head lifts towards the balcony. 'You wouldn't want anything to happen to your family, would you?'

A weighty, painful sensation almost anchors me to the floor as I absorb Aurum's threat. At that very moment, his gaze shifts towards Sarilyn, and a fleeting struggle flickers in her eyes enough for me to notice. She reaches to her side when she locks eyes with me, yanking at a hidden lever.

The arena beneath us trembles and sand scatters and dances as up ahead, the ground opens. From the depths, a cage rises, containing Gus, Freya, Link, Rydan, Idris and Iker, but no Illias.

My emotions surge and crash into me as they cry out my name – Idris ferociously slamming his arm against the bars. I'm about to run for them when Aurum's laugh booms across the stands, and the cage is swallowed up by the ground once more.

'*Or*,' he says, motioning to my left. 'To Illias?'

Another hatch opens on the left beside the one I came out from. All I see are brown curls and drabs completely ripped and dusty from the arena, before my heart sinks as Illias lifts his head.

My name slips from his lips in a half-whisper, but I'm already running towards him. I clutch his face between my hands, tears flooding down my cheeks as I take in the dark circles beneath his brown eyes. He looks at me, muttering how sorry he is we were all caught, and I shake my head, furious and broken that he can even think of that right now.

'So, Nara,' Aurum says coolly. I don't need to look at him to know he's grinning. 'Are you going to protect your brother by fighting against Darius, or let him die alongside you and everyone you love?'

Darius and I turn to each other. The answer is clearly written across his face as his eyes flit over to the daggers and then to me.

I shake my head at him, which fuels his determination as he stalks towards me, but not before picking up a dagger. When he's centimetres away from me, he pushes the blade into my hands and raises it to my chest.

'Don't,' I whisper, my voice cracking at the same time.

'It's not a choice.'

'You told me we would get out of this, and we *will*.'

He doesn't respond to that. 'You get your brothers out of here.' He gives me a stern look. 'Understood?'

'Don't be the one to self-sacrifice now, Darius.' I grab his hand and press it against my heart. He stares at our hands intertwined, my grip tight enough to not let go. 'You can fight Aurum's control; you did it in Aeris; you can do it now.'

He focuses solely on our hands, his eyes like fire burning through them. There's a gloss in his gaze, and each breath he takes is as if it pains him.

'When it hurts,' he whispers, but it's not to me. He is saying it as if he is trying to remind himself.

Aurum's irritated scoff can be heard from the balcony. 'This romantic goodbye is getting rather tedious, don't you think?'

Without wanting to, both Darius and I raise our heads to look at him.

From here, I can see the half-grin on his lips as he says, 'Shall we begin?'

There's no time to protest, no time to fight, even if it is impossible right now.

My head swivels to where everyone is by the stands, then to Illias behind me and finally to Darius, balling his fists as he closes his eyes.

I say his name, but Aurum already has that tight hold on him.

'Three,' Aurum calls out, and I start panting in panic.

Ruvyn is beside Sarilyn now with a trumpet in his hand and a look of guilt on his face.

'Two.'

'Darius, don't listen to him!' I demand, but flames lick their way up his forearms.

As I look up one final time at Aurum, he leans forward in his seat. A smile slices across his vile mouth.

'One.' Aurum's sadistic whisper is aimed at me, and at that moment, the trumpet sounds, setting everything in motion.

CHAPTER THIRTY

D arius lunges for me and I instinctively slide to the ground, evading his grasp. Twisting onto my back, I see him rise from the sand, and my gaze shifts to my brother.

'Illias, run!' I shout, but he remains rooted to the spot. 'Illias!'

Darius conjures up a fireball, aiming it directly at my head. It misses me as Illias hits him from the side, landing on the ground. My heart is pounding against my chest like a relentless drum as I get up, watching my brother try to help me, but I can see Darius about to overpower him, and I run to them, hearing Darius say to my brother, 'Get away!' He's trying not to fight him, suppressing every bit of puppeteering power Aurum drills into him.

Yanking Illias off Darius by the waist, I tumble backwards. The arena emits a forceful whoop as Darius slowly stands, sand dusting his hair and his eyes fixating on me with deadly intent. Shadows encase him, shrouding him completely before deep claws sink into the ground, and a roar reverberates through the arena. Illias covers his ears, and I catch a glimpse of Aurum leaning back with a sinister grin. He's loving every second of this.

As I glance back at Darius, hesitation grips me. His dragon form is the epitome of powers I have always thought it to be. And though usually when I have seen his complete dragon shape, he's given me mischievous looks, played with me and flown across the skies, now he bares his teeth, a groan resonating from his chest. Slit golden eyes lock on to me and Illias, his silver scales gleaming like a full moon. Just then, my heart shatters as a fiery glow illuminates his throat.

I rush to get Illias and myself up just as Darius's mouth opens wide, unleashing a torrent of searing flames. I'm running with my brother along the arena's edges as Darius's flames roar and twist in pursuit.

'On the other side, there's a trap door that leads to a cage where everyone is!' I say to Illias as we slide to a stop once Darius ceases fire, leaving behind a scorched trail on the ground. I can see from the corner of my eyes as Illias looks at me, our legs stretched and bending at the knees, ready to run again at any moment. 'Try what you can to open it!'

'Are you crazy?' he yells over the cheers from the crowd.

'He's under control to hurt *me*,' I explain, keeping my eyes locked with Darius's. 'I can handle him, but if you get in the way, Aurum will use him to hurt you too.' I finally look at my brother, my voice betraying my outward composure. 'I can't let that happen.'

Darius is already turning to me.

The air crackles with smoke and ash. Illias's eyes glisten with tears just as the ground quivers with another rumble of Darius's roar.

'Go!' I order Illias, slamming my dagger into his hands. He falters, stumbling back before he turns and takes off.

With no weapon in my hand, I glance at where the Elf threw the others. They are at the centre of the arena, but Darius is already charging at me before I can think of it. The gap between his torso and legs looks promising as he gets closer. I slide underneath him, sand and gravel scraping my arms before I escape beneath his tail.

I don't look back as I sprint towards the few daggers left. I can almost feel them in my reach when Darius intersects, landing in front of me, and I slip onto the hard ground.

I'm gagging and sputtering as sand gets in my mouth, and I groan, trying to stand. It's a hopeless act because as I twist on my back, Darius's claws come slamming down on me. They're so big that none of them slice through me, but the weight of his leg crashes against me, holding me down in place.

'Darius!' I shriek, flailing my arms out at each side, trying to escape. I wheeze as I struggle to breathe beneath him, but he doesn't listen to me call out for him. His eyes are on me, lethal and beautiful at the same time, as he bares those razor-sharp teeth with a growl.

I can hear the distant cries of children, but I can only focus on Darius right now. The hold he has on me won't let me move an inch except for my arms.

Searching the ground for something, my neck strains and the tendons in my arms ache. The tips of my fingers finally touch the end of a hilt, and though it's a bit far out of reach, I don't stop trying to grab it.

There's a chant from the crowd. 'Burn her! Burn her!'

I don't have to look at Darius to know that fiery glow is already rushing up his throat, ready to burn me alive.

I'm squirming, desperation clinging on to the remnants of my chafing breaths.

There's a yelp.

The blade meets hard skin and bone, making Darius roar in his dragon form. He lifts his leg off me, and I cough, grabbing on to my chest as I try to regain my strength. By the time I'm stumbling on my feet, I turn, and Darius has shifted back into his human form. Blood streams down his arm as he clutches it tightly with the other.

We're both breathing heavily and audibly as we look at one another. The look he is giving me is devastating enough. He knew he was hurting me, and it hurt him all the same.

A sudden wince from him cuts our stare off as he presses his hands to the sides of his head, and I whip my head back at Aurum. He's watching us with perverse satisfaction gleaming off his features.

Beside him, Sarilyn's brows are drawn, her fingers nervously twitching in the air as she rests her elbow on the arm of her chair.

When I fix my gaze back on Darius, he's shaking with fury, his fists again clenched before our eyes dart to the other two blades left.

I shake my head, but that doesn't stop him as he rushes to grab one.

Immediately, Darius strikes, skilfully weaving the jagged blade between his fingers as he turns and slices. I try to deflect as much as I can, and with every backward movement, I look at him with an anguished plea.

'Please!' My voice is lost in the chaos of the arena, and before I know it, my back hits the edge of the enclosure, and I raise my blade to counteract his coming down on me.

Metal sparks fly as the blades connect, forming an X between us.

We push against each other, my knuckles whitening against the grip of my hilt. It doesn't take him much effort; he's too strong for me, and the blades are nearing my neck.

I grit my teeth, sweat loosening my grip on the weapon. I'm whispering Darius's name again, a last effort to get him to hear me.

Agony contorts his features as a searing jolt of pain slashes across my collarbone, the dagger now cutting through my flesh. A cry escapes my lips, hoarse and strained, until I can no longer feel the cold blade against my skin.

Before the blade can do more harm, Darius grunts, stumbling back as he presses his hand to the left side of his chest. Blood seeps between the crevices of his fingers as he falls to his knees, and Illias stands at my side with the dagger he used on Darius in his hand.

'Illias, no!'

He looks down at the weapon in his hand like he is unfamiliar with it; his two fingers latch on to the hilt as he stammers, 'I'm sorry.'

Guilt claws at the cavity of my chest.

'Nara, kill me,' Darius croaks.

My world crumbles before me.

Eyes wide and frantic, I look at him. He's pale and weak, and Aurum might as well have already killed me, making me see him like this. 'No,' I say, stumbling with each backward step I take. '*No.*'

'You have to.' Darius groans in pain, digging his fingers into the sand as he's overcome with Aurum's manipulations.

Through blurry eyes, I shake my head once more. 'You can fight him off, Darius, you can—'

'Nara, *please.*' He's crying. I don't think I have ever seen him cry like this. It's as if his soul is cleaving in two.

I sob, looking towards my brother for help.

The Galgr's vision is coming to life right before my eyes, and I can't do anything about it.

My hesitation leads Darius to charge at me. I push Illias with all the force that is left in me as I'm tackled to the ground.

Darius is on top as he captures my wrists, slamming them down until I release the blade in my hands.

We're both still crying even as Illias attempts to get up. Darius sees him and fires a coil of shadow around Illias's legs, like a ball and chain, so he cannot move.

With one hand now released, I manage to elbow Darius across the face, knocking him off me as I rise, picking up Darius's dagger and placing it behind the waistband of my trousers while holding the other in front of me.

My legs weaken second by second as I square off with Darius. Shadows curve and shape into a sword at the edge of his fingertips.

Glancing at Aurum, I see he's still grinning. He knows how this will end. With me dying. He will cheat. He will use Darius all he likes and have fun while doing it.

My eyes quickly jump to Sarilyn. She gives me a fierce stare, clenching her fist. Her chest heaves with deep and fast breaths; it's odd, it's unfamiliar, like she doesn't want me to lose.

Tell me. I remember her saying. *If it means saving Zerathion, is the Golden Thief worth dying for?*

I keep my gaze fixated on her, knowing every second I stand here can cost me my life.

I tilt my head to the side, and something triggers my memory.

The night in Terranos. When we captured the Galgr.

When the deities of Solaris and Crello created this world, they couldn't stay in it for ever. The skies needed them for the world to survive and knew they had to eventually sacrifice something.

What did they sacrifice?

Their lives.

The reminder tunnels out of me like a rush, and I gasp, almost tripping on my feet.

I drop my dagger and glance back at Darius. He's frowning at me like he knows I have thought of something but can't help the twitch of his hands, readying to attack.

My chin tips up as I look at Aurum one last time and throw him a smile.

He doesn't like that one bit. All amusement fades from his one eye as he leans forward, anger twisting his lips into a frown. He flicks his fingertips, and at that, Darius winces, edging towards me with the makeshift blade at his side.

I take a step back at each swing, my composure calm, yet my heart bucks wildly.

'Nara, what are you doing!' Illias yells, fear and worry potent in his voice as he pulls at his leg to try to free himself.

'Goldie,' Darius whispers painfully as he strikes again, and I take another step, knowing we are nearing the edge of the arena again.

I don't say a word. Instead, I map out his features, the hard contours of his face, the stubble along his jaw, the pout of his full lips. His eyes.

In that final sweep of my gaze, my back collides with the wall, and in tandem with Darius's blade thrusting into my abdomen, I swiftly draw the other dagger from my waistband, digging it deep into his heart.

We go still. It doesn't register at first. The impact is so quick, so shocking, that I don't feel anything. The crowd around us fall into stunned silence. A chilling numbness creeps along the sides of my stomach as my breath mirrors Darius's, both laboured.

Darius lowers his gaze to the dagger embedded in his heart, the blade sinking all the way to the hilt. Exhaustion seeps deeper into my consciousness, and my breath remains heavy as Darius slowly lifts his head, locking eyes with me. Tears trace down his face, yet amidst it all, an unexpected sense of liberation emanates from him.

'It's okay,' I whisper, choking back on a mouthful of blood. I delicately touch his chest; his eyelids are getting heavier. 'It doesn't hurt.' I'm not lying. I feel nothing.

As he yanks out the dagger from his chest, he lets out a sob that breaks me to pieces, unable to hold myself together. I watch as he collapses to the ground, knees first, then the side of his body.

Time slows as consciousness slips away, and my brother's frantic cries become distant echoes. I fall beside Darius, lying on my back with my head turning towards him. I observe his still form. He's no longer breathing, no longer here with me. 'Until next time, thief,' I whisper, giving him a watery smile.

And then . . . I draw one last gasp of air before it vanishes, leaving nothing but silence.

Chapter Thirty-one

A gentle breeze sweeps through me, bringing on the scent of caramelised sugars – a nostalgic smell that takes me back to my childhood.

Strawberry pies that Idris would buy for me at the market whenever I behaved.

I have my eyes closed, the sun tickling my face as I run my hands through the long grass beside me. I turn on my side, carefully sitting up. I blink wide awake as if I have taken the longest nap in time and stretch my arms out, smiling wistfully as I spot my cottage up the hill.

Flowers bloom all around me, buttercups and white clover. I stand up, going onto my bare tiptoes, feel the soft white silk of my dress.

Inhaling the fresh air, I grin up at the sky and head back home, twirling along the way with the skirt of my dress billowing out below me like smoke.

As soon as I enter my cottage, I'm warmed by the cosy embrace of the crackling fireplace. Smoky notes mingle with the subtle hint of Illias's paint pots and brushes – a scent that was strong enough to stick in anyone's nostrils, but I always found them to be comforting.

A fumbling noise in the kitchen triggers my curiosity. I wonder if it is Idris already trying to cut a slice of pie for me, or if Iker is rummaging through the cupboards, scrounging for food that Idris has not touched or tried to cook himself.

My feet pad along the wooden floorboards, the antiquity of our home giving way under my weight as it creaks. I stand by the doorway of our small kitchen and frown, watching as long golden blond hair flows behind a tall and broad back. Calloused hands knead the pastry on the counter, and freshly washed strawberries gleam brightly from the sun at the other end near the unfixed cracked window.

As if he senses I am standing here, staring, the man turns.

My chest heaves with the shocked gasps of what I'm seeing. A gentle smile that I only remember now in memories and dreams appears in the flesh. Brown docile eyes meet mine – the same colour as Iker and Illias's.

'Father?' I choke out.

He shakes his head. 'Think again.'

I frown, my mind running circles from disbelief.

Images start to form. Blurry at first, but soon it's all I can see.

The arena.

Aurum.

Darius and I before we . . .

I look up and whisper my realisation. 'Solaris.'

He smiles, moving towards me, yet I can't seem to unfreeze myself from this very spot.

I place a hand over my abdomen, feeling where Darius had stabbed me. 'How—'

'This is not my true form,' Solaris says. 'It is only what you wish to see. In this case, you chose your father.'

Short puffs of air release from my chest. I glance at the kitchen, then Solaris as my father. He looks exactly like the day I last saw him. He has let his beard grow – the kind that would scratch me when he kissed my cheeks and turn copper in the sun.

I press my lips together, forcing myself not to cry as I blink a few times. 'And is he . . .' I don't dare try to finish the sentence, but Solaris reads me well.

Looking at me with that serene smile, he says, 'He is well. Content among the stars, as is your mother.'

The thought relieves me more than I thought anything ever would.

Solaris jerks his head for me to follow him out of our cottage and into the fields of my once home. 'I have waited centuries for this moment, Naralía,' he says, turning to me. 'The moment when you and I could finally speak.'

My eyes wander the lands, the unfurling grass and pathways that lead deep into the Screaming Forests. I wrap my arms around my body, breathing in the illusion of this place. 'Is Darius—'

'With Crello, yes,' Solaris completes what I had thought would be the case. I glance at him. 'But of course, you know that.'

I shrug, then remember I am not talking to my father. I am talking to a deity. 'You and Crello sacrificed your lives to be together,' I say softly. 'So did I.'

'And as did Darius.'

We stare at each other in silence, until he asks, 'Did you think it was going to work?'

I cast my mind back to my last moments in the arena. Sacrificing our lives was never on the cards, until I remembered the Galgr. It was a shot in the darkness, and I believe even Solaris has to know that. 'No,' I answer truthfully, 'but I believed in him.'

Solaris's smile elicits a twinge in my heart. I clear my throat. 'So, what now? Will I ever see my brothers again?' *Will I see Darius, Freya, Link and Rydan?*

Solaris turns and starts walking again. 'That is up to you.' He stops to pick up a buttercup. 'I've watched you all your life, Nara.' He's staring off into the distance, and it is such a strange sight to behold, knowing it isn't really my father who is talking to me. 'I have seen your highs and your lows, and I have understood you far better than most.' When he turns to face me, he hands me the buttercup, his blue eyes digging fiercely into mine. 'I am you.'

'Then what am I to do?' My words come out like a plea. I feel stuck, unsure of it all. 'I do not want to let anyone down.'

'And you won't,' he whispers, touching my shoulder. The touch is delicate, almost encouraging. 'There is a reason why I picked you, Nara. You fight just as fiercely as you love.'

A million worries crash against my chest. I pick at the buttercup between my fingers until nothing is left but the stem and the sticky residue of honeydew. 'What will happen if I choose to accept who I am?'

'Then you will become the true immortal vessel you were meant to be.'

Immortal.

I'd no longer need to fear a future without Darius, but . . . my friends, my brothers. They will age, whereas I'll remain unchanged. I'll have to witness them grow old, perish and depart from this world, leaving me behind.

'And if I don't?' I whisper.

'You already know the answer to that.'

I meet Solaris's gaze, finding a smile on his face, yet I can't muster the strength to reciprocate. Instead, I redirect my attention to my cottage. Smoke gradually rises from the chimney, momentarily veiling the sky. Even so, the sun manages to pierce through it, casting a radiant glow upon my home.

'I will let you decide,' Solaris says after a moment, the sound of his boots crunching on the grass fading as he walks away from me.

I clench my eyes shut before whirling my head back around. 'Wait!' I wet my lips as Solaris pauses far away and turns. 'I have one last request.'

Solaris tilts his head, a glimmer of understanding passing through his eyes as if he knows what that request is.

Without uttering a word, a soft glow emanates from his body, casting a golden light that dances around him. Slowly, it overtakes him until I can no longer see my father's face as he gradually disappears, leaving behind a trail of stardust in the air.

'Lía?'

My eyes widen.

Whirling around with my heart lodged in my throat, I'm met with the sight of my father standing by the front door of our cottage. He looks the same as Solaris did when the deity took his form, yet this time, it is different. Every instinct in me affirms that it's truly him, and without a moment's hesitation, I dash towards him.

My arms encircle the middle of his frame as I bury my face into his chest. The familiar scent of spices from our village's market and the jasmine candles he would light yearly for my birthday envelop me, confirming that he is real – that my father is here with me right now.

He laughs, returning my embrace, reminding me of Iker's laugh – short bursts of wheezing chuckles. 'My Lía,' he says.

I'm a mess as the flood of tears trails down my cheeks, and my father draws back, capturing my face with his large, calloused hands.

'Look at you,' he whispers, emotions betraying his usual deep voice. 'You're all grown up.'

I smile, feeling the sting of pain inside my chest as I cry. He looks the same, never changing. Built like Idris, long flowing curls like Iker and Illias and eyes like mine. He left, while we all had to grow up without him. 'I've missed you so much.'

There's a wistful sadness in the way he looks at me as he wipes a tear away from my cheek with his thumb. 'I know,' he says, confirming that he has been looking out for me all this time.

The idea of it has the ache in my chest intensify. 'I suppose you never saw me falling for a dragon shifter.' I chuckle, sniffling as I look up at my father.

He smiles. 'I also never saw you falling for someone ordinary. Ever since you were a child, your mother and I would laugh whenever a boy from our village would come up and confess that they liked you. You'd usually scare them away some way or another.'

A sombre laugh escapes me as a distant rumble echoes around us. Glancing over my shoulder, my brows furrow before returning my gaze to my father.

His eyes carry a poignant sorrow, causing my stomach to plummet. 'Time is running out.' He takes a deep breath. 'I think it is time we said goodbye.'

No.

I need more time. This isn't enough.

I shake my head at him. 'But I'm not ready.'

'Yes, you are.'

'No, I— I'm not. You know that I am indecisive. I can't make the choice—'

'Naralía.'

I had not noticed I wasn't looking at my father as my head now lifts at the sound of him saying my full name. I see a different type of sadness in his gaze this time, almost as if it is bittersweet – perhaps he's going over our memories together, the moments we will never get back.

I draw a desperate step towards him. 'Stay.'

'You know I cannot.'

The air turns cold, and from behind my father, I can no longer see my cottage.

In a last attempt to keep my father here, I latch on to him like a child, wrapping my hands around him and locking my fingers behind his back. 'Don't leave me.' My voice breaks as the wind picks up, and I shut my eyes.

'I never left you,' he whispers. 'I've always been there.'

I don't care, I don't care, I don't— 'Then *I'll* stay, I'll stay here with you.'

'But that isn't what you truly want.'

A cry breaks from my chest as my shoulders shake in his embrace.

'You already knew your decision from before, Lía,' he says. 'I am not part of it.'

I sob, holding on to him tightly. I don't want to let go, and most of all, I don't want to say goodbye again.

He kisses the top of my head. 'I'm so proud of you.'

I shake my head, my mind wishing to stay here for at least five more minutes while my heart knows I can't.

'You can wake up now, Naralía,' he whispers. 'The world is waiting for you.'

A chill descends over my body, darkness wraps me in its embrace, and my eyes flutter open to the skies above as I gasp for air.

CHAPTER THIRTY-TWO

I blink as my eyes adjust to the swirling colours and ethereal light of the sun above me. It isn't blinding brightness, but it is enough to bring back the memories of what happened.

Sitting up, I will myself forward. The arena is silent, but my head is thrumming with noise. I look down at my chest, running my hands over the bloodstain on my clothes with no sign of wound or gash on my skin.

A muted groan catches my attention and I turn to the side, seeing Darius stir. I scramble over to him, frantically prying his shirt open to see his skin miraculously healed.

'Of course you will find any opportunity to undress me, Goldie,' he murmurs, and my eyes flicker up to his face, where he is already looking at me with a lazy smile.

Something lights within me, and I choke out a half-laugh and a half-sob. I hardly wait for him as he rises onto his elbow, and I throw my arms around his neck. He buries his head into my hair, and before we can even so much as kiss, a glow emits from below his chest.

We part as he lifts his shirt, and the symbol of lines and an arrow-head fade into nothing.

Our eyes meet, an unspoken understanding passing between us.

'Nara?' Illias says in disbelief as I look at him, and a smile starts to appear on our faces before a guttural roar splits the arena.

Rising to our feet, Darius and I whirl our heads towards the balcony. Aurum's furious gaze locks with mine, but it is Darius who looks up at him undeterred with a cunning smirk on his lips like he has been waiting for this moment for far too long now.

Aurum raises his hand, smiling as he snaps his thumb and fore-finger together. Nothing happens. Darius's smirk grows, and for the first time, Aurum's face pales.

'Secure the prisoners!' he commands the Elves, his voice rumbling through the arena grounds. Some of the Elves look torn for a moment between their loyalty to Aurum and the horror of seeing Darius and me alive. 'Now—' Aurum's order is abruptly cut off by the piercing caw of a bird. I gaze skywards as a shadow glides over us, revealing the majestic form of a phoenix with a legion of dragons trailing behind.

'Lorcan,' I whisper with a smile. At once, flames descend upon the stands and people start to flee.

Illias says, 'I'll try to find a way to get everyone out of the cells!' He turns away from us, sprinting past everyone to get to the passages that lead towards the dungeons.

I don't even get to tell him to wait for me when screams tear through the stands as Elves charge our way. Shadow tendrils wrap around my waist, pulling me towards Darius's chest before an Elf's sword slices at the ground.

Disorientated, I look up at Darius as he grins at me.

I tell him, 'We're getting out of here, like you said.'

'And you found a way.'

I smile, my eyes flickering past him. 'On your left.'

Understanding my every word, he twists as I slide out of the way of an oncoming attack onto the ground. Darius gracefully manoeuvres through the Elves, dodging, using his powers and striking each Elf down with such fluidity.

He hasn't been able to do this in so long without Aurum manipulating him that I can't stop watching him with a mixture of admiration and determination for his success.

I forget where we are for that moment until an Elf charges towards me, lifting a spear above his head. I react instinctually, raising my hand to block the blow when a beam of magical energy shoots from my palm, sending the Elf reeling back with a powerful blast.

I glance at my hand with wide eyes, feeling the pulse of energy course through my veins as it throbs and burns for me to use it again.

What will happen if I choose to accept who I am?

Then you will become the true immortal vessel you were meant to be.

My lips twitch with a smile of disbelief.

The Galgrs were always right.

Gus was right.

'Miss Nara!' Tibith shouts, and I look up as he runs towards me. 'I told you that you have powers!'

Lorcan is behind him. 'Sorry we're late,' he says, helping me up.

I consider the thousands of questions I have for him, whether he orchestrated all this with the remaining shifters or how he is after knowing Hira was his mother all along, but there isn't time for that. Not now. Not in the middle of this.

Nodding in appreciation, I glance over his shoulder, where I spot Leira and Aelle with violet swirls of magic dancing from their fingertips while Fernah dives across the arena with other Ardenti dragons behind her.

'Rydan,' I suddenly say.

Lorcan frowns.

'Rydan, Freya, Link, my brothers . . . Gus – they're all locked in a cage,' I add, panic scratching the surfaces of my heart because I have no idea if Illias is safe having left for the cells. 'We need—'

The ground quakes beneath our feet and my attention is drawn to the rising cage – my brothers, desperately scanning the chaos to find me. However, my focus shifts to the balcony, where a jolt of shock pulses through me as I see Sarilyn's hand resting on the lever. Her gaze is fixed on me with a strange smile that paralyses me.

A split second later, Aurum grabs her by the arm and shouts something in her face. She mutters something back, enraging Aurum as he backhands her across the cheek. Fury wraps around me, making me start towards the balcony, but Lorcan pulls me back as an arrow cuts across me, narrowly missing me.

I whip my head towards the one who has fired it and watch as he reaches behind him to grab another arrow. Still ramped up with rage, I clench my fists. 'Get Tibith to Darius,' I order Lorcan, never taking my eyes away from the Elf.

Whether he is doing it or not, I don't know as I march across the arena. The Elf aims the arrow at my head, and with a flick of my hand, the ground splits, making him stumble. His bulging green eyes widen even more as he desperately tries to nock the arrow, but I am already nearing him.

I grow angrier, the accumulation of everything that has happened fuelling me as light from my hands turns blinding, and I snap the Elf's hand with the motion of my fingers. He screams, attempting with his free hand to use his powers, but failing, and as I raise my palm, a distant voice snaps me out of it all. There's a grip on my wrist, and I turn my head, staring at deep blue eyes that make me think of my mother.

'Idris,' I whisper softly. I look behind him, where all my friends are now free, and then Ruvyn is beside them.

Our eyes meet and he sends me a decisive nod.

He freed my brothers from the cage.

He chose *me*.

'Leave the Elf to us,' Idris says to me as my eyes cut to him. 'It's Aurum you want.'

'You'll lose either way,' the Elf chuckles from the ground. When I look at him, sweat beads down the side of his head, his straggly long hair sticking to his neck. 'Whatever you are—' His words are cut short into a gurgle as a dagger made of shadows punctures a hole between his eyes.

I glance past him, watching Darius stalking towards us. His eyes blaze a golden colour that I haven't seen except when he is absolutely mad. His lips part, a snickering comment likely brewing.

'Nara!' Freya's voice comes out as a frightened gasp. All of us turn to find her in front of Aurum as he wraps a hand around her throat.

Rage sluices through my veins, my legs aching to propel myself forward, but I know better. Idris and Iker, however, let their desperation take over as they rush ahead, and Aurum's grip tightens, causing Freya's chin to lift more.

'Careful.' Aurum grins as my brothers freeze. 'One more step, and I'll snap her delicate little neck.'

I can see Freya's hand at the side, attempting to conjure up some of her magic. Sparks of violet power crackle beneath her palm.

'The stones,' Aurum says, shuffling backwards with Freya in his grasp. 'Give them to me.'

My eyes snap to the necklace around Freya's neck – the one harbouring the magic of the Isle of Elements portal. She gives me the same wild look as we try to come up with the next step.

'You're rotting away,' I tell Aurum, planting my hand out to the side when I sense Idris ready to run again towards Freya. 'The Isle can't give you anything. It will just take and take until it destroys this world.'

The maddening look in Aurum's one eye never yields. 'Don't test me, Nara.' His fingers dig into Freya's neck and a strangled cry leaves her lips.

At once, her magic manifests, and she raises a purple-stricken hand, blasting his face with dust.

Aurum's menacing growl reverberates through the air as he forcefully releases Freya, sending her tumbling to the ground. She clutches the pendant, but the desperate grip proves futile against the brute force of Aurum as it slips from her fingers. The protective shield opens with a crack, and a flash of light erupts, unleashing a force of power up into the air.

My pounding heart echoes around the arena when Aurum's gaze lands on the pendant and the portal. He begins to laugh – a sickening winner's laugh that sends a thick wave of nausea over me – as he sees the opportunity to grab it.

At the same time, Darius and I yell out, 'No!' as we both lunge for it, before Darius's golden eyes turn silver, burning bright as he conjures a blast of water from his palm. It hits Aurum straight in the chest, sending him back against the arena wall and causing it to crack.

Darius slows down, shock making him stumble as he glances down at his hands. His fingers flex as if he knows this is something new, something I can only imagine is thanks to Crello.

But instead of dwelling on it, we have no time. I snatch the pendant off the ground, closing it along with the portal. I'm watching Idris and Iker running towards Freya when Aurum rises to his feet, a look of lethal vengeance in his gaze as gold swirls encompass him, and he emerges from them as a dragon.

CHAPTER THIRTY-THREE

The hollow roar ricochets around the walls as Aurum slams his claws onto the ground. He's just as big as Darius, carrying a menacing undertone within his red and gold exterior. The slim muzzle shows thousands of scars, matching the one that rests across the same eye where I stabbed him and making the colour of it a milky white.

I swallow.

Darius doesn't step back from his uncle's dragon form. Instead, he shifts and challenges him.

'Nara, get the portal out of here!' Idris yells at me. He and Iker have each of Freya's arms on their shoulders as they help her sluggish body stand.

Darius and Aurum are tumbling over each other before Aurum's teeth plunge into Darius's neck. His cry burns through me and my legs twitch to go to him.

'Nara, now!' Iker says, and the command seeps into my bones as I drag back a slow breath and run.

Large and even smaller dragons swarm the arena while the Elves fight against the saved Venators and shifters.

Fernah, my mind automatically whispers.

I hear the distinct rasp of a growl that belongs only to her. She responds instantly, as if she had *heard* me herself, and closes the distance between us with a thunderous roar. Adjusting my pace to a slower stride, I seize the opportunity as she swoops by, leaping onto her back. Urging her forward, I press my heel into her side, prompting a surge of momentum as she lifts us into the air.

I tightly grip the pendant while Fernah dodges between the Ardenti's flames and the Umbrati's shadows unleashing from their mouths. Leaning into Fernah, I urge her higher, chasing the exhilarating freedom from where the dome looms above the arena.

A fleeting smile of relief passes through me, but the serenity is soon shattered by a distant cry, a painful echo that jolts me. My head whips around, dread tightening my core as I search for Darius. But I can't see him anywhere, only Aurum chasing after Fernah and me.

He's closing in on us with malevolent speed, and I yell for Fernah to dodge his impact. Yet, it's not enough as he collides with Fernah's flank.

Everything slows down before me as she loses her balance, and I slip from her harness.

A guttural 'No!' escapes me as I plummet from the sky. The wind tears at my clothes, and I watch in horror as Fernah becomes smaller and smaller the further I drop.

I gasp, desperately reaching for anything within my grasp, fully aware there is nothing in sight. Summoning magic to my fingertips, my veins ignite with surging power just as large silver wings close around me, forming a protective cocoon.

The impact isn't strong enough to hurt me as we land in the arena and the wings unfold. I roll out of them onto the ground, coughing as sand cloaks the air, and see Darius shift into human form. Without so much as a groan, he comes towards me, urging me to my feet. Fresh blood trickles down his neck and chest, but he doesn't care; he only cares I am safe.

My fingers gently glide across his cheek just as Aurum lands opposite us; the resonant boom of his claws meeting the ground shakes the arena. As he transforms, Aurum locks eyes with me, ruthless and unyielding as he stalks towards me.

In that second, Darius snatches the pendant from my hand and steps away from me as he raises it high. 'Looking for this?'

Aurum stops, his head tilting almost unnaturally towards Darius.

Darius chuckles, his gaze quickly darting to the side of me. 'Tibith.' He tips his chin up at Tibith, who has suddenly appeared. 'Catch!'

The pendant travels through the air before Tibith grabs it in his paw. He squeaks, and my eyes widen, telling him to run, right as Aurum cries out in anger and charges towards him.

Darius cuts him off, swinging his fist into his face. Aurum stumbles back, but Darius continues, not allowing the tiniest break as he pummels him to the ground. When fire consumes Darius's hand, Aurum successfully captures his wrist, sending a hit at Darius's jaw.

A surge of fury spikes my blood as Aurum takes advantage, his fingers delving into the wounds that now mar most of Darius's chest and abdomen. Determination fuels me as I conjure a ball of light between my palms.

Aurum looks feral as he bares his teeth. 'You're a pain in my existence, *nephew*.'

Darius hisses in pain, attempting to resist Aurum as he pushes his hand back. 'Likewise.'

Summoning all my strength, I redirect the gathered light straight at Aurum, ensuring he is knocked off Darius.

He grunts, blood staining his nose, but retaliates, coming for me.

My vision blurs with the colour red, and I launch another surge of magic, pushing him back. Despite weakening him for a moment, he doesn't give up. He's relentless – but so am I.

Another advance from him is met with a hit of my magic and a cry that tears from my throat.

Wave after wave of anger channels into my power as I give him all I have against him, and he lets me.

'Nara, wait—' Darius says, but when my next blast has Aurum laughing, I yell and run at him.

Elves are already on Darius, making him unable to get to me as he parries their attack.

I throw my fist back, ready to delve deep into Aurum's chest with my power. He snatches it midair and twists me around so my back hits his chest. I thrash in his hold, only to hear his cold laughter in my ear.

'Look at them,' he says.

I don't know what he means, and I don't care as I shake my head to escape him.

His fingers grip my chin, holding me in place. '*Look*,' he grits.

Panting through clenched teeth, I see what he is referring to as I watch Darius taking on dozens of Elves at a time, trying to get to me, Lorcan helping him from the other side, my brothers and friends on the far end, shielding Freya, then Tibith shaking on the ground.

He's clutching the pendant beneath his body as Elves surround him.

'Even as Solaris and Crello, you and Darius are nothing against me.'

'At least I'm loved,' I spit.

He stills. 'You little—'

In a sudden movement, I jerk my head backwards, hitting him square on the chin. He lets go as a low guttural grunt escapes his lips.

I don't wait for the pain in the back of my head to subside as I rush to where Tibith is.

Elves come at me with swords and spears, and I duck as one of them slices across me. The blade collides with another Elf behind, unintentionally striking him.

'Tibith!' I call out to him, when I notice Gus is already hurrying towards him, telling Tibith to launch the pendant at him.

Just as Tibith does as he's told, Aurum comes between us in dragon form, his wings knocking the pendant onto the ground, causing the rift to open again.

Time freezes. The three of us stare at the pendant. Gus is the first to lunge for it, followed by Aurum's roar as he slices at Gus with his claws. Gus dodges, sliding across the ground.

I'm the last to race for it, am just about within reach when I'm rammed into by Aurum's now human form.

He's straddling me, his lips curling into a snarl. Before he can speak, I kick him off. The portal is within my sight, I'm so close, so, so—

I'm pushed, my feet giving in as I fall headfirst onto gravel. A sharp sting shoots up my shins before I raise my head, and the Isle of Elements stands ahead of me.

No.

I scream as a hand fists my hair and lifts me up from the ground. I cast a glance at Aurum, who is inside the Isle, holding on to me.

The arena is still in view from where the portal is, a few steps away from us. There's a faint-coloured shimmer covering the rift like the first time I ever saw it, but it is so different now. It's . . . dying.

I try to run, but Aurum pushes me back down onto the ground. I land on my back with an aching quake inside my head.

Everything is a haze. I'm blinking in the hope of focusing, but all

I can see is Darius on the other side, yelling my name as he races towards the portal and shifts into a dragon mid-sprint.

Aurum is saying something I can't make out, but I know what this must mean from the sneer on his face as he calmly reaches for the pendant.

I stagger up onto my knees, bile rising in my throat as I crawl and grab Aurum's leg. He kicks me in the abdomen, making me double over with a strangled cry. I clutch my stomach with both hands, helplessly watching Aurum now holding the pendant.

I think I see Gus for a moment, but Darius still seems so far away.

He won't make it.

He won't make it in time.

And as Aurum closes the pendant, someone jumps through the rift, falling onto their hands and knees.

Dark hair falls forward, and when the person turns to look at me, the realisation hits – it's Gus.

CHAPTER THIRTY-FOUR

The sky splits with a thunderous crack above me as I shift onto my side. A dull ache throbs at the back of my head, but I push it aside. 'Gus?' I croak, and he turns to me, steadying me as I rise.

My eyes meet Aurum's as a mischievous gleam dances in his working eye.

'*You*,' I seethe, wrenching away from Gus's grip. Aurum grins, tracing his thumb across the pendant Freya made.

In a burst of rage, I raise my hands, intending to spill every drop of Solaris's power upon him. Yet nothing comes.

What?

I look at my palms, lips parted in astonishment, as I desperately search for what I must have done wrong.

Aurum chuckles, revelling in my confusion as I attempt to use my powers again and fail. 'Even Solaris needs to recharge her powers when they've been overused.'

No, no, no—

'You knew this,' I say, realisation dawning on me as to why he wouldn't fight me back in the arena.

His smile is like a viper, poisoning me with just one look. 'You can't always use magic and expect to be fine, can you?' He sighs in amusement. 'A shame you used it all on me.'

Searing rage flares through me as I take a step towards him, but it's Gus who storms his way, his fists balled at the sides.

'Ah!' Aurum holds out a finger while calmly pocketing the pendant in his coat. 'I wouldn't try anything, Augustus. Not with that wound that isn't healing near your heart – looks like you were struck with Neoma blood.'

I turn to look at Gus. Part of his shirt is ripped, exposing a cut on the left side of his collarbone and down to the upper part of his chest, coated in bright blood. I hadn't even noticed.

Gus shakes his head at Aurum. 'Aurelia was right about you.'

Aurum's smile falls. 'Aurelia is dead.' His one visible eye narrows. 'So I wouldn't dwell on her words too much.'

My fists clench as my chest falls and rises in harsh waves.

'Now.' Aurum claps his hands and rubs them together. 'Shall we get going?'

'The Isle won't help your state,' I tell him as if that will do much when I am dealing with a psychotic man.

Aurum's eye latches on to me, the green in it darkening to something sinister as he slowly walks up to me. 'Then I will use the one thing they can't deny.' He grins in my face. 'Solaris's vessel herself.'

My palm flies out to connect with his face, but his reflexes are still too sharp as he takes hold of my wrist and extends his other hand towards Gus, who suddenly grimaces in agony, collapsing to his knees and clutching his chest.

My face pales. 'What are you doing?'

The wound near Gus's heart tears open, unravelling and extending, as if Aurum is magnifying his injuries by using the very thing I don't have right now.

Magic.

Rivernorth magic.

I look between him and Gus, panic cinching my gut. 'Stop!' I yell, trying to pull away from Aurum, my free hand trying to grab at him to stop his power from causing more harm. 'Stop hurting him!'

Aurum whips his hand away, stumbling slightly on his legs as I notice another rotting tear appear on his neck.

When his grip loosens, I yank myself free and kneel in front of Gus.

He's swaying, drawing back long breaths as I scan the wound on his chest.

'It's okay,' he says weakly. 'I'm okay.'

I shake my head. 'I can heal it,' I whisper. I did it once with Darius when he had Neoma blood in him. I can do it again.

'How sweet,' Aurum says from behind. 'A father and his daughter-in-law, looking out for one another. If only my nephew could see this precious moment.' He starts to laugh. 'Then again, he hates your guts.'

My molars grind together.

Aurum must notice my intentions as he tugs me away from Gus, making me stand. His fingers dig into my upper arm, turning me to face him. 'Don't even *think* about helping him.' I squirm in his hold. 'You're with me.'

In my peripheral vision, Gus struggles to rise. He presses a palm to his chest and winces as Aurum jerks his chin, forcing him to go ahead of us.

'Now,' Aurum says to us both. '*Walk.*'

The cave where the power source lies crumbles and shakes once we enter. Aurum still holds me tightly, his eye wide and gazing around in lunacy as he follows the golden light, paving the way to Solaris and Crello's magic.

I put as much distance between us, hoping to slow him down as much as possible so that I can regain my strength in power. But he's as ruthless as they come.

Gus's breathing seems to worsen, as does the gash on his chest. Regardless, he keeps looking back at me, ensuring I am okay.

As we turn the corner, Aurum jerks to a stop, his grip loosening.

The cascading waterfall of Solaris and Crello's power gently flows into a pit with the four pillars standing in place around it.

Though I have seen this all before, nothing prepares me to witness the last standing element barely functioning.

The flame. Now, it is a tiny flicker of what it once used to be.

My heart yearns to fix it.

'Beautiful,' Aurum says, mesmerised. The enchantment of the power source is messing with his already screwed-up mind.

'Don't you see how weak the Isle is?' I hiss at him, but he doesn't care. Why would he? 'You'll achieve *nothing*.'

Aurum's gaze is fixed on the waterfall as he chuckles in ignorance.

I look over at Gus, who is also staring at the ditch.

Dread scrapes along my skin, knowing his thoughts must be straying to everything he wishes to have.

There's always an urge with the Isle. The king of Terranos already warned me once, yet even when I was here with Darius, my mind would drift to other hopes and wishes rather than what we needed. I was ready to ask for my parents back, for the Tibithian and the Ardenti dragon I killed to be alive again.

For now, though, I need to get Gus and me out of here.

My gaze shifts to a rock the size of my hand on the ground beside me, the edges sharp.

Keeping my eye on Aurum, I inch towards it.

'Do you know what I'm going to wish for, Nara?'

I freeze, but luckily, he still hasn't turned around, so I snatch the rock from the ground and make my way to Aurum. I don't answer him either because I know what he wants. He wants all four kingdoms at his feet. He wants to save himself from the rotting corpse he will become.

'A new world,' he muses, and my stomach turns. 'Zerathion has become everything I despise. Starting with you, Nara.'

My fingers clench around the rock, numb to the edges embedding into my skin.

He wants to eradicate all the people of Zerathion. It is so much worse than we had all thought to begin with.

'A human,' he spits, disgust filtering through his tone.

I close in on him. 'I'm not human any more.'

He scoffs, aware of my presence behind him yet unwilling to face me. 'You'll always be a human deep down.'

I feel something warm and thick trickling down my hand. I can tell it is my blood from the rock. 'Then . . .' I swallow. 'Let me show you what a human can do.'

As he turns, I smash the rock across his head, blood splattering all over my face – whether it is mine or his, it doesn't matter.

Watching him crumple to the ground with a hiss, I rush over to Gus, helping him by placing his arm around my shoulder. My hand reaches for his wound, and I take a long, steady breath, concentrating on healing it.

'Nara—' Gus says, but a force abruptly stops me, slamming me against the opposite side of the cave.

My body vibrates with intense pain as I gasp and drop onto the ground. My vision quakes, everything spinning before I'm grabbed by the throat and lifted off the floor.

'Do you know why I hate humans so much?' Aurum's face comes into view, the palpable waves of his anger reaching out and drowning me. 'Because they are fragile, yet they cling to their illusions of strength. They are nothing. Merely useless beings on earth that dare to defy those above them.' His voice tightens along with the grip on my neck. 'They're liars, and worst of all, they destroy *everything*.'

I wheeze, staring at the patch of gold covering his eye. 'You . . . you fell in love with one, didn't you?' I ask him between gasps, and his expression darkens.

'No,' he says. 'But they did kill my witch.'

My chest compresses from his hold as I try to make sense of his words until I'm let go, and I plummet, gagging and coughing for some air to make its way back into my lungs. I look up through blurred tears, finding Gus standing near the waterfall pit with Aurum on the ground.

Aurum lets out a laugh, lifting himself to his feet. 'You really are like your son.'

Gus cracks his neck to the side and rolls back his shoulders. 'As long as he's not like you, I'm fine with that.' Shadows coil and dance across Gus's body, his powers coming to life as he unleashes them.

Aurum counters with a rush of air from his palms, disintegrating the shadows. I wince, attempting to stand as Gus lunges at Aurum, his shadows slicing through Aurum's clothes. The ground quivers, sending a rumble of rocks tumbling from the walls.

I'm blinking and crawling on my elbows towards the ditch. Gus and Aurum are on the ground, but I can't make out who is on top of whom through the mist in my eyes. There's this raw energy of shadow and light distorting my reality.

'Gus,' I say, but I don't think his name really leaves my lips.

Something is then thrown to my feet.

All I catch is the brassy gleam before I realise it is the pendant to open the rift. As I grab it, my knees slam onto the ground, my head lifting to find Gus amidst the shadows.

A gust of wind circles the cave. I can hear their struggles as I finally focus on Gus battering Aurum everywhere possible.

He fights like Darius. Savage and more human than a dragon.

Gus notices me as he turns his head, but that crucial moment allows Aurum to send Gus tumbling back against the edge of the pit.

'No!' I scream, lunging to my feet and running towards Aurum and jumping on his back. I put my all into hitting and scratching before he pulls me off him. I land on my forearms, glaring up at him as he looks at me. I find the strength to grin maliciously at the state of his bloodied face, the ruined clothes and the decayed cuts along his neck and chest.

A seething energy emanates from him; it's almost suffocating. 'How I would love for Darius to be here while he watches me rip you apart.'

I tip my chin up at him, gritting my teeth. 'Fuck. *You.*'

He raises his hand to strike me, but Gus's arms wrap around his neck, dragging him backwards.

Growls escape Aurum as he spins around, but Gus adeptly dodges each blow Aurum aims at him. Their feet are close to the edge of the pit. They're on the precipice, going at each other's throats. One wrong move, and Gus will plunge into the hole.

'Gus, stop—' I yell at him as he sends another punch Aurum's way and seizes the collar of his coat. He twists Aurum around so his back is to the pit. 'No—'

'I hope you rot along with the rest of those who served you.'

I shake my head, and my legs move of their own accord as I sprint to intervene. If Gus pushes him in, the flame will die.

Aurum's head sways, bloodied teeth exposed as he laughs. 'If I rot,' he says, 'then you'll rot with me.'

Wide-eyed horror fills me as Aurum clings on to Gus and pushes himself backwards into the pit.

My hand reaches out, fingers brushing the back of Gus's shawl, but not enough to catch him as he steals a final glance over his shoulder and closes his eyes.

I call out his name, the sound scratching the surfaces of my throat as I collapse onto the ground with my chest halfway over the pit. I watch them both drop into the abyss, and sorrow pierces my chest as silence falls. My gaze shifts to the pillar, and the Isle seems to wail in agony as the flame extinguishes.

Mountains crack, the cave shatters and the waterfall releases its last bit of magic into the pit, shaking me to despair.

'No,' I whisper, paralysed, and as I look down into the pit, chilling fear grips me by the throat.

What appears to be a crack along the walls of the ditch soon oozes a black substance that looks like tentacles reaching towards the surface. Staggering back, I witness a surge of green shadows and inky liquid erupting from the pit.

Shrill roars and cries fill the air as creatures – no, dragons – emerge. Their bodies are comprised of shadow and decay as they swarm above me. There are dozens of them, with still more flying from the ditch.

A rotten hand then slams against the edge of the ditch, and

without waiting, I rush out of the cave, knowing who the person is, climbing out of there.

Rocks fall around me as I reach the outside, where once-grey clouds have turned pitch black.

'Nara.' The singsong voice of Aurum echoes from the cave. 'No point in hiding now! After all, it was Gus who made the wish, not me.'

My chest cracks, but I don't look over my shoulder.

His maniacal laughs near, and I run.

I slip and slide down the sloped pathways, debris coming down on me like rainfall as I dodge and cover my head.

I pick up my pace and focus on getting as far from the cave as possible. Yet my throat burns with lodged tears, picturing Gus by the pit, his eyes closing right before he fell in.

I think of Darius, and a sob wracks my body.

The shrieks of ruined dragons follow me as some are now out of the cave, flying high in the skies. I grip the pendant, ensuring I still have it before throwing it to the ground as it opens the rift ahead of me.

I can see the arena through the portal. I can see my home.

My leg muscles burn, and I cry out for help as I leap through the rift, falling to the ground. The first person I see is Darius, and I let out an anguished sob as I push onto my hands and knees, trying to stand but buckling under my tired weight.

Darius grabs me by the waist, then grips my face in his hands. He's repeatedly saying my name, but I can't seem to respond, my head lolling back and forth.

When he asks me about Gus, I shake my head. Sharp pains pierce my chest all the way to my heart. 'I'm sorry,' I say hoarsely. That's all I can manage to say. 'I'm so sorry.'

The instant realisation on his face destroys me, but he tucks me into his chest, not allowing himself to show any other emotion.

I pry myself from his hold, staring as I see that the whole arena is in flames, bodies burning in the distance.

Darius is covered head to toe in soot – his own doing, I imagine. I look on and find Illias on the side with freed Venators now standing behind him, and Leira and Lorcan with my brothers and friends. They're okay. They're alive.

I shake my head, murmuring, 'The portal.'

I twist around where the portal is still open.

Lightning strikes the sky inside the Isle, and through the portal, far beyond the destruction of the Isle, I see Aurum gracefully navigating through the dragons surrounding him. Decay coats him head to toe, dark veins protruding from his mottled skin as our eyes lock, and he maintains a steady stride like nothing can hurt him.

I feel Darius shift while holding me, preparing to go in there himself.

My frantic heart won't allow it.

I go to reach for the pendant when my eyes land on a dagger on the ground.

Something wild snaps inside me.

Lorcan seems to realise as he says, 'Nara, don't.'

I don't listen as I lunge for the blade and kneel before the pendant.

Aurum pauses from a distance, his head tilting as shadows slither around his ruined face like serpents seeking refuge in his mess.

I stare at him with the dagger poised in my hand, and that is when he registers what I plan to do. He breaks into a sprint, a torrent of fury within his gaze.

Flipping my finger at him, I swiftly bring the blade down upon the pendant.

This is for Gus.

A surge of air courses through the space around us, almost sending me back.

I hear Aurum yelling in the distance and slam the blade down again. This time, sparks fly off the pendant as it shatters into pieces, severing the connection to the Isle of Elements.

Aurum's remaining eye is the last thing I see before the portal vanishes and I succumb to exhaustion, not having realised I've dropped myself back into Darius's arms until he whispers in my ear, 'You made it out, Goldie. You made it out.'

I rest the back of my head against his chest, my brothers and friends coming to stand by Darius and me. All of us glance at the sky as dark clouds roll in, and for the first time in the history of Emberwell, it rains down upon us, calming the fire.

PART THREE
THE BATTLE OF THE SKIES

DARIUS
A MEETING WITH CRELLO

I sit up on the wooden floorboards. A musky scent hits my nose as I glance around at the familiar cottage, and the sun streaks through windows covered by long, tattered curtains. I carefully stand as a melodic voice hums what sounds like a lullaby from behind me.

I whirl around, my fists clenched, until I see a female. Her back is turned to me, tending to some freshly washed clothes, but I recognise the long dark waves of her hair all the same.

She stops humming and lifts her head without looking at me. 'It is so good to finally meet you, Darius.'

I'm deathly silent.

She chuckles, sounding just like . . . *her*. 'No, I am not your mother,' she answers what is already going through my mind as she turns, those green eyes shimmering like the day she – my mother – died. 'I am only a manifestation of her. My true name, however, is something we have in common.'

She speaks with a celestial grace to her. One I believe belongs to a deity.

Crello.

She smiles, showing the white gleam of her teeth, but the thought of someone else sporting my mother's face vexes me.

'Where am I?' I ask without glancing at my surroundings. I already know exactly what this place is. What I care to know is why, when it no longer exists.

'Your old home,' Crello says, sliding delicate, thin fingers across the cracked wall and carved wooden artwork. 'At least, this is what your mind first thought of when you died.' She looks at me. 'It is your haven.'

The memories of what happened barge into my mind, unwelcome. Images of Goldie crying as she plunged a dagger into my heart, as mine did with hers, haunt me on a loop.

'Nara,' I whisper.

'She is safe,' Crello says quickly. 'Much how you are, too.'

I scoff, giving her an unkind stare. 'How can we be, when we are dead, and you have my mother's face?'

'Your mother is what your heart wishes for. She may not be here, but you may speak to her once we are finished.'

I cock my head to the side. I want to get out of this place and find Goldie, and I need to see for myself that she is okay, not take the word of a likely hallucination in between a state of life and death. 'Finished what exactly?'

'Making a decision.'

Sighing, I cross my arms over my chest. 'All right, then. My decision is that I wish to leave this place.'

Crello laughs, unaware that I'm deadly serious, or even if the deity does know, it doesn't seem to care. 'Do you see that?' She looks towards my left, but my gaze never follows. 'It's the pendant your mother always carried. A sign of who she once was.'

I grit my teeth and stay silent without turning my head. I don't understand why my mind took me to this place. It's riddled with horrible moments of hiding, my mother's death, and the times she would tell me of a future where she was still alive.

'And who you are now,' Crello states.

Anger rises in my chest and Crello can sense it. Whatever she thought would work is failing as the cottage around us disappears, replacing the worn floorboards with grass and overgrown trees.

'Give it back!' a young voice shouts, and the instant recognition makes me turn.

In front of me are two boys, one copper-haired and the other with dark, scraggly hair and a bunch of cuts and bruises on his face.

Lorcan and me.

'Why do you even want this?' Lorcan flails the crescent carving high up in the air, his right palm pressing against my chest. 'It's nothing but a piece of junk.'

Funny, I have always known how neglected I was back then, but seeing it now, I was skin and bone. Anyone could have snapped me in half.

'I said, give it back!' The younger me lunges at Lorcan once again, only for me to land on the ground as he lets go of me. My knees and elbows scrape against grass and mud, the usual look I donned back then whenever Lorcan and I went head-to-head over the stupidest things.

Except this time, I remember what happened.

To this day, I can still feel it. How much rage I had in me.

Lorcan's laugh echoes throughout the woods. His eyes close as he clutches his middle, not knowing how much power was coursing through my veins at that moment.

I watch as this version of me gets up from the ground and rushes at Lorcan, releasing a guttural cry when shadows form at my fingertips and fly out at him.

Lorcan's eyes widen and he ducks right as these shadow blades glide past the current me and lodge into a nearby tree trunk.

As a child, the anger in my eyes dims and my brows rise in fear.

I'd only gone through Ardenti's powers and the beginnings of mind manipulation. Shadow was entirely new to me, and it made me terrified despite what my mother might have once told me.

'I'm sorry,' I'm whispering as Lorcan steadily rises to his feet. 'I'm so sorry.'

He has a hand over his cheek, and when he withdraws it to look at the blood staining his palm, past me starts crying.

Sobs wrack my chest uncontrollably. 'Please don't tell him,' I beg. 'Please?'

Rayth.

I meant Rayth.

Lorcan slowly walks towards me, hands raised as if approaching a wild animal out of its cage. 'I won't,' he says. 'I promise. I'll say I fell.'

And he did promise. It was just never enough.

That night, I was punished, not because Lorcan was hurt but because I was outside when I never should have been.

'Why did you show me this?' I look down at my side, the corner of my eye catching Crello's silhouette.

'Because on this very same day, you made yourself a promise,' she says. 'One where you would make yourself known to the world.'

When she comes to my side, I feel the need to look away.

I hear a soft sigh. It dares me to turn and face the image of my mother.

Crello stares at the trees, a serene smile coating her lips. When she notices my attention is on her, she says, 'Everyone always says that the Rivernorths were the first dragons to be born.'

'Were they not?'

'There is always a mother, is there not?'

The corner of my lip lifts. 'I suppose so,' I murmur.

'When we created this world, we also made the first piece of land, the first tree . . . the first dragon.' Crello's gaze flickers over to mine. 'A dragon who possessed fire, mind, shadow and light like the Rivernorths. The ones to be born first were those by the rivers, and the next were what are now known as Umbrati, Ardenti, and finally, Merati. But because the Rivernorths were the first kind, they were something new, something powerful. And so, when the mother of dragons perished after the final birth of Meratis, Solaris and I made sure there would be another one day. Another source, for a newer generation. *You* – and Nara.'

I shake my head. 'I never asked for this. Neither did Nara.'

'We know,' Crello whispers. 'But sometimes sacrifices have to be made.'

Like today.

'So, Darius, I ask you this. Are you willing to become more than just a shifter?'

I stare at her, the answer on the tip of my tongue.

I never say it.

I don't think I need to as Crello smiles at me.

'Goodbye, Darius,' she says and starts to walk away.

'Wait,' I say, grinding my teeth at what I am about to ask. 'You said I could speak with my mother.'

Crello bows at the waist. 'As you wish.'

She disappears from my sight.

'Shit,' I mutter, running a thumb over my brow. Nerves gut me like a fish as I wait for something to happen.

After a minute, I hear my name spoken softly from behind me, and my heart and mind instantly tell me it is her.

CHAPTER THIRTY-FIVE

NARA

'What about this one?'

I look over my shoulder as Link holds up a bright yellow gown – rather sore to the eyes. A few other dresses lie behind him on the settee of the dressing chambers inside the castle.

'Link, I adore you most of the time,' Rydan says with a hand on his chest, 'but your style is worse than the Ambrose family.'

Freya grimaces as she nods in agreement, and I frown at them.

Link pouts, throwing the frilly dress onto the bed. 'Should we not have a seamstress or maid for this?'

'We do.' Freya nods.

'Sarilyn does,' I correct her. 'Or did.' I turn back to the assortment of jewellery in front of me that is safely placed within a glass case. 'The majority died at the hands of Aurum.'

The room becomes quiet.

It's only been a week since I trapped Aurum inside the Isle of Elements; a week since Gus sacrificed himself to save me. We have managed to lock Sarilyn away and send the Elves back to Thallan, both dead and partially alive, per Darius's wishes.

Yet, even with that, the people of Emberwell still fear for their lives. Our world is crumbling by the second; our crops are dying; other kingdoms are suffering from the change in weather patterns, and then Darius . . . Darius is not himself. He hasn't been for a long time, ever since Aurum captured him, but now it is different. Despite gaining his powers back and embracing the Crello side of him – figuring out new powers tied to water each day – I often awaken at night to find him drinking in another room. Even Freya has tried to speak with him, but she can only go so far with tuning into his emotions. He likes to play it all off with humour, and Freya falls for it just like I always do.

'This one looks good enough,' Rydan says, cutting through my daydream.

'Oh, that one is gorgeous.' Freya crosses the room as I turn to look at the three huddled together, all ogling a golden gown.

I recognise it as one of Sarilyn's. Its cape sleeves resemble ethereal wings as they flow from the shoulders and touch the floor, while its heart-shaped bodice looks like it can mould to any figure.

My friends might admire how it looks, but I, on the other hand, can't shake the queasy feeling it evokes within me.

Still, too much wafting through gowns has made my head pound with useless thoughts that I don't wish to endure any longer.

'I can just envision it!' Freya is beaming excitedly, her bronzed cheeks reddening. 'I could even style her hair into—'

'I'll let Darius know,' I cut them off with a nod, waltzing towards the double doors.

'Nara, wait,' Freya calls out, and I stay put. I keep my eye on the doorknob, knowing that if I look at her, that glow of happiness might just fade. She has tried so hard to keep it all together for me. 'Iker told me that Lorcan wanted to speak to Darius.'

My shoulders relax as I release a slow breath. 'I know,' I say softly and leave the dressing chamber.

Regardless of the times I've been inside this castle, the long corridors seem endless as I turn and search for Darius. He's inside the sitting room, murmuring something to Lorcan, when I stop just outside the door and dip behind the wall.

I peer over the side, hoping Darius won't catch my scent. He is always ever so perceptive when I am around.

Lorcan stands while Darius lounges on one of the quaint chairs by the long windows. His legs extend comfortably and his chin tilts upwards. He contemplates the ceiling as if that is more interesting than listening to his brother.

'You can't win them all over,' Lorcan is telling him. 'Remember, in their eyes, you are still the criminal that Sarilyn hunted for years.'

Darius huffs out a chuckle, levelling him a look. 'You're forgetting you also hunted me for years.'

That doesn't go down well with Lorcan. His jaw ticks. 'Under Erion's influence.'

'Yes, that makes it *much* better.'

'I thought we could get over this petty squabbling. You got the girl – you even married in secret – and all of this belongs to *you.*'

I stifle the annoyance building up in my throat. I don't like how Lorcan referred to me as a prize in a game. Our relationship is a complicated one that no one can fathom. Yes, he has saved me many times, even risking his position in Aeris to come get us, but our history still lingers there on the brink of a precipice. And no matter what I do, he and I need more than a week's worth of talking things out.

'I never *got* her.' Darius shoots up from the chair, his face metres away from Lorcan's. 'This was never a competition for me. None of it was.'

Lorcan huffs, but Darius points a finger to his chest, his voice low.

'I cared for you because you were my only family,' he says. 'At least I thought that until Gus.'

I might not see it on his face, but I know it hurts him just as much. He hasn't said it to me, and I don't think he will for a long time, but I can feel it. I can feel how much he blames himself for never having forgiven Gus to his face.

I let my guard down, choosing to walk away but not in the most stealthy way. Lorcan's eyes flit over to the doorway, spotting me, and Darius's gaze follows.

He turns and smiles as if nothing has been said. 'Spying on us, Goldie?'

Lorcan looks at me pensively, wondering if I heard it all.

Throwing him off course, I stroll into the room, rolling my eyes. 'I don't need to spy on you to know you most likely talked about how much you love yourself.'

'I think you've just unlocked another power from Solaris.' Darius chuckles as I reach him. He crosses his arms over his chest as he dips his head closer to mine. 'All knowing.'

I squash down the flutter in my stomach with a haughty grin.

The atmosphere turns sour when my eyes find Lorcan's; I can almost taste the acid burning my tongue. Darius notices himself, his smile fading as he takes a step away from me.

I wonder if it is his way of wanting not to rub what he and I have in Lorcan's face.

'Lorcan was telling me how we should approach the public today,' Darius says.

Lorcan's expression turns sombre for a second, but he shakes it away with a clear of his throat. 'Yes, um—' He scratches the back of his head, not looking directly at us. 'It's important you show them they can be safe under your command.'

'I am not looking to command.' Darius sounds so serious that Lorcan sighs and runs a hand over his face in exhaustion.

'That's a problem we keep encountering with him.'

And Darius calls me stubborn.

'Command is just another way of controlling others.' Darius turns his back to us as he walks towards the windows and leans his his arm over his forehead, watching the garden outside, the dying trees . . . the barracks now occupied by shifters and surviving Venators. 'That is exactly what Sarilyn and Aurum did.'

Lorcan looks as if he is close to losing his patience. A vein pops up on his forehead. 'How do you expect to be king if you refuse to keep order in Emberwell—'

'Unity,' Darius simply says. 'Make them understand that dragons, goblins, pixies, humans and more are all the same.' The window reflects his gold eyes as he never takes his eyes off what's outside. Darius never wanted to be king, and now it feels like his only choice.

I draw closer to him, placing my hand on his arm. The touch makes him turn to look at me. 'What if they don't want to understand?'

A shadow of pride and longing reaches his eyes before they snap to Lorcan. My head swivels to see him staring at us both. 'Then,' Darius says, 'we give them time. And no matter what, we will always try to help the people of Emberwell get back what they lost, whether they approve of my future reign or not.'

CHAPTER THIRTY-SIX

I'm poked and prodded as Leira and Aelle fit me into Sarilyn's gown. Aelle works the laces at the back as Leira fluffs out the bottom of the silk skirt.

Tibith is on one of the settees watching, while Freya is behind me, pinning all my hair up with pins and pearls, which I had told her not to. I didn't want the three of them to treat me like they were my maids, but they were just as headstrong as me.

'Well, you look like you can't breathe.' Iker chuckles, barging into the dressing chamber with Illias, Idris and Link behind him.

I cut him a glare, holding on to the ornate dresser as if my life depended on it.

'I can still fight you in this,' I warn him, and his palms fly up in defence.

'Don't listen to him, Nara,' Freya laughs. 'He's just upset that Tibith ate his breakfast this morning.'

I laugh, but it sounds like a wheeze as I try to control my breathing. Idris, for once, smiles as Illias bursts out into raucous laughter alongside a giggling Tibith.

'It was delicious bread, Mrs Nara!' Tibith kicks his little feet as my brothers settle beside him on the settee. 'I couldn't help it! Darry told me that any bread I see will always be mine!'

'Perhaps you should tell that husband of yours that bread is meant for sharing.' Iker looks at me pointedly.

Idris grumbles something under his breath, frowning as he shifts his big frame against the cushioned seats. A twinge of regret plucks at my heart, knowing how devastated my brothers were to find out Darius and I had married in secret. Most of all, Idris. Like most families, they wished to have witnessed their youngest sister marry without the fear of certain death.

They didn't disapprove of Darius; they admired him, in fact. After the fight at the arena, Darius was there to make sure they got everything they needed, but that didn't stop them from being their usual overprotective brothers, always wanting to talk with him in private.

'Oh, how I remember the first year of marriage,' Aelle says wistfully, giving Leira a sideways glance as she turns me to face them.

Leira chuckles, fixing my cleavage. 'It is still that way.'

'I would rather not think of my sister in a marriage at all,' Idris mutters, and I don't think he intended for all of us to hear, yet we did.

Freya chuckles lightly, waltzing over to me in her usual beloved purple attire. She holds a circular silver piece of jewellery shaped like a sleeping dragon in her hands. It is the same one I was looking at earlier today.

'I thought this would be fitting,' she says, rising on her tiptoes as she places it around my neck.

I touch the carved scales that rest above my collarbones, and both Aelle and Leira move out of the way to reveal the mirror at the end of the room. I look so small from this angle. The dress, however, almost seems to swallow me up with its thick layers of gold.

'Show them you're the queen of dragons.' Freya squeezes my upper arms with a grin as she admires me in the mirror.

I tilt my head to look at her. 'You know I am not.'

She gives me a look resembling Leira's expression whenever she tells someone off. The same dark brows furrow as she pouts. 'Fine, then, the queen of all creatures.' She is back to grinning. '*Solaris.*'

The contents inside my stomach jump with a nervous thrill. In many ways, it still feels wrong to be called that when I am not the true Solaris. I am only part of her, a reincarnation, yes, a vessel, of course, but not a deity to be worshipped.

I glance back at the mirror, thoughtfully tracing my fingertips over the dragon necklace. Below it, Darius's coin still rests upon my skin. I smile. 'I like the sound of being queen of all creatures.'

'Once a Trapper, now a keeper,' Illias comments, strutting over with Link clinging to his arm and my other two brothers right behind. 'You look stunning, Nara.'

I smile, clutching his hand in mine and giving it a slight pinch.

Idris's gaze then lingers on Freya, his stoic expression not matching his words as he says, 'That gown is very nice on you, Freya.'

She smiles like she didn't expect him to say that. 'Thank you.'

Idris nods, his eyes flitting elsewhere while Freya unabashedly continues staring at him.

On any other occasion, I would smile proudly that Idris managed to say something other than a complaint, but then I see Iker's despondent gaze beside him, and my heart feels for them both.

'Right.' Leira snaps her fingers, and Freya seems to jerk out of her trance as she turns to her. 'We should head to where Darius must now be.' She and Aelle try to usher my brothers and Tibith out, but Idris is a mass of unmovable walls. After a moment, she gives up and shakes her head. 'Don't take too long.' She points at him as everyone else leaves. 'I mean it.'

I chuckle, watching as she slowly closes the door, and I turn to my brother. A frown splits my forehead as his eyes roam my poised hairstyle and lightly dusted cheeks. 'What is it?'

He shakes his head. 'It's just that the first time I visited you here in the city, I thought you looked so different. A Venator in training, your fighting garments, the friends you'd made . . . But I was wrong.'

I don't know what to say. A lot has changed since I stepped foot in this city, and I can't tell if Idris hates that or is just learning to accept it as we go along.

'I mean,' he says, 'you are still you, just . . . grown up.'

Ah. Now I see.

The side of my lips quirks as I fight my own battle not to tear up. 'I still love to carve – when I'm not fighting against my enemies, of course.'

He chuckles briefly with a nod. 'And you still love strawberry pies. Even when I tell you that too much of it will upset your stomach.'

I gasp dramatically, swatting his arm as we begin laughing. It quells my nervous heart to see him content. It was always Idris's job to make his siblings happy. He just never realised I was trying to do the same thing.

As our laughs fade, his expression softens into something melancholic. He glances at the ring on my finger and sighs. 'I would have liked to walk you down the aisle, Nara.'

'I know,' I whisper. 'Maybe one day, if the world is better and healed, we could do it all again.'

He nods, not looking me in the eye, as if he knows that might be too much of a far-fetched idea.

A lump bubbles inside my throat, and I try desperately to swallow it.

Idris kisses the top of my head, telling me he will see me in the throne room, and leaves.

I sigh, smoothing down my gown, and follow him shortly afterwards.

I'm near the throne room when I hear gentle footsteps behind me. I pause. So do they.

I slowly turn to find Ruvyn. His hands are behind his back as he rocks back and forth on his feet.

I huff out a laugh. 'Ruvyn, I told you already. You don't need to treat me any differently.'

After I wrote to Arlayna to make sure Ruvyn's mother was safe, he decided to stay with me out of gratitude, respect and a keen desire to now serve me.

'It's hard not to, Lady Nara,' Ruvyn murmurs, bowing his head as a soft strand of dark hair falls over his left eye.

I start to protest, but Lorcan appears from far down the hall.

'Nara.' He inclines his head before sliding his gaze at Ruvyn.

Ruvyn takes the hint that Lorcan wants to speak with me and retreats to the other side of the hallway, far out of hearing distance but not so far that he cannot see me.

'Are you all prepared?' Lorcan asks. He's still wearing Aerian clothes.

'Yes,' I lie, and he believes it.

He nods, allowing an awkward spark to linger between us as if he is uncertain where to go from here.

I stare at him, like I always do, unsure of what to think. Since finding out that Hira was his real mother, he hasn't spoken about it, and I wonder if it is because he feels that he cannot.

To this day, I still remember him telling me about the mother he thought was his. How she died in childbirth and never met her. Knowing it was Hira rather than someone else makes all the sense in the world.

They might not resemble one another in their looks. In fact, they couldn't be more opposite in that aspect, but their phoenix side . . . they embodied one another through fire, and now they will never get that again – all because of Aurum.

'We've made sure that the perimeter of the castle is guarded by shifters,' he starts to say. 'I know we do not have actual guards that can—'

'Why are you here?' I blurt out, shaking my head at my inept way of speaking to him. 'I mean . . . after everything, you could have returned to Aeris, yet you chose to stay here with us.'

He releases a somewhat tiresome sigh. 'The Aerian leaders weren't all that impressed after I decided to come to rescue you,' he says. 'Instead of mourning Hira, I came here. I wanted to mend things with Darius, but . . .'

'It's proving more difficult than you thought,' I say as he shrugs, pretending it doesn't bother him when it does.

Darius is still coming to terms with who Gus was to him and the role he must step into now that Aurum or Sarilyn isn't here.

'He does need you,' I tell Lorcan. 'I think . . . he needs you more than anyone. It's just that—'

'He's struggling.'

While I may have some insight into what happened during those three months Darius was with Aurum, the undeniable truth remains – I didn't live it the way he did. He was breaking, and like the Galgr said, there is nothing to fix that, but there is a way to heal it, maybe with time or all of us here at his side.

'I think it's time we went in,' Lorcan says.

I look back at Ruvyn, nodding, though it is hardly a nod in the first place, as my mind only thinks of Darius.

Lorcan walks past me and I turn to him before I can stop myself. 'Lorcan?' I call out. He jerks his head back to look at me. 'Thank you for not leaving us behind. It means a lot to him. To us.'

A whisper of a smile flickers across his lips as he bows and walks towards the throne room.

CHAPTER THIRTY-SEVEN

As soon as I enter the throne room, Freya jumps on me, eagerly grabbing my arm as she drags me through the hall. She makes sure not to go near the still-broken pillars smashed along the floor or certain walls where the structure might break if one of us even leans against it.

'We really need to get this place fixed,' she mutters, her brows screwed up as dust dances through the air where the littlest bit of sun fixates on the centre.

'We haven't necessarily had time,' I quip.

She chuckles as we look at each other.

'Witchy,' a deep, teasing voice says.

I whip my head back around as Darius walks over to us from the open balcony. My chest burns, and I have to swallow hard when I look at what he is wearing.

Just how I dressed up to receive the people of Emberwell, he did too. The problem is nothing can ever look bad on him. A simple black jacket with gold thread to match my dress and dragon scales sewn into the epaulettes showcases just how devastatingly beautiful he is.

'Darius,' Freya says, eyeing us both in amusement. 'Take good care of her. You know I still can't forgive you both for marrying without me there.'

I chuckle, patting her arm before letting go. She strides off in the other direction where my brothers and Tibith are.

'Always a pleasure seeing you, Freya,' Darius calls out to her, but his eyes are only on me. His gaze languidly sweeps over my dress as he steps towards me. My breath quickens. 'You look horrid,' he murmurs. 'I should really rip that dress off you. Save me the trouble of having to look at it.'

I smile up at him. 'I could say the same about you, but I would much rather get rid of those trousers.' My eyes slip to the bulge suddenly straining against his dark clothes, and a devilish grin sneaks up on my lips. 'They're not your colour.'

Darius's gaze drills into mine like I am about to be his undoing at any moment. I can see behind his ravenous stare that he desperately wants to grab me and take me out of here.

The torment inside him excites me as I grin even wider, my nerves about what will soon happen on the balcony fading into nothingness.

'Stop right there.' I hear Rydan's dramatic flair of a voice from the side, and I curse him internally. 'Am I witnessing Ambrose turning all soft for someone? Or do I say "Rivernorth" now, since you are married?'

I slowly turn to face him with a glare, but he doesn't seem to care.

'Have to say, I'm too used to Ambrose . . . Either way, this is nothing if not a miracle! Albeit I am jealous, but then again, can you just imagine the amount of people who are crying on the inside knowing the Golden Thief is taken?' He shakes his head with incredulity. 'I mean, I should know; I am one of them.'

I might just strangle him.

Darius just half smiles, half laughs, enjoying this, and now I might just strangle both of them.

'Rydan.' Lorcan comes to my aid, his expression blank and unfriendly. 'Are you done?'

'Speaking of jealousy.' Rydan bunches his lips to the side, whispering towards us before he spins on his feet. 'Lorcan! You look dashing. Being a phoenix really suits you.'

Lorcan doesn't react to Rydan's blatant teasing remarks. 'Go prepare the dragons.'

'Why can't Link do that?'

'Link is out. Crowd control.'

I can tell Rydan is pouting.

'Then what about Freya? Many of the whelps love her, or even Tibith. Look at him. He has no care in the world right now—'

'You are about to make me lose my—'

'Rydan,' Darius interjects before Solaris forbids Lorcan murder Rydan in front of us all. 'Why don't you go see to it that the dragons are being well kept? I trust the shifters are doing so, but I can't have them trying to feast on the people of Emberwell. It could ruin my image.'

Rydan's eyes widen comically. He straightens and places a hand on his chest. 'It will be my honour, Your Excellency.'

I almost snort as he bows and loses his balance. I turn to find Lorcan hasn't moved from his position at all. He lets himself smile for a split second before following Rydan out of the hall.

'Is he always like this?' Darius asks.

I sigh with a hint of amusement. 'Afraid so.'

He chuckles. 'Then I like him.'

When we turn to each other, I forget how much air he knocks out of me with just the way he looks.

Then my eyes slip to where Leira and Aelle are standing by the balcony, scanning the crowd from behind the intact pillars. By the nervous looks they are sharing with each other, the sight of it must not be comforting.

'Are you ready?' Darius says softly to me.

I glance back at him. 'No,' I answer.

His smile quite doesn't reach his eyes. 'Neither am I.' He reaches for my arm, pulling me close so that I can smell that rosewood scent mixed with something so muscular and primal that I want to bask in it like one would in the sun.

He kisses me, hard and without a thought that everyone including my brothers is in here. It's a kiss that tells me he needs it to survive all of this. When we pull apart, I'm left panting, aching for more. I grasp the collar of his jacket, my forehead touching his chin.

'Now I am,' he says, his voice full of yearning.

Suddenly, so am I.

Darius doesn't wait for someone to announce us to the public. He grabs my hand and takes me with him towards the balcony.

Leira looks at us in confusion, and before she can say anything, we have already stepped out.

My stomach plunges with unease. I had never realised how wide the castle's courtyard was before. I suppose after spending most of my time worrying about other things, I didn't notice it when I stood here at night on Noctura.

The civilians from the city extend far as out into the central area, past the ruins of the Neoma tree and the sectors of the castle. From where Darius and I stand, it looks as though we are staring into a pit of fire with red jackets, orange frocks and bright clothing further back. The clothes are the only bright part of Emberwell as the grass, trees and flowers around wilt.

As some start to spot us, they quieten, and others murmur to each other.

My hands are clammy in Darius's hold, but he doesn't let go. Instead, he tightens his grip.

So many are staring at me like I am pointless, disgusted that I should even be wearing something as elegant as this dress.

Or perhaps that is my own thoughts.

Lorcan and my brothers quickly come out, flanking Darius and me. The crowd looks murderous. Our aim is to reach an understanding between mortals and dragons, but the atmosphere here feels more like a public execution – *our* execution.

The atmosphere crackles with tension as I clear my throat and scan the sea of hostile faces aimed at us.

'Thank you all for coming today.' I sneak a glance at Darius to find his jaw clenched and his breathing uneven. I steady myself with a slow exhale. 'We know that for the past few days, things have quickly deteriorated, not only in Emberwell but all of Zerathion.'

I am met with a few scoffs and murmurs from people who disagree. A priestess wearing the colours of fire stands at the front of the courtyard, shaking her head with her followers.

Darius steps forward, our hands tightly joined as he decides it is his turn. 'After Aurum's defeat, we can only promise to protect—'

A shout erupts from the crowd, and then another says, 'You killed my husband.' The young woman's finger is aimed straight towards Darius. 'Bit him under Aurum's command! How can you promise us anything?'

Darius tenses, his free hand clenching at his side. He glances over at me as if expecting me to look at him with the same disgust as other people.

Bit him under Aurum's command.

My heart begins to crumble into ash.

Darius looks away, back out into the crowd. 'It was not my choice.' his tone carries an undertone of anger, not at the woman but at himself.

'He's a monster,' someone else says, and my anger floods me.

'He's not—' I try to say, but when I glance at Darius he looks lost, like he accepts it.

Lorcan steps towards me, a warning brewing in his jade eyes.

I don't care.

'He is not a monster.' I raise my chin to the crowd. 'He has done more to save your lives than you could ever do for someone you know.' I'm teetering on the edge of rage, staring out at everyone's faces that I can make out.

A man from the other side pushes past a few people, yelling out, 'He's a thief and a killer, related to that psychopathic shifter! And you are nothing but a commoner who ruined Queen Sarilyn's reign. Why should we listen to anything you both say when our world is in ruins because of you!'

The crowd cheers, and now Idris steps up as if he is willing to say something himself to defend us. I raise my palm to his chest to stop him when a three-toned whistle pierces the air, and the sounds of distant roars become clearer.

Dozens of our saved dragons fly overhead in the courtyard as the civilians scream. I look at Darius and realise he is the one who called upon them.

Fernah soon joins us, her wings flapping as she descends beside the ledge of our balcony. Others perch themselves on pillars, staring down at the fearful humans.

When the people's cries dwindle upon seeing that the dragons aren't attacking, Darius steps in.

'You can call me every name in the book,' he says. His expression looks calm, but his voice – it's one I could fear. 'I encourage it even. I *am* a thief. I *am* a killer. And I am also related to Aurum Rivernorth. Nothing will ever change that.'

'Darius—' I whisper.

'But these dragons.' He gestures to them all around us, Meratis, Umbratis and Ardentis. 'They are not harmful. As a matter of fact, they are just like all of you. They feel, care, hate and love just the same.'

No one dares to speak up this time.

'All you have known under Sarilyn's command is that you should fear our kindness, and maybe you should. But we aren't so different from you all. So, go on, hate me all you want.' There's a cruel smile to him as he spreads his arms to the sides. 'I implore you to. There is no successful reign without a hater now and then. But just know, I already promised myself one thing, and that was that I will protect you and this world, and I will do it at all costs with her' – he slides a glance my way, his gaze softening – 'by my side.'

I can't help but stare at him, partly bewildered and partly in awe.

He grabs my hand again, his usual shameless smile paving his lips. 'Ladies, gentlemen,' he says. '*Haters*, have a nice evening.'

We don't get to answer any questions as he turns us around and stalks back inside the castle. I just manage to hear a protest from the crowd as the doors close, and I glimpse Lorcan's pale and stressed face.

CHAPTER THIRTY-EIGHT

As I shake my head, I can't help but pace back and forth across the sitting room. Darius seems more composed than I am as he leans against the wall by the windows, Tibith resting on his shoulder.

No one else is here with us. Right after our public speech, I made sure to send everyone away. The thought of Rydan and Lorcan or my brothers talking to me at the same time would have sent me into a nervous collapse. They have seen too many of my tragedies to bear another one, so the last thing I want to do is do it in their presence.

I let out a frustrated breath, longing to pull my gown apart with my bare hands as I nearly trip over the bulk of the skirt. 'This is ridiculous,' I mutter, turning to face Darius. 'Why did we even dress up when we know they still don't see us as anything but the reason this world is a mess?'

'I suppose the strategy to blend in wasn't so horrible when we initially considered it.'

I shake my head, knowing it was a foolish plan to begin with, yet

Darius and I still went along with it, even when, deep down, we knew the people wouldn't listen to us straight away.

'You're not really mad about the gown.' Darius shoots me a glance. The sun is setting, casting a golden glow over half of his face as the other half lies in shadow. 'You're mad about something else.' He steps off the ledge and walks up to me. When I try to look away from his beguiling stare, he delicately hooks a thumb beneath my chin and turns my head. 'What is it?' His soft, hushed voice is too irresistible. Despite myself, I immediately open my mouth to answer.

'When they called you a monster,' I say quietly, 'it felt like you believed them. You know that it isn't true, right?'

He pauses for a second as if my statement has surprised him. I feel his fingertips running over my jaw as he nods and visibly swallows.

He does that lately.

If a thought bothers him, he doesn't like to bring me down along with it. And while he is usually good at hiding it behind a façade of witticism and distracting me with his touch, this time I can see right through it.

Then it hits me.

Darius has only ever known what it is like to be hated, to be called a monster, and he thinks this will always be true.

Grasping his hand, I place it on my chest. 'Darius—'

Ruvyn bursts through the double doors, his face flushed. 'I tried to make them wait—' Following him, a procession of men clad in regal blue uniforms stride past with spears made of shells as they pave the way for another figure.

Darius carefully turns in the other direction, placing his hand on the small of my back as the man ahead looks at us with a less-than-friendly stare. In the golden room, his crown made of broken lapis lazuli shards shines, and the stark contrast between his rich, bronzed skin and white frosted hair is mesmerizing.

It's the ruler of Undarion.

I know because the first time I laid eyes on him was on the night of Noctura. Back then, he was laughing while in conversation with others. He looked so welcoming yet unapproachable for someone like me. Now, the level of disgust in his expression makes him look . . . ordinary.

'So, this is what Emberwell is faced with now.' His voice doesn't suit him. It's higher than expected. 'A criminal as the future king, and his whore.'

The insult stings my skin, and I consider my response, but Darius has already snapped into action. His anger is so palpable I can feel it vibrate onto me through his hand.

'I suggest you be careful of how you speak about my wife, Hedris,' Darius says almost menacingly. 'I would hate for your kingdom to be without a leader.'

Hedris's eyes – too pale to be blue – enlarge. 'My, my, you haven't been crowned yet, and you are already trying to threaten those above you.'

My fists clench at the lack of respect he blatantly has for us. Ruvyn looks over at me, waiting for my approval to kick him and his lackeys out.

I shake my head, signalling for him to leave. If something goes wrong, he can alert my brothers.

He seems to hesitate at my request for a second before he storms away.

When Hedris sees Tibith peeping around the corner of our legs, his eyes drop to the floor. 'How intriguing,' he says. 'We exterminated that species in our kingdom because they served no purpose for us.'

As a reflex, Darius and I step forward to shield Tibith.

'What is it you want?' I demand. Arlayna had already forewarned me that the people of Undarion were furious over the treaty. They were rule followers. Always have been – unlike the Aerian's.

Hedris looks at me. There is no kindness behind his eyes. 'I want you out of here. Neither of you are fit to rule over a kingdom, we already witnessed that today.'

I scoff. 'And what? You take over instead?'

He considers it while his men around him cast sly glances at each other. 'I have an army at my disposal, loyal followers, and I'm respected among others. What do you have, except for people who cannot differentiate between a dessert fork and a fish fork?'

'Well, of course, you would know,' Darius says, and by the amusement in his tone, I can tell he is about to make things worse. 'You can't be eating your own kind with a dessert fork. At least have a little respect for your people.'

Hedris's face darkens. 'I am giving you a warning here. Stand down and hand the reign over to me—'

'Or you'll have my head on a platter. I've heard it all before.' Darius sounds bored, a smirk playing on his lips. 'So, I think I'll pass.'

Furious, Hedris's nostrils flare. 'You're making a mistake here.'

I take a step away from Darius, narrowing my eyes. 'What is it that you would do differently if you were to take over instead of us?'

Hedris gives me the side eye and blinks as if he hadn't anticipated me speaking up once more.

'Suggest another treaty so that kingdoms can't so much as communicate with one another?' Again, I move an inch forward, the heaviness of my gown making it hard to walk any quicker. 'Feel more powerful than the rest for ruling two kingdoms rather than one?' I cock my head to the side. 'Tell me.'

I'm near enough that Hedris's men can attack me at any given moment if Hedris orders it, and even closer, I can see the twitch in his right eye.

'You don't know the first thing about ruling,' he tells me in a quiet, wrathful voice.

'Perhaps.' I lean into his face. He is so much smaller now that I have him in front of me. 'But at least I know how to treat others right.'

That only manages to infuriate him more. To be told that he is worthless, without a heart.

Satisfaction pulls at my lips as I turn to face Darius and Tibith. I can just about make out Darius's smile before it morphs into something furious.

I quickly spin around in time, raise my hand, emitting a bright white light, and twist my fingers in the air, snapping Hedris's hand before he can use his powers to attack me.

He howls in pain, causing his lackeys to surge forward, swords drawn out at the ready. But their weapons transform into black mist as Darius comes by my side, his hand wielding shadows.

'What are you?' Spit forms around Hedris's mouth as he tries to heal his broken hand with water coming from his fingertips.

I smile and simply say in his face, 'Solaris's vessel.'

'That's impossible,' Hedris hisses, his face contorting into another fierce glare.

One of his men tries to pull out another weapon.

'I wouldn't if I were you,' Darius says casually, lifting his hand and observing the shadows go from finger to finger. 'I forgot how much I missed using magic.' Lethal gold eyes cut to Hedris. 'Think of all the pent-up power I could use if you so much as breathe in her direction.'

Another of Hedris's men audibly gulps, which humours Darius

all the more. Tibith springs past us on all fours and starts growling at Hedris.

Shock flickers across his pained expression as he stares at Tibith.

'You should leave.' There's a condescending tone to my voice as well as a warning.

Hedris brings his furious gaze up to Darius, and something about his silence tells me this is far from over.

He stumbles back, hauling his men along with him while Darius, Tibith and I stare on, making sure they leave.

CHAPTER THIRTY-NINE

After our encounter with the leader of Undarion, I spent the evening in the dining room, eating with my brothers, courtesy of Leira's cooking. Idris, of course, was unimpressed to learn that an Undarion king had insulted me, but by that point, none of it had any significance to me.

Afterwards, walking along the hallways, I head back to mine and Darius's chamber. Cracking the door open, I peek inside and see the golden tassel curtains drawn with Tibith peacefully asleep on Darius's side of the bed. A candle beside the dresser in the corner flickers and crackles, giving me enough light to see that Darius isn't here.

Something in my chest sinks as if someone has tied a sandbag to the end.

I close the door quietly enough to ensure Tibith doesn't awaken, then rush back down the halls, searching for Darius. As if his scent carries a beacon, I come to a stop outside the throne room. I look in and find him leaning back against the throne – the only thing not ruined from our attack to free Darius – his fist beneath his jaw and a furrowed stare at the floor.

The soft patter of my boots is the only sound that echoes in the vast hall. Darius doesn't look up, but he knows I am here.

Tonight, the moon looks exceptionally bright. A sight we didn't think would happen for a while after the Isle of Elements.

Staring at the only light source inside the throne room, I say, 'Why aren't you asleep?'

'Beds are uncomfortable,' he mumbles.

'And that throne is any better?'

'Well, I am supposed to be the future king. I should start getting used to it.'

His irony doesn't ever slip past me. I approach him, slower this time, and he looks up at me.

'You know you do not have to take over,' I whisper. 'If being king isn't what you—'

'It is not so simple to give up a crown, Nara,' he mutters. Our gazes lock on to each other for a few tense seconds. Then he sighs and looks towards the moon. 'You know, if it were a normal night after stealing from one of the jewellery shops, I'd be drinking away at Gus's den.' He smirks to himself. 'He'd probably tell me something along the lines of how I need to better myself. You know, the typical things a father should say to their son when they're rebelling.'

Now I understand.

The guilt is slowly eating away at him.

'They say it's honourable for us to have one of our dragons use their fire to burn us after our passing, but I couldn't even give that to him.' He leans forward, dropping his head in his hands. 'There is nothing left of him. *Nothing.*'

I lower myself in front of him and try to pry his hands away, but he doesn't let me as he shakes me away, saying 'No,' in such a broken voice.

'Darius,' I say helplessly. I'm so used to him being the one there to protect me, humour me and build me up, that this hurts too much. Sadness and empathy wash over me as I stare at him, wanting to pull him away from the throne and leave.

Something wet smacks against my skin, and I look up between the gaps in the broken ceiling as it leaks, with sudden rain dripping down onto us.

'We need to go.' I press the palms of my hands against Darius's knees. I don't care so much about getting drenched; I only care for him. 'Darius—'

'I lied to you that day,' he cuts me off abruptly, lifting his head. I still. 'That day in the dungeons.' There's a gloss in his eyes, brightening the gold rings around the iris.

I think I know what he is going to tell me.

The moment when I asked him if he remembered what Aurum did to him, he told me no.

I brace myself for his answer. He can see the fear written on my face.

'I remember every damn thing that happened,' he whispers, but the clarification just makes my chest burn. 'And I wish I couldn't. I wish I couldn't remember a damn thing.'

My exhale sounds like a sob as I close my eyes.

'I wish I could forget the faces of each person I had to kill against my will.' His voice wavers. 'How they begged and pleaded for their life, to not be bitten.'

I shake my head as if that will make me get rid of this heaviness inside my heart.

'I'm broken, Nara.'

My body quivers, but not from the rain, as the Galgr's words come back to me in the most haunting way.

'*If he is breaking, then he must do so alone.*'

'I'm the one thing I desperately didn't want to be,' Darius says. When I open my eyes, I see the rain mixing with his tears.

My arms wind around his neck with an instinctive tenderness. He hugs me back tighter, his body trembling as I shut my eyes, determined to take every little bit of pain away from him. But I know I can't.

I can't fix him.

I don't *want* to fix him.

I just want him to fly.

'He can't do any of that to you any more,' I tell him without a care that my silk nightgown is entirely soaked.

'It will never leave my mind,' he says into the crook of my neck, his breath shaking as he exhales.

I tighten my grip around his neck, my knees aching from kneeling for too long. Yet it doesn't matter to me. Not one bit. 'What else did he make you do?' I whisper, not eager to find out, but needing him to not keep it all to himself any longer.

It takes him a minute to answer me, and when he does, his voice sounds like he's been screaming for hours. 'He would coerce me into using a blade on myself, making me count how many times I could do it before I lost consciousness.'

The confession flies at me like a dagger and I flinch in his arms as my anger surges. I tamp it down for his sake.

'I tried,' he says. 'I tried so hard not to let him in, but every single day, I failed.'

My exhale comes out shaky. 'That time I came down to the Aerian dungeon, you were counting,' I explain to myself more than him. 'It was your body's way of remembering.'

He nods, running a hand through my hair.

It should have been me, not him.

And though I wouldn't have survived to the extent that Darius could during that time, I would have endured it all the same.

Darius and I are silent, embracing one another for a long time; two souls longing for a better future and a better life together where no one suffers.

I release him, leaning back. The rain has subsided; our clothes are soaked and sticking to our bodies like a second layer of skin. Through the subtle silver light, Darius looks incredible. The water has only made him glow ten times more. It doesn't matter whether he believes he is broken or not; he is the moon, carrying the celestial scars that shape our night.

He caresses the side of my face, cupping my cheek as he stares at me. I tilt my head slightly into his hand, letting my lips touch his skin.

Pondering on my past, I say, 'The day my mother died, she told me she felt better.' With a gentle tug, I pull his hand away from my face and clutch it instead. 'She even got up and dressed herself. I thought everything was back to normal . . . I thought that maybe the following day, she could take me to the village where they sold quality carving tools.' I'm not looking at Darius. My vision is a cloudy haze as I lose focus. 'I also remember arguing with Idris that day, telling him I was going out to capture butterflies. He said he didn't want me going out when my mother wasn't stable. I told him he was blind not to see that she was better. My mother didn't want me to go out either; she wanted to spend time with me, and I suppose, in her own way, she knew she was dying. She just didn't want to tell me.'

When I do decide to glance at Darius, he's already staring at me with thundering intensity. He must be wondering why I am telling him this, but either way, he wants to hear it. He wants to *understand*.

'I never did end up catching butterflies that day,' I say. 'But I did pick up an antique teacup for my mother. It was my way of saying sorry that I still left for the day. Only when I got back, she had already succumbed to her illness.'

Darius leans forward, shaking his head. 'Goldie—'

'I broke that teacup.' Memories of the ceramic shards all over the floor cut into my heart. 'Out of anger, grief, love.'

A spark of acknowledgement crosses his eyes, and he finally sees what I am trying to say. 'Did you fix it?'

I smile, shaking my head. 'No. I got a new one and broke that one too.'

He chuckles as if he should have known that was something I would do.

'I broke it and used the pieces as well as the scraps from other teapots to put them all together to craft my own teapot.' I laugh. 'It was hideous, absolutely hideous, but it was *mine* to call ugly.'

A glint of amusement tips the side of his mouth into a smirk. 'Are you trying to say I'm hideous, Goldie?'

I laugh, annoyed yet pleased to see his old self. 'Always,' I whisper, grinning.

I let us bask in this small moment of laughter, before it subsides and we're left in silence.

I lick my lips, then press three fingers to his heart. His chest rises and falls at a symphonising rate. 'I don't care if you are broken,' I say, staring up into his eyes. 'Or if you can't forgive yourself for what has happened in your life. I only care that we are here together, we have a purpose, and we cannot and will never be daunted.'

The expression on his face is so serious, yet the look in his eyes as he stares at me is full of admiration.

Without a word, he slips his palm behind my neck and pulls me towards him. Our lips almost touch as he rests his forehead against mine and closes his eyes. The warmth of his breath as he sighs sends a welcoming shiver down my legs. 'I'd be so lost without you in this world, Nara.'

I smile, whispering against his lips, 'Then it's a good thing you found me.'

He answers me by capturing my mouth with a slow and lingering kiss. Without another thought, I wrap my arms around his neck and melt against him.

We are both still drenched from the rain, and the feel of his clothes sticking to his muscled body makes me ache for more. Unbuttoning his shirt, I run my fingers down his chest, sighing into his mouth as his tongue slides in, tasting me and savouring every drop.

'I want you,' I breathe, rummaging for a way to unhook his breeches. 'All of you. Always and for ever.'

I receive a low groan in response, his hand fisting the back of my hair right as his cock springs free from his trousers. Straight and ready for me.

Our heavy breaths drown out the sounds of distant rumbling, and I stare at him in wonder, almost salivating.

Like a cautious animal experimenting with something new, I reach for him, cupping his wide length. He grunts in pleasure, growing thicker.

'You don't need to do anything, Goldie,' he says, his voice low and heavy.

I look up at him, my breasts tightening at the sight of his hooded eyes.

He has probably done this with other men as much as he has with women.

I shake my head, determined I can do it. I *want* to do it. I *want* to learn on my own.

Leaning forward, I part my lips and gaze up from beneath my lashes, meeting his eyes.

I start off slow, swirling my tongue against the tip.

His head drops back against the throne, and I cannot tell if it's beads from the rain or sweat that trail down his abdomen.

'If you keep teasing me like this, I'm going to lose it, Goldie.'

I pause, smiling with my tongue still out. I grip his shaft, squeezing it gently and making his hips jerk at the sensation.

His reaction only makes me want to do it more, to show him a side of me no one has ever seen and will never experience except for him.

'Nara—'

I take him into my mouth, cutting his words off. He swears under his breath, and for just one moment, I'm lost, not knowing what to do or how to please him, but as he rocks gently against me, I find my rhythm. Slow and languidly.

He fists my hair between his fingers, writhing beneath me. Deep moans release from him, and I continue sucking and sliding my lips up and down him until he is shaking.

Madness takes over me, my own body betraying me as it aches for his touch on me, too.

As my movements quicken, his breaths become choppy, and his legs tighten up against me.

I know he is nearing the edge, but just when it seems like he is about to give in, he summons the strength to resist and effortlessly lifts me onto his waist. I squeal in delight as he surprises me with his sudden action, allowing him to rise while my legs remain securely wrapped around him.

He switches us around, my nightgown gently gathered at my thighs, with my legs gracefully elevated upon his shoulder and his face buried between my thighs.

I almost let out a scream but stifle the sound with the back of my hand, knowing the echoes might alert someone.

My desires consume me, driving me to move with an intensity that matches Darius's strokes.

With a swift motion, he tears my nightgown apart, revealing my wet breast. I'm squirming and panting as his tongue dances along my throbbing centre.

I say his name like a prayer as his touch caresses my body, and the palm of his hand traces a path across my skin, up my abdomen, chest and, finally, neck. I lean my head back against the throne as he firmly grasps my throat, holding me in place.

'I love you,' I whisper, and he pauses. I almost protest once again but he leans over me, the tip of him nearing my entrance before he slides into me.

I gasp at the sensation as his forehead rests against mine.

'I will never tire of hearing you say that,' he says with each thrust.

I bite my lip. 'And you?'

'You already know what I feel.' His movements become faster, my pleasure reaching its peak. 'No word will ever suffice for what my love for you is, Goldie.'

My heart soars.

'My Crello,' I say.

'My Solaris,' he whispers.

And right then, we lose ourselves to each other, over and over again.

CHAPTER FORTY

T he air is brisk and harsh today.

I'm feeding some of the dragons cooked meat. The Ardenti seem to prefer it raw, likely due to their ability to burn it themselves. Fernah enjoys it when I feed it right into her mouth, and I chuckle as she swallows. She seems harmless, though she could so easily have bitten my hand right off.

Everyone else is in the castle fields. Freya is with Iker, laughing at his jokes and smacking him across the chest at whatever foolish thing he might have said. Leira and Aelle are in their own romantic embrace, though their gazes seem sad as they stare at the dried-up trees. I think about telling them what Aurum told me once – that they killed his witch. But then that would be going down a path I shouldn't tamper with since Aurum is no longer here.

On the right, Idris is petting a dragon he has recently gotten close to – an Umbrati named Enox, covered in deep purple scales. The male dragon is the only creature that can make Idris laugh more than once within five minutes.

'What are you, the dragon's personal slave now?' Rydan laughs while walking towards me from the right, with Link and Tibith beside him.

I huff, contemplating whether I should feed Rydan to Fernah. 'Better than ever having to be *your* slave. I'd rather deal with the dragon's droppings.'

Link chuckles, settling down on the crisp yellow grass, as Tibith approaches me.

'Is there bread in there, Mrs Nara?' He stands on his tiny paws, trying to look inside the bucket I'm holding.

I raise it higher, not wanting to make him queasy from all the fresh meat. 'Sorry, Tibith.' I tilt my head apologetically at him. 'I'm sure Darius will get you some.' I cast a glance out into the fields, finding him right away as he strolls out of the castle garden doors, freshly bathed and wearing a black cotton shirt as if it were not cold outside. *Dragon pig*, I think with a smile. 'There he is now.'

Tibith gasps with delight just as Darius spots me from afar. The side of his lips tilts upwards, reminding me of last night's *activities*.

I burn bright red.

'Darry, Darry, Darry—' Tibith rolls around me before catapulting himself towards Darius.

I watch the tender moment of them reuniting as Darius laughs, drops onto the grass and takes Tibith into his arms.

Joy permeates the recesses of my heart, causing its rhythm to beat more vividly than ever. And when Darius's eyes find mine, my heartbeat intensifies.

I place the bucket down with a smile and take up a spot between Rydan and Link. Tibith has now retaken Darius's attention, pouncing on him.

Fernah's whelps circle me, Naryx pulling at my boot while his sister Zuru growls at him. I'm smiling blissfully at their interaction. A sibling bond always gets to me.

'Have you gone to see Sarilyn yet?' Rydan asks me, taking a wad of grass into his hands.

I drag back a breath, the cold air prickling my skin like tiny needles. 'I've been doing my best to avoid the dungeons,' I say.

The first night Sarilyn was incarcerated, Darius and I spoke for hours about what we should do with her. He hates her for every suffering she has put him through, even worse when he knows what I went through with her. Yet . . . I can't imagine I would be satisfied if she was to die.

I should despise her, but all I feel is pity.

The promise I made her the day before I fought Darius at the arena tastes sour in my mouth. I remember how I wanted to put her through the same payment I'd received from her long ago.

'Lorcan told me she's been asking for you.' Link leans forward, capturing my attention.

'Did he?'

He nods.

'I can't imagine she wants me for anything good,' I mutter, gazing back at Zuru and Naryx, then towards Tibith and Darius, still playfighting in the grass.

We're quiet for a few minutes, the three of us staring out into the fields.

Finally, the silence starts to get to Rydan. 'You know what sucks, Ambrose?' he says. I cock an eyebrow in his direction. 'Feeling like you equate to nothing.'

I frown. *Where has this come from?* 'You don't honestly believe that about yourself, do you?'

Rydan answers me with a shrug, twirling another wad of grass in his hands.

'Lorcan shouted at him,' Link tells me. 'He is just taking his words too literally.'

I shake my head. I'll have to talk to Lorcan later about fixing his patience with others, or with Rydan in this case. No one gets on Lorcan's nerves more than Rydan does. What Lorcan fails to notice is that it's Rydan's way of showing affection.

'It's not because of that,' Rydan mumbles, his already pouty lips jutting out as he stares at the grass. With a sigh of defeat, he looks at me. 'You're going to be queen someday alongside Darius.'

My stomach dips at the image of me wearing the crown Hira had shown me.

'Freya is a witch and learning new ways to cast spells with Leira and Aelle. Your brothers are content just seeing you thrive; Link can't stop kissing Illias in every corner of this castle—'

Link turns bright red, choking on his saliva, but Rydan doesn't seem to care.

'The Venators and shifters are . . .' He pauses and grimaces. 'Well, they're not exactly getting along, but that will likely sort itself out, and I am just here, annoying everyone with my presence.'

Link and I share a glance, guilt weighing us both down.

'Rydan,' I say softly, planting a hand on his shoulder.

'I don't want to lead,' he confesses quickly. 'And I don't wish to become a ruler of anything. But I do want to be something.'

I find myself rubbing my hand along Rydan's back and nodding. I know that feeling all too well. At least I did when I left Emberwell to go in search of the Elemental Stones.

'Why do you think I joined the Venators?' he adds. 'I mean, yes, I hardly took it seriously, but at least I wasn't nothing back then.'

That seems to be the story for many who joined the Venators. What Rydan needs to understand is that he has never been just *nothing*.

I remember the moments he would sneak up on me, figuring certain things out that I would have missed, or calculating what move to do next up against another trainee. He always knew what he was doing; he protected me from bullies, and he didn't leave me when he found out I had gone against Sarilyn.

The flap of a crimson dragon wing from the corner of my eye makes me look to my left. A few of them are brawling, baring their fangs. Then I feel a tickle of fur on my free hand, and I know it is neither Zuru nor Naryx. I glance down and see a scarlet songbird nuzzling its head against my fingers.

I smile. It shouldn't be here; it should be hidden in the woods and the trees with its family. But quickly, I realise that I am family to most animals out here. With the grass becoming inedible for animals and leaves slowly dying, creatures are seeking me for guidance.

Puffing my chest out, I return my gaze towards Rydan. If my future is to protect life, so could his, in many other ways I might not be able to. 'Have you ever considered becoming something along the lines of a Tracker?'

'Tracker,' he says slowly. 'Like the phoenixes?'

I nod, allowing the songbird to perch upon my forefinger. Bringing it closer, I say to Rydan, 'You are quite the solver.'

He grins, excitement returning to the deep brown colour of his eyes. 'I am, aren't I?' But then his smile falls, as if he is realising something. 'But Lorcan would sooner have my head on a stick than let me join the Trackers. I'd also need to be a phoenix to even enter.'

'*Or . . .*' I release the bird into the air, hearing it sing as it flies. 'He might be pleased to have someone at his side.'

Rydan shakes his finger at me. 'That's a good joke, Ambrose. At least you're finally learning how to properly interact with others.'

I nudge his shoulder before noticing how quiet Link is. I lean forward. 'What about you, Link?'

He purses his lips as the harsh air blows golden strands away from his forehead. 'I'm not sure,' he says. 'I'm quite content where I am right now.'

'That's because you have someone worth being happy for,' Rydan teases, but there's a hint of jealousy beneath his tone.

Link frowns at him. 'Not necessarily. Before you guys, I had no one. I was just some frightened orphan until I met you all. I'm just glad I'm not alone any more.'

His words have my heart twisting into a knot, and I look at him with the most loving smile before my gaze lands on his neck as he touches the necklace that Illias gave him long ago.

Rydan heaves out an explicitly long sigh and flops onto his back on the grass with his arms wide open. 'Why must you always be so profound, Link?'

'Because at least one of us has to be.' Link grins at him.

Rydan chuckles, pounding his fist against Link's side, and I laugh along with them. As I smack his hands, Rydan curls up into a ball, pretending he's injured. Link and I are wheezing with laughter before the three of us settle down once again.

We each sigh with a smile.

Then, out of the blue, Rydan asks, 'Do you think Sarilyn switched sides because she knew Nara was a Solaris reincarnation?'

My chest suddenly feels heavy.

'Maybe,' Link says, mystified.

'She's just doing anything to stay alive,' I mutter, wishing we could go back to messing around instead of talking about Sarilyn.

'Or she could genuinely know more than she's let on.' Rydan raises his eyebrows at me. 'She did speak with a seer once, and they are practically impossible to come by unless you capture one of those creatures from Terranos.'

He's thinking of the Galgr.

'*Or . . .*' Link drags out the word. 'If you happen to have a friend who is half witch.'

Rydan waves a hand non-committally. 'A witch telling you a rhyme is hardly the same as a seer—'

'Freya would slap you for that,' Link comments, holding back a smile.

'She's become too comfortable with that hand of hers.' Rydan shudders. 'The other day she hit me because I asked her who she would rather bed, Iker or Idris—'

Oh, Solaris.

Link's mouth drops. 'Why in Solaris's name would you ask her that?'

'I was just trying to help. She has no idea both are pining for her and clearly needs a nudge in the right direction . . .'

Rydan's words trail off when a distant rumble reverberates through the earth. The air vibrates with something ominous, and I clutch the dried grass as my gaze whips to the birds scattering from hidden treetops and the dragons, growling as if sensing danger.

The ground beneath us begins to shudder and convulse, and I take in a sharp gasp of air as Link and Rydan hold on to me. Darius is already running towards us with Tibith panicking on his shoulder. Idris is yelling my name, while Iker covers Freya with his body on the ground, and everyone else scatters inside.

I clench my eyes shut, unable to move from the ground. I hear faraway cries from the city, and I imagine the look of terror in people's eyes as they stumble and seek stability from the things around them.

Our world is in ruins because of you!

Neither of you is fit to rule over a kingdom.

Tell me, if it means saving Zerathion, is the Golden Thief worth dying for?

My gaze snaps wide open at the last whisper of words inside my head, and then, as abruptly as it began, the trembling subsides, leaving a strange stillness in its wake.

Darius slows down to a stop, metres away from us, and I quickly rise to my feet, panting.

'Nara?' Rydan says from below.

'I have to go,' I rush out, my legs stumbling as I make my way towards Darius. He grabs me by my forearms and searches my face with furrowed brows.

'Wait, Nara—' Rydan says, his head peering down beside him. 'The grass.' He sounds bewildered, but there's no time.

I look to my left as my brothers and Freya start jogging towards me. I face Darius, saying in a low voice, 'If my brothers ask where I am going, just tell them I won't be long.'

Rydan says from behind me, 'Wait, Nara, the grass—'

'I'll be back soon!' I yell at them, slipping away from Darius's grip as I run off in the other direction.

CHAPTER FORTY-ONE

The entrance to the dungeons stares right back at me as I stay still, contemplating it all; my memories of staying here, and the damage that caused, never ease. Since Aurum, the cells are emptier than they used to be. Our only prisoner now is Sarilyn.

A fetid smell makes my nostrils twitch, and I shake my head before stepping inside the narrow hallways.

Behind me, Ruvyn says, 'I should warn you; this isn't a place that's safe for you after what just occurred—'

I pause and spin on my heel. He accompanied me to the dungeons, and as much as I am glad, he is taking this role as protector too seriously after the events with Aurum. I need to do this on my own. 'Ruvyn, I'm more than familiar with how the dungeon works and what safety measures to take if this place comes crashing down on me.' I cock an eyebrow as he shuts his mouth. He knows not to argue with me. 'I won't be long.'

He nods, straightening his back and standing tall.

I leave him there and walk quite a distance until I reach Sarilyn's cell. It stands opposite the cell which used to be inhabited by the shifter who fed me information long ago. Now it is long abandoned, with the remains of bones and blood scattering the cobbled ground.

Darius never did kill that shifter when they fought. And I never saw him again. I can only imagine he was shortly after killed by Sarilyn, or even Aurum.

'Naralía.'

My head snaps forward at the sound of Sarilyn's voice.

She appears behind the bars, smiling, though she seems to lack the cunning edge. Her usually luscious long hair is now matted, and dirt and grime cake her dress. Regardless, she still has an ethereal beauty to her.

'Have you finally come to check if I am alive or not?' She grins before falling into a fit of coughs as if she hadn't spoken in weeks, since we locked her in here.

I step towards the bars separating us, the sconces on the wall outside her cell illuminating me enough for her to see me better. 'The day I trapped Aurum inside the Isle of Elements, you helped me. Why?'

Sarilyn leans her head to the side. 'Shouldn't you be out there, protecting your thief and his people?'

I turn away from her. This was a stupid idea, so, so—

'I felt the ground shake down here.'

She doesn't wait for me to look at her. She can likely tell from how still my body is that I'm panicking on the inside.

'It's getting worse, isn't it?'

I drag back an audible breath.

She chuckles. 'Sooner or later, this world will be forgotten, left at the bottom of the ocean to rot.'

I whirl around, angry words on the tip of my tongue that are quickly cut off by someone else's voice.

'Nara,' Darius says firmly. I look over my shoulder as his eyes flit from Sarilyn to me, contemplating whether to drag me away from her or stay.

Sarilyn gasps humorously. 'Oh, look, if it isn't the dashing prince – or should I say "king"?'

He ignores her, looking at me now. 'We shouldn't be down here.'

'Why not?' Sarilyn gets the words out before I can. 'Does it bring back memories?' She pouts mockingly.

I step back, watching Sarilyn and Darius interact. Their tension clouds the dungeons, masking the must already in the air.

Darius's jaw works back and forth as he glares at her. 'Don't.'

When I look at Sarilyn, she is no longer smiling. Her gaze thins and I'm suddenly back to feeling angry over her having witnessed Darius's torture for months.

'Why did you save us?' I ask once again, and this time, the demand in my voice makes her coil back from the bars. Her face hollows, her lips forming into a pout as she sucks on the inside of her cheek. 'Like I told you once, I'm on whichever side I see winning.'

I shake my head, taking a step towards her. 'No, that's not it. You told me once that you saw something in me, enough to believe the words once spoken from a seer, so don't lie to me, Sarilyn. Don't be like Aurum; tell me why.'

There's a poignant pause that lasts a lifetime.

Then, her lips tremble as she smiles. 'Because you're me.' She looks past me to where Darius is. 'It is only that you got the better Rivernorth.'

I steal a glance over my shoulder. Darius watches me thoughtfully from beside one of the lit sconces.

'The one who does love,' Sarilyn says. 'The one who would sacrifice his life just to see you smile.'

Darius's eyes never leave mine. I can see in his gaze the silent promise to Sarilyn's words. And Sarilyn herself, of course, knows this because she saw it. She saw how Darius was, even when Aurum tried to make him forget me, saw how he acted when we were together inside the throne room on the night of Noctura. She's known from the start.

Always.

My heart softens until it's malleable enough to mould in my hands.

'Everything I did to you was out of spite, Naralía.'

I glance at Sarilyn, her throat wobbling as she speaks.

'I wanted to *break* you like I was broken all those years ago,' she says between gritted teeth before stepping back and raising her chin. 'And I will never apologise for that.'

For the first time against Sarilyn, I don't fight off the smile that peels back my lips. It's strange. For someone that I despised with my whole being, I now understand her – maybe even admire her.

I believed for so long that Sarilyn broke me. That day in Melwraith, I cried my soul out to Darius and lost all my confidence. And to this day, I fight with myself. I fight to have hope, not just for me, but for everyone else.

'Thank you,' I whisper, a weight lifting off me.

Her eyes narrow, confusion likely muddling her thoughts. 'For what?'

'For making me see that you're just like everyone else,' I tell her. 'Normal.'

Her lips – no longer carrying the gold gloss she used to wear on them – curl into a slow smile, and something mutual forms between us.

I turn my back to her, now facing Darius. His smirk reassures me that he's proud of how I handled myself. I walk over to him, ready to get out of this place.

'Oh, Golden Thief?' Sarilyn calls out.

We both snap our heads to her, my eyes going round when I see her pull out an object from the skirt of her gown. A hint of gold glints as soon as the firelight from the sconce hits it, and Darius turns to stone.

The Rivernorth pendant.

She passes it through the cell bars, the chain dangling from her fingertips. 'Aurum almost destroyed it when he pried it from that man's hands – Ivarron.'

My mind snaps to the very moment Aurum told me he killed Ivarron. I suck back a sharp breath, shooting Darius a look as he heads towards Sarilyn. He knows how complicated my relationship with Ivarron was, yet that never stopped him from comforting me over his death on the first night in the castle. It must have hit me harder than I thought, considering I was silent for most of the night, but I was also mourning Gus, and Darius cared more about how I felt than how he did.

'Why are you giving it to me?' Darius takes the pendant from Sarilyn, staring at it as if it might disappear soon from his grasp.

'I'm defeated,' Sarilyn says plainly, and her voice has a certain numbness.

My brows pinch, never having thought in a lifetime that Sarilyn Orcharian herself would admit to being defeated.

Darius must feel the same as he says, 'You never give up. So why are you giving this to me?'

'Eventually, we all give up.' Sarilyn's gaze flickers past Darius's shoulder to look at me. 'It just took me three centuries for that to finally happen.' She turns away from us. 'I suggest you make your way back to your friends. They won't want to be alone once this world collapses.'

I don't say what she would expect me to or what I truly wish to answer with. 'Goodbye, Sarilyn,' I tell her instead, already knowing I will be coming back here. And it will be to tell her that the world still lives on.

CHAPTER FORTY-TWO

Illias is running towards me as Darius and I return to the castle fields. He wraps me up in his embrace and my arms are stuck to my sides as he tightens his hold, practically breaking my ribcage.

'Let her breathe, brother.' Iker taps his shoulder, laughing when Illias releases me and slaps Iker's hand away.

'Why on earth would you leave?' Illias ignores Iker, his usual worried eyes scanning me from top to bottom.

'I went to see Sarilyn.'

As soon as the name leaves my lips, all three of my brothers widen their eyes as if I have just sprouted ten arms from my body.

'Why?' Iker says, baffled. 'To have a friendly conversation while everyone else is wondering what is going on?'

I sigh. 'Listen, I have already despatched Ruvyn and Lorcan. Right now, they are rounding up a team of Venators to assess any damage to the city and its people.'

Regardless of what I say, my brothers don't look the least bit pleased.

'You're all safe, which is what matters,' Darius cuts in when he sees me struggling against my brothers' concerns.

Idris shifts his attention towards Darius, drawing my gaze in his direction. Darius's fingers delicately toy with his mother's pendant while his left hand rests inside his breeches pocket. His gaze is fixed on my brothers, emanating an air of profound respect that seems to resonate through the four of them.

Footsteps echo against the ground from behind us. Freya, Link, Rydan and Tibith pant as they come to a stop. They look exhausted, yet Freya's eyes are so bright. They twinkle from a distance and radiate something that makes me believe she is overjoyed despite the recent tremor.

'Finally,' Rydan huffs, seeming out of breath.

I frown.

'You need to come see this,' he says, his expression the most serious I have ever seen it.

Freya and Link share a sideways glance before gesturing with their chins to follow them.

'This isn't something Tibith did, is it?' Darius teases as we all begin to walk behind. Tibith's eyes go wide in protest as he clambers up Darius's leg. 'If so, he should be pardoned immediately.'

I chuckle but none of my friends even loosen themselves up a bit. That sets my stomach off. 'Rydan, is—'

'Look,' he cuts me off, coming to a stop and staring at the ground.

My brothers, Darius and I glance downwards at the same time. An odd silence permeates the air.

'Grass,' I say, cocking an eyebrow up at Rydan. 'We are looking at grass.'

'No, don't you get it?' He runs a frustrated hand over his face when I don't say anything. 'It's *grass*. Bright green grass that is *healthy*.'

My eyes wander back down to the fields covered in dead grass. Yellow and lifeless.

'Before you left, us three were sitting here.' Rydan motions to me and Link. 'It wasn't green; it was all dry and crumbling in our hands, but then *you* stood up after the tremors, and it was different.'

His words begin to dawn on me.

I was clutching the earth beneath me so tight when the shaking began; all I wished for at that moment was to be able to mend this world.

'Whatever you did, Nara,' Freya says, shaking her head with a smile, 'your magic grew it all back.'

'You healed it,' Darius whispers, his eyes on the grass as he smiles. *Healed it.*

The story behind it is that it bleeds real blood. Some say it's Solaris and Crello's blood from the creation of this world. Others think it's cursed and are waiting for the reincarnations of the sun and moon to bless it and make it sacred again.

Turning to Rydan, the memory of him saying that long ago flickers like an ember flame, igniting an excited spark in my eyes. In a moment of impulsiveness, I reach out and cup his face, kissing his cheeks. 'You magnificent solver.'

Unruffled, he shrugs, his lips curving into a smug smile. 'It's a gift.'

I shake my head, my grin never dissolving as I turn to Darius, and without needing to say a word to each other, he can already read my mind.

'Inform the shifters we'll be in the city,' he says to everyone. The earth rattles once more, and Darius immediately shifts into dragon form. As the wind picks up, my brothers step back and I climb onto Darius's back.

We take off not a second later, heading straight into the centre, where dozens of people storm the streets, children in their mothers' arms, men picking up broken debris from taverns and past Venators in ordinary clothing, helping them.

I jump off close to the ground before Darius can land. Some scream in terror at the view of a dragon by the pavilion, and others near enough faint by the bridge overlapping the streets.

I spot Lorcan among them and he frowns at me, confusion evident on his features.

Instead of letting him know, I rush towards the Neoma tree, slowing down once I am a few feet away from it.

I can sense Darius right behind me as I say, without looking back, 'Do you think this will work?'

A pang of melancholy strikes my chest as I stare at the once-vibrant tree. Its gnarled branches reach out to me like fingers.

'I trust wholeheartedly that it will, Goldie,' Darius says softly.

I pray that it will.

People from the city begin to surround the pavilion, staring in unease and confusion. My brothers and friends arrive with a few shifters following behind. They find me by the tree, and I release a trembling sigh.

Darius has already rounded the tree and is now facing me.

There is no sign of life.

When I first came here and saw it, I never thought it was salvageable. Aurum had destroyed it beyond saving, and now, as I stand here before it, all I want is to see its marigold leaves alive again.

I feel the rough bark against my fingertips. Gently shutting my eyes, I search for a flicker of existence – for a pulse. And suddenly, as if it senses me, a wave of warmth courses through my veins.

I open my eyes only to find Darius also with his hand on the tree.

I gaze at him with a smile, my hand delicately touching the rough surface of the tree. As the air fills with the earthy fragrance, my eyelids flutter closed, allowing me to bask in the comforting warmth that emanates from deep within us.

As my power begins to flow from the depths of my soul, I focus on the Neoma tree, drawing enough strength to heal, heal, *heal*.

A soft glow then brightens the surrounding area and I dare to peek.

My eyes widen at the breathtaking sight. Around Darius and me, a radiant golden light emerges from the trees roots, spreading like liquid sunlight.

Whirling patterns float gracefully around us, enveloping us in a tender embrace as if we were underwater. One by one, delicate buds form, swell and burst into vibrant marigold blossoms.

I can't help but let out a chuckle as I gaze upon the branches, witnessing their growth unfurling like flickering flames. It's stunning; it's *everything*.

I gaze downwards and lock eyes with Darius, as his powers and mine coax the tree back to life.

We did it, my eyes are saying.

We did, his eyes whisper back.

And then a powerful surge of bright light pierces the sky with a thundering roar.

CHAPTER FORTY-THREE

Darius and I take a step back from the tree, staring at the sky as the world goes quiet.

I glance at him, fearing we have done something wrong despite healing the Neoma tree. But as we start to walk towards one another, a child from the crowd yells, 'Look!' and we stop.

Carefully lifting our heads, we see specks of gold dust falling from above, little by little at first, and then enough to cover the ground like snow.

'Noctura,' I whisper, holding out my hands to collect it all. Excitement and relief wash over me, finally realising that Darius and I made the Neoma tree the new power source. That it was always going to be the Neoma tree, nothing else.

Gasps fill the pavilion, and people cry, saying it is a miracle as they bow down to us.

I look to Darius and my brothers and friends, and I smile so wide that my face could split.

'My Solaris,' Darius whispers, sliding beside me and turning me to face him.

The people of Emberwell begin to celebrate, throwing bundles of gold dust into the air.

'My Crello,' I say, before noticing he has taken the Rivernorth pendant out from his pocket **and he's holding** it in front of us.

I carefully lift the pendant from his open palm. Its golden exterior catches a soft glint of light as I lean in, deciding to drape the piece around his neck. 'There.' My voice is a warm breath of air as I whisper. 'It is back where it truly belongs.'

Darius's eyes are on me, not the pendant, as I take a step back to admire it on him. I last five seconds before my gaze flickers up to his lips.

The tension dissolves into jubilation as my brothers hoist me into the air, their victorious cheers ringing in my ears. Balancing atop Iker and Idris's sturdy shoulders, I find myself soaring above the crowd while Illias stands before me, his fist thrust high into the air. There are tears in his eyes, happy ones that pull my chest tight with adoration.

Darius watches us with his hands in his pockets and the most handsome smile on his face. The people around continue their overjoyed celebrations, and when Lorcan joins us beside Darius, his gaze on me severs as he turns to face him.

This is the first time that I see Lorcan smile at Darius as he extends a hand for him to shake, only for Darius to pull him into a brotherly embrace. I laugh at the wide shock on Lorcan's face, his hands outstretched at his sides before he gives in to it.

I savour the moment like it is the last meal I'll ever receive. In fact, I savour it all. This day, this exact place and the hope we have instilled in others.

My brothers then set me down as Freya, Leira and Aelle come bundling towards me.

'You've saved us,' Leira whispers, an overwhelming emotion clutching her throat as she touches my cheek. 'You've saved this world.'

I shake my head, smiling bittersweetly.

Freya cuts in, enveloping me in a hug so tight I chuckle. 'I'm so proud of you, Nara.' Tears are in her eyes, prompting mine to kick in.

Everyone seems so at peace right now, and I don't want it to ever end.

Link and Rydan steal Freya from me and start playing with the gold dust while my brothers come back to me with Tibith by their side. I pick him up, grinning as he squeals in delight, and I spin him around as shimmering gold falls all over his fur and nose.

'I always knew you had magic in you, Mrs Nara!'

'You did.' I nudge my nose against his and scrunch up my brows. 'You always did.'

'This is going to be a pain to remove,' Idris huffs from the side as he glances at his golden-coated arms.

I throw my head back and laugh, placing Tibith down before grabbing Idris, Iker and Illias. I pull them all into an embrace, making sure I kiss all three on their cheeks.

Iker pretends to be disgusted as he wipes at his skin, but I know he is happy and proud of me. They all are, and that is all I want from them right now.

I then turn to go and find Darius, but ultimately see Ruvyn standing amidst the crowd. He has this childish smile on his face as he watches a little girl draw shapes on the ground. He straightens into a guard-like posture when he spots me and bows his head at me.

I jab a finger in his direction, wanting him to enjoy this moment just as much. He gets the hint when he chuckles and loosens his shoulders.

At that moment, arms wrap around my abdomen, lifting me off

the ground as I'm spun around. I squeal and laugh, knowing who it is by just the warmth of their hands.

As I am put down, I whip around, facing Darius. I place my hands behind my back, hiding the gold flakes covering them and grinning. 'I got you something.'

He raises a brow and smirks. 'If it is not you naked, Goldie, then I highly doubt I'll want it.'

I pretend to ponder that thought. 'Not even if it is me naked and wearing . . .' I bring my hand out from behind my back, showing him all the gold I have collected. 'This all over me?' It will certainly leave areas where scrubbing clean won't do anything, but it's worth Darius's reaction.

He closes his eyes with a groan and drops his head into the crook of my neck. 'Oh, you are cruel.' I gasp as he hoists me over his shoulder and my friends stop to watch the commotion along with my brothers. I can feel my cheeks flame bright red in response to Darius's laughter as I wiggle in his tight grip.

'Idris is going to kill you,' I tell him, too embarrassed to look at my brother as I train my eyes on Darius's backside.

He chuckles. 'At least I'll die a happy man having had you tonight.'

I cover my face to stop myself from smiling, but it is nearly impossible.

When we arrive back inside the castle, we hardly make it to our chamber before he drops my feet onto the floor, his hungry eyes all over me as I don't waste any opportunity in grabbing him by the collar of his shirt and slamming my lips against his.

We're clawing at each other's clothes, kissing between each break with an aching, fervent thrill. His bottom lip runs over my chin, leaving whispering kisses along my skin that make me feel reckless.

Shimmers of gold coat my face and hands, and I paint it along my breasts, eliciting a groan from Darius.

I bite my lower lip, chuckling when he grips my bottom and lifts me onto the bed. His chest collides with mine, smearing the gold onto him now, but he loves it. He loves it so much.

'You make me act so irrational sometimes, Goldie,' he murmurs against my breasts, and the vibrations of his voice hitting the peaks of my nipples almost make me moan.

With eyes half closed in arousal, I look at him with a smile. 'Sometimes?'

I can feel him smirk, and then he's kissing me, worshipping me, loving me.

His palm comes between my thighs, causing me to arch my back and my eyes to roll in ecstasy. He doesn't even need to do much, and I'm already tipping over the edge.

'I was already addicted to you before, but seeing you naked, covered in gold for me?' He shakes his head breathlessly, his fingers circling my entrance. 'I'm infatuated.' He nuzzles his nose against the curve of my neck. 'Obsessed.' He now gently captures my lower lip with his teeth. 'Enamoured.'

A shuddering moan breaks past my lips at the word, and in an instant, he pounds into me with an intensity that takes my breath away. I cry out, only to be silenced by a tender kiss. And as he thrusts in and out, I sink my nails into his shoulders, making him hiss against my lips.

Every moment spent like this with Darius is different. He is never just one thing. He makes love to me, but he can also fuck me to oblivion. And I'll always beg for it to never end.

When he pulls out enough to make me whimper, our eyes lock on each other, before he thrusts into me once more.

My legs tighten around him, my breath quickening to match his. I can hardly contain myself any longer. I'm trembling with an overwhelming surge of pleasure, wave after wave. It sweeps me away like the tide, leaving me utterly powerless over my own body.

And after he lets out a deep, satisfied moan at his own release, I succumb to exhaustion within seconds.

CHAPTER FORTY-FOUR

I jerk awake to the sound of a crash in the next room. Gasping, I turn to look at Darius, still asleep beside me. He doesn't stir as I try to rouse him, and I wonder if it is just my imagination playing up when a shadow passes below the doorway.

Sickness lingers in the back of my throat as I still and suddenly hear the groan of heavy doors echoing all the way here.

Darius never moves, and my heart starts to hammer. I slip away from the bed, using a robe to cover my naked body as I flee the chambers barefoot in search of the noise.

I might be overreacting – I know my brothers or even Ruvyn could be awake and roaming around the castle, celebrating – but something in my gut tells me otherwise.

The double doors to the throne room are slightly open, enough for the dim glow of the moonlight to filter through the stained glass as I enter.

My fingers brush against the cold, rough surface of the wall, a futile attempt to ground myself as my breath stutters and I creep past the pillars.

A creak comes from behind me, and I whirl to find nothing there.

My eyes narrow, silence puncturing the room until I turn again, and all the warmth inside me drains as I face Aurum. His once-familiar features are now twisted into something grotesque, cracked skin oozing with a black substance across his withered face and a sickly aura of decay that makes my stomach turn.

'Hello, Nara,' he hisses, the words seeming to crawl along my skin. *This is just a nightmare. Wake up, Nara. Wake. Up.*

He looks around the ruins of the throne and open ceiling, a green shadow circling him. 'I see you have yet to fix things around here.'

I fight to keep my voice steady, taking a few steps back. 'This isn't real. You're not here.'

His lips curl into a semblance of a smile, half of his cheek missing, showing the inside of his mouth. Bone and all. 'Where do you think I am?' He's starting towards me, slowly, delighting in my discomfort. 'The Isle?'

I shake my head, forcing magic to my fingertips.

He halts in his tracks, a faint amusement playing on his lips as my palm casts a glow. 'Now, how impolite of you,' he says, his voice laced with a chuckle that never reaches his eye. 'I only came here to warn you, Nara, nothing more.' His gaze locks on to mine with a sinister flare that sends a shiver down my spine.

He picks up his pace again, taking a stride for every step I take back until he's closed in on me and yanks me by my hair towards him. I'm paralysed with anger, trapped in believing this isn't real, that I will wake up.

And Solaris, I hope I do.

'That when you're at your happiest,' he says, his rotten flesh making me gag up close, 'surrounded by those dear to you, basking in a triumph that should have been mine . . . know that I'll be lurking in the dark, waiting for the perfect opportunity to strike.'

I seethe, my nostrils flaring as I let out hard breaths, staring at the cold resolve in his eye.

'And I will make sure to meticulously dismantle your world, piece by piece. Because when I come back, you will know.'

He can't, I trapped him. I . . . saw him, I . . .

'You freed me without realising it, Nara.' The laughter that punctures his words is breathy. 'And for that, I'm granting you these fleeting moments of peace.'

I shake my head, dread washing over me. It's not true. It can't be. 'No,' my voice cracks.

Aurum nods as shadows erupt from behind him, forming into slender fingers as they reach out towards my throat, and I scream.

I scream and thrash, slamming my powers into him until everything is covered in shadows, and all I hear are Aurum's chuckles travelling through the air around me.

I'm suffocating on my own cries, my body convulsing as every bit of my power erupts uncontrollably.

'Nara!' A distant cry calls out to me, but I never stop.

I'm drowning. Each breath I take is a battle.

'Nara, stop!' Suddenly, Darius's voice cuts through the chaos as he pins my hands down against something soft.

I gasp, eyelids fluttering open as I look up at Darius straddling me. Blood drips from his bare chest, where ash covers certain areas in the shape of a hand. My hand.

'He's here,' I say between sobs, my voice shredded from screaming. 'He's—'

In an instant, Darius lifts me up, his arms encircling me as he draws me into his embrace. He cradles my head, pressing me close against the steady beat of his heart. My fingers grip him with ferocity, terrified he'll disappear.

He strokes my back, a soothing rhythm that slowly chips away at my paranoia. My tears soak into him, and all I can say is how sorry I am that I hurt him. But it doesn't matter to him as he shakes his head, his heart practically breaking just seeing me this way.

As my gaze lifts to look at his face, it catches on the door instead, standing ajar – the same way I left it in my nightmare.

The morning after falling asleep in Darius's arms, Link comes rushing to tell Darius and I how the barracks have erupted in an argument between the existing Venators and shifters.

Luckily, he can't tell how exhausted I look, nor does he notice how I destroyed our room by unleashing an uproar of magic here last night. He would eventually tell Illias if he did, and I'd have to deal with him, Idris and Iker worrying.

When I enter the barracks alongside Darius, I realise that Link wasn't lying when he said it was chaos. The entire food hall has a dozen shifters and Venators screaming at each other from across the tables.

'Full-fledged dragons aren't supposed to be inside here,' a former female Venator says to Relyari, a young shifter who has an Ardenti dragon beside her, looking as if it is about to burn the Venator alive.

Relyari glares at her, saying something back, resulting in other Venators joining in and insulting the dragon.

'It's been like this since breakfast,' Freya sighs, coming between Darius and me.

I spot Leira and Aelle holding back some other shifters from trying to murder the Venators before Rydan and Lorcan barge through the doors.

'Who started it?' Darius scans the crowd, his gaze sharp and inquisitive. A figure darts by, but Darius's reflexes are quicker. He snatches the culprit by the back of his shirt, halting his escape. A smirk curls the corner of Darius's lips as he identifies the guy he's holding. 'Cutler.'

Cutler cowers into his shirt, sheepishly smiling. 'How . . . how are you, Darius?'

Tibith emerges from between other people's legs and his ears flutter at Darius. 'It was him, Darry!' he shouts. 'He told the humans that they don't belong here!'

Cutler's face pales at Tibith's accusation. The rioting in the background starts to die down, faces turning towards us.

Darius keeps a firm grip on Cutler. 'Is that so?'

'I didn't mean it,' Cutler blubbers out. 'I promise!'

Truth be told, I believe him. Cutler has always been a menace, ever since I first met him at the den. His mouth gets him into trouble more often than not.

I sigh, deciding I want this all to be over. The remnants of the nightmare stick to me like a second skin, leaving me with a bad taste in my mouth and an aching throb in my temples I wish I could shake off. The sooner this is settled, the sooner I can rest.

Mounting one of the tables, I clear my throat, gaining everyone's attention. My brothers appear then and flank me, with Ruvyn standing sentinel by the doorway.

Suddenly, I'm out of words to say. All I can see is Aurum's face, his laugh ringing in my ears and his promise to ruin my life.

My breath comes out fast, and it is not until Darius releases Cutler, his concern etching a direct path to me, that I realise I'm on the verge of unravelling. But Freya gets to me before him, climbing onto the table and looking at me with a reassuring smile.

Gathering courage, I nod at her, turning to everyone else. 'After Aurum's defeat,' I swallow at the name, 'I thought we had all moved past this feud that separated the Venators from the shifters.' I shake my head. 'I guess I was wrong to think that.'

Disappointment washes over their faces, both shifters and Venators I once worked with.

'The world of Zerathion needs more than just Darius and me healing it,' I say, more to myself than to them. 'It needs unity against other threats, because they will never go away.' I look at as many faces as I can. 'There will always be something, and I need *all* of you to be here to protect what is ours.'

My eyes land on one of the Venators I knew through Erion: Niamh. She survived through Sarilyn and Aurum's rule. Now she seems rougher around the edges and less timid than when I first saw her, following Erion about with her big, round eyes. A scar runs across her pale cheek as she turns her head to the side and looks at the others silently for a moment, considering my every word.

'Then what do you suggest we do?' She speaks up, narrowing her eyes at me.

At least this is a start.

'Talk,' I say, then look towards the rest of the shifters merging with the Venators. 'Get to know each other as a person, not as a shifter or a Venator. Train together, show the other what you know. Become allies rather than rivals.'

A little girl, her pigtails frayed at the edges, emerges from the throng, her eyes wide and hesitant as she tiptoes closer to the woman beside her. Her gaze flutters towards me before it settles on Darius. As I look at him, the smile he casts at the little girl, so tender and imbued with hope, tugs at my heart. It seems to put the girl at her ease, and she flashes him a toothy smile.

'What if that doesn't work?' Roman, another former Venator, interjects, shattering the fragile bond of unity in that fleeting instant.

'It will.' I glance at the shifters. 'And if you doubt my words, you can always listen to the beat of my heart and tell me if I am lying.'

There are a few who widen their eyes at my abrasive words.

Some individuals are taken aback by my direct words. Others smile.

'And the Rümens? Are they—'

'Most herds were killed after Aurum returned,' Lorcan joins in. 'You would be lucky to find any still alive.'

The thought makes my chest ache. Rümens might have been vicious creatures, but they deserved to live, including those who became Erion's victims.

'All right, then.' Roman doesn't look too convinced. 'What about a leader? We still need someone to guide us as your future warriors.' He lifts his chin. 'What say you, Deputy? Ready to come back as General this time?'

We all focus our attention on Lorcan, and I search for any reaction that might tell me he still wishes for that title.

His gaze briefly slides over to mine. 'No,' he says, looking back at Roman. 'But I do know someone who is worthy of that title.' He glances at Freya and smiles. 'Freya Demori.'

Freya's eyes widen as everyone turns to look at her.

'I think she would make an excellent leader,' Lorcan says, 'far better than her father did.'

I look at Freya, her surprised expression making me smile as I grab her hand and give it a good squeeze. Her mouth opens then closes, unsure of what to say, but I know she would make an excellent leader. She already is one.

The pack of shifters and Venators mesh as one, glancing up at Freya curiously.

She slips free from my grip, and as the crowd erupts into discussions, I go up to Lorcan.

'You did a good thing there,' I tell him, watching as Freya shakes the hands of the Venators with a bright smile.

He lifts a shoulder. 'I was never a good deputy to begin with. Who knows what I would have been like as a general.'

'You were an excellent deputy, Lorcan,' Darius says, approaching us. He chuckles, rubbing his thumb along his lower lip. 'And I don't say that lightly.'

Something warms in Lorcan's expression. 'Thank you.' He bows his head. '*Brother*.'

I watch them give each other a respectable nod, and it moves me. They still have a long way to go, as decades of miscommunication ripped them apart, but at least . . . they're healing together.

'You were great up there,' he whispers against my ear, and I smile, lowering my head. 'Gus would have been proud.'

'Of both of us,' I whisper, lifting my chin to look up at him. There's a spot of gold dust on the side of his neck, and I wipe it away.

He murmurs a chuckle under his breath. 'I guess not all of it came off.'

My smile soon falters when my eyes fall to his chest.

'I'm sorry about last night,' I murmur, grimacing at the memory of what I did.

He frowns, capturing my face in his palms. 'Why are you sorry? Because you had a nightmare?'

I shake my head, lowering his hands from my face. I glance at everyone inside the barracks, talking and paying no heed to us. 'What if . . .' I lick my parched lips. 'What if it wasn't just a nightmare?'

Darius stares at me. Every muscle in his body suddenly coils as if he is ready to search the lands just to keep me at peace. 'He's still in the Isle, Goldie. He can't hurt you from there.' His jaw tenses as he shakes his head. 'I won't let him.'

I exhale a quivering sigh and nod. Darius wraps his arms around me, pulling me to his chest.

'Don't let him haunt your dreams,' he says, his voice deep and troubled. He still has nightmares about Aurum, too. 'It's the one place I can't protect you.'

I close my eyes. 'But I can't protect you from yours.'

'You protect our world. That is enough for me, Goldie.'

CHAPTER FORTY-FIVE

'A free pint of Flame Spewer for the saviour of Zerathion!' A wooden mug is shoved in front of my face as I stop by a stall in the streets of Chrysos. After the nightmare the other day, I busied myself by visiting the city more often.

I eye the flames spitting atop the tankard and jut a brow upwards at the burly vendor giving it to me. The same one who once insulted me the first night I ever came to this city.

I doubt he recognises me from that night, but I remember him.

Freya glances between us, a grimace marring her usually soft features, expecting the worst. Yet I smile at the man instead and take the drink, downing it while maintaining eye contact with him.

'Thank you,' I say, the vendor's eyes widening as I hand him back the mug and walk off with Freya.

She snorts as I hook my arm with hers. 'I truly have no idea how you handle a drink like that.'

'It no longer contains goblin blood,' I reply, content with that thought. 'Darius made sure creature cruelty was banished from the city.' I say that just as some pixies fly past a few giggling children.

'And the rest of Emberwell?'

My lips screw together. 'We're getting there.'

There are still nearby towns and villages where animals may be captured and sold now that the treaty is broken. I can envision Hedris taking on the role of a buyer, although the thought is rather sickening.

'Is he always going to follow you around?' Freya suddenly asks, subtly trying to glance behind us at where Ruvyn walks a few paces slower than us.

I chuckle. 'He did that with Arlayna. I think he enjoys it.'

Freya raises a brow.

I shake my head in amusement. 'Looking out for others, I mean.'

Freya laughs, butting heads with me, and I suddenly feel for Ruvyn. He's still young, and I assume he will eventually return to Terranos for his mother, but with Thallan ruling, I doubt he wants to cross paths with him.

'Ambrose!'

Freya and I come to a halt. We exchange a knowing glance full of amusement before we turn and see Rydan bundling down the street. He nearly stops at one of the stalls, hesitating as if tempted by something, but ultimately declines and joins us.

'What is it now?' Freya asks an out-of-breath Rydan.

He holds up a finger, needing a moment as he doubles over and tries to catch his breath. 'Your brothers—' he wheezes. 'And Darius—' Another wheeze. 'Are together.'

I stare at him.

'As in together, *together*,' he rephrases slowly, 'giving him the almighty brotherly talk, I'm sure.'

Oh, Solaris.

'You came all this way to tell us this?'

'Frey Frey, do not start with me.' He lets out an exasperated breath. 'I overheard Idris tell Iker and Illias to be prepared to test him, which I'm assuming is not a good thing—'

My eyes widen, which only makes Freya burst out into laughter. 'Where are they?' I ask.

'In one of the taverns in the city—'

I swiftly take off down the street, leaving Rydan with the words still in his mouth. 'Stay here,' I say to Ruvyn as I pass by him.

'Wait,' Rydan calls out to me. 'What are they going to ask him?'

Questions I do not want to even imagine.

Intimate ones, threatening ones, and possibly even embarrassing ones. None of which have concerned me in the past, but now I find myself unwilling to tolerate my brothers' attempts at superiority when faced with someone like Darius, who has a knack for saying all the wrong things just to get under someone's skin.

I search the streets, passing by various taverns until I land on one named The Hickory and see that it is the most crowded.

Raising my brows, I enter through the wooden double doors and scan the heady-scented place. A few patrons are chatting and looking towards the far corner, so I storm over there and come across Darius, Tibith and my brothers sitting around a table with jugs of ale stacked upon others.

I blink like an absolute fool, not knowing what is happening as I stare at the four who are roaring with laughter. Even Idris is smiling.

My gaze is coated with suspicion as I near them. Tibith jumps onto the table, grinning at me. 'What is going on?' I demand.

Darius looks up, the side of his mouth tugging into a smile. 'Your brothers were just telling me about the time you pretended to be Iker.'

Iker's face is bright red from laughing. 'It was convincing until I broke the bed trying to sneak in.'

'It wasn't that convincing,' Idris grumbles, lolling his head to the side to look at him.

Still in shame at this outcome, I sink into the chair beside Idris. 'Did you . . .' I lean into him while staring at Iker, Illias and Darius. 'Did you do—'

'He passed.' Idris smiles, already knowing what I was trying to ask.

My head snaps to Darius, his smug smile telling me everything.

'Mr Iker asked Darry why he chose you of all people as his bride!' Tibith lets slip out, ever so innocently.

Iker snorts out a chuckle. I glare at him, and if this was like the old times in our village, he knows that I would have chased him around with a poker.

'All right, all right.' Illias raises his palms. 'The point is that we know . . .' All three of my brothers share the same look. 'You and him are right for each other.'

'That, and also that you're both reincarnations—'

'Regardless,' Idris cuts Iker off. 'We're happy for you. Both of you.'

I can't contain the joy that bubbles out of me, and it must be contagious because my brothers stare back at me with their eyes sparkling with delight.

Darius places his hand on my thigh, and I glance at him with my heart full and face flushed.

As my brothers converse with a bubbly Tibith, I discreetly reach for his hand, savouring the warmth of his touch. Our fingers naturally entwine, and he lifts our hands to his lips with a tender gesture, kissing my knuckles.

I shake my head with a smile at the suggestive gleam in his eyes.

'Oh, Nara,' Illias says. I turn my head to see him leaning back into his chair with the biggest grin on his face. 'Did you know Idris has been very into writing lately?'

I think I hear Idris growl at him, which makes Iker and Illias chuckle.

Surprised, my brows scrunch together as I look at Idris and say with a smile, 'Really?'

He plays with the rim of his tankard. 'It helps pass the time,' he grouses.

'For when he's writing down his feelings, rather than saying them.' Illias picks up his mug and smiles into it, much as Darius does right now, watching us interact.

'I have only written a few things; my spelling isn't exactly up to scratch,' Idris says hastily, then sighs. 'But I must say, I do . . . enjoy it.'

'He's trying to take after his young brother.' Iker stretches his arms over the back of his head, eyes squinting as he dons a lofty smile. 'It's only natural.'

Idris simply rolls his eyes, prompting Iker to laugh. It gladdens me that they are getting on again and relying on each other rather than arguing for the sake of it. That is the last thing Freya would want.

I tilt my head, my eyes on Idris. 'I'd like to see what you have written so far.'

He shakes his head. 'It's nothing special, Nara. It's just words.'

His humility reminds him that he has never thought highly of himself. 'Words written by a special man.'

He casts me a glare that softens when he realises I mean it.

'Would anyone like a fourth round?' Iker drums his hands against the table when the barmaid comes past.

Illias slides Iker's mug far away from him. 'You've had enough.'

I relinquish a sigh, knowing what is to follow. Iker will start an argument with Illias, Idris will intervene and become frustrated, and eventually, we will all be kicked out for disruption.

'How about a game of Liars' Dice?' Darius suggests right as Iker is opening his mouth to insult Illias.

My head snaps at him, but he simply casts me a small, knowing glance.

Tibith gasps, thrilled. 'Can I play too, Darry?'

'Of course.'

'Liars' Dice?' Iker asks.

Darius leans forward, tilting his head to the side. 'You never played it when you were at the den?'

Illias shakes his head, a scoff escaping his lips. 'Most of our time was spent practising what we would do if Sarilyn found us.'

A slither of guilt works up my throat, but I swallow it. They are with me now. Safe and free from the people who would try to harm them back in our village.

'Well.' Darius looks at me, the corner of his lips quirking into a smile. 'There's always a first time for everything.'

I hum at him gleefully, distinctly remembering that I won the first time.

Beneath the table, Darius places his hand on my thigh again and squeezes punishingly. I jerk, almost hitting my knee against the wood, and he chuckles while my brothers and Tibith have no clue.

My cheeks burn and Darius looks at my brothers as Iker and Illias consider playing the game. When they agree to a round, Darius lifts his mug in a toast to them before draining the last remnants of mead. With a resounding thud, he slams the tankard onto the table and deposits a few dice inside as he fixes me with a simpering smile.

The look might as well turn me into a puddle of liquid as I fight an eye roll but fail.

'How do we play?' Idris suddenly asks, surprising me with his keen interest in participating.

Darius leans forward, his golden eyes sparkling with anticipation and excitement as he starts to explain the rules.

CHAPTER FORTY-SIX

C hrysos Street at night is bustling with life as my brothers bid us goodbye and retreat to the castle after a few rounds of Liars' Dice.

Darius told me he wanted us to stay behind for a little bit to witness the different districts without him having to use glamour, or us having to run from danger at every corner.

Not long ago, this would have never been possible. But now it's quite surreal. It's a dream just to be with Darius and see him smiling at the people of Emberwell as they greet him and give him their thanks and praise for restoring their home.

A young girl with long golden hair stops us in the middle of the street. She must be about five, and she looks up at us with beaming blue eyes and a toothless smile. 'Can I say hello to him?' She points to Tibith perched on Darius's shoulder.

Tibith, gleeful as always, giggles, and Darius nods at the girl before he gets down on one knee to match her height. The little girl grins, reaching a small hand towards Tibith's head to pet him.

My heart swoons at the sight.

'What's your name?' Darius asks her.

'Mira,' she replies, and during that second, her mother calls from down the street.

Darius chuckles. 'You remind me of someone, Mira. Someone extraordinary.' When he looks at me, I realise it is me who she reminds him of. Back when we were children, I gave him the golden coin that I now wear proudly around my neck.

By the time our stare breaks, Mira's mother is catching up to her daughter and apologising, thinking she had disturbed us.

'She was very nice, Darry.' Tibith waves after them. 'Maybe she can be a friend.'

I place both hands on my hips. 'Don't you have plenty of friends already?'

'There is always room for more, Mrs Nara!'

I throw my head back, laugh and turn to find Darius staring at me with a smile. My eyes narrow, and my lips purse at him in amusement. 'Did she really remind you of me?'

His smirk promises a smart-assed answer. 'Same toothless smile.'

I nudge him playfully, which only causes him to snatch my wrist and pull me straight towards him. My body fits into his perfectly as his lips come down to kiss mine for a yearning second.

A satisfied hum leaves my lips as I look up at him.

'You know,' he drawls. 'Now that you're a power source of immortality yourself, I can imagine our future filled with smaller versions of you and me running around.'

My heart reacts like never before, dancing with a new-found rhythm that pulsates joyfully. Each beat rushes through me, and I think of the day Faye told me how mortals and shifters could never bear children. It would kill us before the child was even born.

Yet now . . .

'What makes you think they'll be running around?' I whisper with a smile against his lips.

He smiles in return. 'Because they'll be adventurous, just like their mother.'

I bite my lip, wanting that more than anything: to grow our family. Perhaps one day, in the near future, when things are more settled between the kingdoms, we can.

'What about me, Darry?'

Tibith shakes the hem of my dress, and Darius and I break apart, chuckling as we look down at a glossy pair of eyes.

'*You*' – I point my finger at him – 'are always going to be number one.'

He smiles and nuzzles his head against Darius's leg.

I think about how perfect our little family is as Darius and I stare at each other for minutes in silence.

Then he whispers, 'I want to show you something, Goldie.' He interlaces his fingers with mine. 'A place, actually.'

I regard him with suspicion. 'Where?'

A smile tugs at the corners of his lips. 'It's a surprise.'

We cross a river – one of the northern rivers – and my eyes widen as soon as we land. Against the background of dust and basaltic rocks, the ground flows like liquid silver, tracing a winding path through the empty land.

Volcanoes that I know are called Helland stand sentinel on either side up ahead, their peaks shrouded in a mist that blurs the line between land and sky. I had always wanted to visit when I was little, and I was sure I would as a Venator, but so much happened in between that it made all trips up here impossible.

Tibith runs past me, scouting the area, leaving me to admire as the day wanes and the sun dips below the horizon, causing the river to mirror the sky's fiery shade.

'What do you think?' Darius asks me.

I shake my head, stunned. 'It's beautiful,' I breathe and turn to him. 'When did you first come here?'

'A few years ago.' He comes by my side and takes my hand, leading us towards the banks of the river. 'I wanted to see where my bloodline came from.'

I gaze at the river, its gentle ripples dancing with a form of magic that differs from any other kind.

'That day at the arena,' Darius says. 'Crello mentioned that before us, there was a mother.'

I cut him a glance, but his eyes are locked on the river. We've barely spoken about the conversations we had with the deities, much like I never told my brothers about seeing my father. It would only make them miss him more.

'A mother?' I whisper.

Darius nods. 'The first dragon.' He looks at me. 'The one that started it all.'

I gaze into Darius's eyes, picturing what this dragon might have looked like and how all dragons came to be; but most of all, the beginning of the Rivernorths.

Darius raises my hand to his lips and closes his eyes. He presses a kiss against my skin and sighs in what sounds like relief. 'When I first came here,' he swallows, 'I used to think about how I never thought I'd see you again.'

A vast array of emotions swirls within my veins as I move closer towards him, my lips now touching his hand on mine. 'And yet you did,' I say quietly . . . lovingly. 'You were always meant to find me.'

His eyes shut as he smiles, lowering our hands to pull me in close. Our noses touch as he whispers, 'I already said this once, Goldie, but *you* found *me.*' He kisses me long and hard, revelling in our love, but even this does not feel like enough. For us, our kisses always feel like our first – that night in the woods, his full lips on mine and the palpable desire we passed off as hatred. It's a fire that never dies out.

As he breaks our kiss, I make a noise, needing more, until he angles his head to the side and shows me a bubble of water floating in his hand.

A surprised laugh rips from my throat as I watch it move and become different shapes. The silver glow from the river glistens inside the ball, and I see mine and Darius's reflections smiling at it.

'Show-off.' I pretend to glare.

Darius gives me a half-smile. 'I do have part of Crello's power now.'

I lift a brow. 'And I Solaris.' To rattle him, I push power towards my fingers as I stretch them out to the ground, crafting a small flower to bloom in the dry land. Instead, all I manage to do is impress him. Pride flickers through the gold sparks of his eyes, and I shake my head at him.

'I was thinking.' He cocks his head, seeming to pull me even closer to him. 'I think it is time we had a proper wedding, don't you think?'

'Is this another way of you wanting to show off again?'

He laughs. 'Not this time, Goldie. Is it a crime to want to marry you again?' He lowers his head and a whisper of a kiss touches my neck. 'And again.' Another kiss, this time on my collarbone, enticing me all that much more. 'And again.' A final kiss on the lips. 'And again.'

It is hard to decline the offer when he puts it that way. Though the truth is, I would marry him a million times if I could.

'My brothers would love to see us get married,' I admit, and a hum rumbles deep in his chest. 'And I do enjoy hearing your wonderful vows.'

He grins.

'I will be there.' Tibith frowns from below. 'Won't I, Darry?'

Darius chuckles. 'You'll be front and centre.'

'And after?' I ask, raising my brows in amusement.

Darius's gaze flickers over to me, arrogance sparkling in his eyes. 'We will dance together.' He grabs my waist, and I tip my head back with a laugh. 'All night, if you are up to it.'

I nudge him playfully in the chest, shaking my head, but my attention quickly shifts as my eyes catch something in the distance. I pause, gazing towards the volcanoes. A wisp of smoke billows out of the top of one, and I swear I see a dragon silhouette disappear in the mist.

'Have any of our dragons left the castle?' I ask, my voice sounding detached for a moment.

'Not that I know of,' Darius says. 'There are likely others out here that are separate from ours. Why?'

I furrow my brows, staring for a second longer at the volcano. I shake my head and look back at Darius when I don't see anything. 'Never mind. I just thought I might have seen . . .' I let my words fade away, a soft smile gracing my lips instead. 'It's getting late; we should head back. Illias will panic if I'm not back for our nightly chats.' *Or* to complain about how Iker clearly cheated at Liars' Dice, making no one a winner.

Darius watches me, his usually light eyes turning dark as if he senses something is amiss, but I have already changed the subject by the time he tries to ask.

CHAPTER FORTY-SEVEN

The days go by quickly. What is a week turns into two as everyone around me plans for a lush ceremonial wedding.

I pay many visits to Sarilyn during this time, much to her surprise. She expected me to let her rot all alone down there after Darius and I restored the Neoma tree, and perhaps another version of me would have. But after the day she mentioned how much she saw herself in me, I found myself compelled to talk to her again. To find out *more*.

Some days, she was quiet, eating away at the food I brought her while everyone else assumed I was resting. Other times, she would tell me of her childhood, her life while training with a sorceress, and how her favourite pastime was to sing.

It seemed so mundane at the time, finding out these things when all I ever imagined was her plotting everyone else's demise in her spare time.

'Does the thief know you are down here?' she asks me one day, then takes a bite out of her apple.

I twitch on the spot, casting a glance at the ground. 'He's no longer a thief.'

She chuckles. 'You didn't answer my question.'

I huff, forcing my gaze up at her. 'No . . . he doesn't know.'

A faint hint of a smile appears on her lips. She takes another bite from the apple, the crunch irritating my eardrums.

I find myself needing to defend my reasoning. 'You did murder his entire family.'

'And yet it shocks me he hasn't already paraded my head around the shifters.'

'I asked him not to.'

She cocks a brow.

'And I don't think he would have been as nice as to parade your severed head in front of the shifters.' He would have wanted to make more of a statement. Something dramatic enough to make me roll my eyes.

Sarilyn hums pensively, turning her back to me. 'What was it like?'

'What was what like?'

She turns her head to the side. 'Your time in Olcar.'

I take a moment to think it over. 'Different,' I end up whispering. 'A lot happened while I was there. The good, the bad . . .' The words trail from my lips as I search through the memories of the Screaming Forests, the first night with Darius, and Aurum's tricks. 'Dusan mentioned you, though.'

Sarilyn faces me and her eyes search mine for something she cannot find. She looks at her palms. 'Yes, he seemed to have never forgotten our time together; well, that was before Aurum murdered him.'

The noise of Dusan choking on his blood has never left me. Although, I don't think much of that day has ever left my mind at all.

'I can imagine the royals of Terranos despising me just as much,' Sarilyn scoffs, falling into miserable laughter.

'For creating the forest?' I go on, 'Killing half of the Fallcrown bloodline? Or is it because you tricked Dusan into falling for you in order to get to the Isle?'

Her lips snap into a thin line. 'I never tricked him,' she grinds out, then composes herself by using her fingers to comb through her matted hair. 'He had just decided that what I wanted was not good enough for him. He wanted peace and a marriage. I wanted an end.'

'Despite it costing you everything?'

'As you already know, I would do it all over again if need be.'

I sigh, surrendering to the quiet that envelops us. I can't change the past; even if I were given the power to alter it, her path towards vengeance would remain the same. I don't believe anything would have stopped her, not even the possibility of falling for Dusan.

Ruvyn emerges into the dim corridor, the flicker of his torch casting shadows across the prison walls. 'I think it is time we left, Lady Nara.' His gaze drifts to Sarilyn's, the lines around his eyes visible as he frowns. He seems to think it is a lost cause, coming down here most days without my brothers' or Darius's knowledge.

With a reluctant nod, I concede, allowing him to lead the way. Yet I barely manage a few steps before Sarilyn's words anchor me to the spot.

'You should know that a Rivernorth is not invincible.'

I slowly turn on my heel and stare at the vacant look in her eyes as she toys with the ripped lace of her bodice.

'Not like everyone believes them to be.' Her gaze slices through the air to meet mine with an almost tangible intensity. 'See, as a child, I grew up seeing them as these powerful beings who nothing could destroy. They were unscathed by steel weapons, magic . . . *anything*. But do you want to know what was in the Northern Blade that killed them all?' She edges closer to the bars, beckoning me with her hand as if she were letting me in on a secret.

I remain motionless, intrigue mixed with wariness not letting me walk away. She leans forward while clutching the iron bars and lets out a knowing chuckle with a playful arch of her eyebrows. 'Nothing,' she whispers, her tongue sliding across her teeth as she watches my reaction.

I reel back, the ground beneath me feeling as unstable as Sarilyn's revelation.

That can't be possible.

Sarilyn nods, taking in my unvoiced questions. 'The Isle created it, yes, but it never gifted it with anything potent enough because it didn't need anything special. It didn't require any poison, magic or spells to doom them. All it needed was my sacrifice, a token of despair, for the Rivernorths to abandon all hope they clung to.' Her eyes widen as she reminisces about what she did all those years ago. 'When I returned to Emberwell, I made sure to dismantle their world bit by bit – to break their foundations and everything they had built in their honour, and once they also saw what Aurum had become, they themselves broke.'

Their legacy was destroyed . . . 'So,' I whisper in realisation, 'they became—'

'Almost human,' Sarilyn finishes. 'And all they had ever known was power. You can imagine why they crumbled so easily. And eventually, Darius's mother met that same fate because she had given up long before that.'

My chest heaves at the thought. I lift my gaze to Sarilyn's, not having noticed how intensely I was staring at the ground. 'You gave up your powers for years, just to end up here?'

'With it,' she says, 'people would have feared me for the magic powers I had, not for who I was without them.'

I try to accept that answer, but the tragedy of it all sets my spine rigid. 'And Aurum?'

Her expression grows cold and distant. 'Aurum' – she utters his name with a venomous disdain – 'possesses no semblance of a soul. He cannot even fathom the concept of hope.' She pauses, savouring the moment as the weight of her words hangs in the air. 'He was born a monster; that is all he will ever be.'

By the time I walk through one of the lounging quarters, Freya and Darius seem to be debating. Freya stands up with her hands in the air, gesturing something grand, while Darius repeatedly says no from his chair. Lorcan is by the fireplace, smiling as he watches them alongside Idris.

When Darius's eyes flit towards the threshold, his eyes light up. 'Goldie.' He rises to his feet and meets me halfway. 'Please tell your friend I will not ride on a horse to our wedding.'

From behind him, Freya huffs as I say teasingly, 'I thought you enjoyed all eyes on you?'

'I'm a changed man.'

Lorcan snorts.

Darius casts Lorcan a look over his shoulder, and I chuckle, though my mind is still consumed by the conversation I just had with Sarilyn.

'Ah, there's my other favourite witch. Do you plan to stay?' Darius says towards the threshold, where Leira enters with a nervous expression.

Already on high alert, the hairs on my neck stand up.

'I have some news.'

I glance at Darius, noticing all the amusement that was on his face has now been stripped away.

'By the look on your face, I assume it's not good news,' he says.

Leira holds her hand out, a cream envelope in her grip. 'It's from the Undarion palace,' she says as Darius takes it. 'It arrived this morning.'

As Darius rips the seal and begins reading the contents of the letter, I turn to Leira, asking, 'Why didn't you say anything?'

She closes her eyes in apology. 'You were nowhere to be found.'

'What does it say?' Freya walks over, trying to get a peek at the letter.

By the muscle ticking in Darius's jaw, it must be nothing good.

He runs a hand over his mouth. 'They're still demanding we stand down from the throne.'

Lorcan and Idris curse under their breaths as I turn away from them all, my cheeks burning with frustration.

'Or what?' I can hear the irritation in Freya's voice. 'He'll declare war on us? This is insane!' She smacks her hands down on her thighs. 'I should have known never to trust a man like that; he always gave me the strangest looks whenever my father introduced us at festivities.'

Idris takes a step towards her, his brows furrowed. 'Did he ever try to do anything to you?'

The question startles Freya and she blinks at him. 'No, he just— he just—'

'He was the type to get away with anything because he rules Undarion,' Lorcan explains. 'He was never born into royalty. Hedris had to build his way up in the ranks until he got what he wanted from Undarion, and now that he has that, he likely wants more.'

'Then why can't he take it from somewhere else?' My brother scowls at Lorcan, not understanding why there can't be a solution to this. He has yet to learn what Hedris is like. He's lucky to have never spoken to him directly.

'Nara and Darius are new to all of this,' Leira says, giving Darius and me a sympathetic smile. 'In his arrogance he probably thinks the two of you don't stand a chance against him and his army.'

'We stand a chance,' Darius states blandly. Suddenly, the letter in his hand ignites in flames. He crumbles the burnt pieces into ashes and then looks up at us with a smile. 'But for now, I guess we can entertain him in thinking that we don't.'

'For the love of—' Lorcan mutters. 'We cannot sit around until he tries something.'

'He is right,' I tell Darius. Who knows what Hedris plans to do if we don't give in to his tantrum. 'What we need is more allies.'

'You could speak to the Aerians,' Lorcan suggests, though I know he immediately regrets it. He clears his throat as all eyes latch on to him. 'They helped once; I'm sure they can again.'

It was Hira who helped, not her sisters. I can't say that, though. My time in Aeris felt too much like torture to now give the rulers a fair chance.

Darius doesn't seem too pleased by the idea of going there. He did spend most of his time there in a prison cell with only me or Gus to talk to.

'What do you think, Goldie?' he says, his gold eyes seeking an answer as he looks towards me.

There aren't many options, and Darius knows that himself, yet it is not only his decision. It is my opinion he wants above his.

I nod. 'I'll arrange a meeting with them, and I'll write to the princesses of Terranos to see if they have any news on Hedris that might be of service to us.'

I hope and pray that they do.

CHAPTER FORTY-EIGHT

D awn has just begun to unfurl across the horizon as I pierce the cool morning air on Fernah's back. Beside me, Darius is in his dragon form, moving at a graceful speed as his scales shimmer between silver and gold from the sunrise.

A few days ago, a letter from the Aerian palace confirmed our meeting.

Nearing Aeris, we soar over mountains and winding rivers that glisten from afar before the palace slowly emerges from the mist atop the floating land. As I glance at Darius, his mighty wings cutting through the sky, my heart begins to thrum with a mixture of trepidation and resolve. I hope that our meeting with the Aerian leaders goes well.

It's our only chance to form an alliance against potential enemies.

As we descend towards the palace bridge, the first rays of sunlight glint off the curved windows overlooking the fields.

A few guards are in armour patrolling the open entrance as we land, and I unbuckle myself from Fernah. She growls at one of the guards as they move towards me, and I chuckle, petting the side of her body.

'Should I be jealous you decided to ride another dragon?' Darius appears beside me, rolling his shoulders back.

I flash him a playful smirk in response, ready to exchange our usual banter, when suddenly, a mysterious woman in a captivating burgundy dress approaches us, her hands concealed behind her back.

'The leaders eagerly await your presence in the grand throne room.' She turns, expecting us to follow.

Darius and I depart from Fernah, gliding through the corridors adorned with artwork that I don't remember seeing the last time I was here. In the vivid paintings, a fierce clash unfolds between majestic red phoenixes and their grey counterparts with soulless eyes that I can only assume are the Rocs.

As Darius and I enter the throne room, both doors swing open. We pause atop the phoenix-shaped marble flooring as we make our way to the room's core. Soldiers surround the entire chamber, and the leaders are ahead of us on their thrones, with Hira's seat in the centre vacant.

My chest burns with uncompromising anger, but I stamp it down as much as possible by plastering on a friendly smile.

'Nara.' Col is the first to speak, her dark eyes already assessing me from head to toe. 'We weren't sure you would come.'

Her sister Ara straightens in her seat, her staff glistening bright red.

'As I mentioned in the letter,' I reply coolly, 'we truly need your help.'

'Why?' Col says flatly. 'Were the Elves already taken?'

Snickering and laughter erupt from Ara and the other warriors around the room.

I curl my hand into a fist at my side, blood pumping fast within my veins as I try to calm myself.

As soon as the laughs stop, I say, 'Hedris is threatening our position on the throne.'

Col doesn't seem to care. 'Pity,' she remarks dryly. 'Perhaps he has a reason for doing that.' Her gaze goes to Darius beside me, and I begin to lose all feeling in my hand. 'You don't exactly seem fit to be the new king of Emberwell.'

I glance over at Darius; his worried eyes had only been on me this whole time. When he sees my scrunched-up fist, a sudden vicious gleam flickers across his gaze. 'You're right,' he tells the leaders. 'I'm not.' He turns to them and starts wandering around the chamber. 'I was a criminal, and still am, if you think about it.'

The warriors are on immediate alert, eyeing him suspiciously.

'As a matter of fact . . .' Darius stops and slowly spins on his heel. 'I already have my eyes on various things I could steal inside this palace.'

His admission has Col and Ara's faces burning.

'And what is stopping you?' Ara says, her tone icy in comparison.

Darius offers her a smug smile. 'Certainly not your guards.' He then shrugs. 'Or you.'

He's testing them; anyone else would be foolish to, but not Darius. He's had years of experience.

I would know.

'Clearly you agreed to this meeting only to reject whatever we might offer you.'

Ara stirs uncomfortably at what Darius is accusing them of.

'Your intention is to humiliate us – or, more specifically, my wife.' He looks over his shoulder at me, then back at Ara and Col. 'That doesn't sit well with me . . . *So*, I suggest we restart this meeting – you can listen to every word *she* says, then reconsider your response.'

He can't see it, but the pride and awe that courses through my veins is formidable.

'Your *wife* caused a great deal of stress to our people when she stayed here,' Col says, her cruel gaze cutting towards me. 'Forgive us if we are not inclined to accept your suggestions.'

I take a bold step forward. 'But you *were* inclined to accept Aurum's offers when he took us back to Emberwell, weren't you?'

'It was you or our people.' Ara lifts her chin. 'What loyalty do you have to us?'

Unbelievable. 'He *killed* Hira.'

'Maybe she deserved it,' Ara says simply, as if Hira meant nothing to her. 'She birthed a child with a human, despite the Aerian rules stating that the warriors chosen to rule the land cannot marry, nor bear a child. She wasn't worthy of the title that was bestowed upon her.'

'But she was your sister, and Lorcan is your nephew—'

'He is an abomination who is not welcome back here,' Col interrupts, her verdict final.

I can only stare at them in horror. It's surprising how Lorcan's heroic act of saving us from Aurum has resulted in such extreme shunning from those who are meant to be his relatives. I knew that the leaders were mad, but not to this extent.

'Hira would not have wanted this,' I say quietly, but still loud enough for them to hear me.

Col leans forward in her chair, her dark eyes narrowing. 'And how do you know what Hira would have wanted? We were her sisters, her guides. You were nothing to us.'

'If you were her sisters, then you should know she loved Lorcan dearly and would have never wanted you both to deny him his true heritage,' I counter, willing my voice to sound strong and firm.

'He deserves to be here,' Darius says with finality, but the two Aerians do not seem to accept that as their knuckles whiten against the arms of their thrones.

Ara turns to Col and they begin a heated discussion that does not reach our ears.

After a minute, Ara gets the final word and Col sits back and stares at us silently, her expression hardening.

'We will allow Lorcan', she starts, much to her displeasure, 'to return to Aeris whenever he wishes, but he will never inherit Hira's place, and we will most definitely *not* join your kind.'

I can sense Darius on the verge of offering a retort, but I gently touch the fabric of his sleeve. His eyes snap towards me as I shake my head. Uncertainty swirls in his gaze as if the Aerians might truly be our only shot, but he knows what I'm thinking. He can see it in my expression.

Lorcan matters more. Their connection runs deeper, whether by blood or not. And he shouldn't be exiled from the place his real mother came from.

At that moment, a solitary clap reverberates through the hall, capturing our attention, and we all turn our heads towards the source of the sound.

Kirian steps out from the shadows, reminding me of how he first introduced himself back in Thalore. He still looks the same. That enigmatic stare in his eyes, and the pale skin tone that matches his softened tousled mane. His piercing gaze lands on the Aerians, shadowed slightly by the dark locks falling across his forehead. The only difference I can see in him now is that he does not look as relaxed as he was in the comforts of his home, wearing a simple shirt and waistcoat. This time, he wears a black coat adorned with a ruffled, cascading jabot, and black leather breeches that hug his muscled form.

Ara and Col rise from their thrones at once while the other warriors unsheathe their weapons, but Kirian doesn't so much as blink in their direction.

'Well, that was dramatic,' he says. 'I was beginning to wonder if a fight would break out. A shame it did not.' He glances at me. 'You must be stepping into your role as future queen, Naralía.'

I narrow my eyes, distrusting his sudden appearance.

'One must not express such atrocious behaviour,' he mocks. 'Or is that a rule that applies only for the princesses of Terranos?' He chuckles. 'I can never keep up.'

'How did you get in here?' Col demands as Kirian drags his gaze to hers.

His smile is sharp enough to bite someone's head off. 'A little Elf told me they would be here.'

Arlayna.

'I would have gone straight to Emberwell, but I had a feeling that you Aerians would turn down their proposal for an alliance.'

Even from a distance, I can see Col's eye twitch. 'We are too busy to form any alliances with them.'

Kirian narrows his eyes. 'Yes . . . but not too busy to form alliances with the Rocs. Or so I heard.'

Silence.

He lets out a deep sigh. 'Shame, really. Perhaps if you weren't so closed-minded, we could find a way to help one another.'

'*Leave.*' Col glares at each of us. 'All of you.'

Kirian's low, derisive chuckle does nothing to ease Col's irritation. 'We will, but first, why don't you direct me to the nearest town?' He glances our way. 'I heard the food here is outstanding.'

CHAPTER FORTY-NINE

I'm convinced my expression has frozen into a permanent scowl as Darius and I observe Kirian from across the table outside a bakery while he savours a slice of spice cake. According to him, the sweet loaf is an Aeris delicacy with its intricate blend of spices, all drenched in syrup.

Not that it matters when that is not what we are here for.

As Kirian relishes another bite, his eyes twinkle with pleasure. Meanwhile, armoured Aerian soldiers parade down the street opposite us. Kirian's attention briefly shifts, followed by a scoff. 'You would think, with all the Aerian soldiers they have, that this kingdom would be better protected.'

Darius lets out a playful chuckle. 'Like your land is?'

'One must take precautions regarding one's people,' Kirian retorts with a derisive smile.

My patience thins. 'Why are we really here, Kirian?'

Wiping his mouth with a napkin, which he then meticulously folds atop his lap, Kirian looks up at me. His stare is bold as if he expects me to draw back in fear. 'The Fallcrowns mentioned the predicaments you were facing with Hedris after the treaty was broken.'

My brows pinch in confusion. 'Arlayna told you that?'

A flicker of distaste shadows his expression. 'Yes.' His voice strains. 'She is quite the . . . *informative* one.'

I find that hard to believe. It was clear from when I last saw Arlayna that she has likely given Kirian hell with each letter they have sent each other.

'What she has failed to mention,' Kirian adds, his gaze flickering towards Darius, 'is that you're a Rivernorth.'

Darius eases back in his chair, his casual manner showing that he feels no threat whatsoever. 'Well, believe it or not, there is more to me than my name.'

Kirian mimics Darius's position, igniting a competitive air of male powerplay between them. 'Still. You hold a powerful title in all of this, Darius. You're the last standing Rivernorth, and others such as Hedris feel threatened by that.'

'And you?' I ask. 'Do you feel threatened?'

'It depends.' He shrugs. 'The only threat you could pose is if you came for my people.'

Which I'm certain Dusan and his forces have tried to do before.

'*But*,' he emphasises with a raised finger, 'I believe we can help each other.'

Darius and I share a look of unease. This is what Arlayna mentioned. Kirian wanted us on his side.

'Hedris believes he has the higher ground, especially now that Terranos is being ruled by someone unknown, and Emberwell by you,' he says.

'And you think forming an alliance with us will help?'

He nods once, shooting me a charismatic smile that doesn't suit his title of shadow king.

'You're a Dark Elf,' Darius reminds him, his voice a mix of

intrigue and arrogance. 'Not exactly a favourite among the Fall-crowns, or any other Elves.'

'And yet the Fallcrowns can't help you. They have their own issues right now, and whether you like it or not, the Aerian leaders won't side with you.'

Much to my annoyance, he is right. The Aerian leaders never warmed to me, and it's clear after our meeting that now Hira is gone, they won't help, even if Lorcan is their nephew.

'You've brought a lot of trouble with you, Nara,' Kirian says, his gaze flitting between Darius and me. 'Your union has.'

The mere mention of union rattles Darius. Despite Emberwell's gradual acceptance of us, scepticism still lingers elsewhere, especially towards a shifter and a former human.

Darius leans in, his laugh carrying an edge of menace. 'Suppose we entertain your offer. What's in it for you?'

Kirian ponders briefly. 'Let's just say I'm not without adversaries,' he confesses with a tight smile. 'Eventually, a time will come when I'll likely seek the same help I'm offering you now.'

The wind tousles my hair, stirring contemplative thoughts about what might come of this as it weaves through the sandy expanses of Aeris, lifting grains of dust in its wake. An alliance with the Dark Elves seems like a death wish, but having no one else at our side if Hedris ever attacks is worse.

'And when that day comes, I hope you both will be by my side, regardless of the situation.'

'And if we aren't?' I ask.

Kirian looks at me, his cold smile indicating the gruesome thoughts that must be running through his head.

'He won't do anything,' Darius says. Kirian's gaze cuts to him with a raised brow.

I frown, noting how casual Darius looks right now. He's smirking as he lounges in his chair and drums his fingers on the table.

'Won't I?' Kirian questions, seeming amused.

'No,' Darius retorts. 'You won't. You're not that stupid.'

'Darius—'

'No, no,' Kirian says to me, crossing his leg over his knee. 'I'm curious to know what he means by that.'

Darius stares at him with a narrow-eyed expression. 'He already knows that half the Elves will never side with him,' he explains. 'Thalorians are seen as outcasts – I would know. My people were too.'

I glance at Kirian to see what his reaction might be.

He simply rolls his forefinger and thumb together while giving Darius a twitch of a smile.

'But of course, everyone knows that.' Darius chuckles. 'And I assume that even though you are exchanging information with the princess of Terranos, you're not guaranteed safety. The High Elves still despise you, and with the new reign in place, they will likely come for you one day. You need as many people as possible on your side, and you know that losing us would only cause you issues in the grand scheme of things.'

A heavy silence hangs in the air between us once Darius finishes.

Then Kirian expels a sigh. 'You got me there, dragon.' His gaze slides to me and then back to Darius. 'Assuming I am never to act upon my threats – you still need me and my people.'

I roll my tongue across my teeth, still annoyed, *still* contemplating.

'It is either us, or no one at all. *So.*' Kirian tilts his head. 'What do you say?'

CHAPTER FIFTY

The door to my chambers swings open as Freya enters with a confident stride, her hands resting gently on her hips and a radiant smile gracing her lips.

The sun has just begun to rise, casting a soft glow on the room. I find myself still wrapped in the comfort of my dressing gown, anticipation bubbling within me because today is the day. The day of the wedding ceremony.

Last night, everyone made sure that Darius and I slept in separate rooms. Though neither of us wanted to be apart, we were excited about what was to come. No more worrying about Hedris – at least for today – or dwelling on our alliance with the Dark Elves.

'You're here early.' I chuckle, throwing my hair over my shoulder and weaving my fingers through my waves.

'That is because,' she drawls, 'I have a surprise for you.'

I raise an eyebrow inquisitively.

She rolls her eyes and flashes me a grin. 'Just close your eyes.'

I comply with her instructions, albeit with a slightly exasperated sigh. 'I hope you know I am not one for surprises.' At least, not with everything that has happened.

Freya chuckles; it sounds distant and echoey like she has just stepped out into the hallway. 'Well, this is one surprise I pray that you do love.'

I can feel the anticipation building within me, my feet eager to take that first step forward. I've never been known for my patience.

'All right.' Freya takes a deep breath. 'Open your eyes,' she whispers, her voice filled with a hint of mystery.

My breath catches in my throat and I blink, because the gown in Freya's delicate hands is unlike anything I have ever seen.

It has a white off-the-shoulder bodice, sculpted to perfection with what looks like white dragon scales. The skirt flows in a cascade of opalescent chiffon adorned with patterns that mimic the scales, while the sleeves drape down like the wings of a dragon. In the middle of the bodice, a gold-cut jewel lies perfectly still, as if it were the heart of the dress.

I am left speechless as I gaze up at Freya, her lips gently caught between her teeth and her eyes shimmering with hope. 'I know that you entrusted me with your wedding dress, and I truly had the perfect one in mind, but then I stumbled across this room full of clutter and old chests—'

A look of concern crosses my face. 'Old chests?'

Freya pauses, looking as if caught in a moment of uncertainty. 'Yes, it . . . was a hidden room, on the upper floors. I found this dress, among other things, inside a chest engraved with the name Aurelia.'

Aurelia.

'This is Aurelia's dress,' I whisper in awe, my eyes lingering on the exquisite gown. 'Darius's mother.'

Freya's joy is replaced by regret. 'Oh, my Solaris, I'm so sorry,

Nara.' She gently places the dress on the bed and grabs both of my hands. 'I didn't . . . I do have the back-up dress if you wish—'

I surprise her by enveloping her in my embrace, causing her to take a few steps back. I hear a soft gasp escape her, followed by a quick recovery once her arms come around me. 'I think Darius will love it,' I tell her.

'Are you certain?'

I nod and take a step back. We grasp each other's hands, and a smile naturally spreads across my lips as I admire the dress. 'I just hope, if Aurelia can see this, that she also loves the idea of me wearing it.'

'Of course she would,' Freya says softly. 'Who else other than Solaris herself should wear that dress?'

I chuckle, feeling too many emotions at once.

'So,' Freya playfully twirls a strand of my hair. 'Shall we prepare you for your momentous occasion?'

My stomach is a knot of nerves as I nod excitedly, and Freya gets to work with my hair. She drags me to the vanity by the window, braiding and pinning my curls into a low updo. We talk, laugh and sing until it is time to put the gown on.

Standing in front of the mirror, I am now clad in the wedding veil Freya had custom-tailored for me, a see-through piece of artwork with the sun stitched across it. The dress, on the other hand, is even more exquisite and it fits as if it were made for me. The white fabric of the skirt cascades like a waterfall made of the purest milk as each fold catches the light from outside the window.

I gently place my hands on the bodice, its scales feeling almost too forbidden to even touch.

It's perfect.

'Gus would have loved to see this.' As thoughts of him consume my mind, my admiration for the dress fades. All he wanted was to be near his son and the love of his life. I can only hope that he is now with her after all these years.

'Darius seems to be in less pain,' Freya empathises. 'He must be coming to terms with the idea of who Gus was to him – and to his mother.'

I stare at the ground. 'There are still days,' I whisper softly as if I'm sharing a secret. 'There will always be days.' Although there is no denying he is better than he was weeks ago. There are rare moments when I notice he is distant, in his own little world, but all it takes to bring him back is to grab his hand and let him see I am there for him. 'I suppose . . . ' I begin to say, but my words trail off as I turn around and freeze upon witnessing Freya completely out of it.

In her gaze, a misty white takes over the colour of her eyes, taking me back to a distant memory of when this happened to Leira. A cacophony of alarm bells goes off in my mind, and I urgently grab Freya by her shoulders.

'Freya!' I shake her. 'Frey—'

I let out a sharp gasp as she snatches my wrist and begins to sing in a low voice, 'From decay and ruin, they reclaim their vengeance—'

Her grip becomes painful.

'Freya.'

'No door can bar; no seal can bind.' The words get louder, echoing through the air.

I struggle to break free, my eyes widening in a surge of panic. 'Freya, wake up!'

'Yet the rivers hold the answer, and the lover who once was—'

The doors burst open, abruptly breaking Freya's hold on me, causing me to lose my balance and collide with the mirror.

Leira and Aelle walk into the room, their faces filled with joy when they catch sight of me. However, my attention immediately returns to Freya as she regains consciousness, her eyes blinking back to normality.

'Freya?' I pant, but she just smiles at me. I inch closer to her. 'Are you—'

'Oh, Nara, that dress is simply breathtaking,' Leira interrupts, her hands pressed against her heart.

Freya gazes at her aunt, oblivious to my shocked expression. 'Doesn't she just?'

'Darius is truly fortunate,' Aelle says, her eyes welling up with tears. I shake my head. 'I—'

'He would argue otherwise,' Freya chuckles, the three of them not giving me a chance to speak again.

There's a gentle tap on the door and Ruvyn steps inside. A hush falls over the room as all eyes turn towards him. With a gentle gesture, he adjusts the folds of his tunic. 'Excuse me, Lady Nara, may we have a moment?'

My lips part, yet no words escape.

'It's of the utmost importance.' He tilts his head downward.

'Very well, very well.' Leira gracefully waves her hand. 'We were just leaving.'

I quickly seize Freya's arm just as she is about to follow Aelle and Leira. Her gaze meets mine, suddenly concerned.

'We need to talk afterwards,' I say quietly, causing her to grow even more worried. 'Don't go too far.'

'What's wrong?'

So much is wrong. *So* much.

'Freya,' Aelle calls out to her, and Freya sighs, casting a longing glance in my direction, assuring me that we will see each other before the ceremony.

She had a vision. A vision that sounds terrifying.

As Freya exits the room, my heart pounds. I turn towards the vanity and press my palms against it. I close my eyes and let loose a shaky breath. 'What is it then, Ruvyn?'

'Sarilyn,' he says. 'She wishes to speak with you.'

I mutter a curse and swiftly turn around. 'Now?'

He swallows and then nods.

She could not have chosen a worse time.

CHAPTER FIFTY-ONE

'Oh, Naralía,' Sarilyn says as soon as I appear behind the bars of her cell. She rises from her seated position on the ground. 'That dress.' She shakes her head and smiles as she stares at it up and down. 'You truly make a luscious bride.'

I'm reluctant to give her any form of gratitude. 'It belonged to Aurelia,' I say it straight, and her brows jump. 'Why did you want to speak with me?' I add idly, seeing as my mind is still thinking about Freya.

Sarilyn blows out a breath and spears me with curious eyes. 'I heard you have allied with the Dark Elves.'

My shoulders tense, and as I move closer, I lift the skirt of my gown so it doesn't collect dirt. 'Where did you get that from?'

'Your little friend who follows you around like a lost pet.' She cocks her head from side to side. 'The Elf.'

I sigh. *Ruvyn.*

'He's quite the chatterbox once you rile him up.'

I should have never brought Ruvyn into all of this. He is the only other companion who knows about my visits with Sarilyn. He is the one who takes care of her necessities. It was only a matter of time before she began to get inside his head.

'King Hedris wants to dethrone Darius,' I tell her. There is no point in evading the situation any longer. 'We are simply preparing ourselves.'

She hums vaguely. 'I thought you never wanted a fight?'

'I don't,' I huff. 'All I have ever wanted is to prevent us from going to war, yet it seems all odds are against me.' My mind circles back to Freya's words.

From decay and ruin, they reclaim their vengeance . . .

My hands feel clammy and nausea tickles my throat as I grimace, turning my head to the side. I don't want to think about what that means, or even think about it at all, but I can't get it out of my mind. Freya felt something – something that happened just to her.

'When I first met with the seers,' Sarilyn says quietly, and my gaze drifts to hers only to find her staring far off at the walls, 'they used to live deep in the woods. I still remember the one I visited. She was living with witches at the time.' Under her breath, a disdainful laugh bubbles up her throat. 'Twin witches.'

I stay rooted to the spot, not knowing whether to speak or even breathe.

'When the seer told me of what could happen, I retaliated by—'

Knowing where she is going with this, I cut her off, gritting my teeth. 'You killed them.'

Her eyes snap my way. 'I made *Erion* kill them,' she says, as if it were any better. 'The twins, but not the seer. I wanted her to know that I could change the future however I wanted. That nothing would stop me, not a fight, not a dragon, and much less a reincarnation of the so-called Solaris.' Contempt colours her expression in a way that reminds me of the old Sarilyn, the one who did everything she could to win.

Yet a moment later, that old loathing cracks and she drops her shoulders with a sigh. 'I suppose, though, that there are times when, no matter what you do, you cannot change the spoken future.'

'That's not true.' I say it in a whisper, as if I'm afraid to admit something I am unsure about myself. 'Maybe . . . you went about it the wrong way. Chose paths that resulted in the opposite outcome to what you wanted.'

Sarilyn's eyes are on me as she considers it. Then she backs away further into her cell and sits down on the grimy floor. She is so used to the dungeons now that the dirt and bones of previous prisoners no longer disgust her.

'Well.' She takes a breath. 'Time is ticking, Naralía. I feel I have kept you down here long enough. I doubt you want to be late to your own wedding, do you?'

No. No, I do not.

Still, something tells me that Sarilyn found an excuse to bring me down here. She might not say it to my face, nor do I think she will ever have the courage to do so, but I know that in some depth of her heart, she enjoys my company.

I don't bid her goodbye. I decide that a simple nod will suffice as I turn my back to her.

'Naralía?' she says. I whirl to her, dragging the light layers of my gown with me in my hands. 'Good luck in your new life.' She surprises me with a genuine smile, despite a certain sadness lingering in her dark eyes. 'I expect you to thrive more than I ever could have.'

The raw and earnest tone in her voice wraps around me, affecting my heart more than I care to admit to myself.

I want to think it is her just manipulating me to feel this way.

I want to believe it is just her way of toying with me.

Perhaps then, it wouldn't make me feel such guilt for someone who caused me so much pain in the first place.

I scold myself as I spare a quick glance at Ruvyn as he comes to fetch me through the flickering, sconced corridor and faces Sarilyn's curious stare.

There will be no going back after this . . .

The air is humid as I walk through the fields back to the castle along-side Ruvyn. For the entire journey back from the dungeons, Ruvyn did not speak a word, nor did he give me a single clue as to what might be going through his mind.

Until now.

As I look at him, he clears his throat, opens his mouth, and closes it again.

I stop and lift a finger at him. 'Don't say a word.'

His lips twitch. 'I wasn't planning to,' he lies, bowing his head. 'Lady Nara.'

I sigh, annoyed that today isn't going how I thought it would.

'Although,' Ruvyn suddenly starts. I send him a glare, which he ignores. 'I do wish to know what you plan to tell everyone once they realise—'

A strange shadow comes from above, as dozens of birds slice through the sky with urgent squawks that cut off Ruvyn's words. Our gazes are drawn upwards, and we watch with intensity as the flock flees from the north.

'Are they—'

A sense of foreboding tears in my chest. 'They're scared.' I glance back down at Ruvyn and am about to speak again when a sharp pain twists inside my gut, and I double over, clutching my stomach.

When the time comes, you'll know.

I shake my head with terror.

Ruvyn is saying my name, asking what is wrong, but I can't— I can't—

We'll see each other very soon.

My throat tightens, each breath escaping me in ragged gasps as I try to straighten and slowly turn on my heels. My vision tunnels, merging all the birds, and I know then that the worst is about to come.

I stumble into Ruvyn, clutching his arms. 'I need you to ring the bells and inform everyone.'

He looks lost, his dark eyes wide with alarm. 'Inform everyone of what? Lady Nara, please. I implore you to calm down.'

'I can't!' I draw in another sharp breath. 'He's coming—he's— Aurum's coming.'

Right then, as if speaking those words into existence, the air becomes thick with the pungent aroma of decay, and from where the volcanoes lie beyond the hills, an unmistakable shade of green shadows fog the sky.

Ruyvn's hands go slack, and I start to back away, my gaze trained on the shadows.

When you're at your happiest, surrounded by those dear to you, basking in a triumph that should have been mine, know that I'll be lurking in the dark, waiting for the perfect opportunity to strike.

As Aurum's words echo inside me, I take off in a sprint, feeling the deep pain of each pounding step of my feet inside my heeled boots.

CHAPTER FIFTY-TWO

A mass of chaos unfolds before me when I return to the castle. I see Niamh, with a few other past Venators, running with their weapons drawn as they mount the shifters' backs and take off from the windows.

Time seems to slow as Darius stands across from me in the centre of the throne chamber, his eyes spotting me instantly. We begin running towards each other, my shoulders knocking against Venators before I reach him. He catches me in his arms, pressing me tightly against him. There is only a moment spared for us to look at what each of us is wearing: him in a gorgeous black jacket with silver thread, and me in his mother's old gown.

'Aurum,' I say, my voice hoarse from screaming at everyone out in the fields to run.

He rests his palm on my cheek and nods, his jaw firm. 'I know.' He looks past me as the bells in the castle's tower ring. 'Come on, we need to get as many people as possible out of here.' Grabbing my hand, he leads me towards the exit. I start to search for my brothers, but the ground cracks beneath Darius and me.

We stumble to a pause, feeling the earth shake and crumble.

'Darius,' I say, before his name on my lips is drowned out by the deathly shriek of a dragon landing on the balcony – a dragon belonging to Aurum. I whirl my head, my heart hammering as the creature shakes the debris from its head and spots us. Soulless eyes dripping in black substance lock on us as it screams again and charges at us.

Its large wings catch against the pillars, but they're no match for the dragon as it breaks through them within seconds.

Venators run at it with their swords but are swiftly slammed against the walls as the dragon's ferocious roar reverberates through the chamber.

Darius tightens his grip on my hand, his eyes set on the dragon ahead. When the dragon leaps towards us, Darius rallies his power, startling the creature as fire descends upon it.

'We need to find Freya!' I shout before the dragon can regain vision. Darius immediately abandons his jacket and shifts. Seeing that I can't do anything other than rip my dress as I climb atop him, I reach for a sword right as Darius takes off.

We weave through the chaos, aiming for the balcony. But the dragon is now hot on our trail, trying to scorch Darius with a green mist that emerges from its mouth. The scent is suffocating as the air fills with that same smell of decay I noticed before.

I glance back to see a group of Venators, including Niamh, aiming their weapons at the dragon again, their faces set with a determination that reminds me they're still hunters – *dragon* hunters – at heart.

Stretching my palm out, I unleash a blast of light, sending the dragon sliding against the ground with a painful cry. This gives us enough time for Darius to break through walls and stone, destroying the entire balcony in his wake. I clutch on to him, gazing at the expanse of Emberwell and the fields below us.

When I look up at the skies, dragons – both ours and Aurum's – paint each other with streaks of fire and rotting shadows. I glance back at the ground, making out figures of people battling against these creatures. Amidst them, I catch a glimpse of orange fur moving quickly through the crowd.

Relieved, I say to Darius, 'They're down there—'

Without warning, one of Aurum's dragons collides with Darius. The impact is so sudden and brutal that it knocks the sword from my hand and tears me away from Darius as I'm flung off his back. I shout his name in panic as I twist in the air, desperately reaching out for something, anything, but all I can see is the blur of green and brown beneath me.

I can only catch glimpses of Darius and the dragon, locked in a deadly embrace, as they claw at each other and spiral away from me. Their roars fade into the distance of forests just as I plummet and crash through the canopy of dense branches and leaves, and finally land on thick grass.

For a moment, the world stops screaming.

I lie there, staring up at the sky, my body aching and my head throbbing.

'Darius,' I croak out as if he can hear me from wherever he is, and as I try to sit up with effort, a sharp pain shoots up my leg, almost blinding me, a wave of nausea following afterwards. I grimace in agony, glancing at the skirt of my dress, shredded and dirty now, and I hike it up to assess the damage.

Horror twists my gut, and I bend over to the side, dry heaving. Nothing comes up, not even when I want it to.

Peering down at my leg again, I wince, seeing it twisted in a way limbs should never be.

I grit my teeth and reach down with trembling hands. I can

already feel my body trying to repair itself, but the pain coursing through me is like no other. I can't wait for it to heal, there's no time.

With a deep breath that feels like drawing daggers into my lungs, I grasp my leg just below the knee with one hand, placing the other hand above the broken bones.

'One, two, three—' A cry mingled with what sounds like a howl, tears from my throat as I pull at my leg. The pain I feel right now is a white-hot explosion, obliterating my senses. I can hear the grind of bone echoing throughout the fields as I breathe harshly through my teeth. For a second, all I see is dark spots swirling in my vision before the pain slowly ebbs away, and I push myself to my feet.

My body protests at every movement, but I will myself to limp forwards and out of the trees.

There, where the fields seem to stretch on for ever, stands Aurum, waiting for me.

I freeze.

'Nara.' He dares to smile. 'There you are. You didn't think I was going to miss your big day, did you?' His ruined face sends a shiver down my spine before he notices what I am wearing. 'That dress,' he murmurs, studying it with hatred in his eye. He quickly douses that flame of rage with a cruel grin. 'Pity it's ruined.'

'How?' I swallow. 'How did you get out?'

'I already told you, Nara.' He takes a step towards me, and I glower. 'You freed me. It turns out that when you healed that tree, a rift opened in the Isle.'

My heart drops, and as if he can feel it himself, he stares at me with a cruel vengeance in his working eye.

The nightmare I had. It was real . . . and the silhouette I saw between the volcanoes . . . it was *him. All of it.*

'And *now*,' he whispers with a chuckle, 'thanks to you and my nephew, I'm finally out.'

I shake my head and charge at him, healing leg be damned. 'You bastard—' I hiss, but he raises his hand, and somehow, I stop.

He grins and cups his ear. 'Do you hear that?'

Through what I thought was silence, I soon start hearing the screams of others coming from the city, the castle, the castle gardens . . .

'It's the sound of your people dying.'

No.

I must have said it out loud because he nods. All I feel is blinding rage as I summon my powers. I send them his way, parrying one of his strikes as the fabric of my dress tears.

Aurum chuckles, finding all of this amusing. 'You should have prepared yourself, Nara. Was my visit to you not enough warning?'

A guttural cry escapes me, and I conjure up a sword of light – something that I have never done before. Aurum stops laughing, and I run at him, swinging that blade in every direction.

Today was supposed to be my special day.

I was supposed to be holding a bouquet of flowers, not a weapon.

And I should have been walking down the aisle in the back gardens of the castle alongside my brothers.

Every swing and hit that I manage against Aurum is useless, his rotting body only fixing itself back up, as shadows dance around him, reeking of the dead. The one thing that makes him stumble back is when a swarm of bees and wasps come out from behind me. They fly around Aurum as if to protect me, and I use the distraction to spiral out a sharp force of power towards his chest.

He grunts, locking his gaze on me.

One moment, he is far away from me, and then the next, he is right in front of me, leaving only a slither of shadows behind him.

I don't have time to dodge him as he grabs me by the neck and lifts me into the air before slamming me back down onto the ground. Searing pain echoes throughout my head, and I try to fight back, but his foot comes down on my neck, pressing until I start to gasp for air.

'You really are a waste of a reincarnation,' he seethes. 'Even the Aerian and Undarion rulers despise you.'

I scratch at him, pushing all the power I have to my fingers to force him off me.

'I guess it is a good thing that they are now on my side.'

My power draws back into me, and I stop fighting him.

Aurum's smile crawls across my skin as he gets the reaction he wants out of me. 'You didn't think it would be my army alone, did you?' he croons, and I scream. I scream for my friends, my brothers . . . for Darius, but my voice is so hoarse, so . . . *quiet*. 'It was so easy to get them on my side once I was out.'

Blood bubbles inside my mouth, and I glare at him. Then, out of nowhere, my eyes drift behind Aurum, spotting Idris as he cries out and raises a dagger over Aurum's head.

'Idris!' is the single thing I say as Aurum releases me and turns, grabbing Idris's arm before the blade can hit. He punches my brother in the face, knocking him back a few paces, but Idris doesn't give up. He never does.

He lunges for Aurum, engaging in a fight that I know my brother cannot win.

'Get away from him!' I try to yell, my vision blurring as I stand and take stumbling steps towards the two figures.

They're on the ground, Aurum pummelling my brother with dark powers swirling within his palm. When Idris swings his other arm around, I hear the sound of bones breaking, and his scream pierces the skies. I rage, seeing red, and blast my power out blindly at Aurum.

As my sight begins to clear, I find myself in a surreal scene where the ground has crumbled beneath my magic, and on the other side lies Aurum, slowly regaining strength from my blow. Without hesitation, I run towards Idris. His face is stained with blood, and I gently shake my head, trying to help him rise with one arm.

'I'm all right,' he says with a groan before I can ask.

'He broke your wrist—' I reach for it, but he moves, hiding the injury from me.

'It's nothing,' he promises, but there's an odd look in his eyes.

'That wasn't very nice,' Aurum spits, now standing and trying to hold in place the flesh of his hanging cheek. 'I guess I underestimate you sometimes.'

My fingers curl as I will whatever power is left at my fingertips.

Aurum just laughs, like my attempts amuse him. 'Save your powers, Nara,' he says. 'This is just the beginning.' His eye slithers from mine to Idris's, and even in this state, Idris clings to me in a protective embrace. 'I only came by to warn you.'

The cries from the city subside, as does the chaos up in the sky.

'You have five days to decide, Nara,' Aurum declares. 'Fight me for the kingdom, or die along with the rest of Emberwell.'

Never.

Never. Never.

I grit my teeth. 'Fuck you.'

'Hm, I would think it over, Nara . . . you might change your mind sooner than you think.' His lips curl into a smile dipped in malice, and he glances at Idris once more. 'One week,' he says again, then calls to his dragons, flying past us like a storm.

Idris and I hold on to each other tightly, my heart pounding as the deafening cries of Aurum's creatures fill the air before he vanishes along with them.

CHAPTER FIFTY-THREE

I yell for help as soon as I make it to the courtyard. Idris and I limp
and stagger, watching the smoke coat the air and flames flicker all
around us. Leira comes through the haze, sees we are covered in
dirt and soot – as is she.

'Nara—'

'I need you to take Idris to the infirmary,' I tell her, not giving her
enough time to worry about me.

She stares at me, her wild dark curls matted and soaked in all kinds
of things. With a slight hesitation, she nods, but Idris begins shaking
his head. I ignore him, letting Leira lead him away as I scan the
wounded Venators and shifters helping each other up from the ground.

My head pounds in agonising pain. Everything is destroyed, my
people are injured, and I can't find Darius, my friends . . .

'Nara?' a shaky voice says from behind me.

I spin around, tears stinging my eyes as I see my two brothers
holding one another. Their clothes are ripped, and underneath the
dirt that covers them I can see a hint of gold and colourful tunics –
attire they wore to celebrate my wedding today.

My lips wobble as I sway towards them. I wrap my arms around each of them before pressing my forehead against Illias's forehead.

'I'm so sorry,' I whisper. 'This was never meant to happen.'

'I know.' Illias nods, but it's not enough. No apology is enough.

As I pull back from him, my eyes trace the familiar lines of his face, the brown curls that look darker against the dust. Then, I do the same to Iker. He pulls me into an embrace, sighing when I mumble another apology to him, too.

But the bittersweet moment shatters when I look up and see Darius emerging from the smog. My heart lurches as I take in the blood splashed across his once-pristine jacket.

His eyes find mine, and his steps quicken, swallowing the space between us until he reaches me, and I collapse into his arms. He peppers my face with kisses, saying how much he loves me over and over again as I nod and close my eyes.

'What did he do?' he says, his voice tense as I open my eyes to look at him. He knows. He always knows.

'He . . .' I shake my head, almost whimpering from the memory of seeing his rotted face in the flesh. 'He gave us five days.'

Darius's brows pull together, his lips parting.

'Five days,' I say again. 'Five days to either fight him in battle or he will destroy more than he already has.'

Concern flickers across his eyes, and he cradles my head against his chest. He says, 'We'll figure it out, Goldie. I promise.'

I lean back to look at him, wanting to make sure that he is actually here with me, but another figure captures my attention as Lorcan strides into the courtyard, carrying the body of someone in his arms. His jaw is set as his eyes meet mine, and I look down at the person in his hold.

Ruvyn.

He is utterly lifeless in Lorcan's arms as blood trickles down the side of his head and mats his hair to his face.

I stare at him for seconds as I bite my lower lip to keep myself from crying. 'His mother,' I whisper. 'He—' I look up, my throat burning. 'He was supposed to be with his mother.'

Darius's hand brushes against my cheek, smearing soot and blood. I don't care; I take in his touch, needing it more than ever. 'He died in your service,' he says. 'Protecting you and this kingdom despite it not being his home. His mother would be proud, and so should you be, Goldie.'

I glance at him just as he wipes away a tear that escapes me. In his eyes, I see the reflection of flames that gives me enough strength to smile. 'We will need to bury him,' I say, then look at Lorcan. 'How many casualties?'

He sighs deeply and shakes his head at the ground. 'It is hard to tell. At least a hundred between the city and the Venators.'

I nod, trying to keep my composure. At the same time, Freya comes running towards us with Rydan and Link. She holds a scared Tibith in her arms before handing him over to Darius to console.

She immediately swings an arm around my neck, whispering, 'You're okay, Solaris, you're okay.'

'As are you,' I say as we pull apart. She has a slight bruise marring her forehead, but other than that, she looks perfect as always. 'I needed to talk to you before . . .' Well, she knows the rest. I clear my throat. 'Freya, do you not remember at all what you told me in my room?'

She frowns, shaking her head at me.

'You had a vision.'

Freya blinks at me, her mouth opening then closing as she tries to wrap her head around that.

'It was a warning,' I emphasise. 'Like the one Leira once gave me. I think . . . I think it is the only thing that can help us right now.'

'Nara.' She sighs. 'I don't even know what I said or—'

'But I do.' My eyes flicker towards everyone else. The weight of what I am about to say might worsen things, but I can't keep it from them. 'I freed Sarilyn.'

I hear Rydan mutter a 'What?' while Freya takes a step back in shock.

'Nara,' Lorcan warns, but I look to Darius for his reaction. He doesn't speak, nor does he look mad.

'She told me,' I say before anyone can interrupt me, 'about the seer who she visited all those years ago. The same seer who will likely know more about Aurum than any of us.'

'Sarilyn *knew*.' Rydan shakes his head. 'She was the one there with him for centuries.'

'And yet she still doesn't know everything.' My mind recalls how Aurum mentioned a witch. '*My* witch,' he had said. I capture Freya's hands in mine. 'In your warning, you said that the rivers hold the answer.'

'I—'

'Just trust me.'

Freya's gaze turns watery as she stares at me. After a moment, she whispers, 'You know I do.'

'Where does this seer live, *if* she is still alive?' Darius says for the first time after I told everyone about Sarilyn.

'Deep in the woods.' I look towards the walls of the castle. 'I can only hope that she never left.'

The revelation hangs heavy over the group. I hold my breath, waiting for someone to at least respond.

'Deep in the woods,' Darius echoes, his voice steady and resolute. 'Tell us when you're ready, Goldie, and we'll leave in search of her.'

Hearing that confirmation from Darius gives me all the assurance I need. The group's collective gaze turns to me with unwavering support, while Freya's eyes fill with fear.

I squeeze her hand the same way she would mine. I glance at the courtyard surrounding us; bodies lie on the ground that was once green and beautiful. There's a silence among us, as we mourn everything we have lost today.

I can't seem to take Aurelia's dress off. Even as it hangs filthy and ripped in parts that show off my skin, I still can't. I buried Ruvyn, wearing this dress. The last thing he saw me in before dying.

Glancing at Darius I see he is sitting on the edge of the bed, his clothes, unlike mine, on the floor, leaving him in just his breeches. The muscles on his chest go taut with every movement of his hands as he pulls off his boots and sets them down with a heavy sigh.

I walk over to him, and he looks up. His hair is all messy, and I just want to run my hands through it.

He slinks his hands around my waist and pulls my stomach towards his lips.

'Freya told me about the dress,' he murmurs.

'I'm—' I bite my tongue, knowing an apology won't fix it.

'I don't care if the dress is ruined,' he says, lifting his head to look at me. 'I care that I wasn't with you when Aurum attacked.'

The darkness inside our chambers doesn't hide the gold in his eyes. His grip is so tight around me that I can't imagine what he must have thought when that dragon attacked us. I almost lost it myself when I couldn't see him.

'I should have known there was more to that nightmare you had.'

He's blaming himself, and I've never hated it more than when he does this.

I straddle him, my eyes levelling with his now. 'We thought he was still trapped in the Isle. We couldn't have known.'

He runs a hand across my back, eliciting a tingle to climb up my spine, and I shift against his lap. 'And about Sarilyn—' he starts.

Shame reddens my cheeks. 'I know I shouldn't have let her out. It's just—'

'You did what you felt was right,' he says, surprising me. 'I'm not angry at you, Goldie. I would have done the same.'

My lips twitch into a soft smile. 'Really?'

He nudges my nose with his. 'Really,' he whispers.

I indulge in this moment despite the horrors we are facing. Sighing, I say, 'Do you think we will ever get rid of Aurum?'

Darius nuzzles himself against my neck and breathes me in. 'One can only hope, Goldie.'

CHAPTER FIFTY-FOUR

Everyone is silent as we stalk through the forests in the far east of Emberwell. The morning has barely settled, yet dark clouds still seep across the sky in ominous waves. It's a reminder that Aurum's attack destroyed more than we thought.

After leaving our dragons a few miles back so as not to spook the seer, my brothers, Rydan and Link now stride ahead of Darius and me, while Freya has her eyes on the ground as she holds on to the strap of her quiver. She looks completely guilt-ridden after what happened yesterday, and as much as I keep telling her it is nowhere near her fault, she still blames herself for what she said.

From decay and ruin, they reclaim their vengeance.

No door can bar; no seal can bind.

Yet the rivers hold the answer, and the lover who once was—

'I've noticed Idris and Enox seem to have gotten close lately.'

Darius's voice gently coaxes me back to reality as he jerks his chin towards my brother.

I turn my head to look, and where Idris is usually so sure-footed in his surroundings, he seems distracted now, his face lacking its usual golden hue as he peers over his shoulder and notices me staring.

'And I thought he would never get used to dragons.' I smile at Darius, but I think he can tell it's not quite there.

Tibith, on the other hand, whirls around in circles a before climbing onto Darius's shoulder.

'I am used to dragons too!' he babbles, and Darius and I chuckle.

'Says the one who likes to rile the whelps up whenever they get too close to Goldie.' Darius smirks, making Tibith huff. 'You should talk to him.' Darius's smile fades as he looks at me. He means Idris. 'It looks like he needs it.'

I bunch my lips to the side as I set my eyes on my brother. His left wrist is bound in a crude splint, the angles all wrong, as if he might have put it back in place himself. He likely never allowed Leira to take him to the infirmary.

Since he came to my rescue yesterday we haven't had the chance to speak about what happened – how he risked his life for me against someone like Aurum. I know what he would have said, though – that he would sacrifice his life if it meant Illias, Iker and I were safe. Much as I would, too.

I nod my head at Darius and walk over to my brother, falling into step beside him. 'How is your wrist?' I ask him, watching as he cradles it protectively against his chest.

'Better,' he murmurs, avoiding my eyes.

It sounds like a lie.

I decide to focus ahead as we move through the dappled light of the dense woods, an unspoken tension hanging between us.

'You're strangely quiet,' Idris says, breaking the silence. 'I thought you would have accused me of lying by now.'

I hesitate as I glance at him. He's trying to find humour in all of this, though it has never been his style. Shrugging, I say, 'I've got a lot on my mind.'

He nods. 'Same here.'

'I was thinking, though,' I say. 'About the times you told me I couldn't train to become a Venator.'

He quirks a brow.

I chew on my bottom lip. 'I wonder what would have been like if you had never let me leave that day.'

Idris stops, so I turn on the spot to face him. 'There was never an if,' he tells me quietly. 'You know yourself it was meant to happen.'

'I know,' I say, my eyes flickering to where Darius now laughs at whatever Tibith might be saying. 'But I'd like to think of a different life in which I went back to our home, shouted at you for not letting me go and then continued on our days undisturbed.'

He gives me a tight smile. 'Me too.'

I don't know what comes over me, but my heart urges me to embrace my older brother. So I do just that and wrap my arms around him. It makes me feel young again. Back then, I would argue with him and later on say how I couldn't sleep. Idris would lift me up into his arms with a sigh and sing this lullaby our mother used to sing to send us all to sleep.

Close your eyes, the day is done,
Rest in my arms as the sun sets,
Let sleep take hold,
And your dreams raise a new beginning.'

As the last note of the lullaby fades in my mind, I smile but it doesn't last too long as an uneasy silence falls upon everyone.

Idris tenses as I step back and glance around the clearing. Dense thickets border it as a rustle from deep within the forest sets every nerve on edge.

Freya nocks one of her arrows in readiness. My eyes narrow against the dimming light, and at that exact moment, a shape emerges.

'Shit!' Rydan yells as the familiar screech of a Rümen splits our eardrums.

My brothers and friends reach for their weapons as Darius stalks towards it.

My heart pounds in my chest and my protective instincts flare to life as I step forward, palms outstretched between everyone and the Rümen. 'Stop!'

The all come to a halt.

The Rümen included.

It cowers, flapping its leathery wings in a form of distress.

'It's hurt,' I say, frowning as I look closer. The Rümen's wings are shredded to bits, blood dripping and painting the grass.

Something palpable connects us as we come face to face. It is a sort of sadness and pain that reminds me that this creature is alone and likely the last of its kind.

I stare and stare at it, at the venom seeping through its sharp teeth, and I hear its weak cry.

A hand then comes across my waist, its immediate warmth and scent telling me it is Darius. I don't notice I am crying until he wipes the dampness away from my cheek, and I lift my head up to him.

'It's not our—'

'I know,' he whispers.

Enemy is what I wanted to say.

But as the Rümen's sudden shriek pierces the forest, it disappears in a flurry, sprinting off and leaving bloody leaves in its wake.

'Wait!' I tumble out of Darius's grip, wanting it to come back, but someone steps out from the trees and I skid to a stop. It's a woman, and her dress is a blend of forest materials that resembles the ones I'd seen Elves wear in Olcar. As she takes another step into the clearing, I notice her eyes are a vivid blue, contrasting with the deep mahogany of her skin. The slightest light catches the contours of her face, highlighting her cheekbones as she takes in everyone's defensive stance as well as the lingering traces of the Rümen.

When her gaze finally rests on Darius, her eyes are alight with surprise. 'Darius?'

Baffled, I look at Darius, but he doesn't seem to know her. He narrows his eyes, moving towards her with cautious curiosity. 'I'm sorry.' His chuckle is low. 'Have we met before?'

'Oh, yes.' She slowly smiles. 'Many years ago. I am the one who assisted the witches that took those markings off your hands.'

The seer.

It's her.

'I was never able to forget those golden eyes of yours.' She chuckles. '*Darius Rivernorth.*'

CHAPTER FIFTY-FIVE

'Apologies for the mess.' Silaria, the seer, takes off her shawl and places it on a hook beside the door, revealing long, glossy dark hair. The inside of her hut is small, with just enough room to fit about ten of us in here, though we can hardly move an inch.

'I haven't had any visitors in years,' she laughs lightly.

'Looks like it,' Rydan mutters with a snort, and Link elbows him.

'Are you all right?' Freya whispers from the doorway, and I peer over my shoulder as she stares at Idris with a hint of worry in her eyes.

Idris is leaning against the wall, breathing harshly, his eyes half closed.

I'm already walking over to him with immense concern, but Silaria's high-pitched whistle makes me jump.

'Pips!' she sings, searching the hut, until she stops and claps with glee as she stares down at the rocky floorboards. 'Ah, there you all are.'

What sounds like a thousand chirping birds turns out to be the excitable commotion as a flurry of Tibithians crowd around her.

I gasp out my surprise at all their different sizes, some bigger than Tibith, and others so small, they could fit in the palm of my hand.

Silaria bends down to stroke one. They purr and wiggle their noses. 'I took them all in years ago after my friends perished.' She looks at us. 'They keep me company.'

The Tibithians spot Tibith by my side and surround him, sniffing his fur with curiosity.

'Hello!' Tibith's ears flap as he waves at them. 'My name is Tibith. What is yours?'

Darius chuckles, and Silaria stands, watching their interaction.

A shadow of humour crosses her bright eyes. 'This might be the first time I have heard a Tibithian speak,' she says. 'It's rare that anyone is ever willing to try to teach a creature to talk.'

'Well, Tibith was always keen to learn.' Darius stares at Tibith, a smile lingering on his lips.

Silaria chuckles. 'And have you thought about letting him go with his own kind?'

'Tibith is family,' I say. 'If he were ever to decide to leave and go on with his kind, we wouldn't stop him. But for now, he is happy here with us.'

She hums in thought before turning her back to us as she rearranges some flowerpots on her table. 'So, what is it that brings you here?'

Darius and I glance at each other. He nods for me to go on, so I step forward and say, 'I am sure you have seen the chaos that has unfolded lately.'

Silaria pauses. 'I tend to stay out of it all,' she huffs, then resumes picking at her flowers. 'Though sadly, my visions do not let me.'

My eyes narrow. 'You saw us coming here.' A seer is not a witch, after all. Their visions come and stay with them even in the darkest of hours.

After a minute, Silaria nods. 'I have seen you in my dreams many times, Naralía.' She turns to me. 'It is nice to finally meet you in person.'

I tilt my chin up at her. 'Likewise.'

She smirks. 'Now,' she says, looking towards Darius and then me. 'What is it you wish to know?'

'Years ago, you told Sarilyn Orcharian about a battle between powerful beings.'

She stares at me, not liking where this is going. 'I did.'

'She made her general kill your friends, the witches, but did you also ever mention to her that Aurum once fell in love . . . with a witch?'

Silaria's eyes carry the weight of past secrets, her gaze shifting to everyone inside her home. 'No, I did not.' Her denial comes out in a whisper. 'But I do know who it was.' She glances at Darius. 'Thanks to your mother.'

Darius tenses beside me. 'What do you mean?'

'Your mother and I were once very close. In fact, she and the twins were my only trusted friends at the time.' She smiles to herself. 'I still remember the day she brought you over. You were such a shy little boy. Up until I handed you a piece of gold jewellery, and then you settled down.'

I can't stop the laugh that comes out of me as I look up at Darius. The image of him so young and shy melts every bit of my heart.

He chuckles under his breath, shakes his head and slides a glance Silaria's way. 'And my mother?'

Silaria turns and walks over to her cupboards, rifling through them. '*Aurelia*', she begins, 'was always an outcast among her family. At least, that is what she always told me. She was considered the weakest among her siblings, which meant Aurum never considered her a threat. He knew he was the greatest king to live, and the more power-hungry he became, the more he forgot about his family. That was . . . until he met *her*.' She sighs. 'Orna.'

There is a pause as the name settles over all of us.

'That is what Aurelia said her name was. She was a witch assigned to him. Their connection tethered to help one another.'

'They fell in love,' Freya says quietly, but everyone manages to hear it, including Silaria as she turns.

'Yes.' She smiles, then eyes Freya with a look of interest. 'You're a witch too. A *halfling*.'

Freya swallows and then nods, placing one hand behind her back; the other is holding Idris's. He seems to be better; whatever is going through his mind is now soothed by Freya's touch.

'As I was saying,' Silaria brings my attention back to her. 'Despite them falling in love, Aurum had this ideology about life that Orna never agreed with.'

'What happened to her?' Illias asks.

'Aurelia knew the relationship was wrong,' Silaria continues. 'Aurum was too possessive, and he became untethered against the sorcerers at the time, killing anyone that even spoke of Orna. All of this soon led to the war, but before it could, Aurelia wanted Orna to leave. Even promised her a better life if she left Emberwell. When Aurum found out, he almost killed Aurelia; luckily, their siblings intervened, but by the time Aurum went in search of Orna, a group of humans who were in favour of the sorcerers had attacked her carriage and—' She is unable to finish her words, swallowing them as if they are poison.

The reality is that she was murdered. How gruesome it was, I do not ever wish to know. But it explains Aurum's hatred for humans ever since that moment.

'Eventually,' she says, 'he found a new witch to aid him in his twisted decisions. But she was never able to replace Orna.'

'What can we do to destroy him once and for all?' I say, my voice carrying this sense of urgency. We have less than five days before Aurum kills more of my people and destroys the kingdom itself.

Silaria sighs, her dark hair covering her sharp features as she looks at the floor. 'I do not know.'

'You do.' I take a step towards her. 'You have to know.'

She lets out a laugh that sounds borderline self-mocking. 'My dear, I may be a seer, but that does not mean I can tell you exactly word for word what will happen within the next few minutes, let alone ten years from now.'

My hope depletes, and I look away, feeling the frustration trying to best me.

'But what I can tell you is that Orna is and always will be his weakness.'

That doesn't make this any better.

'And what are we supposed to do with that information when she is no longer alive?' Darius raises his brows at her expectantly.

Silaria simply smiles cryptically. 'She doesn't have to be alive to end him. Have you ever thought that perhaps the place where life was given to him is also the place where it can be taken away?'

Her words coil around me like a serpent, whispering knowledge into my ears that I can decipher completely.

'What—'

My question is severed by the sudden sound of a body hitting the ground with a weight that drags the breath from my lungs.

'Idris!' Freya yells, and I spin around with my heart in my throat, finding my brother crumpled on the floor as he claws at his splint.

We all rush to him, a flurry of hands trying to hold him down as he writhes in agony, and Silaria marches over to see.

'Idris,' I plead. 'Look at me—'

'I'm sorry,' he says, glancing over at Freya. 'Forgive me.'

Freya and I look at each other; our worry is so potent that it taints the air around us with dread.

'What's wrong with him, Mrs Nara?' Tibith's voice is a distant cry, lost in the chaos of my mind right now.

Darius acts quickly, ripping the dressing off his wrist just as Silaria looks at my brother. Immediately, she takes a frightened step back, her expression solemn as she turns to look at me, like this is the one thing she had not seen coming. 'I am so sorry, child.' That is all she says before I glance down at Idris's wrist, and my worst fear comes to life.

There, etched into Idris's flesh, are the unmistakable marks of a bite – marks that match where Aurum grabbed his wrist only yesterday.

CHAPTER FIFTY-SIX

The doors to the barracks infirmary swing wide open as we carry Idris into one of the bays. He lets out a pained cry and writhes as we carefully lay him down and examine the area where the bite has begun to spread.

'What happened?' Lorcan bursts into the infirmary, taking in the agonising sight before him.

Darius says something to him, yet I tune everything out, focusing solely on my brother. Gasping for breath, his complexion is drained, his face covered in perspiration as he desperately reaches towards me, my brothers and even Darius. 'Nara,' he gasps, and I hold on to his hand.

'Why didn't you tell me?' I whisper, my heart trembling with fear as I steal a glance at Iker and Illias across from me, their composure barely intact.

'There's nothing you could have done.' There is a hint of sorrow in his tone, but I shake my head, refusing to believe it.

'No, I could have done something. I still can.'

Freya runs towards us from the entrance, and Link and Rydan

trail behind. When Freya sees the bite has become worse, with the dark venom filling Idris's veins, she can't help but stifle a gasp with her hand.

No, no, *no*.

'If we can just delay it,' I say, 'I can find something, we—we can search for a cure. There has to be one. There's always been a cure for everything.'

Darius locks eyes with me, his gaze filled with urgency as he bites his wrist, drawing out blood. I watch him lean over my brother, ready to give it to him, but Lorcan pushes his way through and stops Darius before a drop can get past my brother's lips.

'It won't work,' he says, his hand trying to seize Idris's arm.

Iker shoves him, causing him to stumble back into Rydan. 'Don't touch him!'

Lorcan's eyes shift towards mine apologetically, like he knows I will be the one to understand. Except this isn't the same as what happened with Erion, and there's no time to waste if I am to save my brother.

I reach out my hand, gently extending it towards Idris's chest. His breaths come in heavy, ragged waves as I close my eyes, feeling my power ripple through me and onto my brother.

Please, please, please—

Idris takes hold of my hand and I gasp as I open my eyes and look down at his face.

As he shakes his head, dark, crawling veins start to appear on his neck. 'Just stop,' he rasps.

Iker and Illias lower themselves to their knees. 'Come on, brother, we need to try,' Illias urges with a nod, but all Idris manages to do is tell us '*No*.'

'Idris,' I say. He looks at me, and it takes all of my strength not to break. 'Don't try to be stubborn now; that is my thing.' I chuckle softly and sink on my knees to the same level as my brother.

He smiles. It's such a rare sight on him, but right now I want his smiles, his frowns, his lectures, and everything in between. 'You got it from me.'

'I got a lot from you,' I tell him, my voice steady despite the tremor of emotions threatening to break free from my throat.

My brothers stare at me and then at Idris. Illias is already crying, and I don't know why because everything will be fine.

'Do you . . .' Idris winces and I thread my fingers through his, trying to soothe him and take all that pain away. 'Do you remember the day I tried to make your favourite pie?'

I give a subtle nod. 'Yes,' I say, smiling. 'You almost burned our cottage down.'

'I still remember Iker covered in strawberries while I was trying to distract you from coming into the kitchen.' Illias chuckles.

Idris's laugh is weak. 'It was a disaster,' he admits, and Iker can't help but crack a smile. 'One I'll never forget.'

'I couldn't get the scent out for weeks,' Iker quips, playing along as his gaze softens.

The memory dances vividly inside the depths of my mind. I can still recall the frantic yells and clashes of pans and dishes while a young me wondered what was happening. It is such a simple story, but for Idris, it means everything.

His grip on my hand tightens, and there is this heartfelt promise in his eyes. A love that gradually fades away as our connection weakens. His breathing soon ceases, yet the glistening tears in his eyes cascade down his face, freezing time altogether.

'Idris?' His name is a whisper on my lips as a profound silence now deafens the room.

Illias weeps softly while Iker's once smile shatters into a thousand pieces with the kind of grief that knows no consolation. He looks frozen in place, and as I look up at Freya, she shakes her head and starts to sob.

No.

'Get up,' I order, my lips tightening as I glance back down at Idris. He doesn't move. 'Idris . . .'

Nothing.

I bite my cheek, drawing blood. 'Idris, get up, come on.' I shake him forcefully, but he is just so still, so . . . motionless.

Get up.

Get up.

Get up.

My words come out angrier each time.

He just needs to wake up. That is all. Once he wakes up, everything will be back to normal.

'Nara,' Darius murmurs softly, and I realise he is now behind me, his hand on my shoulder. He doesn't try to pry me away from my brother; he simply lets me know he is here and that he won't leave me unless I want him to.

But why would I tell him to leave?

Idris is just resting. He'll wake up soon.

'He is okay,' I whisper, smiling as tears blur my vision. 'Just get Leira and Aelle in here.'

'Nara, no.' Iker's voice breaks, and my gaze snaps towards him. He is crying unabashed, and it is the most I have ever seen him cry in so long. Not since our father's death.

I shake my head and look down at Idris. His face is even paler now, all that golden colour consumed by a shifter's bite. 'Get up, Idris,' I say to him and *only* him.

He never answers me.

My lips wobble and I whisper, 'Please?' I can taste the salty tears as they slide down my face. 'You made a promise to Father that you were always going to look after me, so fulfil it. Get up and tell me we will work this out. Argue with me, tell me how annoying I am, just do something!'

From the corner of the room, Freya's sobs turn into devastating whimpers. I cast a desperate glance in her direction, begging for her help, but she breaks down and turns to Rydan, who wraps his arms around her in consolation.

I feel the tears streaming down my face, hot and relentless as they carve paths down my cheeks that sting. 'Get up!' I yell again, my voice raw and commanding.

Hands reach out to pick me up, but I push them away, not realising it is Link until I look. 'No!' I cry and he clutches his chest in sorrow. 'He is going to wake up.'

I glance around at everyone else. Lorcan can barely look me in the eye, while my brothers just hold on to Idris.

'Nara,' Rydan says, still holding Freya in his arms. 'I think we should—'

'He's not dead!' I shout, but that isn't what Rydan was going to say. It is almost as if I needed to say it out loud to deceive myself. 'He—' I stare at them all like a mad woman. 'He—'

I crack.

As soon as my gaze lands on Darius and he looks at me with that twisted anguish in his eyes, my soul ruptures and I let out a wailing scream.

I scream and cry and shout for my brother to come back.

'Don't leave me,' I sob, my chest aching with grief. *'Please—'*

Darius then grabs at me, pulling me into a tight embrace despite me now hitting and scratching at him to let go.

He lets me do it even as exhaustion consumes me, and I bawl into his arms. He holds on to me, rocking us back and forth on our knees. I don't know how much time passes, but soon enough, I order everyone to leave, except for Iker and Illias. And for the rest of the night, I remain by Idris's side, my cheek lying on his chest as I sing our childhood lullaby.

CHAPTER FIFTY-SEVEN

The smoke from the pyre that Enox has lit aflame outside the courtyard twists and writhes towards the sky, carrying the essence of my brother with it. I stand silently among everyone close to me, mourning him as my gaze stays fixed upon the flickering flames that consume Idris.

I'm no longer crying. There's nothing left in me *to* cry.

The scent of burning cedarwood is heavy, and the cries of everyone around me burden me with even more sorrow. It's then that I feel the presence of a dozen beings behind me.

Turning to look, I see the faces of different creatures staring at me. Deers, rabbits, dragons – all of them look to me for comfort and safety. Tibith walks past them with Fernah at his side. He looks so small beside her, and his eyes glisten with tears.

I smile at him to let him know I am okay. But that would be a lie. Everyone knows it would be.

Shifting my gaze towards the pyre, I squeeze Darius's hand. I don't look at him, but I know his eyes are already on me.

I could have done something. We could both have together. I

know it. I want to at least believe it – that as Solaris and Crello's vessels, there might have been a way.

Come back, my mind says. *I need you, Idris.*

Yet, as his body turns to ashes, I know he never will.

I stand inside my brother's room, staring at the tools he used to craft weapons and straps. The bed is made, the pillows are fluffed and ready for him to lay down on.

There is a knock at the door and I peer over my shoulder to where Darius now stands against the jamb. He walks inside and I search the depths of his gold eyes, seeking to borrow his strength for myself as he comes to a stop.

'He's gone,' I whisper, my voice breaking.

And yet everything that belonged to him remains intact.

Darius's gaze holds mine, unflinching, before he wraps me in his arms. My body aches for the release of tears, but I can't cry. I'm numb; I'm broken; I'm barely surviving.

'Leira found this while cleaning our room,' he says as we separate. I glance at the folded parchment piece in his hands. He sighs. 'Illias, Iker and Freya all received similar letters to this.'

I stare at it. At my name scribbled across the opening.

A letter.

He wrote us each a letter.

I remember he had been practising how to write lately. The letters must have been the last things he wrote.

My chest feels heavy, and with shaky fingers, I take the letter out of Darius's hand and unfold it to read.

My dearest sister,
By the time you read this, I might not be here.

I knew after I was bitten that there would be no cure, and no matter what you did, we just would not have had enough time.

I do not fear death like most would in these circumstances. I always knew I would be the first to go, although I often thought it would be due to you scaring me half to death whenever you rebelled.

I'm glad to know that wasn't the case in the end.

You have made me the proudest bruther, Nara, and I hope you know that, but please, look after Iker and Illias. They need you.

And . . . tell Iker that I would be delited if he ended up with Freya, because I know that I will never have children nor a wyf to share my life with, but he still can.

For as long as I can remember, I have always beleeved my true purpose was to look out for my siblings and I think I did just that.

So, Nara, my little sister whom I'll miss, keep chasing that adventure, there is always more to come.

With love, your brother,
Idris

I read it once. Then twice, then a third and a fourth time, memorising his messy writing, the misspellings of a few words and the way he writes his name at the end.

'He always knew,' I say quietly. Part of me wishes I could find the strength to be mad at him for it, but it's impossible. I want him back. I want to prove to him he could have the life he thought he couldn't.

I want to smile and feel happy, seeing him with his own children and wife.

I want to argue with him every day if it means he will return.

'Goldie,' Darius whispers, tracing his thumb across my cheek. 'I hate seeing you like this.' He drops his forehead against mine, our eyes closed. 'Tell me. Tell me what to do, and I swear I'll do it just to see you smile.'

I shake my head. 'I want him back.'

'I know,' he says. 'And trust me, I have thought of every solution to bring him back.'

And I believe that.

Darius would even trade his life for my brothers if he could.

I shift away and turn my back to him, my eyes scanning Idris's room all over again. 'There is one thing we can do.' My voice sounds hollow as I think about every choice I have made in my life that has led me here. 'I want to fight.' I whirl around, my blood pumping with rage as I remember Aurum's threats and the fact he did this. He bit my brother, knowing the outcome.

Darius stares at me, his expression giving away nothing. And then he starts to smile that smile that always brings me to my knees. 'I believe it is time we called in that favour from Kirian.'

I don't say a word. I just march up to him and kiss him ferociously. It is a clash of grief and resolve, fierce and gentle all at once, like a storm that not even someone as powerful as Aurum can stop.

I have strived tirelessly to avoid engaging in prophesied battles, believing that by doing so, we could preserve lives. I was wrong. Because, in the end, it isn't just about fighting a war. It is about standing together, past enemies and all, for the one thing that matters most.

This world.

CHAPTER FIFTY-EIGHT

The ground beneath my boots quivers as we approach the looming silhouettes of the scorched lands, surrounded by Helland
volcanoes. The Rivernorth lake lies at our side, and the air is
thick with the scent of must and sulphur. To my right march shifters
and mortals with full-fledged dragons by their sides, and to the left,
my two remaining brothers, my friends and Darius come to a stop. All
of them wear silver armour, in contrast to the armour I have on.

The gold and black breastplate I wear belonged to Aurelia. Its
intricate pattern resembles dragons, while the shoulder pauldrons
sweep back in regal arcs that remind me of wings. They are tipped
with gold, just like the gilded gauntlets that extend over my forearms,
flexible yet unyielding.

With the looming battle on our hands, we only had days to prepare. Mere *days* of plotting and planning while we waited for the
Thalorians to arrive.

Speaking of Thalorians, behind my friends is Kirian with his
troops, all on horseback and wearing dark gear that features their
emblem of a star.

Darius dons armour like Kirian's, save for the helmet which Kirian has placed over his head.

My hair flows freely behind me as the first sign of Aurum's approach comes from the volcanoes. There's a shift in the air, where his dragons soar across the sky.

I tighten my grip on my sword – a weapon I carved and forged with Idris's tools. My pulse quickens at each shriek and the drumming of hooves from where the Undarions appear with their legion. Hedris is at the forefront of his army, malice dripping from his gaze. To his right are the Aerians and their leaders.

My eyes go to Lorcan, but he remains stoic while staring at his aunts. Col and Ara hold on to staffs imbued with ancient rubies that match their fighting gear.

'Nara, Darius.' Aurum approaches us. His eye, cold and devoid of mercy, finds mine across the battlefield, his usual gold eyepatch covering the other eye that I took from him. Shadows bask in his glory as he grins at the people by my side. 'I see you chose correctly.'

I step forward, my stance unyielding. 'You killed my brother.' Even now, I can't contain the rage festering deep in my veins.

He shrugs, his lips twisting into a mocking smile. 'He got in the way.'

That is all it takes.

As soon as he utters those words, my anger erupts and I raise my sword and let out a cry that echoes throughout the skies. Darius charges and shifts midair, followed by everyone else as they cut through the enemy ranks. I run at them with a ferocity that blooms within me.

Clashes of steel and magic rage on as my power weaves through soldiers like an animal capturing its prey. Light pierces through their armour, and I enjoy each gurgle and cry that emits from their lips.

'Mrs Nara!'

I whirl to the sound of Tibith's voice.

He comes forth with a dozen of Silaria's Tibithians behind him, all parading in their own kind of battle gear with leaves and paint smeared on their fur.

I grin.

'Where do you want us, Mrs Nara?' he shouts, right as one of Hedris's men comes for me, and I shoot my hand out to blast him.

'Safe!' I shout back, my gaze searching for Freya, who now has her hand raised. She fires a ball of purple-dusted magic at someone while leading a batallion of Venators. 'Head to Freya! And stay by her side!'

Tibith nods at my order as I run in search of Aurum. I call for Fernah and the ground trembles as the opposing sides each use their powers. She comes by swiftly and scoops me up into the air and I scan the terrain. Kirian and his troops have dominated the Undarions, shadows and blood becoming one.

Through the haze of ash and ember, I spot Aurum by the river, watching the battle unfold.

'Fernah, down!' I order, her roar unleashing fire across the ground. I hold on to her, my gaze locked on Aurum as she dives for him.

Fernah's wings beat with a rhythm that matches my racing heart. As we spiral downwards, a shockwave of her fierce cry sends ripples through the air. But then, at that moment, a sudden warmth pierces through the dust and ash.

A phoenix rises from the ground, its cry a clarion call that makes me wince as Fernah veers away from it. I cling tighter to her, feeling the searing wind that trails in the phoenix's wake. It circles above Aurum as if guarding him, and I let out a guttural growl of anger.

Fernah lands back on the ground, and I leap off with my sword in my hand. I strike, dodge and slice across throats as I pass through enemies.

Up ahead, Darius is unleashing his flames upon Aurum's dragons. He looks ethereal in the sky, raining terror on them all. Shadows and water drawn from the rivers fill the air around him, and I wish to be up there by his side.

But my focus quickly catches sight of Link, outnumbered and struggling, the glint of his armour dimming beneath the swarm of Hedris's soldiers. The noise that bursts from my throat is frightening. I sprint towards him, propelling myself to where Link parries and dodges a soldier's attack.

A stream of water shoots from one of Hedris's men's palms, but I block it with my power before it can hit Link. The light from my hand blinds the soldiers for a moment, giving me time to slam into the closest assailant.

I swing my sword around, severing heads and coating myself in their blood. I yell out my rage, jamming the tip of the blade into one of the men's chests. He gags and splutters before I draw it out, and a dozen dead bodies lie in a circle around me.

Turning to look at Link, I march up to him and grab his shoulders while searching him to see if the blood that is on him is his.

'It's not mine,' he says, and relief blooms inside my chest.

I scan the terrain as the battle rages on, with phoenixes circling the air. 'Where are Iker and Illias?'

Link swallows, his hair damp with sweat. 'They were with Rydan, near the volcanoes.'

My hands fall from his shoulders as I lift the sword, with the blood of Hedris's men still dripping from it. 'Here, take this.'

Link frowns, shaking his head as I place the blade's hilt in his hands. 'But it's yours.'

'I don't need it!' I tell him as I back away and turn to run off in the opposite direction.

I begin to shed off my gauntlets, fury burning in my gaze as I focus on the rivers. Kirian is on the other side, looking unfazed as he unleashes dark tendrils of shadow magic to repel the oncoming warriors.

The air cracks with the collision of magic and weapons as I push my feet to the maximum strength.

A woman clad in royal blue armour intercepts me, releasing a harrowing cry as she brings her blade down on me. I roll onto the ground, twisting my head as the dagger slams into the dirt beside me. I release a blast of light from my palm, sending her to the ground. As I rise, her pale face screws into anger and she tries to lift herself back up, but I don't let her. My expression is cold and relentless as I throw another burst of my power her way.

She screams and all I can think about is how much *I* screamed when Idris died.

I think about the bite and how bright red and bruised it was.

I think about how pale he looked and how much pain he was in.

I think . . . I think about how this person can be on the side of someone whose only desire is to destroy every piece of land on this earth.

I lift my hand, beckoning magic to my fingertips, but someone stops me as they capture my wrist. I can't seem to calm myself as fire burns through my nostrils and I turn my head to where Darius is now by my side.

He doesn't yield his hold on me. A storm swirls in the gold rims of his eyes. 'Nara, stand down.'

I can't believe he is saying that. 'Darius—'

'He *wants* you to be drained of every power you have inside you right now.'

I can only stare at him, realising the truth behind his words.

'Think about it!' He shakes my arm, which seems to steady me back on track. 'What has he done up until now?'

Nothing. He has done nothing but watch.

Just as he did back at the arena, letting me waste all my energy so that he could overpower me.

My gaze softens as Darius stops trying to open my clenched fingers, and our shared fury is momentarily quieted. The woman on the ground scuttles back, the contempt in her gaze palpable as she watches us turn our attention to her.

'Well, isn't this a wonderful sight.'

My spine turns to steel at the voice coming from behind us. I can feel an undercurrent of rage brimming beneath Darius as we turn to find Hedris with a group of soldiers backing him.

Hedris's gaze slices between Darius and me. 'The thief telling his bitch to calm down.' His words are a deliberate provocation, and it works as I try to run at him.

Darius stretches his hand out to stop me, his jaw tightening as the muscles on his neck go taut. The pause that follows feels like the beginning of a thunderstorm. 'Say that again,' he dares, his voice low and hinting at the temper that lies just beneath his surface – the temper I have witnessed a hundred times before.

Hedris sneers. 'Your. *Wife*. Is a—'

'Sire.'

Hedris halts at the voice of one of his men. Every head then turns, sees the soldier's hands trembling as he grips his weapon, a terrified look on his face.

Then one by one, Hedris's soldiers all begin to turn their swords on themselves.

Hedris looks on in horror at his men as each one slits their own throat against their will. Darius watches the scene unfold with a smirk on his face, his Merati powers snaking their way through the soldiers' minds.

A growl rumbles deep from within Hedris's chest as he whirls to us, his eyes practically bulging with unrestrained anger. He extends his palm out at us, a swirl of dark water aimed right at us.

'You—'

One minute, he is snarling at us; the next, his head is rolling onto the floor as his body stays standing. Then his knees buckle, and he collapses.

My eyes stretch wide, disbelief etched into my every feature as a figure appears, her blade dripping with the remnants of Hedris's blood.

Nonchalantly, she cleans her blade on her leather garb. 'I never truly liked him.'

'Sarilyn,' I whisper.

CHAPTER FIFTY-NINE

Sarilyn meets my gaze with ferocity. 'I thought you might need some help.'

I choke out an astonished gasp. She didn't run away after I freed her. No, she came back.

'*What are you doing?*' The memory of Sarilyn asking me that the day I let her go comes at me in flashes.

'*Doing what you would never have done for me,*' I had said before burning through the iron cell with my power.

Darius steps forward, his expression unreadable as he stares at the person who made his life a living hell.

'Thief.' Sarilyn's acknowledgement of Darius isn't laced with the venom it once might have held. Instead, there is a flicker of understanding that echoes between them.

And suddenly, a smirk tugs at the corner of Darius's lips. 'Sarilyn.'

Sarilyn's posture is relaxed yet undeniably commanding, like it has always been.

'I never thought of you as the cavalry type,' I say, and she laughs.

One of Aurum's dragons comes crashing down on us, and Darius whirls around me, slamming his shadow power at the creature.

Sarilyn throws me another blade. This one is shorter than the one I gave Link. 'I thought I would try something new,' she tells me as she skilfully thrusts her sword through an Aerian.

I had never seen her fight this way.

It is almost alarming.

'Naralía!' Ara's mocking voice comes calling from the other side of the battlefield. I whirl to find her slowly marching her way up to us, flames dancing in her palms.

'Go,' Sarilyn says. 'I'll handle her.'

I look at her, wondering if I should, but all she does is give me a gaze that warns me not to test her. So I dart off, paving the way to Aurum. Until someone bumps into me and sends me to the ground.

I am taken aback by the sudden force, gasping for air as I desperately try to regain my footing, only to be met with a powerful kick to my stomach. I let out a cry of agony, doubling over as I gaze into the furious eyes of Col.

With her staff raised high, she prepares to strike me, but I swiftly dodge her attack only to catch a glimpse of Ara, almost overpowering Sarilyn. I tightly grasp my blade, swinging it towards Col, but she grabs my arm before sending a powerful blow to my nose.

I see stars, blood pouring from every direction.

'You should have never come into our lives,' Col hisses as I struggle to recover. With a swift motion, she forces me to the ground, her staff poised dangerously close to my neck. Instinctively, I catch it with my hands, my arms straining from trying to push it away from me. Col doesn't yield. Her face is manic. 'Where's Loverboy now, hm?'

My face burns as I let out a raging scream at her.

Don't waste your powers, don't waste your powers, don't—

I can't stop myself.

I inhale deeply, allowing my thoughts to intertwine with the presence of the earth beneath me, the vast expanse of the sky above . . . and the creatures that roam this world.

I need you.

All of you.

A tremor ripples through the land, shaking the ground. Col's gaze quickly lifts, and at that very moment, I feel it – the cries of every bird, the deafening roars of dragons coming to my aid, and more.

When Col looks down at me, I smile, all toothy and bloody. 'Run.'

She releases her staff, stumbling backwards while I roll onto my front and witness the flurry of animals rushing past me. Col lets out a piercing scream as she transforms into her phoenix form. But as she takes flight, Enox seizes one of her wings in his jaw. Fernah then grabs hold of the other, ripping the phoenix apart.

Ara sees this, her face contorting in horror as she drops everything and runs towards her sister.

I spit blood onto the floor as I stand and look around me breathlessly while drowning out the cries of Col and Ara. Whether they are dead or not, it doesn't matter to me.

Lorcan has a new family, one that's a hundred times better than them.

The view of the river now becomes clearer as I swipe the dagger off the ground and make my way towards it.

Aurum stands by the riverbank. As if he senses my approach, he turns to face me with a smirk that speaks of malice and ruin. 'Nara,' he greets me, as if we are friends.

I don't falter as I meet his gaze with my own steely resolve. 'Just fuck right off,' I say breathlessly and lunge for him.

He swerves and laughs, the sound unsettling as it ripples across the river's surface. 'I can see why Darius loves that filthy mouth of yours.'

I don't respond with words. Instead, I channel my energy, feeling the familiar warmth of my power coursing through my veins. With a furious cry, I unleash that power towards him, but he counters it with a dark wave of his own magic. The impact of both our powers sends a shockwave through the ground, and the river's waters churn in response like they are protesting against us.

We collide again and again, my power draining every second, yet I can feel Aurum's surprise at my resilience.

When I manage to hit him, he laughs.

'There it is!' His yell is almost a cheer, his grin viperous. 'That is what I wanted, Nara. For you to fight me like the reincarnation you're meant to be. Pity it took killing your brother—'

I scream my rage at him as I lash out and throw everything I have at him, my soul, my life, my *pain*.

He pushes it back at me, and every bit of exhaustion overtakes me, sending me flying back. Everything spins, and I can only look up as Aurum prepares to hit me once more; yet he never does. Darius steps in front of me like a shield, blocking out Aurum's magic.

Aurum hisses, shaking his hand as if he's been burned. He tuts. 'Oh, nephew, nephew. Why must you always intervene at the most inconvenient times.'

Darius doesn't waste time in pitiful conversation as he launches himself at Aurum, their magic clashing before both shift.

I can only blink as Aurum's new look as a shifter comes into focus. I can see the exposed bone and rot in his chest and wings, the sharp teeth on display through the gaping hole in the side of his maw.

They connect in an almighty blow, Darius fighting for us and our land, and Aurum fighting for his own gain.

I try to stand up, my voice hoarse from screaming as horror clutches my chest, watching Aurum latch on to Darius's neck. He lands heavily, dust coating the air, while I rush towards him. His body shifts back, and Aurum descends to face us.

I'm helping Darius sit up when Aurum lets out a low, hateful laugh in his human form.

'Oh, how I could revel in this moment for ever.'

I glare up at him.

'Hello, sweetheart,' Sarilyn's voice croons from behind him. Aurum stills before he turns and sees her there by the river, her smile cold and ruthless. 'Missed me?'

Aurum's smile strains, not having expected Sarilyn to still be alive. 'Sarilyn. What a surprise.'

She looks around. 'Seems familiar, doesn't it?'

'I wouldn't know.' Aurum's chuckle sounds taunting, reminding her of how he switched with another soul. An innocent one.

Sarilyn's anger brews deep within her like a silent, oncoming storm. 'I doubt this time you will be so lucky.' She strikes first, seeming merely to entertain Aurum as he doesn't use his powers on her.

My gaze focuses on the river, its waters glistening under the tumultuous sky.

Yet the rivers hold the answer, and the lover who once was . . .

'Yet the rivers hold the answer,' I repeat out loud.

Have you ever thought that perhaps the place where life was given to him is also the place where it can be taken away?

My heart races as Freya and Silaria's words ferment inside my mind.

Sarilyn and Aurum are close to the water's edge, fighting one another as if Aurum was a mortal now, just like her.

'The river,' I whisper, and glance at Darius as he narrows his eyes, trying to decipher my cryptic words.

I slowly rise, curling my fingers into fists. 'Orna,' I say, the word drifting through the wind. I say it louder. 'Orna!'

Aurum freezes. His hand stops halfway through the air as he is about to strike Sarilyn. He turns to me, his eyes wide and untamed. 'What did you say?'

I start to walk towards him. 'Her name was Orna.'

Sarilyn looks on like I have lost my mind.

'Solaris,' I whisper, gazing at the dull skin that is now covered in welts and rotting away. 'She would hate the man you have become.'

His one remaining eye burns into me with an intense fury, yet for just one moment, I see vulnerability there.

It makes him almost . . . *human*.

'Take that back,' he seethes.

'No.' I huff out a hostile laugh. 'If she could see you now, she would be disgusted.'

Darius appears by my side. 'You're alone.' He joins in taunting him. 'Even the only family you have left wants you dead.'

Aurum stumbles back slightly. 'Do you think that you can ever get rid of me?' He smacks his chest. 'I will *always* win. Always!' Spit flies out of his mouth as we corner him.

'You can't win,' I say, 'if you no longer exist.'

He is in the river now, his armour sloshing against the waters.

'We create,' I grit between my teeth. 'We destroy.'

He becomes furious, raising his palm at us, but no power comes.

'And who is to say,' Darius angles his head, watching Aurum frantically try to conjure any bit of power he has, 'we can't take a life away.'

Aurum tries to speak, but it's too late as I lift my hand, and Darius hovers his hand over mine. Our palms glow bright as our magic becomes tethered to one another. A whirlpool emerges from

beneath Aurum, and he starts to shout obscenities, desperately clawing at everything in sight.

I begin to see the memories of Idris flash through me. The night
I lost him, how he cared for me, how much he loved me.

Every ounce of my being is infused with that power and strength.
Darius clings to me as if I am his beacon of light, and I stare and stare
at Aurum. His furious roar echoes through the air as the relentless
force of the water engulfs him, pulling him and all his creatures into
the swirling vortex of the river.

A gold and silver light then erupts from the water in a brilliant
cascade, piercing the sky and silencing the battlefield. As it dims,
returning the river to its original state, I stand still, paralysed from
the shock of it all.

I finally turn to Darius. We're left panting, staring at one another
in disbelief. Sweat, ash, blood and so much more coat our faces, but it
doesn't matter. Not in this moment as he closes in on me and captures
my lips, his hand resting on the back of my now tangled hair.

'He's gone,' I whisper, needing it to be true.

Darius nods, his forehead rubbing against mine. 'He's gone,' he
affirms.

A phoenix lands on the ground in front of us, a bright light
emitting from its body before it shifts and out comes Lorcan. He
stares at us in shock before coming over and embracing Darius with
a slap on his back. They part, their hands on each other's faces as
they smile.

Sarilyn looks at me from where she stands by the river and bows
her head to me.

I return the gesture just as Lorcan taps my shoulder, and I turn to
hug him. When I look back, Sarilyn has disappeared.

My smile falls, but I accept that she must go.

I hear the clangs as swords drop to the ground, and Aerians and Undarions turn to face each other, accepting defeat.

'Darius!' Freya emerges from the throng of Dark Elves carrying an unconscious Tibith in her arms. There is panic in her eyes. 'He's not moving, he—'

Darius and I immediately look at one another, and without needing to say a word, we run towards her. Gently taking Tibith from Freya, Darius kneels on the ground, his hands cradling the small, lifeless body. Tibith's fur, usually bright and soft, is now matted with the grim residue of dust and ash.

Tears swirl in my vision as I hear Darius whisper his name, and I crouch opposite him, lightly brushing my hand over Tibith's head.

'Come on, Tibith,' Darius begs. 'We need to celebrate our victory – and we can't do that without you.'

The world around me feels unbearably still, the silence stretching on as I sob quietly.

'Tibith,' Darius says again, his voice cracking.

Then, barely audible, a soft sigh breaks through the stillness. My breath catches in my throat as I see a faint movement beneath Tibith's tiny chest.

I watch, not daring to blink as he stirs again, and those wide eyes flutter open.

'Hello, Darry,' he says, giving him a feeble wag of his ears.

Relief sweeps over Darius's face as he chuckles and scoops Tibith further into his arms. He doesn't let go for minutes, and we just sit there, crying and staring at each other, relieved and exhausted.

Link and Rydan come jogging over to join us. My brothers gather by my side, their presence a comfort as Illias kneels beside me and wraps an arm around me. Leaning my head against his shoulder, I take in this moment. All of it.

Kirian watches us from a distance, his usual scary demeanour now full of pride and gratitude.

'Did we win?' Tibith asks, making me focus on him instead.

My laughter is mixed with tears. 'We did,' I whisper, looking up as the rest of the survivors gather around us and a sense of sombre victory settles upon us all.

Aurum is gone.

And Emberwell survived.

CHAPTER SIXTY
SIX MONTHS LATER

D arius and I, our hands intertwined, gaze out at the crowd of shifters and humans. Their smiles and awe reflect the unity we have wished for them for generations. We now sit on the castle's thrones, mine specially crafted for me, an exact replica of Darius's, while the grand hall had to be rebuilt after the damage caused by Aurum's pets.

The gown I wear is a shimmering, lustrous off-the-shoulder white dress embroidered with threads that glint like the sun. The bodice is adorned with a prominent sun emblem that rests at the centre of my chest.

To my side, Darius's attire mirrors mine, not in design but in essence. The white of his tunic is pristine, with the symbol of a crescent moon glowing upon his chest. He looks like he was born to wear it. A wreath crown of starlight and moons sits atop his head.

The same one Hira once showed me.

I look towards Lorcan on the other side of the hall, silently thanking him once more for fetching these crowns after the battle ended and we got the news that his aunts had survived – much to my dismay, but they at least surrendered.

My brothers and our friends stand beside us now, cheering us on as I smile at them, savouring the look on their faces and the proud gleam in their eyes. When I glance over at Darius, he looks at me, lifting our intertwined hands to his lips and kissing them softly. I laugh, the halo shape of my crown almost slipping with the tilt of my head.

The head priestess of Emberwell steps forward onto the dais. She wears a golden robe cut from rich fabric similar to ours. A white tassel hangs from her waist, and as she bows to us, the hood of her robe covers her eyes but not her tender smile.

'We welcome you as the new rulers of Emberwell,' she says, raising her head. 'King Darius Rivernorth of the moon, and Queen Naralía Brielle Rivernorth . . . of the sun.'

I rest my elbows on the balcony, staring down at the celebrations in the courtyard. From up here, I can see Freya being spun around by Iker, her curls wild and free as she tilts her head back to laugh. Rydan once again seems to be pestering Lorcan about something, although he does manage to get a smile out of him, while Link and Illias hold each other tenderly, swaying to the sound of violins.

Releasing a happy sigh, I turn my attention to the golden hues of sunset, which wrap the world into night.

'I knew you would be out here.'

I straighten and turn around to see Darius smirking as he leans against the wall.

'You mean you saw me from down there and decided to come up here.'

He laughs, pushing himself off the wall and making his way towards me. He wraps a hand around my waist, swaying me gently as I look up into his eyes. 'You can't prove that.'

I chuckle and pinch his arm. He nips at my lip in retaliation. 'So,' I say, a little out of breath as he pulls away. 'How are you finding life now that you don't need to steal?'

'Boring.'

I laugh again.

'Boring because you no longer have me tracking your every move?'

He squeezes my hip. 'No,' he drawls. 'Although it did take you a little while to finally capture me.'

I smack him with one of my glares, but a laugh rumbles through his chest as he leans in and kisses me.

'Now,' he says against my lips. 'What is on your mind that made you want to come up here on your own?'

Curse him for knowing me too well.

I tip my head back to really look at him. 'I guess I was just feeling overwhelmed.'

He hums. 'And?'

'And . . .' I drag out the word. 'I guess I am worried that as queen, I won't be able to live up to everyone's expectations.'

He sighs. 'Goldie—'

'No, I know what you're going to say, but none of it will ever stop me from thinking I can't do it. I still want adventures; I still want us to be able to go to sleep without the stress of paperwork or criminals in our kingdom. I just . . .' I release a flustered breath, unable to finish what I have to say.

Darius cups my face in his hands, forcing me to look him in the eyes. 'You want adventures? Done. You're worried about paperwork? We won't be the only ones doing it. We'll have others, our friends, our allies. Criminals? If they're anything like I was, then they should worry about who the new queen is because I heard –' the corner of his lips lifts – 'she is a ruthless one.'

I shake my head at his ability to have such power over me with just his words.

'I mean it, Goldie.' His gaze makes my skin warm and tingly. 'You're not alone in this. You never will be.'

I smile, kissing his lips just as I hear the faint footsteps of a little orange furball.

'You also have me, Mrs Nara!' Tibith says, bouncing on his feet, his belly protruding after eating so much bread from the festivities.

Music drifts over the fields and up to the balcony as I chuckle.

'I'll always have you,' I say, my eyes flickering back up at Darius. 'Both of you.'

'In that case,' Darius says, backing up. 'Why don't we go on a little adventure. The three of us.'

Intrigue lifts my lips into a smile. 'Where to?'

Darius's gaze sweeps over me. 'Where would you like to go, Goldie?'

I ponder the infinite possibilities as I saunter up to him and swipe at the invisible lint on his shoulders. 'Surprise me,' I murmur against his lips, and he grins. Seconds later, he has shifted into his dragon form, and Tibith and I clamber onto his back.

He lifts us into the skies, Tibith and I surrendering to peals of laughter as Darius weaves us through billowing clouds, sweeping over the views of Emberwell. I gaze upwards and close my eyes as I smile, promising myself this journey will be a new adventure.

And Solaris, will it be a great one.

I 'm standing inside a cottage, shifter children running around as I make the final adjustments to Illias's tunic. He looks around nervously and tries to brush my hand away.

I smack his fingers. 'Stop fussing, you look wonderful.'

'You say that even when I have paint all over my face.'

I smile up at him. 'Because it's the truth.'

Illias looks like he is about to disagree when Iker knocks on the door. 'Everyone's waiting—' He freezes when he sees Illias. 'Are you going to cry, brother?'

'And give you that satisfaction? No, thank you.'

Iker and I both laugh, which doesn't amuse Illias in the slightest.

Shaking my head, I pat down the lapels of his tunic and take a quick breath. 'Nervous?'

He nods, and my heart swells, thinking about what is about to happen. Last year, when Darius and I were finally able to marry in front of our loved ones, Illias found the courage to propose to Link during our celebration.

It is somehow poetic that, on the third go, we were able to have a proper ceremony, and my brother gets to have his moment.

'Well,' I say, biting my cheek when I feel a lump in my throat. 'You shouldn't be. You and Link deserve this.'

He offers me a gentle smile. 'I know.' Then, something in his expression changes. 'Do you think Idris is watching?'

Pain flickers inside my chest, remembering the death of our brother.

I glance at Iker, who straightens off the wall and walks towards us. The three of us stand together, missing one person to complete our circle.

I can feel my eyes begin to water, so I blink them away. 'I do,' I whisper, grabbing Iker and Illias's hands. 'And I also think he will wonder why we are taking so long.'

They chuckle and I exhale a long breath.

'Ready?' I ask.

'Now more than ever,' Illias says, and I smile, linking arms with him on one side while Iker grabs the other.

We step out of the quaint cottage and venture into the woods where the shifter's den used to be. As Iker and I guide my brother down the makeshift aisle, a carpet of lush ferns and ancient, inter-twining roots, the dappled sunlight filters through the trees, casting a kaleidoscope of light around us.

The people we love rise from their wooden seats and turn to face Illias with a smile. The forest is alive as dragons, pixies and goblins we have come to know circle the clearing. I look to my left, where Lorcan bows his head to me in respect, then at Leira and Aelle in the next row, grinning at us.

Giddiness rushes through my veins as I acknowledge them all.

As we approach the end of the aisle, where Link is standing

beside Freya and Rydan, wearing a tunic similar to my brother's, Tibith is there waving excitedly in his usual furry self, my eyes find Darius. He is the one who will bind my brother's marriage to Link. It was Illias's fervent wish, and he obliged, causing my heart to almost burst from my chest when they first told me.

Now, seeing him standing there, everything else fades away. It's just him and me, two souls lost in a love they share so deeply. Just the way he looks at me with such tenderness fills me with an over-whelming sense of happiness I can't control. I don't think I ever will be able to.

He flashes me a teasing smile and I blush, never bored of that cheekiness within him.

As we finally reach the front, I gently hand my brother over to Link. Iker embraces them both before Illias turns to me, and I rest a hand against his cheek.

Tears swim in my vision as I smile. 'It's a great day to get married, don't you think?'

Illias chokes out a sob, grabbing my face and kissing me on the forehead. When he takes his position opposite Link, my heart cries, knowing that I am letting him go, just as I will have to let go of Iker when he marries Freya next year, and just as I know that one day they will be my past.

At least, for now, they are my present and my future.

~Acknowledgements

I cannot begin to explain the emotions I feel after finishing Nara's story. When I first started writing this, I was in a low state of mind. I wasn't sure if I was ever going to get out of it and to this day, I have my moments, but one thing that I will say is that writing this book saved me, and for that I am eternally thankful.

Mum – Mami, you are one of the biggest supporters in my life. Ever since I was little, you've been there through my many phases of wanting to be a singer, then a hairdresser, then a baker, an artist and so much more! You never once told me I couldn't do it, or that it was a dream too far-fetched. So, thank you for always believing in me, I love you lots.

Dad – You have always been my inspiration and the one who makes me laugh at the silliest situations. I could never imagine not having you here asking me when my next series will be out, or when you say 'Me río porque te quiero' whenever I ask you why you're laughing at me. I don't ever want to stop asking you that question. After all, your answer is my favourite thing in the world.

George – You are likely reading this right now and thinking 'Yes, I'm mentioned!' and to that I smile as I write this. You have been with me through my highs and lows, and I still don't understand how you put up with me. That is why I created Darius using you as my inspiration. Your cheeky, flirtatious personality as well as the hilarious comments you make are the reason I first fell for you six years ago. I cannot wait for more adventures with you and to show you how many more storylines I can create.

My siblings – Eddy and Noelia. Although you both still don't like to read, I want to say how thankful I am to have you. Eddy, I have always looked up to you as my big brother and as a best friend. Noelia, you are the little sister I look out for and hope to make proud. I love you both.

Areen and the team at Wildfire – I can't believe we are at the end of Nara's journey. I couldn't have done it without you and everyone's help as you guided me through the publishing process. Once again, thank you so much, Areen, for taking a chance on a story about a grumpy girl, a cute little furball and a devilishly handsome thief.

Mi familia – Aunque todavía no sabes lo que dicen las palabras de este libro, sé que algún día podrás leerlo en español. Los quiero a todos por siempre estar ahí para mí a pesar de que vivimos a 1,489.78 km de distancia.

Yaya Mercedes – Hola Yaya, terminé el libro! Sé que no llegaste a leerlo en español, pero me imagino que de alguna manera estás con tus superpoderes allá arriba en el cielo viendo como termina la serie. Sé que estarías orgulloso en este momento y espero que algún día puedas decírmelo en persona. Voy a estar esperando. Te quiero siempre. Tu nieta.